PRAISE

THE INEVITABL

"A Los Angeles lawyer defends a professional safecracker accused of murder in Rucker's debut legal thriller.... Earl's a shrewd, worthy protagonist, surrounded by exceptional characters, including reliable investigator Manny Munoz and second-chair district attorney Samantha Price. This novel certainly doesn't skimp on twisty plot turns, but retains an understated, authentic approach to the law."
  — *Kirkus Reviews*

"An absolutely smashing first novel. Simply what the best legal thrillers have been all along. Rucker's debut delivers the same intelligent and compassionate punch as those first memorable novels of Grisham and Turow. *The Inevitable Witness* will appeal to readers who like old-fashioned storytelling mixed with modern courtroom drama. A powerful tale written by a man who knows what it is like to stand before a death-penalty jury – a tale driven by characters you care about and believe in. As I read the book, something in Rucker's style reminded me of the great books of Raymond Chandler and Erle Stanly Gardner...thoughtfully constructed suspense where murder is an element in a sophisticated thriller...not a blood-soaked rampage."
  — Thomas Eidson, author of *St. Agnes' Stand* and *The Missing* (Random House)

"Veteran defense attorney Ed Rucker knows the realities of the darker side of his profession and has transformed this experience into a gripping work of fiction which is as detailed as the notes on his yellow legal pads and as harrowing and absorbing as the work of the best of today's L.A. Noir masters. If I ever got in a jam, I'd want Rucker's lawyer-hero, smart and dedicated Bobby Earl, standing for my defense."
  — Jon Wilkman, author of *Floodpath* (Bloomsbury Press)

"Ed Rucker takes us inside the mind of those who practice the law, those who enforce it and those who cannot help themselves but to bend and break it."
  – Richard Lourie, author of *Hunting the Devil* (Harper Collins)

"Ed Rucker's compelling novel manages to be both wonderfully entertaining and intellectually satisfying. *The Inevitable Witness* delights with a cast of off-beat characters, a richly-evoked L.A. setting, flashes of wit, an insider's critique of 'the system,' and plenty of plot twists and surprises."

> — Elisabeth Gitter, author of *The Imprisoned Guest (Picador),* and professor, John Jay College of Criminal Justice

"I downed the book in two sittings, the pages flew by, and I was sorry to have to leave Bobby Earl to his next adventure. Tightly plotted, no strains on belief, and lots of 'Wow, I didn't know that.' What if a policeman got shot? And you were charged with the crime? And the DA wants the death penalty? And in fact you didn't do it? I would recommend two things: read this book, then find an attorney as good as Bobby Earl, the crafty, witty and insightful lawyer who is the star of The Inevitable Witness. You couldn't be in better hands, and you can't read a better book."

> — Steve Greenleaf, author of The *Tanner Detective* series

THE INEVITABLE WITNESS

Ed Rucker

ISBN-10: 0-9913274-7-0
ISBN-13: 978-0-9913274-7-8

Front cover illustration and book design by Fiona Jayde

Chickadee Prince Logo by Garrett Gilchrist

Visit us at www.ChickadeePrince. com

First Printing

ED RUCKER

THE INEVITABLE WITNESS

Ed Rucker has been a criminal defense lawyer his entire career, trying over 200 jury trials, including 13 death penalty cases and several high profile cases. He has received numerous awards, including the L.A. Criminal Bar Association's "Trial Lawyer of the Year," and the LA County Bar Association's "Distinguished Career Award." He is listed in "Best Lawyers in America," and was elected to the American Board of Criminal Lawyers. Among his cases have been several high profile cases which he has drawn on to portray the role of the media in our judicial system. He is the co-author of *California Criminal Practice*, a 7 volume set in its 4th edition, published by Thomson Reuters.

More recently, at the request of the government of Ukraine, he spent two years guiding the creation of a national legal assistance program for the defense of criminal cases in their country.

THE INEVITABLE WITNESS

Chickadee Prince Books
New York

To Susan

CHAPTER 1

Los Angeles, June 2010
Late Sunday Night

Officer Terrance Michael Horgan knew he was dying. He lay on his back, staring at the ceiling. He could sense life slowly ebbing away, could feel the wetness of the blood spreading on his Hawaiian shirt.

He knew he was alone now. Why, he thought, when I heard the door open, didn't I notice that the footsteps sounded wrong? I could have slipped out my back-up gun. What was I thinking? I've always been so damn careful, so damn smart. But not this time. He remembered his surprise when he saw the gun pointed at him, the taste of metal in his mouth as he fought to tighten his loosening bowels.

Horgan's mind kept shouting that this should not be happening to him. He was too young, not ready. He was "The Man," tougher, smarter than everyone else. If he hadn't come here tonight, he would have been in a bar, laughing with his buddies, watching the women come in. He would have pulled a woman close to him, drinking tequila shooters with a hand on the curve of her shoulder, touching her neck and feeling the strands of her hair between his fingers, looking over the room, daring anyone to challenge him.

Not now, for Christ's sake, he pleaded. Not like this. Not on the floor of a fucking Chinese restaurant. Officer Horgan tried to raise his arms, but there was no feeling from his chest to his legs. To die alone, he thought. And for what? Why? A man should know why. He didn't want to shut his eyes. He didn't want the light to go out. But it did.

Two Hours Earlier

In the moonlight, the alley ran like a cement canyon between the darkened buildings. Along the walls, dented garbage cans and dumpsters were tattooed with gang signs. The alley seemed worn and tired, somehow not a part of the city's great commercial machine. Not even the night's rain could wash away the years of grime and the rancid odor of garbage mixed with urine, the result of the alley's unenviable selection as the toilet of choice for the homeless.

A garbage can lid suddenly rattled as a tom cat leapt to the pavement and stared at the back door of the Looh Fung Restaurant. The tall, slender man in the doorway turned quickly and met the cat's stare, then turned back to the door. He wore a crisp white shirt, bow tie, three-piece wool suit and a grey fedora. Unusual in Los Angeles in June and even more so in an alley in Chinatown at midnight on a Sunday night. Two heavy leather cases rested beside his highly polished shoes.

To any passer-by, Sydney Seabrooke might appear to be a shop owner fumbling with his keys. But there were no keys in his hands. From his inside coat pocket he retrieved a small case of finely tooled leather, and selected two short "L" shaped metal rods. Replacing the case, he inserted the thin rods into the keyhole of the shiny Grade 1 commercial dead bolt lock on the grease-stained door. Within a minute, he heard the reassuring click of the last tumbler falling into place and the bolt disengaging. He was inside.

Seabrooke snapped on his flashlight and listened. Silence. Now he could relax. He looked about with disdain. A Chinese restaurant. Not his usual fare. High end jewelry stores and bullion deposit vaults were more to his taste. But a contract was a contract. A dim grey light filtered through the front street window, revealing lonely dining tables shrouded in their white cloths. The pungent smell of cooked fish and steamed pork lingered in the air. Vinyl-covered booths stood along walls hung with prints of craggy mountains and fishing boats. In the eerie blue light of a large fish tank, fat cod slowly glided, unaware of their coming fate. His gaze fell on the booth where earlier that afternoon he had enjoyed a passable shark fin soup, followed by an excellent roasted freshwater eel, while he sketched the restaurant floor plan.

He strolled into the second dining room, where the light from his flashlight revealed another door in the back, next to the kitchen entrance. He turned the handle and saw a surprisingly large office with a battered wooden desk, file cabinets and several telephones. These held no interest for him. As promised, a heavy combination metal safe sat next to the desk. He retrieved his leather cases, set up a floor light and hung his coat and hat carefully on the back of a chair. He focused his pale grey eyes on the safe. He ran his hands through his short cropped grey hair, then stretched to release the tension in his shoulders. At fifty, Seabrooke was as nimble and confident as a man two decades younger. He knew he was still at the top of his game, the acknowledged best in the business – known in the trade as "The Professor."

From a thermos in his case, he poured himself a cup of Earl Grey tea and sat down to study the safe. As his concentration deepened, all other thoughts fell away, and he felt a sense of calm but intense exhilaration. The contest of wits had begun.

He recognized the safe as a Schwab, good quality, probably 1950's, most likely with a Sargent and Greenleaf combination lock. But there was no time to listen for the tumblers and figure out the combination like they did in the movies. Too bad; that was fun stuff. But this safe probably had false tumbler notches anyway. He would have to drill. But this old beauty would undoubtedly have a "relocker," a sheet of tempered glass inside, between the safe door and the combination lock. Drilling in front would break the glass that released spring-loaded bolts, which would block the lock mechanism, resulting in a frozen block of steel that even the proper combination could not open. He would have to take the more difficult route and drill from the back. The drilling was the easy part, where to drill was the question. The alignment had to be perfect, no easy task since the placement of the locking mechanism varied from box to box to defeat just such attempts.

Once he drilled a hole, he could insert his viewing device, a fiber optic borescope with a flexible tube and look inside at the action of the tumblers. He knew that a small metal box covered the lock mechanism to prevent this, but there was always a keyhole on the back of these boxes to allow a tool to be inserted to change the combination. His only chance to view the tumblers was through this keyhole, so there was no room for error.

After some careful measurements, he made further mental calculations, feeling grateful that his father had been a mathematician. Seabrooke's renowned facility with numbers was the one inheritance his father could not deny him. He reached into a case and retrieved a drill rig armed with powerful magnets, which enabled him to clamp the rig firmly to the back of the safe. They would hold the drill in precisely the correct position. Running his hands over the surface, he judged the outer skin to be more than standard milled steel, probably hard plate. He took out a small wooden box, and selected a tungsten-carbide drill bit and began.

Thirty minutes later the drill punched through. Seabrooke detached the drill and returned it to its case. Then he took out his borescope, with its thin telescope-like tube with a light attached by an electrical cord to a small battery case. The view was murky, but he could tell that the hole was lined up perfectly. He reached around to the front of the safe and slowly turned the combination dial until he saw the first of the four tumblers fall cleanly into place. When all four tumblers were in place he would be able to turn the locking lever and retrieve his prize. He continued slowly manipulating the dial, until only one tumbler remained.

The clanking of the security gate on the front door shattered the silence. The sound of the security gate sliding open was like the swish and clump of a guillotine. Seabrooke froze. This was not supposed to happen. He had been instructed to break in at this exact time and assured that no one would disturb him. He grabbed for the floor lamp and snapped it off. In a panic, he fumbled in the dark for his tools, scrambling to shove them back into his leather cases. A key scraped in the front door lock and then another, as if someone were searching for the right key. Christ, his mind screamed, he had to get out of here. Seabrooke snatched up his coat and hat, jamming them under one arm and heaved up his cases. He stepped quietly to the office doorway and peered out. In the main dining room, the front door swung open and illumination from the street suddenly swept across the floor like the beam of a search light. Too late for the back door, he would be seen. Seabrooke moved to his right and eased through the swinging door and crept into the kitchen.

As he crouched in the dark, he could hear someone moving about. Oh, please, he pleaded silently, don't come into the kitchen. A chair creaked in the office. Then silence. Seabrooke tried to quiet his breathing which sounded to him like a bellows in the silence. He waited. It seemed like hours, but he knew it was only minutes.

The thud of the front door shutting broke the silence. Then footsteps. Someone else was here. An angry shout hurtled from the office. Muffled voices spoke in clipped, angry tones. Suddenly gunshots exploded. The booming sounds felt like blows inside Seabrooke's head. He began to whimper. Then he heard the front door open and close.

***

That same Monday morning, to the west of Chinatown, where the city bumped up against the Pacific Ocean, Bobby Earl leaned against his kitchen counter; a sweat-drenched Cal Berkeley tee shirt clung to his chest and back. He pulled a plastic jug from the fridge and gulped cold water, letting it run out both sides of his mouth. His running companion, a lanky black and tan hound dog, loudly lapped up water from his dish, then slowly walked into the living room, his jowls dripping a wet trail across the floor.

In his late thirties, Bobby Earl had been a criminal defense lawyer for over ten years. His mouth had an upward curve as if anticipating at any moment the world would produce the punch line to a good joke. Under tousled brown hair, his broad clean features were divided by a broken nose that gave his face a rough-hewn look, more masculine than handsome, a face to trust rather than admire. And that was what mattered. Juries trusted Bobby Earl. And that was where he had been for the last four weeks, in a jury trial. This morning he was due to give his final argument and he had spent all week-end planning it.

He was bone tired. Trials always took it out of him. If he didn't give his all, he felt like he was cheating. But this morning he had gone for a run on Venice Beach. Somehow a run always seemed to revive him, clear his head. Unlike the lean physique typical of a runner, his square body had the hardened bulk of a youth spent on the laboring end of a shovel. Still, he relished the challenge of the soft sand, pushing himself, sucking in the damp salt air, walking home on drained wobbly legs. In the early morning he could let his dog off his leash without fear of getting a ticket from the puppy police. The big hound delighted in lumbering after the shore birds who would squawk their annoyance at being disturbed as they circled and settled back down. The comical sight was worth the time it took to hose the dog off back home.

Earl replaced the water jug, it was time to focus. For the entire trial, his mind had been in a vice grip of concentration; now was no time to let down. Nothing was more important than the final argument. This was where everything had been leading. From every witness, with every question, he had been collecting the pieces to a story. Now was his chance to breathe life into it, to tell it, to sell it. But it was also a time of risk. His way of delivering a final argument required a certain level of openness, a willingness to reveal a part of himself beyond his role as a lawyer. And that was where the risk came in, because if he lost and his client was convicted, it was not just about being defeated as a trial lawyer or failing his client. The jury's verdict was a judgment of him. He had stepped outside his role and asked for their trust. He had spoken from the heart and they had rejected him. He could not help it; he took it personally. Any time he lost it took a piece out of him. That was why the cases that stuck with him were not his triumphs but his defeats. But now was not the time to think about losing.

An hour later, he was striding along the eighth floor hallway of the downtown Criminal Courts Building. Each time he entered the courthouse, he felt like a traveler who was returning home. There was a sense of comfort that came from knowing each cog and piston that drove the great engine called the criminal justice system. He knew the unwritten rules, whose word you could trust, whose hand was on which lever of power. All the skills and gambits they never taught in law school. And this was a world that knew Bobby Earl, too. He was, as the saying went, the trial lawyer you called when you "fixed bayonets." If asked, he would probably have said that a criminal courthouse was the one place where he felt most at home.

But in the courtroom a few hours later, after the D.A. had delivered his final argument, Bobby Earl did not feel his usual confidence. He sat at the counsel table as the jurors shuffled back to their chairs, picked up their notebooks and reluctantly settled in, as if bracing for a long bus ride. Bobby Earl stared straight ahead seeming to wait for the judge, appearing not to look at the jurors. But he was keenly aware of their movements, just as he had been of each expression, murmur or glance during the trial. And right now he did not like what he saw. The jurors were not looking at him; they were avoiding his eyes. Any defense lawyer knew this was not a good sign.

The jurors' gazes swept past him and fell on Roger Kelly, the District Attorney, with his silver grey hair and dignified bearing. Last year, after Earl had pulled off his fourth straight homicide acquittal, the DA's office had taken notice. This time they had sent one of their best. And there he sat. Roger Kelly had just delivered his final argument and it had been brilliant.

Acknowledging the jurors' looks with an almost imperceptible nod, Kelly made a show of putting his legal pad back in his briefcase. The empty tabletop before him clearly said there was no need to take notes on Earl's argument. This case was over.

Earl could feel the nervous tension in his client. Johnny Granarian had good reason to be nervous. He was on trial for first degree murder. Granarian was a very rich and very successful nightclub owner who had spent so much time snorting giggle powder up his nose he had been incapable of leaving his house. This did not stop the steady parade of young women lured to his door by the opportunity to "audition" for his nightclub. Each Monday morning, the club's manager brought the week's cash receipts to the house so Johnny could skim off the top to avoid taxes. The party rolled on until one afternoon a thug showed up with a very large gun and robbed Johnny of his cash and nose candy, shooting his bodyguard in the process. A week later, this same thug was found beaten to death in his apartment on Dreamland Drive in Hollywood.

The media had dubbed the case the Dreamland Murder. But in Los Angeles, notoriety had a short shelf life. You had to fight to keep it in the public's "need to know" crosshairs. Bobby Earl's refusal to give interviews about the case or even return reporters' phone calls did not help. Now the only spectators in the courtroom were the usual geriatric court watchers.

Judge Nancy Bonner had returned to the bench and had taken her seat beneath the great seal of the State of California. She rearranged a stack of jury instructions and put them to one side. A short strand of pearls lay on top of her black robe, and a smile crinkled around her eyes. As a former prosecutor, she knew Earl was in trouble after Kelly's argument. Out of a sense of fairness, she had taken a short recess after Kelly concluded. "Mr. Earl, you may give your closing," she announced.

Most lawyers would say that cases are never won in final argument. To Earl, that might be true for some cases, but not for a close one. Right now, he knew this case was slipping away from him. The atmosphere in the courtroom was flat, with no sense of anticipation, no spark of interest. The jurors just wanted to be released to finish their job, and Earl knew where that would end.

He turned and put an arm around Johnny Granarian's shoulders. "Listen to me. It's like an icebox in here. I've got to shake them out of this, so no matter what I say, no matter what," he emphasized, "you look straight ahead. No reaction. You got that?" Johnny's eyes widened and his breathing got short, but he nodded in agreement.

Earl pushed his six-foot frame out of the chair. At 175 pounds he was ten pounds lighter than when the trial started. The stress and long nights had taken their toll. He buttoned his off-the-rack dark blue suit coat and walked over to face the jurors. They were gazing past him across the room or down at their notes. He stood for several seconds in silence, moving his eyes along the two rows, trying to make contact. Occasionally one juror would glance up, then quickly back down again.

He began to speak in a low conversational tone. "You remember when we first started on this journey together, Judge Bonner read you an instruction on the law? The judge told you that under our law, before you could find Mr. Granarian guilty, the prosecution had to prove his guilt beyond a reasonable doubt. You probably already knew that. A wall of protection against the power of the state. But in reality, it's just a bunch of words. And words don't protect anyone." Juror number five, the postal worker, looked up, and number eight in the back row put down her notebook to gaze at him with a puzzled expression.

"You know in old Soviet Russia they had a wonderful constitution, a magnificent document that guaranteed all kinds of freedom. That was supposed to be the law. But it didn't work that way, did it? And you know why? It was just a bunch of words. There was nobody who put any power into those words, who made the words mean what they said. So what's the difference here?" Earl paused to look at them. "You are." A couple more jurors glanced up. Juror number four, the schoolteacher, was listening now but still had his arms folded across his chest. "You decide whether to put meaning in those words. If you decide that proof beyond a reasonable doubt just means it probably happened, then that's what it will be." He paused. At least they were all looking at him now.

"If you convict Mr. Granarian on that kind of proof, you know what happens? Nothing. That's right. Nobody jumps up and says, hey, that's not right. Mr. Granarian and I will stand here in silence and accept the consequences, because that's our system. Because you, not the words, are the benchmark of justice in our community. If you decide rubber stamping the prosecution is the protection you want us to have, that's what it will be." He made eye contact with each juror, one after another. Several had leaned forward.

"So that brings us to Mr. Granarian. My guess is you don't much like him. You know what? Neither do I." Juror number four unfolded his arms. "What a waste of a life, drug addiction and chasing young women. For a smart man, he sure made a mess of his, didn't he? So what has that to do with what you're doing here? Well, if you decide to put real meaning into those words, it should have absolutely nothing to do with it. And I'll tell you why. If we start using one standard for those we like and another for those that disgust us, then we really are in trouble. It's a slippery slope. What comes next is one standard for those like us and another standard for those '*other*' people. You start with one group, then another until one day it may be your turn." They were listening now.

"There is only one way to do your job. You have to forget who is sitting in that chair and just give meaning to the words. Did the prosecution give you enough evidence to erase any reasonable doubt, or not? So let's talk about the facts, the hard facts, not what the prosecutor wants them to be, but what they are."

He had them now. Some picked up their notebooks. Juror six, the truck dispatcher, nodded to himself and glanced at his neighbor. From the corner of his eye, Earl saw Roger Kelly, the D.A., reach down and pull out his legal pad. Earl was no longer worried; the room had gotten a lot warmer.

"But first, let me tell you a story. One I think just might apply here. It's about my grandmother. She was a no-nonsense farm girl who, during the depression, got blown to California from the dust bowls of Kansas.

Whenever she heard a story that didn't quite add up, maybe a little short on facts, she had this saying. 'It sounds like there's a fish in that milk bottle.' Strange, huh? I knew better than to laugh at my grandmother, nobody got away with that. But one day I asked her what it meant. It seems that during the depression, some farmers would add water to the milk they sold to make it go farther. A few thinned the milk so much, it was said that a fish could swim in it." Several jurors smiled in appreciation. "And I think that's the problem with the prosecutor's case. It's thin on facts. He's got a fish in his milk bottle."

CHAPTER 2

While Bobby Earl was making his argument, Detective Jack Tanner was pacing impatiently around the tables at the Looh Fung Restaurant, smoking a cigarette while he thought through how he would organize the investigation, how many "bodies" he would request. He wanted to get started. More than that, he needed to get started. The first hours of an investigation often proved the most vital, and this waiting was pissing him off. This was the killing of a cop for Christ's sake. The forensic people were finished. Every crevice of the office had been dusted for prints, swabbed for DNA, photographed and videotaped. The physical evidence had been cataloged and bagged. Everyone at the scene had been logged. The coroner had gone through his examination, as if Tanner needed to be told that the gaping holes in Officer Horgan's chest were from gunshots and were "most likely" the cause of death. It was 10:30 a.m., and he was still forced to wait.

He glanced over at the corner table where his boss, the Head of Homicide, huddled in conversation with the Deputy Chief, discussing Department politics over Styrofoam cups of coffee. They were the ones who had decided he had to wait, everybody had to wait, until they found the Head DA. All this so the DA and the Chief could make a joint statement at a press conference. If everyone was released, the Deputy Chief had explained, there was bound to be a leak to the press and it would be on TV before the Chief had made the announcement. That type of PR blunder was not going to be on his head. So the real police work would just have to wait.

Standing at the open front door, Tanner flicked his cigarette into the street, where groups of uniformed officers and lab personnel sat on the hoods of cars or in the backs of vans, all under orders not to use their cellphones. A sweating Chinese workman, bent under a sack of produce, hurried past. Tanner stretched in the early morning haze, working out the kinks from the long night. A veteran of the homicide squad, he was always among the few considered when a high publicity case was to be assigned. He was smart, tough and ambitious, with a reputation for getting results, one way or another. So the brass never asked to see his play book. But most important, he could speak in complete sentences in front of the television cameras.

At thirty-five, he had inky black hair, a firm jaw and dark eyes that refused to reveal what he was thinking. Perhaps that mystery was what women found attractive. Rather than the rumpled sports coat typical of detectives, he wore a freshly pressed, expensive pale grey suit with muted stripes and ruler straight creases. Recently married, it was rumored that he still played away from home and had more than a professional relationship with a certain female DA.

Detective Tanner ducked under the police tape into the now-deserted restaurant office that earlier had been crowded with hooded technicians in zip-up plastic coveralls. Klieg lamps on tripod stands lit the room with the harsh brightness of a surgery table. Cardboard numbered squares marked the location where photographs were taken. The smeared pool of blood on the floor scented the air with the smell of death. Tanner grimaced as he surveyed the scene. We all want our deaths to be meaningful and dignified, a fitting exit from life's stage. But he saw death as it really was. You die alone, your body bloated and discolored, clothes soiled with shit and urine, a comic expression on your face, drooling spittle, and blank staring eyes that somehow always looked cheated. And the stench, of course, always the stench.

A noise roused him from his thoughts and he turned to see Sergeant Richard Walker standing in the doorway with his tool box.

"You the safe man?" Tanner asked. Walker nodded as he looked around the room.

Sergeant Walker was a lean wiry man in his fifties with a sun-weathered face and short, steel-grey hair. As LAPD's "safe man," he chased the professional "safe crackers" and opened the safes of drug king-pins for the Narcotics Squad. He was the only safe man now, since his partner retired. When he had received the call this morning, he had asked for a description of the type of safe. Then he immediately drove directly to the home of the only man, still at liberty, capable of "attacking a box" of this quality – Sydney Seabrooke. He found what he had suspected. The hood of the Professor's car was slightly warm, as if it had been driven late last night.

"Nice of you to join us," Tanner said sarcastically.

"I had to check something," Walker replied evenly.

Tanner was irritated, but he quickly decided that he wanted answers more than he wanted to upbraid an old man who looked sixty if he was a day.

"What's up with the anointed ones?" Walker jerked his head toward the Department heads at the corner table in the other room.

Tanner smiled appreciatively at Walker. He was starting to like the old guy. He motioned Walker to follow him. In the corner, on a gurney lowered to the floor, lay a grey body bag. Tanner leaned over and zipped it open. "Meet Officer Horgan. Terrence Michael Horgan, LAPD," Tanner said, gesturing to the body bag. "You know him?"

Walker stared at the young, handsome face with a stubble beard. He looked almost serene, except the light had gone out of his eyes. "No, but I knew his father, Captain Frank Horgan. Good man."

"I knew Terrence Horgan," Tanner said flatly. "He was an asshole." He paused, looking down. "But he was one of us. So that makes it personal." He turned a stern face to Walker. "And I intend to find the motherfucker who did this." He zipped up the bag and indicated that Walker should follow him. "Get me into this thing." He nodded at the safe. "I don't want any surprises," he said, and went into the next room.

Left alone, Walker examined the safe, running his hands searchingly over the steel surface. Squatting at the back, he looked closely at the fresh drill hole. Nice clean entry, he thought, fingering the hole. Easier to go in the front, but the guy probably figured it had a re-locker plate. Smart move.

Opening his tool case, he pulled out his borescope. As he inserted the tube in the drill hole he could see the tumblers through the keyhole of the lock case. Beautiful job, he thought with professional admiration. Lined up perfectly. A real pro. Three of the four tumblers had already fallen into place. That was strange. All that was needed was one last turn. He reached around to the front of the safe, and slowly turned the combination dial, watching as the last of the four tumblers slipped into place.

He stood up. "Detective Tanner," he called. When Tanner joined him at the door of the safe, Walker turned the handle and the thick steel door swung silently open.

"Oh, fuck me," Tanner said, in a tone mixed with surprise and exasperation. Bundles of crisp hundred dollar bills, still in their clean bank wrappers, were stacked neatly on the floor of the safe, row upon row, thousands and thousands of dollars. "Hendeley," Tanner shouted, clearly angry about this unwanted complication. Detective Frank Hendeley immediately stuck his head in the doorway. "Get the fingerprint guy in here. I want everything in here printed. Everything. And where the fuck is the owner of this dump?"

"We found him, he's on his way," Hendeley said and darted away.

"Property," Tanner shouted, still staring into the safe. Another head replaced Hendeley's in the doorway. "After this is printed, make an inventory of everything in here." He looked up and fixed the young detective with a hard stare. "And count the money with a witness." He turned back to the safe. "Make sure you start numbering where you left off with the other property," he added.

Tanner turned to Walker. "Can you tell me if they got into this thing?" Turning back, he said softly to himself, "Why wouldn't they take the money?"

"I don't think so," Walker said. "Whoever drilled this was a pro, I can tell you that. Calculating where to make that drill is complicated, and it was right on the money. Once that was done, they could have opened it the same way I did. Three of the four tumblers were already in place. One more turn would have done it."

"Maybe they were interrupted." Tanner squinted at the safe.

Walker shrugged his shoulders. "Neither of the restaurant doors was forced, so I can probably tell you if somebody let them in or if they picked the lock. But I'll have to pull both locks."

Tanner nodded, still staring at the safe. "Fine," he mumbled quietly.

Walker went in search of the property custodian to explain he had to remove the back door lock. The property man was responsible for any physical evidence found at the crime scene until it was booked downtown. This protected the chain of custody for court and required only one witness to testify where everything was found. Walker saw a young detective in shirtsleeves, seated like a mother hen with a clutch of plastic bags spread out on a table. "You want to come with me?" Walker asked. "I've got to pull the back door lock."

"Sure," the young man smiled, "but maybe you can help me?" He picked up a plastic bag and handed it to Walker. "I got this on my list, but I don't know what the hell to call it."

"Where'd you find this?" Walker asked.

"It was on the floor, under the desk in there." He nodded toward the office.

Walker pushed down the plastic to outline the object. "It's a borescope," he said thoughtfully. "You use it to look inside a safe, once you drill a hole in it."

The young man picked up a clipboard. "How do you spell that?"

"Wait here a minute," Walker said, "I need to get something."

In the dining room, Tanner and Hendeley sat across the table from a young Chinese man dressed in a designer dress shirt, blue slacks and rimless eyeglasses. Tanner liked working alone, that was why he kept Hendeley as a partner. Hendeley took notes during interviews, wrote reports and did the scut work. That way, when they closed a case, there was no question who got the credit.

"Mr. Lee," Tanner said, "you want to explain to me what an LAPD officer was doing in your restaurant in the middle of the night?"

"Officer Horgan often came here," Lee said calmly. "Usually to use his safe."

"Your safe, you mean," Tanner shot back.

"No, it was his safe and his father's before him," Lee replied, unfazed. "I don't even know the combination."

Tanner fixed him with an appraising look as if trying to decide whether Lee was deliberately playing with him or was just plain thick. After a moment, Tanner leaned across the table. "Mr. Lee," he said in a menacing whisper, "I have a dead police officer in there and I am a little short of patience right now. So, I would strongly recommend that you tell me what the fuck is going on and that you start right now."

"Look," Mr. Lee began, no longer so calm, "my grandfather and Officer Horgan's grandfather had an arrangement. I don't know what, but my grandfather gave Mr. Horgan a five percent share in our restaurant. We, of course, honored my grandfather's word, so the arrangement has passed from father to son. Officer Horgan inherited that interest a few years ago. Just recently I suggested we might change the arrangement. Now he just used the safe and ran a house tab. He had a key and came and went as he pleased."

Tanner turned to Hendeley. "Check it out with property." As Hendeley left he turned back to Lee. "I suppose there's a deed or contract or something."

"It wasn't necessary. My grandfather gave his word."

"Interesting," said Tanner, "now let me tell you one. I don't think you even knew Horgan. He was on loan to the Feds, working dope. I think he came here to make an undercover buy and got popped during a rip-off." He paused to watch Lee's reaction. "So tell me, where were you last night?"

"Detective," Lee said deliberately, "why would I have anything to do with something like that? I own five restaurants around the city. I am a businessman." He leveled a stare at Tanner. "I was at home with my family."

Hendeley returned and joined them. "It was in Horgan's pocket," he said, holding up a key. "It works the front door."

Walker returned from his truck, pulled on a pair of surgical gloves and removed the borescope from its plastic bag. Fitting a jeweler's loop to his eye, he began to scan the surface of the tool. "I'll be damned," he muttered. Swimming into view were the initials R.W., crudely engraved on the tube.

"When you list this," Walker said, "put down it has the initials R.W. on it."

The young detective looked puzzled. "I don't...."

"I'll explain later," Walker said. It must be two years ago now, he thought, as the memory came back to him. When he and his partner were working nights, they would routinely drive through the jewelry district downtown before returning to the Glass House, as LAPD Headquarters was known on the street. This was prime hunting territory, both for them and their quarry. That night, they spotted a familiar car pulling out of an alley. The driver was a high-end operator they had never managed to nail. Figuring him for a fresh score, they pulled him over. No such luck; he was clean, but his tool cases were in the trunk. So they booked him for possession of burglary tools. Not much, but something. Then the case got thrown out of court for an illegal search. Walker could have lived with that as just one of the breaks of the game, but then the defense lawyer decided to rub his nose in it. He got an order from the judge that Walker and his partner had to hand the crook back his tools. That really pissed them off. They got engraving tools and spent all weekend carving their initials into every item, but so small it wouldn't be noticed. You never knew what might turn up. And now this.

Walker went looking for Tanner. He wanted to tell him the guy they should be looking for was Sydney Seabrooke.

CHAPTER 3

It had been three days since he finished the trial. Sitting at his kitchen table, eating his usual breakfast of cold cereal and coffee, Bobby Earl was cooling down from his morning run while reading the sports page. His black and tan hound dog sat on the floor, noisily licking his genitals.

It felt good not to be in trial, when every waking thought was focused on the case. On Monday, after the Johnny Granarian trial ended, he had felt completely drained. He never knew how deeply he immersed himself until it was over. He had dived deep for that one. The DA had made him work for it. And the jury asking for a re-read sure didn't help. He had to sit silently before them, his facial muscles aching from a forced expression of confidence, as the court reporter droned on. It was torture second guessing himself as he heard questions he wished he could re-word, answers he should have probed. And all the time, studying the jury out of the corner of his eye for any indication of what they were thinking. But in the end, he heard that glorious word "not" before guilty. It was like being shot at and missed.

A small TV stood on the kitchen counter next to jars filled with pasta, trail mix and dried fruit. In the years since his divorce, Earl had taught himself to cook a few simple dishes and liked to keep the kitchen clean and orderly. Ever since he was a small boy, he had been proud of his self-reliance. Perhaps too much so. His former wife, Judy, had tearfully pled with him to see this need for self-sufficiency as merely a fear of letting someone else into his life. It had proved a bridge too far for Earl.

The television host introduced a report on the weekend's "tragic incident" from Charlise Howard, "who was at the scene." Earl looked up. An attractive blond reporter was speaking solemnly into the camera. "Yesterday, the LAPD turned out in force to honor one of their own. In a ceremony attended by the Mayor, the District Attorney, the Chief of Police and a roster of prominent politicians and clergy, Officer Terrence Horgan was laid to rest. Officer Horgan was shot and killed late Sunday night in the line of duty." A photo of Horgan in uniform filled the screen, the polished visor of his police cap leveled over a pair of cold eyes that had the bluish grey color of a razor blade.

Earl studied the screen. There was something about those eyes. He had seen that look before on men who were holding their anger in check but hoping for any excuse to let it explode. It reminded Earl of the type of guy you could find in any bar that had sawdust on the floor and cheap beer. The type who was there for only one reason, to look for a fight. It didn't matter if they won or lost, just as long as they got to hit somebody.

The camera pulled back to the reporter, Charlise. "Officer Horgan was a decorated hero on the force, awarded the Medal of Valor for bravery in a pitched gun battle with a fleeing bank robber. This tragedy should remind us all of the selfless sacrifice these men and women make every day protecting us and our families. Sadly, this time Officer Horgan made the ultimate sacrifice." Charlise paused. "K-NEWS has learned that a suspect is already in custody, a man with a criminal record." A photo filled the screen as the reporter continued to speak. "This man, Sydney Seabrooke, is being questioned by officers in connection with the killing. He is being held without bail and charges are expected to be filed later today."

The image of Seabrooke was obviously a copy of his booking photo, which Earl figured had either been leaked by the investigators to attract witnesses or sold to the media by someone in the photo lab. So much for any chance at a fair line-up in the future. In the photo, Seabrooke stared out with eyes that appeared frightened and confused. Not the typical face of a cop killer, if there was such a thing. But one thing is certain, Earl thought, if he's good for it, it's a guaranteed death sentence.

He got up to shower and dress for court, but still stood watching. The TV was showing Horgan's family at the grave site. Two older men with stern, dignified faces and captain's bars on their squared shoulders stood beside straight backed women in dark glasses. Across the open grave, a white-gloved honor guard waited stiffly at attention. On command, they raised their rifles and fired the first of the salutes. Earl turned off the television. It was time to get to court.

As usual, the courthouse hallway was crowded. Earl weaved through a group of jurors who were complaining about court delays, and passed a pair of uniformed cops huddled on a bench, studying their police report, memorizing the difference between court truth and street truth.

Bobby walked on and pushed through the doors of Judge Michael McKeene's courtroom.

Court was in session, so he sat down on the hard wooden bench in the front row of the public section. He was there because the judge's bright eyed clerk had hailed him in the hall, just as he left his last morning appearance, and informed him the Presiding Judge wanted to see him. A request from the Presiding Judge required compliance, but also, he was curious. He and Judge McKeene had never exchanged a civil word on or off the bench. Moreover, Judge McKeene's restless ambition had shifted lately in a political direction, so Bobby Earl, as a devout non-joiner and conscientious objector to committees, would seem to be a person of no use to the judge.

Up on the bench, McKeene sat impatiently, staring over the top of his glasses at the DA, a journeyman prosecutor who was droning on with his standard closing argument at a jury fighting hard to stay awake until the lunch break. The judge's clear eyes and steady gaze exuded a sense of crisp, no-nonsense competence. At the same time, there was an understated but clearly cultivated sense of the showman about him. Rather than the traditional black judicial robe, he wore a red ermine-trimmed academic robe that, as president of the USC alumni association, he donned for the university's commencement ceremonies.

In the past, Earl's appearances before Judge McKeene had resulted in tense exchanges. McKeene's highest priority, as the supervising judge, was to goad the judges into reducing the time they spent conducting their jury trials, thus improving the all-important judicial statistics for his courts. If any judge proved reluctant to embrace this regime, McKeene would declare him in need of some "freeway therapy," and transfer him to the most distant, unimportant courthouse McKeene could find. As a defense lawyer, Bobby Earl considered this preoccupation with speed akin to judging a stage play with a stopwatch.

McKeene noticed Earl and got to his feet, signaling that the DA was finished. When Earl was ushered into chambers, the judge was behind his desk, tipped back in his leather chair, staring up at the ceiling, talking affably on the telephone. Shed of his robe, he seemed relaxed in a starched button-down dress shirt, red tie and red suspenders. Without glancing over, he waved Earl to a chair and continued his conversation. In his right hand he absent-mindedly squeezed a small rubber ball to ensure his handshake was convincingly firm. On the table behind him, a sterling silver filigreed frame displayed a photograph of his smiling blond wife, beaming teenage son, and grinning yellow Labrador. His wife's town and country look was a comfortable transition from her sorority days at USC.

The judge finished his telephone call with a hearty laugh, turned and marked something in his calendar. When he looked up at Earl he stared flatly for an instant, seeming to shift mental gears. "Ah, yes. Mr. Earl," he said with a strained smile.

"Your honor," Earl nodded.

"You're aware of the Sydney Seabrooke case, I take it," McKeene said, switching to a business-like tone.

"As much as anyone in LA who hasn't been in a deep coma or taken monastic orders."

McKeene ignored this attempt at levity. "The defendant obviously doesn't have the money to defend a capital case and the public defender is unavailable due to a conflict." McKeene stared at Earl as if expecting a reaction. Not getting one, he said pointedly, "I've decided to appoint you."

Now McKeene got his reaction. Earl raised his eyebrows in surprise. If a poll had been taken among all the lawyers capable of trying a death penalty case, Earl would have thought he ranked last on McKeene's list to be appointed. Most judges found Earl's intense advocacy style a burden, one that forced them to make too many legal decisions and consumed too much time in trial.

"Judge, thank you for your confidence in me," Earl said diplomatically. "But I don't take appointed cases." To Bobby Earl, submitting a bill to a judge with whom he had just been fighting never seemed like a good business plan. He charged his clients a flat fee, a fixed amount. Paid in advance. Then he did what it took to get the best result, no matter how much time or effort was needed. That was the way he liked it.

"I know, I know." McKeene waved his hand dismissively. "No appointed cases. Something about being compromised. Not wanting to feel dependent on the judge who's trying your case to get paid."

"Something like that," Earl said pleasantly.

"Well, I took care of that," McKeene declared. "Instead of the trial judge, you'll submit your hourly bill to Judge Nelson, the supervising judge over in civil. You'll be paid. There won't be any hassle." McKeene paused to study Earl. "I've designated this a highly complex capital case, which puts it outside the normal compensation schedule. So I've arranged for you to be paid at twice the normal rate."

Now Earl was truly puzzled. Why this effort to get him, of all lawyers, to take this case when there was a line around the courthouse of lawyers willing to sacrifice some of their bodily extremities for a chance at such a publicity magnet. "That's very generous of you, judge," Earl said, playing for time.

"You haven't asked where the case is being assigned," McKeene replied with a grin. He waited a beat, but Earl said nothing. "Right here," McKeene beamed. "I'm going to try the case myself."

This was one move that Earl *could* figure out. It was well known that McKeene wanted to run against Carmine Cavalli, the sitting DA, in the next election. But such a decision carried more than just political risk. Under California law, McKeene would have to resign from the bench in order to run. Earl knew a savvy guy like McKeene would not take that plunge unless he had favorably calculated his chances of winning. Everyone knew he had the money for such a campaign, or more accurately, his wife's family did. But he needed more than that. He needed what the politicos called name recognition. That was where the Seabrooke case would come in. The trial of the case would create a cottage industry of publicity in LA and Judge McKeene knew how to focus the television cameras. Presiding over this case would make him a household name. Now all he needed was something to run on, an issue, a scandal, something negative about the current DA. But that was McKeene's problem to solve. What Earl *couldn't* figure out was why McKeene needed *him*.

"This case is going to make you, Earl," McKeene said, as if Bobby Earl's acceptance was a foregone conclusion. He looked through hands formed to outline an imaginary television screen. "You know how it works. Being seen on television is a lawyer's ticket to the high rent cases. It doesn't matter if you win or lose, just as long as you're seen on television." McKeene looked at Earl out of the corner of his eye. "You think Sharon Epstein, the TV darling, is a great trial lawyer?" he asked. "Please." He drew out the word, and turned back to the wall with a mirthless chuckle. "But the clients climb over each other to hand her their wallets."

"That may be true, judge," Earl said, "but there's one thing." He paused to get McKeene's attention. "Why me?"

McKeene swiveled around slowly to give Earl an appraising look, as if seeing him in a new light. "Why Mr. Earl," he smiled as if sharing a private joke, "because I want a good defense lawyer on the case." Then, in a serious tone, he explained. "This case is going to be on television every day. I don't want to sit up there like some kind of time keeper while the DA marches over the defense like Sherman through Georgia. I want a trial. I want a defense that puts up a fight, one that's not afraid to take on the DA." He paused. "You never know what might turn up."

Earl had not expected a straight answer and he had not been disappointed. If McKeene really wanted a spirited defense, it would constitute a historical first for him. The last thing McKeene wanted was to be known to voters as the judge who presided over the acquittal of a cop killer. A strong defense couldn't be the reason McKeene wanted him on the case.

McKeene stood, the interview concluded. "The arraignment is tomorrow," he said, already looking down at his desk.

Earl got up and left the judge's chambers. He was seething with anger. He hated McKeene for his smug assumption that Earl was one of those self-promoters who had his nose rammed up any ass that offered him an opportunity for publicity. But what else could McKeene have concluded, he thought, berating himself for meekly bowing to McKeene's will. In truth, he always made an effort to discourage media interest in his cases. If the media showed an interest, he went into a "prevent" defense, delaying the case in the hope that the media's short attention span would be exhausted. While publicity might promote a lawyer's career, it was never good for the case. Publicity shoved any case off the normal judicial tracks. If a prosecutor or trial judge thought the media was interested in a case, they immediately raised the stakes. Judges, just like the DA, had to stand for election, and the best way to protect their jobs was to give the public what it expected. That meant being seen to satisfy the public's perceived demand for harsh justice. "Get tough on crime" was the watchword. In a publicity case, you could count on the legal rulings coming down heavily in favor of the prosecution, sentences being doubled and the victim being canonized. Suddenly everyone had veto rights over any plea agreement.

Earl walked out into the deserted hallway. During the lunch break, the courthouse inhabitants fled the building as if responding to a fire drill. He flopped onto a wooden bench. He was a storm of conflicting emotions. The truth was, he wanted the Seabrooke case. He had never lusted after money or position. He had only one abiding ambition, to be recognized as a great trial lawyer. Maybe it was just plain vanity, but he wanted to walk into a crowded courtroom and feel the stir among his colleagues that such respect engendered. He had honed his skills in scores of jury trials. Now, he felt ready. He wanted to put his skills on display. Like a dancer or musician after years of practice, he wanted to perform before an audience. Trial work was what he did, the essence of who he was. This case was destined to be enveloped in a blanket of publicity no matter what he did, so this would be his stage.

He reached into his coat pocket for his cellphone. He needed an investigator. He called Arthur Munoz. You did not survive thirty years of Police Department politics and retire as Head of the Robbery Homicide

Squad without knowing where the bodies were buried or how to throw a few elbows in the clinches. Munoz had worked with Earl before and seemed pleased for another chance. He agreed to meet Earl at Jimmy's Diner for breakfast.

Five floors above the hallway where Earl had called Munoz, the offices of the District Attorney were humming, processing the paperwork that distilled the tales of human misery into the sterile numbers of Penal Code violations and mere entries in columns of crime statistics.

As District Attorney of Los Angeles County, Carmine "Rocky" Cavalli had a spacious office on the top floor of the Criminal Courts Building, looking west over the city's business district. He leaned back in his green leather chair, hands entwined behind a head of thick black hair, and swiveled to gaze out the window. In the three years he had occupied this office he had never grown tired of the view. On rare occasions, when the Santa Ana winds were blowing, he could see as far as the Palos Verdes Peninsula and the Pacific Ocean. But he was forty-five, and this was not the view with which he intended to end his career. The State Attorney General's office in Sacramento had a broader view, a State-wide view. But first Cavalli had to hold onto this office, and the election was only a year away.

He turned back to the room. His dark eyes and engaging smile stared back at him from a solid wall of framed photographs in which he was paired with all the current political players. He felt a tingle of excitement, because today he was going to make some real decisions. Not the usual mind-numbing administrative ones about budgets or staffing or promotions. No, today's decisions were about politics, with Byzantine plots, shifting alliances and conspiratorial intrigues. This was the game in which he thrived. Today he would be a master of the universe. Today, he would decide who would try the Sydney Seabrooke case.

The Chief of Trials, Bob Bishop, sat at the mahogany conference table, leafing through a thick case file, making notes on a yellow legal pad. As a career prosecutor, he had earned a reputation as an able trial lawyer, but he had gotten tired and retreated into administration. Phil Ruzzi, Cavalli's campaign manager and political guru, slouched at the end of the table, dressed in his trademark black turtleneck sweater.

"So what kind of a case have we got?" Cavalli asked as he moved from his chair to sit on the edge of the desk.

"From what I can see," Bishop replied, glancing up from the case file, "it looks pretty good. Not a walkover but, given it's a cop killing, there's enough here for a jury to be satisfied convicting."

"Hell, then maybe I should try it myself," Cavalli said with an expansive gesture. There was not a chance he intended to take that risk, but he liked to keep alive the pretense he was still a trial lawyer.

"Sure," said Ruzzi the politico, sitting up in his chair. "Why go through an election campaign? Let twelve morons decide it. You lose the case, you lose the election. Sounds fair to me."

Cavalli smiled. He had anticipated that response. "So, who should we give it to? Who can win it and not become a matinee idol?" The unspoken memory in the room was that it had been just such a chance selection that had catapulted Cavalli into office. A relative unknown, he had been selected by the DA to prosecute the Goldberg brothers, accused of killing their wealthy parents when discovered acting out a sexual fantasy with a dominatrix in their parents' bedroom. Media hints of childhood abuse created a public appetite for any salacious details. Cavalli, with his telegenic good looks, affable manner and ready availability to the cameras, was perfect for the part of the fearless champion of those engrossed in the unfolding media morality play. When it later came to light that the sitting DA had engaged in the normal overreaching for campaign funds, Cavalli ran against him and rode in on a tide of self-righteousness.

"How about Roger Kelly?" Bishop suggested. "He's our best trial lawyer and he knows how to get a death verdict."

"Who's that?" asked Ruzzi.

"He's tried some of our biggest cases," said Bishop. "He's smart, articulate, a Stanford grad. Sort of preppy looking, from an old Pasadena family."

Ruzzi looked at Cavalli and raised a concerned eyebrow.

"Who else?" asked Cavalli.

"There's always Jim Jessup," Bishop replied unenthusiastically. "He's steady, dogged, not real imaginative, but knows how to put on a case."

"What's his background?" Ruzzi asked.

"He's divorced, so he has the time. Sort of a messy custody fight, as I recall. He's a career man."

"Good," Ruzzi said. "Let's put somebody young as second chair. Preferably a woman. It makes for better demographics."

"Samantha Price," Bishop offered. "She's been in felony trials only a few years, but she's bright, a hard worker and has gotten some good verdicts for us."

Cavalli looked puzzled. "Wait a minute. Isn't she the one who tried to get around my policy on filing Third Strikes?"

Bishop sighed silently. "Not exactly. She didn't think life sentences were appropriate on small-time thefts or burglaries just because of the priors. She thought the Third Strike needed to be a violent felony to pull a life."

"Now I remember," Cavalli said. "She's Honest John's daughter, right?"

"Yeah," Bishop nodded, remembering his old mentor. When Bishop joined the Office, back when trial DA's could use their own judgment about their cases, John Price had been the DA everyone looked up to. Not only a fine trial lawyer, he had been the embodiment of the principle that a prosecutor's first obligation was to see that justice was done. It seemed such an antiquated notion now, when the idea of treating a defendant as anything but guilty and a lower life form was considered a sure sign of feeble-mindedness by his colleagues. Bishop smiled, remembering a past when John would sit each morning in the vacant jury room of his trial court as defense lawyers came in, one at a time, to run their cases by him. If he agreed with them, he would reduce the charges or even dismiss the case. If not, the case went to trial. No wonder his daughter didn't think that piling on the years to a sentence was the only mark of a good DA.

"So why are we even considering her?" Cavalli asked.

"Because, this is not a case where we're going to be cutting any deals. It's a cop killing. It's going to trial and Jessup is going to need help. She's smart, knows the law and is a first-rate trial lawyer."

Cavalli looked at Bishop with a question in his eyes.

"Rocky, I have seen her in trial," Bishop said earnestly. "When the bell rings, nobody is more competitive. Nobody. She wants to win."

Cavalli stared at Bishop as he thought. "Okay," he said finally. "But make sure she knows Jessup is in charge."

"Will do," Bishop said.

"All right, what else?"

"We have a choice about where to file the case," said Bishop. "It was close enough to Pasadena, so we could file there and we would get a much better jury pool. If we file downtown we're bound to end up with some blacks on the jury, and you know how they feel about the LAPD."

"Pasadena would fuck up your news coverage," Ruzzi protested. "The media room is right here, and the press is set up to operate out of here."

"I'll need to make some comments most nights, so let's file downtown," Cavalli said. "Now, in which court is the case going to be set?"

"I hear McKeene's going to keep it." Bishop stared down at the table. "He called me to schedule the arraignment."

"The son of a bitch," Ruzzi spat. Both he and Cavalli were well aware of McKeene's political ambitions. Ruzzi had been working the phones to convince the opinion makers that Cavalli's reelection was inevitable and they'd better get on board. To Ruzzi, choosing sides was a zero sum game. Bet on the wrong horse and forget about having your phone calls returned.

Cavalli smiled. "I figured as much. It's what I would have done." He turned to Ruzzi. "Don't worry." He turned back to Bishop. "Paper him."

Ruzzi turned quizzically to Bishop, his official translator of legalese. "At the start of any case," Bishop explained, "each side has one shot to disqualify the judge, no questions asked, simply by filing a one-page form. This paper automatically kicks the judge off the case." Bishop turned back to Cavalli. "We only have one challenge, you know. If we do this, McKeene can send us to whomever he wants, so it's not going to be a soft landing."

"I don't give a shit," Cavalli shot back, "as long as McKeene doesn't get it." He turned to Ruzzi. "Okay, let's schedule a news conference."

CHAPTER 4

It was late that afternoon, by the time Bobby Earl finished his last court appearance and drove back downtown to the Men's Central Jail. He wanted to meet his new client before tomorrow's court appearance so he wouldn't have to introduce himself for the first time amid the crush of a media circus. He pushed his ID, Bar Card and visitor's slip through the slot in the Deputy's glass booth and stepped through the open gate.

Some sounds would always resonate in his memory. The solid smack a fast ball made when it hit his catcher's mitt and the clang of metal as a jail cell slammed shut. He stood still as the steel barred gate rattled shut behind him. It was always the same. For a moment he felt trapped. Under the harsh light, he scanned the rows of long narrow tables stretching the length of the attorneys' visiting room in the Men's Central Jail. Crammed shoulder to shoulder, lawyers perched on anchored wooden stools talking over a low wooden divider to uniformed inmates. The much-lauded confidentiality of these attorney-client conversations depended upon how hard the inmate on the next stool tried to listen. A bored sheriff's deputy sat behind a desk next to the inmate entrance. He was busily stamping visitor passes, as a line of inmates looked anxiously around for their lawyers. Over the din of conversation, the deputy shouted out the name of a lawyer and directed an inmate toward the raised hand.

Earl calculated he had spent enough time, over the years, confined in this room, waiting and talking, to equal a short prison sentence. He took a seat at one of the open-ended glass booths along the wall that offered the illusion of privacy. These were reserved for interviews with clients facing the most serious of charges. Earl figured that Seabrooke just might qualify.

An hour later, a rhythmic jangle of chains announced Seabrooke's arrival. Escorted by two large deputies, hands cuffed behind his back, shuffling in ankle chains, he was trying, with great difficulty, to maintain a dignified posture. The deputies shoved him onto a stool opposite Earl and recuffed one hand to a bolted steel eyelet on the table. Seabrooke stared at Earl with eyes that flickered between fear and arrogance. Under a receding hair line, his narrow face was pale. His blue inmate shirt hung loosely on his narrow shoulders and thin, spare frame.

Earl introduced himself and explained he had been appointed to represent him. Seabrooke sat mutely staring at him. Earl passed a business card over the divider and described how to call collect on the jail phone.

"Do I have a choice in the lawyer that represents me?" Seabrooke asked in a calm voice.

"Not unless you have the money to hire one on this kind of case," Earl replied.

Seabrooke looked down idly at Earl's card. After a moment, he asked, "Have you ever handled big cases? I don't remember seeing your name in the papers."

"Publicity is usually not good for a case. I generally try to discourage it."

Seabrooke nodded. "Where did you go to school?"

"Berkeley, then Boalt Law School," Earl said.

"That's the public school up north, isn't it?" Seabrooke asked.

"Yes," Earl said, somewhat amused at the turn this conversation was taking. "Where did you go to school?"

"Princeton. My father was a professor there in the mathematics department,"

"Really?" Earl said, pretending to be impressed. "And when did you graduate?"

"I didn't. I found the whole experience rather boring," Seabrooke said casually, then asked, "To which house did you belong? I think that's what you call them. We had luncheon clubs."

"You mean a fraternity?" Earl asked incredulously. "None." He paused. "I didn't realize this was a job interview," he said with a smile.

"Oh, I thought it was," Seabrooke said in mock surprise. "I've already had another offer to represent me."

"And who was that?" Earl asked.

"Jay Silverton. Do you know him?"

"Oh yes," Earl said flatly.

"He's agreed to represent me without a fee. He felt that with all the public interest surrounding my case, after he won an acquittal we would be offered a book contract and could divide the proceeds."

Earl knew exactly what someone like Jay Silverton would do with this case. Soak it for as much publicity for himself as possible until it got close to trial, then concoct an imaginary "conflict" to get off the case, not having done a minute of preparation. Why expose your incompetence when faced with a jury after you've been seen on television, which, as everyone knows, means you must be a great lawyer.

"Mr. Seabrooke," Earl said, fixing him with a steady gaze. "The last time Jay Silverton saw a jury was in the movies. You are being charged with a capital offense. The prosecution will seek the death penalty. You need a trial lawyer. There are not going to be any deals in this case. It is going to trial."

He paused, then spoke slowly, emphasizing each word. "They are trying to kill you." He regretted having to speak so bluntly, but Seabrooke needed a dose of reality. He paused to measure Seabrooke's reaction. Every client reacted differently when faced with this sobering news. Earl had seen it met with everything from resignation to outrage, from denial to false bravado. For an instant Seabrooke's mask slipped and Earl could see the fear in his eyes, but just as quickly he raised the mask again.

"In that case, you've got your work cut out for you. You see, I'm innocent."

"We'll get to that, Mr. Seabrooke. All I wanted to do tonight was introduce myself and warn you not to discuss your case with anyone in here. Not anyone. There are men in here to whom you're just a piece of merchandise, a high-priced item they can sell for a ticket out of here. All they need is a little information and they'll make up the rest. So you must not discuss anything about your case with anyone." Earl waited in vain for a reaction. "The sheriffs always have a couple 'house snitches.' Somebody they can count on to produce a confession. In a case like yours, they will probably stick one of those near you."

Seabrooke nodded and looked down, as if finally coming to terms with the grimness of his situation. After a moment, he looked up. "Let me tell you what happened."

Earl never wanted to hear a client's version of events until after he learned what the prosecutor knew and had discussed it with the client. It was a given that people reacted differently when first charged with a crime; most were frightened, some just angry they had been caught, others were confident the case would evaporate. But all of them had one thing in common. They lied. They might lie out of shame or fear or guilt or even distrust of their lawyer. But they lied. The lie might be about the facts of the case or the reason behind what they'd done, a trivial detail or the key to the case, but it would not be the truth. Earl's concern was not that the lie breached some unspoken moral pact or imagined bond of trust between lawyer and client, but that it might hurt the case. Clients rarely recognized the facts that would resonate with a jury and on which a case would pivot. But once they lied, they blindly clung to the lie, and that meant Earl would be stuck with it. It was best for them to wait to unburden their souls.

"There'll be plenty of time for that," Earl said pleasantly. "We are going to be spending a lot of time together."

"I understand," said Seabrooke. He looked at Earl for the first time with a plea in his eyes. "But, I need to tell you."

Earl could see that this was not a request he should refuse. "All right," he said and sat back.

Seabrooke paused to gather his thoughts. "I am a thief. A professional thief. I have a certain talent. I can open safes. With enough time, any safe." He eyed Earl, who nodded. "A few days before these, uh, events, I was in custody right here."

"What for?" Earl asked.

"Violating my probation. I had pled to a trivial misdemeanor. Trespassing."

Earl's eyes squinted a question.

"I was discovered in the back room of a large exclusive jewelry store. They suspected I was studying their security system. They were right. But all they could charge me with was trespassing, to which I pled guilty and was put on probation."

"So what was the violation?" Earl asked.

"The judge had imposed this ridiculous condition barring me from the premises of any jewelry store. I didn't take it seriously and besides, it interfered with my livelihood. By a quirk of fate, I was seen in a store by my probation officer and arrested."

"Who was the judge?" Earl asked.

"Malcolm Ferguson," Seabrooke said.

Earl smiled. Ferguson was infamous for imposing bizarre probation conditions, such as requiring a pick-pocket to wear boxing gloves in public, or a purse snatcher to wear tap shoes so women could hear him coming. "So why not bail out?" Earl asked.

"The good judge imposed an extremely high bail and at the time I was experiencing a lack of liquidity." He paused. "More to the point, a lack of access to my funds. In my line of work, it's prudent to take precautions against the current criminal forfeiture laws. To access my funds requires me to travel, which my incarceration, of course, prevented. You might call it a Catch 22."

"So how did you make bail?" Earl asked.

"As I said, I have a skill. With it comes a reputation. I was approached with a business proposition by a local bondsman. He agreed to post my bail, without a fee or collateral, if I would do a certain job."

"Who was the bondsman?"

"Johnny Aradano," Seabrooke said.

Earl knew him. A former prize fighter, a local LA favorite, turned bondsman. He had an office across from the jail with a sign over the door proclaiming "I will get you out if it takes ten years." In spite of this attempt at humor, Aradano had a lot of customers.

"What was the job?" Earl asked.

"I was told there was a safe in this Chinese restaurant that contained a large amount of cash. My work had to be accomplished late Sunday night, between midnight and two a.m., after which I was to meet Aradano to divide the proceeds."

"Did Aradano tell you how he knew there would be money in the safe?"

"No. He just said he had a source and it was solid."

"All right. So what happened?"

"I was interrupted. Before I could finish, I heard someone opening the front door, so I fled," Seabrooke said.

"Did you see who it was?"

"No. I had no intention of confronting him. I don't engage in violence. I am a craftsman, not a thug."

"Where did you go?"

"To the appointed place to meet Aradano."

"How did that go?" Earl asked.

"Not well. He was angry. He said I was trying to cheat him by keeping the money. He was somewhat appeased when I pointed out that if I wanted to cheat him I would have merely skimmed most of the cash and showed up with the remainder. Plus, I enjoy a reputation for absolute reliability. After that I went home."

Earl nodded and sat quietly, absorbing the story's significance.

"Do you believe me?" Seabrooke asked.

How many times had Earl faced this same question? It was not something he usually gave much thought to because his belief or skepticism did not enter into it. The client's story was merely the hand Earl was dealt and he played it as best he could. Clients always thought he would work harder on their case if he thought they were innocent. Actually, he always worked hard. He was driven by the demands of his own standards, his own code, his own moral fabric. Even if he knew the client was guilty. In fact, he preferred not to believe a client was innocent. It merely added to the pressure. But he had learned that working hard to satisfy one's own personal code was not something a client would understand.

"Mr. Seabrooke," Earl said, "I think you are too smart to lie to your lawyer."

Seabrooke stared at him, as if deciding whether to accept this compromise, then nodded.

"You mentioned your father. Can I call him for you? He's probably quite worried," Earl asked.

"My father and I have been estranged for several years," Seabrooke said.

"Anyone else you'd like me to contact? A wife, relative, friend?"

"To speak to my wife, you would need a translator. She speaks very little English. She's Thai."

"You speak Thai, then," Earl asked.

"No," Seabrooke said flatly.

Earl gave him one more caution against talking about his case and left. This was plenty for their first meeting. He would wait to see the prosecution case before he started to juggle the pieces in the hope that there might be something here to weave a defense around, a story he just might sell. The chance to put on a defense, to put up a fight, was what exhilarated him. He knew the noble mission the justice system ascribed to defense lawyers: they policed the police, forcing them to obey the laws that protected not just the criminals but all citizens; they challenged the weight of evidence the State said was sufficient to lock someone up, keeping the bar high enough to protect the innocent. The defense bar, protectors of the rule of law. This was undoubtedly true, but it was not why Earl was a defense lawyer. He was drawn to the battle, the exhilaration of a jury trial, when he felt totally alive, totally focused. For that short time, everything else faded away. There were moments in court which came closest to those he had felt on the college playing fields, the pulsating excitement mixed with the fear of failure, the simple truth of victory or defeat. Except in court, the prize was someone's life, the ultimate competition. A true blood sport. It might not be noble, but it made him one hell of a trial lawyer.

The drive home from the jail on the Santa Monica Freeway, at a steady five miles over the speed limit, then dropping onto a few side streets, took less than thirty minutes. His old wood-frame bungalow sat a few blocks from the ocean and Venice Pier. He'd had the interior completely gutted, installing modern fixtures and hardwood floors. It was, as he described it, the house that murder built. Paid for with the accumulated fees from four murder cases.

As usual, his saggy-jowled hound dog, Henceforth, waited at the front door, his broom stick tail banging happily against the wall. Earl realized the dog's name was an unfortunate choice. When he first got the dog, he had taken care over the choice of a name, so much so that each evening when he returned home with that day's inspiration, he would solemnly announce to the young dog, "Henceforth, your name shall be ..." After several days of these reversals, the only name to which the dog would respond was "Henceforth." Looking at the large dog, whose tongue was flopping to one side, Earl thought that if the conventional wisdom was correct, that having a cute dog was a good way to attract women, he'd have to find some other way. Seventy-pound, sad-eyed Henceforth did not fit the bill.

He walked down the hallway lined with the framed self-portraits he had requested from each client charged with murder. More than mementos, the drawings were a subtle effort to allow him a look inside, to penetrate the walls everyone threw up to protect their secrets and avoid the pain. Some clients refused, some drew idealized versions or cartoons, but sometimes the drawings revealed what the client refused to say in words, something that Earl could use in the case. And sometimes what emerged was just plain scary.

Almost without exception, Earl managed to find in each of his clients an element of humanity he could identify with. This allowed him to see them as people, fellow human beings, not just the sum of what they had done, or another criminal case. It was not that he deluded himself about their flawed characters or any danger they might pose. He had seen too much of what human nature looked like when the thin veneer of civilization was peeled away and the fear of consequences evaporated. He well knew what people were capable of when the brakes came off.

He put on a pair of jeans and a tee-shirt, then he padded barefoot into the kitchen to feed Henceforth and throw some pasta into a pot. He popped open a beer and turned on the television. A stern-faced Rocky Cavalli was speaking straight into the camera from behind a podium sprouting a dozen microphones and emblazoned with the county seal. "As District Attorney of Los Angeles County, I can assure you that this cowardly act will be prosecuted to the full extent of the law, with all the resources of my office. We will seek the death penalty as the only punishment fitting such a crime, a crime which strikes at the very fabric of our society. Mr. Seabrooke will be brought to court tomorrow, and we will demand a speedy trial so that justice may be done."

Earl picked up a dish towel that jogged his memory. On it was stenciled *The Owl And The Pussy Cat Went To Sea*, with a picture below of a row boat with its two hapless passengers staring warily at each other. Below was printed *A Recipe For Disaster*. It had been left by Ashley, his latest former girlfriend. Beautiful Ashley, with her dancer's legs and an art gallery on Melrose Boulevard. Like the others, she had been unable to find a place for herself in his life, always crowded out by his clients. Once he dove into a case it always seemed to consume him, he could never find room for anyone or anything else. Maybe deep down he doubted that he was smart enough or talented enough to devote time to both, and it was always the case that won out. Sometimes he worried he would end up alone, a trial lawyer with a string of not-guilties and no one with whom to share it. But more often, he worried that this idea did not bother him more than it did.

CHAPTER 5

The next morning, it was barely six a.m. when Earl walked into Jimmy's Diner, but most of the regulars were already there. In the red vinyl booths, solitary figures sat hunched over coffee cups, breakfast plates and newspapers. A stout, middle-aged waitress with a rhinestone name tag that read "Millie," circulated with a pot of coffee, joking and chatting with the customers. Arthur "Manny" Munoz, the investigator Bobby had hired to work on the case, was sitting at the back, his bulky frame covering the vinyl bench. His muscled forearms lay on the table like two fallen tree trunks. He grinned as Earl approached. Munoz was a large man with the strength of an ox, but his demeanor was disarming, not threatening. He made people feel comfortable, like a familiar pair of old house shoes. People were willing to talk to Munoz.

"So we're back in business," he said, shaking Earl's hand.

"Looks that way." Earl slid into the booth facing Munoz.

"But, shit, Bobby, a cop killing? The jury won't even leave the box to vote."

"We'll see, we'll see." Earl waved at Millie for coffee. "So what did you find out?"

Munoz pulled out a small notebook. "I made a few calls to some 'old timers.' Seems your man hit the jackpot. Horgan was LAPD royalty. Father and grandfather before him. Back when the Irish ruled LA, before we Mexicans took over." Munoz grinned.

Earl raised his eyebrows in dubious assent.

"It seems the grandfather was a bag man for old Mayor Reilly, collecting from our yellow brothers in Chinatown. The mayor got a taste and let them keep their gambling parlors, whores and opium dens. They had an interesting system. When the newspapers would moan about corruption and vice, grandfather Horgan would explain to the Chinese that he would have to stage a raid, and they would negotiate how many people had to be arrested for the paper's photo ops. When they did their so-called 'raid' and kicked in the door, the designated fall guys would actually raise their hands."

"Very civilized," Earl said.

"But you got to hand it to the Chinese," Munoz chuckled. "Since grandfather Horgan negotiated the mayor's piece, some of the Chinese gave Horgan an interest in their own restaurants. The ones they used to front their operations. That way he was negotiating against himself."

"Very clever."

"Over time they dropped the whores and opium and concentrated on gambling. Exclusive clubs, members only. So it passed to Horgan's father to make sure they stayed under the radar and to give them a heads up if the vice squad was sniffing around." Munoz paused. "I knew his father. A real hard ass from the old school."

"That explains the Chinese restaurant," Earl said. "The safe was probably where the grandfather parked the take back in his day, until it was time to deliver it downtown."

"Yeah, but those protection gigs for the old bulls were shut down when the new chief took over." Munoz said. "That, at least, was one thing the pencil pusher got right."

"But what was Horgan doing there?"

"Oh yes, Horgan the younger. He was a piece of work. Must have made the old man proud," Munoz scoffed.

"What do you mean?"

"He was one of those cowboys who had watched too many *Dirty Harry* movies. His personnel jacket must have read like a civil rights lawyer's to-do list."

"On television, they said he was a Medal of Valor winner," Earl said.

"Oh, yeah, a real hero," Munoz said sarcastically. "He gets involved in a high speed chase with a bank robber. The bad guy turns up a dead end street and stalls out. He's just sitting there. On the radio tape you can hear the dispatcher yelling to proceed with caution because there's a hostage in the car. Right after the warning, you hear Horgan open up, blasting away at the car. Kills the bad guy and puts a through and through into the hostage."

Munoz looked at Earl for a reaction.

"Some hero," Earl replied.

"So now the brass has a problem. Do they prosecute one of their own? LAPD royalty? Admit he just plugged a civilian? No fucking way. They muscle the coroner to say he can't determine who shot the hostage, so they blame it on the bad guy and give Horgan a medal."

"I would love to have been a fly on the wall when that was decided," Earl said.

"Oh, they were not pleased with young Horgan. Right after the medal ceremony he was loaned out to the Feds to work undercover drugs. Somebody must owe somebody good for taking him off their hands."

Millie appeared at the table to offer a refill.

"No thanks Millie, gotta run." Earl turned to Munoz as he got up, "Good work, Manny. I'll call you after I go through what I get from the DA today. I'm glad you're on board."

The benches in the cavernous courtroom were filled with lawyers and their bailed-out clients waiting for the judge to appear and call their cases. In the front rows, news reporters huddled together, chatting and laughing like a group of school kids on a field trip. They were entirely uninterested in the misery around them, unless a case had a sensational or unusual angle their editors or producers would consider newsworthy.

The felony arraignment court was like a judicial clearing house. Defendants were officially told the charges they faced and were assigned a future date for a preliminary hearing. In theory, a preliminary hearing required the prosecution to present enough of its case to satisfy a judge that it should proceed to trial. Not necessarily enough to prove the defendant guilty, but at least to raise a reasonable suspicion he had done it. The benefit to the defense was a chance to preview some of the prosecution witnesses and cross-examine them.

Earl checked in with the clerk and scanned the room. Facing the judge's bench, behind tables cluttered with telephones, filing bins and stacks of case files, were the harried prosecutors and public defenders permanently assigned to this court. These were the dispatchers who voiced the required legal responses, noted the court dates in the files and later passed the files on to the lawyers ultimately assigned the case. In the dark humor of the profession, they were there "to move the meat."

In the jury box, which in the arraignment court was never used as intended, sat those prosecutors with a serious case who chose to handle this appearance themselves. Earl spotted his DA, with whom he had crossed swords before. Jim Jessup was a sour-faced, middle-aged man with a fringe of grey hair like a nest around his shiny bald spot. His jowls were beginning to droop, as if giving in to the weight of his down-turned mouth. He wore the same plain grey suit as always, which Earl figured came off a rack of identical ones in his closet. Jessup was methodical to a fault, checking every box, calling every witness, fighting over every issue. A trial to him was about tactics, not about rights and justice. It was about winning. But he was honest, a virtue not always shared by all his colleagues. There would be no October surprises, no unrecorded confession suddenly appearing from a detective's pocket in the middle of trial.

"Jim, how are you?" Earl said, offering his hand. "I see you wore something for the cameras."

"Counselor," Jessup said, keeping his seat.

Earl knew that Jessup, like most prosecutors, identified defense attorneys with their clients and accorded them the same level of respect.

A young woman stood up next to Jessup. She had sun-lightened auburn hair, pulled back behind her head and wore a pale blue pants suit. Shaking Earl's hand, she said, "I'm Samantha Price. I'll be assisting Mr. Jessup. Call me Sam."

"Nice to meet you," Earl said. Her firm handshake fit her broad-shouldered, athletic body. She met Earl's eyes with a steady gaze and a guileless smile that conveyed a quiet confidence. While she was not a classic beauty, her tanned face had a wholesomeness and openness that made her seem genuine and unaffected. *Shit,* Earl thought, *the jury is going to love her*. There was none of the "just try me" hard-eyed cynicism that some of her female colleagues felt obligated to adopt. Lacking older women role models, most young women DA's had chosen to emulate the female television prosecutors on *Law and Order*, which meant exuding a toughness just short of announcing "mine are bigger than yours." Earl had planned on playing off a glum-faced prosecutor. She would give the prosecution a whole different look.

"So what have you got for me?" Earl asked Jessup. At this stage in the proceedings, the legal rules, called "discovery," required the prosecutor to turn over all the relevant evidence in the case to the defense, so the defendant would know some of what he was facing and could prepare for the preliminary hearing. In reality, the defense only got the highlights, a bare-bones outline of the prosecutor's case. The bulk of the evidence was held back until the case reached the trial court.

Sam reached into her briefcase and handed Earl an inch-thick folder of papers. "This it?" Earl asked, thumbing through the pages.

"You know the drill," Jessup said. "You'll get the rest later."

"OK, shall we pick a date for the prelim?" Earl suggested.

"What for? You know we're going to the grand jury."

Earl had anticipated this would happen. In a major case, no DA wanted to expose his witnesses to cross-examination before trial, so instead of a preliminary hearing, the law permitted the DA to present the case to a grand jury. It was a secret proceeding, without the presence of the defendant or his lawyer. During the proceeding, the DA called his witnesses before a group of citizens, hand-picked by the judges, who sat for a year and heard only these special cases.

"You sure you've got enough?" Earl asked with a smile, holding the folder of reports in the palm of one hand as if to measure its weight.

"For a grand jury?" Jessup asked, taking the question seriously. "As the saying goes, they'd indict a ham sandwich if I asked them to."

The bailiff called out for order over the noise in the room and announced the judge was taking the bench. Papers rustled as everyone rose. The door to chambers opened, and John Albert Thompson strode in. A successful civil lawyer, he ran the arraignment court smoothly and efficiently, all the time hating the assignment. His reward for bringing order to this normally chaotic process was an extension of his tour for another year.

"Let me take a case out of order, so we can get some of these people out of here. *People versus Seabrooke*," the judge announced.

Earl stepped to a podium facing the bench and identified himself as Seabrooke's lawyer. Jessup announced for the People, leaning against the jury box. Several news photographers quietly left their seats in the audience to step past the bar into the lawyers' area and took up kneeling positions with cameras at the ready, like marksmen anticipating a shot.

"I have a request here," the judge said, holding up a piece of paper, "from several media outlets to be allowed to photograph and film the proceedings. Any objection?"

"Yes, your honor," Earl replied. "There may be an issue of eyewitness identification. I can't represent there is one because I just received the discovery. But displaying photographs of Mr. Seabrooke at this stage would certainly prejudice any future identification process."

"There's no ID issue," Jessup said. "Besides, his photo has already been shown on television."

"Unless the People will stipulate," Earl said, "that they will not be offering any eyewitness identification evidence at trial, my objection stands."

"I'm going to err on the side of caution," the judge said. "The media request is denied. Bring out the defendant."

The photographers returned to their seats and shrugged a question at their reporters. A steel door at the side of the courtroom silently opened and Seabrooke hobbled out in chains. There was a buzz of conversation, and the bailiff shouted for silence. Earl turned and smiled at Seabrooke and waited for him to slowly join him at the podium.

"Your honor," Earl said. "I am making a formal request that my client's restraints be removed."

The judge stared at Earl with annoyance. "Counsel, this is just an arraignment. There is no jury here. You and your client will be out of here in a minute."

"That may be true, judge. But while we're in this courtroom, no matter how briefly, my client, like any defendant, deserves to be treated with dignity, and to appear without restraints. As the Court knows, the United Sates Supreme Court agrees with me on this point."

The judge heaved a sigh at what he considered a waste of time. He stared hard at Earl for a moment, then turned and nodded at the bailiff. When the chains had been removed, Seabrooke rubbed his wrists, straightened his shoulders and said under his breath, "Thanks."

The formalities of the arraignment were over quickly, as the judge had predicted. Earl entered a plea of not guilty and waived the requirement that the prosecution publicly read the charges. Jessup told the judge the prosecution would seek a grand jury indictment, to which Earl made a motion that the transcript of the testimony given before the grand jury be sealed and only be available to the parties, not open to the public. This produced a stir from the reporters. The judge granted the motion, but said the transcript would be sealed only temporarily until the trial judge could decide the question.

As Seabrooke was being led back to the holding cell, the judge called a short recess so the audience could thin out. The reporters and photographers noisily gathered their belongings and funneled out the door, followed by a scattering of "court watchers" who spent their days routinely following any publicity case around the courthouse.

A trim young black man with close cropped hair, wearing a dark blue suit, approached Earl. "I'm Deputy Morris, the Sherriff Department's press officer. I assume you intend to make a statement to the press."

"Do I have a choice?" Earl asked with a resigned smile.

"Not unless you want to be filmed running to your car as they shout questions at you."

"So what's the routine?" Earl asked.

"I'll escort you out of the building. In front of the courthouse there's an area we have designated for the press conference. There's a piece of tape on the pavement. That's your mark. Stay on it. The cameras are all set up for that spot. The press has a 'no go' zone of ten feet in front of your mark, so they won't mob you."

"Sounds like it's a good thing I played rugby in college."

The deputy did not smile. "After you have made your statement, it's up to you if you want to take questions. Usually they need about thirty seconds of video, if you want to give them more to work with, that's your call. Once you finish, I suggest you return with me into the building to give them some time to clear out. Any questions?"

"Nope. Let's do it."

In the hallway, Earl was approached by a short man in a plaid sports coat. "Mr. Earl, I work for Thomas Glass. Do you have a moment?"

Earl knew Thomas Glass. Everyone in the court system knew Thomas Glass.

"What's up?" Earl asked.

"Mr. Glass has requested that you join him for lunch tomorrow at the Redwood Room. Twelve thirty."

An audience with the great man, Earl thought. How charming. Thomas Glass had a television show called *The People's Voice*, on which he and selected guests held forth on the city's criminal justice system, its participants and any current case worthy of their attention. Glass was known in the courthouse as The Thumb for his ability to tip the scales of justice. His reputation had been established when he called for the defeat of a well-respected judge who was up for reelection. On his television program, Glass singled the judge out for coddling criminals. He was labeled the "Santa Clause Judge" who gave away the courthouse. The judge ignored Glass as a shameless self-promoter, safe in the realization that a sitting judge, short of an accusation of child molestation, was always re-elected. When the judge was defeated by a previously unknown opponent, it sent a shiver down some spines, but was viewed as an anomaly.

But one group paid attention to Glass's campaign, the insurance companies. They approached Glass and offered to fund a campaign against the Chief Justice of the California Supreme Court. She was causing them trouble, or more precisely, money, by leading the Court in protecting a consumer's right to sue for injuries. Glass attacked the Justice over her handling of death penalty cases, an issue about which there had been no previous concern. After a year of Glass's lamenting the Court's failure to uphold every death sentence as "the will of the people," the voters did not reaffirm the Chief Justice. This time a cold wind of fear swept down the halls of the courthouse.

After that, any case that drew The Thumb's televised attention suddenly became toxic. Prosecutors suspended their own judgment and substituted what they guessed would appease Glass, judges abandoned long-held sentencing practices and doubled or tripled sentences to avoid his censure. Perhaps his most damaging practice was to begin examining cases on air while they were being tried, criticizing a judge's rulings or a defense attorney's performance, always ready to provide an explanation for any shortfall in the prosecutor's case or suggest the existence of a missing piece of evidence.

"Tell Mr. Glass I'll be there," Earl said, knowing he had no choice.

The sound of clicking cameras announced his appearance as Earl pushed through the courthouse doors and into the sunlight. He tried to look assured as he walked to his designated spot. Facing him was a tightly packed scrum of reporters and cameramen, bristling with microphones and lenses. The cameramen, who all seemed tall and sturdy, jostled each other to protect their reporters' position of access while aiming their shoulder-held cameras. Behind them, the television vans parked on the sidewalk, each with a tall antenna sprouting up from the roof like some super weed.

Earl looked into the cameras with a bemused smile. "Thank you all for coming," he said in a clear voice. The scrum fell silent.

"It is often said that the road to justice is long. Today, Mr. Seabrooke and I took the first step on that road by entering a plea of not guilty. We intend to work diligently over the coming months to marshal the evidence to prove just that. At the end of this road lies a trial before a jury from our community. Mr. Seabrooke and I have complete faith in the fairness of our jury system. Therefore, it is only appropriate that I respect that system and present our case in a courtroom to a jury and not engage in a duel with the prosecutor over the merits of the case in the media. A trial by jury, with rules forged over centuries, is the finest vehicle yet devised to arrive at the truth. Mr. Seabrooke and I look forward to that test, confident that the truth will emerge and Mr. Seabrooke will be acquitted. Thank you for your attention."

Earl turned and walked back into the building. The reporters erupted with a chorus of shouted questions. "Is Seabrooke guilty? Do you think he deserves the death penalty? What did he tell you happened?"

As the courthouse door closed behind Earl, the mass of reporters turned as one and scurried to their designated filming spots. Earlier that morning their cameramen had divvied up the locations on the pavement where the reporters could do their on-camera commentary with the courthouse in the background. Each location was chalk marked with the call letters of a TV outlet, to avoid any dispute. The reporters stood at their spots, adjusting their clothing, brushing their hair and striking the proper pose to deliver their lines.

Without looking back, Earl walked out the south exit and headed for his car.

CHAPTER 6

The next day, Detective Fred Brown sat in a small, windowless room deep inside the Los Angeles Men's Central Jail. He was waiting to interview a snitch. The metal chair across the table was empty, as were the gun-metal grey walls of the room. He had arrived early, hoping to avoid the heat. Fat chance. Brown took off his jacket and loosened his tie, but his sweat-soaked shirt still stuck to his back. He was hot and irritable and needed a beer. It had been thirty minutes and they still had not brought down his man. He silently swore to himself that the wait had better be worth it. This moron had left his prints behind at two of his armed robberies. It had been Brown's case and an easy one for a change. The guy was bought and paid for. A conviction this time around would be his Third Strike which meant a life sentence. So if this puke wanted to trade information on some other poor asshole for a break on his case, he'd better have some heavy chips to play with.

Talking to snitches, he silently complained, was always a pain in the ass. For starters, he had to use this airless oven, rather than the attorneys' visiting room, so they would not be seen talking with a cop. He didn't particularly care if some snitch got "shanked," but not before he had served his purpose. The whole process of dealing with snitches was irritating, but what was he supposed to do, he had to clear cases. It always amused him when he talked to some of his wife's friends. They actually thought he solved cases by following clues like some smartass Sherlock Holmes. Like he had that kind of time. He cleared most of his cases with confessions, and a bunch with snitches. The rest just got cold.

So that was exactly why Brown was here. To talk to Jake Snyder. When it came to working the system, Brown had to admit, the son of a bitch was lights-out. The best, a natural. He always found someone a little higher on the food chain to trade. Snyder would testify against his own mother if it would cut a few years off a sentence he was facing. Snyder just needed a little squeezing to make sure he wasn't holding something back for the next time.

Rising from his chair, Brown paced the room hoping to circulate the air. The last time he saw Snyder, he had wanted to cut a deal in exchange for some rumors about a supposedly dirty cop. As if snatching away some poor cop's pension was supposed to put lead in his pencil. Besides, this unnamed cop was on loan to the Feds, the very guys who wouldn't piss on you if you were on fire. So no thanks. Let them deal with it. He was interested in his own damn cases. So Snyder better give him something good and it better not be about some drug dealer or whorehouse. Those fucks in narco and vice could clear their own paper.

The door swung open and Jake Snyder stood in the doorway. Brown nodded at the deputy standing behind him, who gave Snyder a rough push forward and shut the door. Snyder shot a resentful look over his shoulder. Dirty blond hair hung over the collar of his blue prison shirt. His deep-set eyes quickly cruised the room, settling on Brown. He attempted a smile.

"Hey, thanks for coming, Detective Brown."

"Yeah, and fuck you too. This had better be good. If you're peddling that tired shit about a dirty cop, I'm done."

"No, no, this here is some major shit. Gonna be my ticket out of here and a big score for y'all."

"Yeah, keep dreaming," Brown said.

"No, listen here. You know that there cop Horgan that got popped. The guy who did him, I can give him to ya'. Gift wrapped." He smiled slyly.

Brown sat thinking. It wasn't his case, it was LAPD, but, Jesus Christ, the asshole killed a cop. Nobody gets away with that. "Jake, you better not be fucking with me or I swear I'll put your fucking face through that wall."

"Y'all think I'm crazy? Why the fuck would I do that? I'm serious."

Brown studied him. "So what have you got?"

"Okay, okay, just listen a minute. I can't tell ya' yet, but...." He raised his hands in a plea when Brown started to get up. "But I've got it. I swear to fucking Christ."

Brown stared at him with smoldering eyes, as if Snyder were an insect he wanted to step on.

"Sergeant Brown, all's I need is a phone. That's all. Just a phone call and I'll have it."

"So go make the fucking call."

"No, I mean one of them private phones, like they got in the office."

Brown sat thinking. "An office phone, that's all?"

"That's all. That's it, I swear."

"You mean one that isn't monitored and doesn't have that recording saying it's a call from the jail?" Brown said with a smirk.

Snyder gave him a cloying smile and shrugged.

"All right. But here's the deal. If you're playing me, I'm going to call you down to the visitor's room and make sure everybody knows what good pals we are. You got me?"

Snyder nodded soberly. "Okay."

Brown got up and pounded on the door. When the escort arrived, Brown told him to send down the senior deputy, he needed to talk to him about a special arrangement.

***

Across the city, in the glare of the morning sun, Earl maneuvered into his office parking space behind an old two-story California Craftsman. An enterprising lawyer had bought the once proud Santa Monica mansion and converted it into law offices. Earl rented space on the ground floor. From the first, he had been drawn by the feel of the old building with its high ceilings and creaky wooden floors that seemed to be whispering they had stories to tell.

Once inside the back door, he fell under the jurisdiction of Martha, the secretary who was part of the package that came with his suitemate, James McManis. A lean older woman with short grey hair, Martha swam at the YMCA each morning before work and did the day's crossword puzzle in ink. She and McManis had been together for twenty-five years and still addressed each other as Mr. McManis and Miss Sullivan. They argued like an old married couple, secure in the belief that neither would leave. She was unmarried, and he was a recent widower. There was a time she had dreamed of this opportunity, but now it seemed to be too late.

"Well, Mr. Important, the press has been calling." She held up a sheaf of phone messages. "I suppose I'll be seeing you on TV tonight and you didn't even get a haircut."

"This is the new look, Martha. Sort of the tortured-artist-turned-lawyer."

"Yeah, well get your tortured soul to the barber tomorrow. Now, what do I do with these?" She indicated the phone messages.

"Into the dust bin of history." Earl pointed at the wastebasket.

"They'll just call again."

"If they do, tell them I'm not commenting or giving interviews." Earl had already decided he would ask the judge for a gag order, preventing both sides from talking to the media about the case. Any chance of getting such an order would quickly evaporate if his comments were spread all over the judge's morning paper. Besides, the defense never won a battle with the prosecution for the headlines. Reporters were dependent upon the prosecutor's office for the inside information on their stories, case after case, year after year. Defense lawyers came and went. That pipeline only stayed open if the reporter adhered to the prosecution view-point.

Earl stepped into his office and shut the door. It was a large room with a fireplace centered on one wall. When the house was young, this room had served as the parlor where the gentlemen retired after dinner for cigars and whiskey. An oriental carpet, a gift from a grateful client, extended to the edges of the hardwood floor. A large old mahogany desk, its top inset with hand-tooled leather, sat comfortably at one end, facing two maroon leather client chairs. Angled near the fireplace was an over-stuffed leather chair with a law book resting, open, on its arm.

On the mantle were the framed photos of two athletic teams. A younger Bobby Earl grinned in both. He had gone to the University of California at Berkeley on a baseball scholarship and played rugby in the offseason. He was never a great hitter, but he knew the art of catching. He called the pitches, so he studied the opposing hitters and knew what to look for. He knew that the way they moved their feet between pitches telegraphed where they expected the next one, or that if the mark the ball left on the bat after a foul was on the barrel, the hitter might square up on the next one. Details made a difference.

At the far end of the room, a fully restored antique Nickel Head slot machine from the California gold rush days sat on a sturdy-legged table. Earl urged each new client to give the arm of the old machine a pull, to impress on them his warning that, as in most things, luck played a part in every case. Starting with which judge they drew or which prosecutor, even the mix of people in the jury pool. An infinite number of things could intrude upon their chances, even with the most skilled of lawyers. As with most everything in life, he had yet to see anyone pull three cherries.

He tossed his coat onto the leather chair, slid the file folder of reports onto his desk, dropped into the high backed desk chair and started reading. Even though he had read hundreds of such files, as he turned the pages, he still felt a sense of anticipation, an excitement, like the start of a hunt. He read the reports, worded in that stilted police speak, not just to learn the prosecution facts, but searching for a hint of something out of place, something that did not fit the official version, something that might widen into a door through which he could march a defense.

Most of the reports contained not a word of substantive information and were generated merely to satisfy some bureaucratic dictate. Jessup, like any DA, had given up as little as legally required at this stage, but there was still enough to start Earl's mind churning. This was no routine case, the questions just kept jumping off the page and bouncing into each other as he tried to order his thoughts. He picked up the phone, called Munoz and asked him to come to the office. He needed a sounding board. Then he grabbed a legal size yellow pad and furiously scribbled the first of what he knew would be endless questions and lists of work to be done.

Within an hour, Munoz had wedged his bulk into the easy chair and was reading the reports. Earl sat pondering his note pad, feet on the desk, feeling perplexed. As Munoz closed the file, Earl lowered his feet and swung round to face him. He quickly explained what Seabrooke had told him about being bailed out to do this job, expecting cash in the safe but being interrupted before the job was completed, then fleeing. Seabrooke had denied even seeing Horgan and certainly had not shot him. Munoz knew that, because he worked for the defense, he was bound by the same rules of confidentiality as Earl was. Munoz also knew not to ask Bobby Earl if he believed his client. An investigator's job was to sniff out the facts, what Bobby did with them was his decision.

"Two hundred and fifty thousand dollars," Munoz said. "Are you kidding me? That's a lot to skim, even from dope dealers."

"So where did Horgan get it?" Earl asked. "And why did he get an interest in this restaurant? I don't buy this honorable ancestor bit. Horgan was doing something for this owner. Maybe they had something going. Maybe that's where the money came from."

"Maybe they were in the drug business together," Munoz said, "and Horgan kept his split in the safe. The restaurant owner wants to steal it, so he goes to Aradano the bondsman and they use Seabrooke. Horgan stumbles onto the plan, figures the owner's behind it, calls him to the restaurant, they argue, owner pops him."

"So why leave the body there?" Earl asked.

Munoz slowly nodded in agreement. "Maybe it was a drug deal gone bad. Horgan used the restaurant for the meet. Gets popped. Our man being there was just a coincidence."

"Pretty big coincidence," Earl said. "Seabrooke was told it had to go down that night, between midnight and two a.m."

Munoz sat for a moment, thinking, tapping the file. "So, it says our man picks the lock to get in and Horgan had a key. How did somebody else get in? Either they had another key or Horgan let them in."

"Which means Horgan knew them or was expecting them."

"Figures," Munoz said. "He had a backup gun, but it was still in his ankle holster."

"But why keep the money in a safe in a restaurant?"

"If it was dirty money," Munoz explained, "there's no way a cop would keep it at his own place. And a bank account or a safe deposit box is the first place Internal Affairs would look." Earl nodded and they both fell into a puzzled silence.

After a pause Munoz heaved a sigh. "Well, ol' Aradano the bondsman is the key. But good luck on him giving up his source for the money in the safe. He might have taken a few too many punches to the head, but he ain't that stupid."

"I'll take a run at Aradano," Earl said. "But what do you make of this tool, this borescope, whatever that is, with a mark on it? It seems an awfully convenient fit for the DA's theory. Horgan surprises our man in the act, our man shoots him and forgets the tool in the excitement. Pretty pat." Earl shook his head. "You think it's legit?"

Munoz thought for a moment. "All cops are tempted to lie about the reasons for searches and arrests, you know, probable cause and all that shit. If the guy is good for it, they figure what's the difference. But actually *putting* a case on somebody." Munoz made a grimace. "And a safe man, at that. That's a real stretch."

"Well, anyway, if this tool is really all they've got, it's pretty thin. After all this time, how are they going to tie it back to Seabrooke? And the safe man's report says the original stop when they marked the tools was thrown out. Why don't you see if you can dig up the original reports? And check out the safe guy." Earl flipped through the file. "Richard Walker's his name."

Munoz wrote in his notebook. "And why don't I work the dope angle a little, see if I can find out what Horgan was working on? Maybe he was mixing with some serious players and got careless or fucked up somehow." Munoz made another note. "The Feds are uncooperative bastards, but I'll make a few calls."

"Good, Manny. The DA is taking it to the Grand Jury this week, so we may know a little more when I get a transcript of the testimony, but I doubt it. Jessup will probably play it pretty close to the vest." Earl shuffled the reports back into the folder. "At least I feel better now that we're getting started."

"You must be getting calls from the press," Munoz said, prying himself out of the chair.

"Oh, yeah. But get this. I've been summoned for an audience with Himself, The Thumb."

"May he rot in hell," Munoz said sternly.

"Whoa, what's that about?"

"You don't know the story?"

"Apparently not," Earl said.

Munoz sank back down. "Several years ago, before he was The Thumb, just some hack reporter covering fires and auto accidents, he arranged to go on a ride-along with a couple rookie patrolmen. He was going to do a 'day in the life' kind of thing about cops. They get a call that night on a crazy, acting up on some citizen's front lawn. They roll on it. The three get out of the patrol car, the two rookies and The Thumb. The ding is a homeless woman and she is screaming avenging angels and streets running with blood. The young cops start to approach her when she pulls something shiny out of her pocket and points it at them. Somebody yells 'gun.' They do as they're trained to do and pop her. It turns out she's got a spoon in her hand, and The Thumb has been filming the whole thing."

"That should have helped, having it on film," Earl said.

"Wait. So the shooting team calls in Internal Affairs and the scalp hunters go to work on them. Each kid says he relied on his partner yelling 'gun,' but each denies he's the one who yelled it.

"I don't like the sound of this," Earl said.

"So Internal Affairs goes to The Thumb. Did he hear anyone yell 'gun'? Funny thing, not only did he not hear it, but for some reason, the mic on the camera was turned off." Munoz smiled cynically. "That night he's on television showing the film and calling for their scalps. The rest, as they say, is history."

They both sat silently for a moment. "Enjoy your talk," Munoz said. "Just be sure to wash your hands after."

Johnny Aradano's bail bond office was across the street from the Men's Central Jail, a few blocks from the courthouse. Earl decided to pay him a call before his appointment with His Eminence, The Thumb. He pulled his car into the small lot of the mini-mall next door, avoiding the glittering shards of glass in front of the Planet of the Grapes liquor store, he parked and got out. Along the sidewalk, Aradano's cappers were posted like sentries to net the families walking to the jail visitation line and shame them into posting a bail they could not afford. Across the street, a line was forming at Rita's Taco Truck, drawn by the rich smell of refried beans and chorizo sausage. On the corner, the morning's crop of released inmates milled idly about, blinking in the unaccustomed sunlight. Mostly drunks and young male prostitutes, they were part of the catch and release program spawned by the over-crowded jails. In the light of day, the transvestites had a sad, clownish look, with their smeared makeup and large feet wobbling in too small high heels.

Inside his small office, Johnny Aradano sat behind a scuffed wooden desk covered with wrinkled bond papers, topped with a fresh pink pad of blank bail forms. A small television on the corner of the desk was tuned to a Spanish language soap opera. On the walls were framed black and white photographs of Aradano fighting in the ring, sweat glistening on his taut muscles as he furiously punched an opponent. Back then he was Johnny "Lights Out," a local boxing hero. He never trained much but, with his aggressive style, the fans were always sure of somebody ending up on the canvas.

But it was not the hard bodied, handsome young man in the photographs Earl found sitting behind the desk. Aradano's face, armored with thick scar tissue, was divided by a nose that first turned sharply right, then left. In a nostalgic touch, his curly black hair was swept up in a pompadour.

"Hey, come in," Aradano said, "You hear the one about the guy walks into a bar with a talking dog?"

"Yeah, he'll sell him cheap because he's a liar," Earl replied.

Aradano was obviously disappointed. "So, what can I do for you?" he asked, reaching for his pad of bail forms.

"I'm Sydney Seabrooke's lawyer."

Aradano stared hard at Earl, then tossed the pad onto the desk and leaned back in his chair. "I hear your boy's in a lot of trouble."

"And I hear you put him there," Earl said.

"What are you talking about?" Aradano shot back.

"Look, I know you set up the restaurant job. You bailed out Seabrooke so he could crack the safe and split the proceeds. I don't care about that. All I want to know is who gave you the information about what was in the safe. Just give me a name and you're out of this."

Aradano leaned forward. "I got a lot of work to do, so if you don't mind." He looked up and nodded toward the door.

"You know there's another way to do this. Maybe somebody might drop a dime on you to the cops. I'm sure they would love to have a chat with you."

Aradano looked at Earl with a smirk, as if an opponent had just hit him and there was nothing behind the punch. "Your boy's not going to do that, counselor, because that would be admitting he was the trigger man. You think the DA would cut a deal with a cop killer to get a piece of an old fighter," he scoffed. "Besides, it would just be his word against mine."

"Well, there is the small matter of you going his bail without a fee or collateral. Somebody might wonder about that," Earl said.

"Hey, I'm a nice guy. I like to help people. Maybe I was doing a favor for a friend."

"I'm sure your surety company would enjoy hearing their bond money was being used for your charitable activities."

"That the best you got? I write more paper for them than anybody in town. You think they're gonna give a rat's ass? Here." He pushed his phone off a pile of papers. "Call them."

Earl sat silently as Aradano grinned at him. "Fine," Earl said finally, "let me have a look at the bail file."

"You got a subpoena?" He paused. "I didn't think so. I guess we're finished here."

"For now," Earl said.

CHAPTER 7

"Mr. Glass's table is right this way." The tuxedoed maître d' led Bobby past the red leather booths filled with wine-drinking businessmen in white shirts and silk ties, past the mahogany bar with its polished brass fixtures and chatty cast of regulars, past the wood-paneled walls hung with framed caricatures signed by celebrities, in appreciation, to Bernard. The Redwood Room, just a few blocks from the courthouse, adopted a more animated atmosphere in the evening when the criminal defense lawyers gathered for drinks to lie about their trial exploits and complain about judges' rulings.

Thomas Glass' regular table was in a corner at the rear. He was a small man with thinning hair, a high forehead and fleshy cheeks that gave his face a soft, almost cherubic appearance. It was certainly not the robust, handsome face needed to read the news on television. Earl noticed, as he approached the table, the slight upward tilt to Glass's lips, as if he thought the world utterly corrupt and knew each person's price. Unlike on television, he wore a cream colored suit with a lavender tie and matching silk handkerchief that flowed out of his breast pocket. Strawberry red cufflinks winked on either side of a fine china plate displaying a filleted fish.

"Mr. Earl, nice of you to join me. May I call you Bobby? Please." He gestured to the chair opposite. "You must pardon me, I couldn't wait. It's Dover sole. Bernard flies it in for me. Quite fresh, quite delicious, you must try it." He raised his hand to call a waiter.

Earl had made certain he would be late. "No thanks, I was held up and now I've got to get back."

Glass gave Earl an appraising look. "I see, a deliberate man, who believes in getting down to business," he said as if he knew this was a fraud. "You don't mind if I continue to eat."

"Not at all."

A cellphone hummed, which Glass retrieved from his suit pocket and put to his ear. "I'll send Francis," he said and clicked off. A glance over Earl's shoulder and the same little man in the plaid sports coat appeared. "Our friend has something for us," he told the man. "He'll meet you at the fountain, as usual. Give him this." Glass reached in his wallet and passed over a bill. Returning to his meal, Glass continued eating, focusing on his plate as he spoke. "I understand you have the Seabrooke case."

"I do," Earl said.

"I want to interview him," Glass said between bites. "On camera, of course. And you would be featured as well, profile of a prominent defense lawyer, shots in your office, endorsements from colleagues. Should attract a huge audience share." He paused and looked up at Earl over his rimless glasses. "You ready to be famous?"

"Sort of the 'public's right to know' coverage," Earl echoed.

Glass put down his silverware and stared skeptically at Earl. "Please, Bobby, don't disappoint me. I heard you were bright. You think the fate of the Republic hangs on what the television public hears about this tawdry case?" He waited as if he expected a response. "This is about my ratings and making you a household name. The lawyer that people in trouble will turn to. It's what's called a win-win deal."

"I appreciate the interest. But an interview is probably not the very best thing for the case right now."

A tall, dignified man approached the table. "Andrew," Glass said, looking up. "You two know each other don't you? Bobby Earl, Judge Sanford."

The judge looked very uncomfortable. "I was hoping for a word."

"Not right now, Andrew," Glass replied. "Give me a call, we'll set something up." The judge hesitated, then he nodded and left.

Glass looked back at Earl.

"As you know, Glass said, "I often have lawyers on my program to comment on cases. Perhaps you'd enjoy appearing and just talking about the case. Maybe a regular feature could be arranged."

"You know, that's just not me," Earl said. "Maybe when the case is over."

"We could start with information you wanted out there. I could certainly get it on the air. Without naming my source, of course. And when I refer to prominent defense lawyers, as I am wont to do, your name would be mentioned regularly."

"Thanks again, but any information I need to get out, I'm sure I'll be able to present during the trial."

Glass made a practiced gesture with his eyebrows that caused a waiter to silently appear and clear his plate. "Perhaps I don't quite understand. When you took this case you knew you would be the object of a great deal of attention. This obviously appealed to you or you wouldn't have taken the case. So why are you playing coy with me? You don't kiss on the first date? You expect me to court you?" Glass asked with skeptical emphasis on 'me.'

Earl checked his temper. "Of course I knew there would be publicity. But by taking the case I was also agreeing to do what was best for the client."

"Maybe you are naive, after all. The DA is appearing on my show tonight. What do you think we'll be talking about? You want his side to be the only one told? Because, be assured, I am running with this story, with you or without you. And if his dish is the only one on the menu I will serve it up, piping hot."

One thing Earl knew, he did not want to make an enemy of The Thumb, because if it got personal, it would be his client who paid the price. The last thing this case needed was The Thumb administering a nightly dose of hemlock to the potential jury pool. "I'm sorry if I have disappointed you, Mr. Glass. Maybe I am being a bit naïve. Let me think it over after I've gotten into the case a little."

"All right, Bobby. Have it your way." Glass smiled as if they both knew this was not going to happen. "Have a pleasant day."

As Earl left, he tried to calm his anger by telling himself his pathetic display of knee bending was merely a necessary part of his duty to his client. It was not the first time this responsibility had required him to eat such a distasteful sandwich, and what was between the slices of bread was never steak. He wished he did not feel the need to exercise self-restraint, that he could feel free to tell an arrogant DA or a self-righteous cop what he really thought of them. But he could not bring himself to see such a display as anything but self-indulgence. It certainly could not be wrapped in a cloak of moral courage, since the inevitable petty response for the resulting bruised ego fell on the client, not the lawyer. The client suffered the vindictive extra charge or served the additional time meted out to appease hurt feelings.

Earl knew that even if he appeared on his show, The Thumb, like any crime reporter, would always adopt the prosecution line. It was useless for the defense to "try" its case in the media. His best move was to get a gag order to prevent the prosecution from using the press to pass on the stuff that would never be admissible in court. Any chance of his getting that order would quickly disappear if Earl appeared on Glass's show to fire the first publicity salvo and then went into court to complain about leaks to the press. But not appearing was a gamble. If he didn't get the gag order, the airways would open up and rain a shit storm of abuse on him and his client. Glass would be happy to trumpet any rumor or discredited story passed to him by the DA's Office, who knew they could never get such "evidence" before the jury.

They had served scrambled eggs with fried baloney that morning, so it must be Monday, Jake Snyder figured. It was hard to keep track in the jail - every day was the same as the day before. But not today, he said to himself. Today was going to be different. He felt certain of it as he swaggered down a cement hallway in his blue inmate shirt, swinging his uncuffed arms, his thin chin tilted upward in a challenge. The muscular guard, following closely behind, directed him with monosyllabic grunts when to turn down another hallway. A group of unescorted inmates appeared ahead, and the guard barked "hit the wall." The inmates shouldered each other as they lined up facing the hallway's institutional green walls. All inmates quickly learned this routine, designed for the safety of the vastly outnumbered unarmed deputies. Very few refresher courses were ever needed. The guard intently watched their backs as he passed, not knowing which of them might be carrying a "shank," a piece of scrounged metal crudely fashioned into a knife, wrapped and inserted in their "keister drawer."

Jake arrived at a wooden door with a large glass window looking into a small office whose sole occupants were a grey metal desk and chair. A cream-colored cradle phone and a black three ring notebook looked lonely and abandoned on the otherwise empty desktop

"This is it, dickwad," the guard sneered, putting a heavy hand on Jake's shoulder and spinning him around. "The sergeant said you was to have privacy to use the phone. So I guess you want to call your boyfriend or some such fag shit."

Jake looked at him with an expressionless face, the hatred buried deep in his eyes. He knew this guard with the biceps bulging under his tight uniform shirt. Now was not the time, he said to himself. But if he was ever on the street and he happened to be carrying his piece, oh yeah, he would love to do this fat fuck.

The guard waited, hoping for a response. "All right, asshole. Fifteen minutes. If you touch anything but that phone, I'll break your face."

Jake stepped into the room and sat down at the desk. A paper clip peeked from under the notebook. He deftly scooped it into his hand as he pulled the phone closer and began to dial. A paper clip was a valuable little item. It could be bent into a key to open handcuffs.

"Yes, operator, do you have the number of Department B, as in boy, of the Torrance Superior Court?" Jake spoke into the receiver in an attempt at a civilized tone. He was scheduled to go to that court the next day on his robbery case. Christ, he thought, was that caper a mistake. He normally targeted only low-level drug dealers, but he had seen an easy mark on the street and could not resist. How did he know some guy would play citizen hero and get himself pistol whipped? With his record, now he was looking at a three strikes case, which carried an 'L.' No way was he going to do Life.

He paused to collect himself and rekindle his old confidence with memories of deals he had cut with the cops before. He was going to get back out there again. He had to. He had the plan now. All he had to do was put the pieces together. The operator interrupted his thoughts with the number and he made the call.

"Department B, bailiff," the voice said.

"Yeah, deputy, this is Sergeant Brown, out of East LA robbery homicide. I was wondering if you could do me a favor?" Jake said.

"What's up?"

"I got this snitch I gotta talk to. Says he's got some hot shit on one of my cases. He's housed in Men's Central. But if I pull him out down there his cellies might make him, which would probably be a benefit to mankind, but not before I'm through with him."

"I hear you on that," the bailiff said.

"So I was wondering if you could put the snitch on the court list for tomorrow and bring him down to Torrance on a dry run. We could talk to him in the downstairs lock-up," Jake said.

"Sure. You got a booking number?"

"Shit, you know, I don't. But he's got a fucked up name. Should be easy on the computer."

"What's the name?" the bailiff asked.

"Seabrooke, Sydney," Jake spelled it out.

"Hey, that sounds familiar. He's not the one who's good for that LAPD cop?"

"No," Jake said drawing out the word. "What have you been smoking?" He made a snorting sound. "That was Seymore or something. This guy is just some burned out old junkie, got caught up in a 187."

"OK, happy to do it, Sergeant," the bailiff said.

"Thanks, I owe you one," Jake said and hung up. He leaned back in the chair and drew a deep breath. That was close. If nobody jumped to it, tomorrow Seabrooke and he would be sharing a bus ride and later a cement bench in the lock-up in Torrance. He picked up the receiver and dialed. "Operator may I have the number for the robbery homicide division at the LAPD headquarters downtown." After getting the number he took a deep breath and dialed. "This is Sergeant Brown out of East LA robbery homicide. Who over there's got the Horgan homicide? I may have something for them."

"That would be Detective Tanner, but he's out in the field," the voice said.

"Is anybody around who's working the case?" Jake asked.

"Officer Hendeley. But working might be a bit of a stretch to describe what he does," the voice chuckled.

"One of those, eh? We got our share over here in the Sherriff's Department, believe me. But let me talk to him anyway," Jake said, knowing this was exactly the type of cop he wanted. The voice shouted Hendeley's name and told him to pick up the line.

"Hendeley," a voice barked.

"This is Brown over at Sherriff's robbery homicide. I understand you're working the Horgan homicide," Jake said.

"That's right."

"Well, I got this gang banger over here with a piece he says was used in the Horgan caper. What caliber was your murder weapon?" Jake asked.

"A twenty-two," Hendeley said.

"Shit. I knew it was bullshit. This is a thirty-two. But I figured I better check. Sorry.

"No problem," Hendeley replied and hung up.

Jake smiled to himself. What a dumb fuck. He picked up the receiver and fingered the rotary dial to a number he had memorized.

"Sergeant Brown, please," he said.

"He's off today. You want to leave a message?" the voice asked.

"Yeah. Tell him Jake Snyder called. Tell him to come see me in a couple days, I've got what he was asking for."

At the same time, just two floors above, Earl was having a very different conversation in the Attorney Visiting Room.

"I've decided to do an interview on television with Thomas Glass," Seabrooke said across the table's wooden divider.

Earl stared at him in disbelief. It had been several days since his last visit. He had not figured Seabrooke for one of those clients who needed constant hand-holding. Maybe that was a mistake, he thought. "What brought this on?" he asked.

"Mr. Glass came to see me and offered me the opportunity of setting the record straight on what really happened. He said he could arrange everything with the jail authorities, so we could film right here." Seabrooke gestured behind him to the attorney interview room. He turned back to Earl, his lips curved slightly in a satisfied expression.

It was unclear to Earl if Seabrooke was more pleased at the prospect of the interview, or at the effect his announcement was having on Earl. It was clear Seabrooke felt he was back in charge.

"I'm sure he could arrange that," Earl said matter-of-factly. "In fact, the DA would make sure it was arranged."

Seabrooke stared back with suspicion, as if caught off guard.

"Let's imagine this interview, why don't we?" Earl said, looking off as if in thought. "The first part will be the questions supplied by the DA that he wants Glass to ask. So they can pin you down before we know what evidence they have. Make sure they know what to expect at trial so they have plenty of time to prepare. Then he'll get to the emotional stuff, photos of the cop, medal of valor stories, edit in interviews with his family, ask you if you feel any regret, that sort of thing. He'll probably finish up saying he doesn't believe a word you said and that you're nothing but a cold-blooded killer. That will make him look strong and resolute, particularly since the guards will be kept off camera."

Seabrooke's stern look clearly said he was not enjoying Earl's performance.

"Have you ever even seen his show? You think this will be some dispassionate search for the truth?" Earl paused. "And what are you going to tell him, anyway? That you were there in the middle of the night to crack a safe and by some wild coincidence a cop happened to get shot and killed in the same place, on the same night, but you had nothing to do with it?"

Seabrooke was silent, but he glared angrily at Earl.

"Let's do this," Earl suggested in a reasonable tone. "Let's postpone this interview for a while. The offer will stay open, believe me. Give ourselves some time to figure out where we're going on the case. We go back to court in a week. The DA has to give us more of his case material then."

Seabrooke leaned back, leaving his handcuffed hand on the table, as he studied Earl. After a pause, he said, "When I was a boy, we had a cook from the South. She had an endless supply of sayings in which to wrap her opinions. One I remember seems apt. 'Why buy a dog if you're going to do the barking yourself?' " He gave Earl a cold smile. "I'll leave it to you, for now."

"Good," Earl said, ignoring the comparison and trying to act as if this was a decision arrived at by mutual consent. "There's something I wanted to ask you." He explained about the tool found at the scene and the cop who said that a couple years ago it had been marked and returned to Seabrooke. "Does that make any sense to you?"

"What kind of tool?" Seabrooke asked.

Earl pulled out the file from his briefcase and thumbed the pages. "It's listed as a borescope."

"I had one. Any real locksmith has one. I don't know if I left mine, I was in a bit of a hurry leaving the restaurant. Who was the officer? Was it Richard Walker?"

Earl nodded. "How did you know?"

Seabrooke smiled. "You might say we're professional rivals. He's the LAPD safe detective who has been trying to catch me for years. A very able safe man. We talk shop on occasion when our paths cross. I think we both enjoy talking about our craft with someone on our own level."

Earl raised a quizzical eyebrow.

"Oh, yes. Neither of us takes this game personally. We each have our jobs to do. You might say it's a question of mutual respect. If Richard Walker says he marked the tool, then, unfortunately, he marked the tool. He is painfully honest." Seabrooke shook his head. "Very clever, I must congratulate him when we next meet."

CHAPTER 8

The next Monday, Earl got to the courthouse early to avoid a long wait in the security line. The DA had taken Seabrooke's case to the Grand Jury and had obtained an indictment. Seabrooke was scheduled to appear on the morning calendar before the Presiding Judge for the case to be assigned to a trial court. As Earl walked down the hall toward Judge McKeene's courtroom, he was joined by George Kennedy, a public defender, wearing an emerald green gabardine suit that set off the sheen of his ebony colored skin.

"Man, this is one of my favorite days," Kennedy said.

"How so?" Earl asked.

"I love watching when it hits them which judge they drew," Kennedy said with a wide grin. "It's like roulette in Las Vegas."

"More like Russian roulette," Earl replied.

Inside the crowded courtroom, the din of conversation signaled that the judge had not yet taken the bench. Through the crowd Earl saw Jim Jessup, the DA, with his back against the jury box, arms folded, ignoring the group of reporters leaning over the spectator rail who were vainly lobbing questions at him. Samantha Price, the second chair DA, sat in the jury box, laughing and talking, the center of attention for a group of young DAs huddled around her, enjoying even this secondhand contact with a newsworthy case.

Earl worked his way through the milling lawyers, shaking hands and exchanging greetings, moving toward Jessup. "Jim," he said nodding toward the retreating reporters, "I hope you didn't trot out that old story about your days with the Weather Underground."

Jessup looked at him glumly from under raised eyebrows. "That's more your style isn't it, counsel?"

Earl smiled. "So what have you got for me?"

Jessup looked down at two cardboard boxes filled with documents. "Sign for it." He indicated a form on top of one of the boxes.

"Don't trust me, eh?"

Jessup rolled his eyes.

"Just want to give you a heads up," Earl said. "I intend to ask McKeene to continue the order sealing the Grand Jury transcript. It'll just be our little secret. For a while anyway."

"Knock yourself out. I'll oppose it," Jessup replied, staring past Earl into the room.

"O.K. Maybe we can at least agree on some dates for our next appearance." Earl opened his calendar book. "I hear McKeene is going to keep the case."

"Let's wait on dates and see what happens," Jessup said.

"Well, well, aren't we full of surprises? Don't tell me you've seen the light and are going to dismiss the case?" Earl shook his head in mock astonishment.

Jessup looked at him. "Let's just wait," he said.

The bailiff loudly announced that the judge was taking the bench. Earl walked toward the back of the courtroom where George Kennedy had saved him a seat.

McKeene bounded onto the bench and stood rather than sat, his red ermine-trimmed robe casually hung open to show his crisp white shirt and rep tie. The news photographers in the front rows leaned forward eagerly, glancing back at their reporters like hunting dogs straining at their leashes.

With a courteous but not too overly friendly smile to the assembled, McKeene picked up the court calendar. "People versus Logan," he called.

A lawyer with a battered briefcase in one hand and the arm of his client in the other, pushed through the swinging gates and stood before the judge. McKeene greeted him by name, prompted by a note on the calendar, and turned to his clerk with a nod.

"Remember," Kennedy whispered, "how they used to actually have a round cylinder they would spin with all the judges' names in it. I liked it better when they reached in and drew the name."

The clerk consulted the computer-generated, randomly ordered, list of judges, then looked up. "Judge Florence Guittierez, Department 105," she announced.

From behind, Earl saw the lawyer's shoulders slump forward and his head drop. All around Earl, grinning lawyers silently elbowed each other and gleefully pumped their fists. Kennedy buried his face in his hands, bending behind the bench in front, his shoulders shaking with laughter. "The brown Brandeis," he wheezed facetiously.

The game of chance continued to mixed reviews from the waiting lawyers. General grumbles of disappointment were quietly expressed at their poor luck whenever a favored judge was assigned and taken out of the rotation. The pleased recipients of such good fortune were, by custom, awarded a surreptitious middle finger salute by their colleagues as they exited. Soft whistles of relief escaped whenever a colleague drew one of the "meat grinders." As the victims walked out, there was no eye contact out of fear their bad luck might be contagious. There would be time later for commiseration over drinks.

After some time, McKeene tossed the court calendar onto his bench and surveyed the room to ensure that all the press was assembled. "*People versus Seabrooke*," he said. Earl walked rapidly to the podium, announced his presence for the defense and turned toward the metal door of the court lockup for his client. The press photographers rose from their seats, only to be pulled back down by their reporters. It was clear to everyone that McKeene was not a judge who would suffer them to take liberties without his permission.

"Before we bring out the defendant, I have a request from the media I need to rule on," McKeene said.

"Your honor, before the Court decides any issues in this case," Jessup said, as blandly as if he were reading his grocery list, "the People are filing a peremptory challenge to this Court."

A sudden hush settled on the room. The reporters looked at each other in surprise, then began writing in their notebooks. McKeene's clerk looked dumbfounded. McKeene glared at Jessup as if he were a worm that had suddenly emerged from his dinner salad.

"On what grounds, Mr. Jessup?" he asked coldly.

"As the Court knows, we don't have to state a ground. Each side has one challenge," Jessup replied flatly.

"Mr. Jessup, before you do that, I think we had best have a little talk with your supervisor."

"That's fine, judge," Jessup said, with the certainty of any bureaucrat following orders. "Mr. Bishop is in the courtroom."

McKeene shot a look into the audience as Bob Bishop, the Chief of Trials, rose solemnly from his seat. They locked eyes for a moment, then McKeene nodded and smiled sourly. "I see that Mr. Cavalli has decided to play politics with our justice system."

All eyes followed Jessup as he walked over to the court clerk and handed her the paper, which she took then stared in bewilderment up at the judge.

"There is, however, one last task I must perform, Mr. Jessup. Merely clerical, of course, to assign you to a new court," McKeene said.

As Jessup walked back, Earl could see his eyes clouding with concern.

"With a case of this magnitude, it would not be appropriate to assign it randomly. Therefore, this case is assigned, for all purposes, to Judge Frederick Jefferson, Department 102. Appear there next Monday. All prior orders are to remain in effect."

Well, thought Earl, there's a curve ball, but not a wholly unexpected one with an election coming up. But if the case was to be tried before Judge Jefferson he needed a scouting report. With Judge Jefferson as the trial's umpire, so to speak, Earl needed to know how he called the balls and strikes. And if he called them the same for both teams. Luckily he knew who to go to for the answers.

Earl walked down the stairs of the parking structure carrying the boxes full of the reports the DA had just turned over. When he reached the third level he put the boxes down. Sam Price was leaning in an open car door, wrestling a brief case and an exhibit chart into the back seat while pinning a thick file folder under one arm and balancing a computer case that was hanging from a shoulder strap on her other arm. The car was a Range Rover whose color was buried under a carpet of dust and had enough mud plastered to the fenders to qualify it as an entry in the Baja Road Race.

"I've got a discount coupon to a local car wash if you're interested," Earl called. "Unless, of course, the car is part of your juggling act."

Sam smiled without looking up, apparently recognizing his voice. She tossed the rest of her things into the car and turned to him, propping one hand on the open car door and the other on her hip. "I guess you don't appreciate performance art when you see it, Bobby Earl. This took me all weekend," she said, gesturing to the car.

"I see. It's apparent you put a lot of effort into your work."

"I do. And speaking of work," she nodded at the two boxes at his feet. "I thought you would need a fork lift to move those."

"You know what they say. Strong back. Weak mind."

"That's not exactly what I've heard around the Office. Kelly's still smarting over losing that murder case to you."

"He didn't lose it. I just had the facts. Which reminds me. I hope you marked all the good stuff in there that helps me. I don't want to miss something."

"You know, I intended to do that but my pen ran out of ink."

They stood for a moment smiling at each other. "Well," he said, "have fun coaching whichever witnesses you're going to meet."

She chuckled. "Somebody's got to tell them what to say."

Earl picked up the boxes then watched as she drove off. What am I doing? he thought. Making friends with a prosecutor I'm about to try a case against is not the best way to keep your competitive edge. It was bad enough that the jury was bound to like her. He had to watch himself. The trouble was that there was something about her that made it difficult for him to keep his distance. Damn it, he silently swore. He couldn't help it. He really liked her.

Leaving the Courthouse parking lot, Earl pushed a disc of Tom Waits' *Heart of Saturday Night* into the car stereo and drove rapidly through the noonday traffic toward his office in Santa Monica. He was anxious to dive into the boxes of reports in his trunk, but first there were certain preliminaries. He grabbed a rare parking space on Wilshire Boulevard, then carried the cardboard boxes into Quick Copy. Slipping a $20 bill to the clerk as an incentive, he said he would return for the copies in a couple of hours.

Back at the office, he called Munoz to tell him to come by later that afternoon for his copy of the reports and then went looking for his suitemate, James McManis. In his late seventies, James (no one called him Jimmy) was the Dean of the criminal defense bar and depository of over fifty years of the history of all things, true or rumored, concerning every player in the Criminal Courts of Los Angeles.

If Earl's case was going to Department 102, he needed to get a fix on Judge Jefferson. Earl knew of him, of course, but had never tried a case before him. Judge Jefferson was retired and was sitting by assignment from the Supreme Court to help clean up the LA courthouse backlog of cases. Earl needed to know how Judge Jefferson ran his courtroom. There might be one Code of Evidence, but what one judge considered relevant might be wild speculation to another, what passed for robust cross-examination in one court, might be witness harassment next door. So before Earl looked at the box of reports, he had to anticipate the condition of the playing field, where the holes were in which he might turn an ankle, the dry spots that offered no traction, the high grass into which to steer an opponent. One clue to that terrain would be to learn about Jefferson, the man, where he came from, who he was. Earl had long since discovered that everyone's past formed a prism, opaque or clear, through which they viewed the world.

James McManis' usual haunt was the first place Earl looked, the upstairs law library. The room was a warren of tall book cases lined with uniformly bound volumes of appellate decisions, like soldiers on parade paying homage to the legal battles they chronicled. McManis was standing in a back aisle, his mane of snowy white hair and shaggy eyebrows bent close to the page of an open book. As always, even here, he wore his suit coat, tie firmly in place, but now the suit coat hung loosely on his frame, as if tailored for a larger man, a younger James McManis, the one the newspapers had dubbed the "Lion of the Courtroom."

"James, you got a minute, or are you in the middle of something?" Earl asked.

"For you, lad, I always have time. But I am surprised to see you up here."

Earl smiled. "You know anything about Judge Jefferson?"

McManis slowly closed his book. "Now that's a story." He gestured to a chair at the library table where his legal pad was lodged among a clutter of books. "Is that where they sent you?"

Earl nodded. "The DA papered McKeene."

McManis nodded in contemplation. "You're a lucky man. You're in front of a real judge." McManis eased into a chair and stared off with eyes hooded with age as he gathered his thoughts. "Frederick Dubois Jefferson, born here in LA, his father was a Pullman porter out of Union Station. After high school, Jefferson joined the LAPD, back when Perkins was the Chief, and ended up the first black to ever make Sergeant. This was back in the days before Miranda, when most detectives were big, meat-fisted men who didn't like wasting time talking to blacks. They preferred a more direct form of communication." He gave Earl a knowing look. "Unlike today, LA at that time had several newspapers, one of which was a black newspaper called the *Clarion*, which began running stories on the police beatings, complete with names and dates. Chief Perkins went berserk over the leak and suspected it was Jefferson, who was promptly assigned to patrol the toughest part of Watts, alone, on foot, at night."

Earl nodded slowly. "Now I see why McKeene picked him. No love lost there for the LAPD. But how did he become a judge?"

"It so happened," McManis continued, "that his beat included the offices of the *Clarion*. The word went out through the neighborhood that absolutely no criminal activity of any kind would be tolerated on Jefferson's watch. And there was none. So, each night Jefferson would take one turn around the block, then go to the *Clarion* offices, to which he had a key, and study law all night. Two years later he sat for the bar and passed."

Earl interrupted. "Oh, so that was back in the day when you could do what was called 'read law' with a practicing lawyer rather than go to law school?"

McManis smiled with approval. "Full marks, young man. Exactly right. Jefferson became the lawyer for the black community. As they prospered, so did he. Made a lot of money. One of the first blacks named to the bench."

"I would have loved to hear the howls when Jessup got back upstairs and told the DA where McKeene had sent them," Earl said.

"I think you'd be making a mistake if you thought Jefferson was carrying water for McKeene. He's nothing if not his own man. And he has a strong sense of fairness, so don't think he's got some all-consuming grudge against the LAPD."

"Too bad," Earl said. "But how does he run his courtroom?"

"Well, it's *his* courtroom. Don't ever forget that. But he likes good lawyering. Likes a good fight. Calls them pretty much down the middle and once he makes a call that's it, move on. He'll give you a fair trial. But from what the media is saying about your case, that's probably not exactly what you're looking for."

Earl thanked him. "Is that desk bottle of yours making an appearance tonight?"

"It will if you'll join me."

Earl promised he would and headed for his office. He wondered what turns his life would have taken with someone like McManis for a father. Earl had never understood his own father. Frank Earl was a brooding man, quick to anger, with a ready backhand, of which Bobby was a frequent recipient. Earl senior ran an asphalt repaving business. From the age of twelve, Bobby worked every weekend and all summer as a member of his father's road crew. By sixteen, he was as strong as a grown man and worked like one. But still, Bobby always had a vague feeling that somehow, for some unknown reason, his father resented him. It was never spoken, never out in the open, just every now and then Bobby would see it in his father's eyes or hear it in his voice. Even as a child he realized this had nothing to do with him; it had to do with his parents and their strange tug of war between love and hate. Some couples learned to forgive one another for what each knew the other would never be. But not his parents.

Bobby could still remember how he would wince at the dinner table when his mother would admonish him to study so he "wouldn't end up on the end of a shovel like your father." Or blush with shame as his mother preened over him while his father warned "you might as well put a dress on the boy and have done with it." What Bobby never could understand was why he ended up in the middle of their crossfire. Maybe that was why, after he left home at 18, he never looked back.

For the next three days, Bobby came to his office in jeans and a sweatshirt, and devoted himself completely to studying the content of the cardboard boxes. Martha held his calls, allowed no appointments, and supplied endless cups of coffee. The foundation of his preparation on any case was always built on mastering the facts, every line in every witness statement, every detail. Some facts were solid blocks and had to be accepted, others might be shaved or shaped to appear differently, others might disintegrate under cross-examination. The prosecution facts must be taken on board or skirted around or plowed right through, but never ignored.

At this early stage, he usually started to formulate his final argument to the jury. The final summation was the framework that guided him through the case. It was the blueprint that decided which lines of investigation might supply support for the argument, what questions needed answering during cross-examination, what evidence to attack and what to embrace as if it were his own. The only trouble with his normal approach was that, as of now, there was no argument to be seen.

Earl wrote his case notes by hand. Most lawyers used a computer to record their notes and organize their case documents. But Earl's relationship with his computer was one of both dependence and distrust, like two enemies forced to share the same life boat. Earl recognized that this was due in large part to his remarkable lack of technological ability. At the same time, he was secretly convinced that his computer was actually an animate object, one that subsisted by occasionally eating an entire brief Earl had spent hours working on and burping up a blank screen. He called his computer Hal, after the runaway computer in Stanley Kubrick's movie *2001, A Space Odyssey*. Earl would not trust Hal with this case.

Besides, the act of writing helped him remember and, more importantly, the handwriting itself was like a second language or code that spoke to him. A heading meant one thing if it was underlined, something else if it was starred or color-coded or given a page citation or question mark. Each mark carried a message that jumped off the page at Earl. By the time of trial, his notes were as familiar to him as the neighborhood where he rode his bike as a kid and as easy to navigate.

The last step was to organize this mass of material so he could find a document when he needed it. Most lawyers would do this by computer, scanning in documents, numbering and indexing them. But to Earl, clicking away on a computer in front of the jury appeared impersonal or mechanical, and it would somehow put a distance between him and the case. Earl used three-ring binders, in which there was a section for each witness with every statement they had made. There were sections for physical evidence, autopsy reports, investigator's logs, final argument ideas and so on. Binder after binder, section after section.

As the binders began to line the shelves of his office, he derived a sense of calm and control from this image of orderliness. Now the only thing missing was a defense.

CHAPTER 9

"Rocky, I want to congratulate you," Thomas Glass told Carmine Cavalli, the District Attorney of Los Angeles County. "That was a very bold move of yours to kick McKeene off the Seabrooke case." With his hands folded in his lap, one leg crossed over the other, Glass gave a bemused smile across the desk at the DA, letting him know he was aware of the political impact.

"We just felt McKeene's penchant for publicity might endanger the defendant's and the People's chance for a fair trial," Cavalli said. "We're all better off in front of Judge Jefferson,"

"So you're pleased it ended up there?" Glass asked.

"Of course," Cavalli replied.

"Of course," Glass repeated with mock sincerity.

"So what can I do for you, Mr. Glass? You know my office always welcomes any opportunity to help the press."

"That's why I came, Rocky. I want to see the Seabrooke Grand Jury transcript," Glass said matter-of-factly.

Cavalli seemed startled by the bluntness of the request. "If I only could, I would. But you know that's not possible. The Court ordered it sealed. I can't, I really have no choice."

"That's unfortunate," Glass sighed. "I have a ten-minute gap in my coming show and this producer," he rolled his eyes as if in disbelief, "wants to fill it with this story which I have steadfastly been resisting." Glass held Cavalli's stare.

Cavalli froze. "What story is that, Mr. Glass?"

"Oh, I shouldn't have even mentioned it. I'm sure I can talk him out of it."

Cavalli, like everyone else, knew that any producer who ever dared to oppose Glass would be typing up his job resume by morning. "No, please, I'm curious."

"Well, if you insist. It seems there's this report that the night Officer Horgan's body was found, you dismissed your driver for the night, disconnected the tracking device on your car and turned off your cellphone. So everyone had to remain at the crime scene for hours until you surfaced."

"There may have been some delay in my responding," Cavalli said, "but no harm done. Cops are used to standing around."

"You're right," Glass said apologetically. "It's just that there's this business about checking into a motel in Burbank."

"That's ridiculous," Cavalli said.

"I know, but this clerk said he can identify you and...."

"What the fuck is this?" Cavalli interrupted.

Glass continued calmly, as if he had not heard. "And the woman he described being with you bears a striking resemblance to Judge Nancy Goodwin. I'm sure he's wrong, but she is such a striking beauty, it's hard to mistake her."

Cavalli stared at Glass with absolute loathing.

"Isn't she the judge who runs the Grand Jury? The same Grand Jury that just indicted Seabrooke?" Glass said. "Well, no matter. I'm sure it will come to nothing. You would never permit yourself to get entangled in such a...." he paused as if hesitant to say the words, "conflict of interest. Would you?"

Cavalli sat locking eyes with Glass, who looked perfectly at ease. After a minute, Cavalli opened a drawer in his desk and laid a thick transcript on his desk. "I have to go to a meeting now," he said in a disgusted tone. "If you'd care to wait, I'll tell my secretary you're not to be disturbed. I'll be gone a couple hours." He walked to the door, leaving the transcript on the desk.

"That's very kind, Rocky. I think I will wait. I have to call that producer and tell him to forget about that ridiculous story. I'll figure out something to fill the time slot."

"I hope you found something we can use," Earl said to Munoz, nodding toward the shelves of binders, "because I've been through the DA's stuff, and I sure didn't find any 'get-out-of-jail-free card'."

Munoz sighed. "Don't get your hopes up."

It was Friday. For three days, Earl had read and reread the material in his carefully collated binders, which resulted in pages of handwritten questions, but no answers. Earl picked up a pen, pulled over a legal pad and leaned his elbows on his desk. "Lemme hear what you've got. Then we'll talk about where we're at."

Munoz flipped open his small notebook. "Well, I did find the partner of Richard Walker the safe man. Name is David Cunningham. He's retired, lives in Las Vegas. And he remembered when he and

Walker arrested Seabrooke at a traffic stop. Seems as safe men they only made a couple busts."

"Good," Earl mumbled as he took notes. "Was he willing to talk to you?"

"Talk," Munoz grinned. "I couldn't shut him up. According to him that traffic stop was the reason he retired."

Earl gave Munoz a puzzled look.

"Seems he and Walker had been after Seabrooke for a long time. Seabrooke was a high end jewel thief. When they saw him that night they did a 'maybe we'll get lucky' stop. They did catch him with all his gear, but no loot. So Cunningham writes it up as a broken tail light stop." Munoz gestured as if striking something. "Then everything was supposed to have been in plain sight on the back seat."

"Right," Earl said skeptically.

"They go to court on the search and Walker tells the DA to put only him on, as his partner won't be testifying. When Walker starts testifying, Cunningham understands why. Walker's not following the script. He just starts telling it like it happened, they stopped a well-known safe-cracker on the chance he had just done a job. No broken tail light, no gear on the back seat, no probable cause. So the judge suppressed the tools. It appears Officer Walker never learned the difference between court truth and street truth. Cunningham couldn't think of enough things to call Walker, and none of them were his name."

"Son of a bitch," Earl said, pushing back from the desk in astonishment. "How come that never happens in my cases?" He paused. "What about marking the tools?" Earl reminded him of the report in which Walker claimed his initials were on the safe-cracking tool that was left at the crime scene.

"Cunningham says it's true. It was Walker's idea. They were so pissed that the court ordered them to return Seabrooke's tools that they engraved their initials on them all in the hopes they would turn up one day and they could nail him. They spent all weekend doing it. Then Cunningham retired, said he couldn't partner with Walker anymore, plus there was rumbling about his filing a false report."

"What a strange bird," Earl said.

"Tell me about it," Munoz replied.

"But maybe I can get Judge Jefferson to exclude the evidence about the tool being marked based on the previous court ruling that the original search was no good. I gotta think about this."

Munoz adjusted his bulk in the leather chair, which squeaked in protest. "I also made a call to a contact of mine over at the Feds."

Earl hunched forward. "And what did you learn from this brave crime fighter?"

"Not much. He did confirm that Horgan was on loan to the Feds. Undercover drugs. But so far my contact won't give up what cases he was working."

"Manny, we've got to see those files. You've been through the discovery. You see a defense in there? I got nothin' so far. If we're gonna have a chance here, we've got to put somebody else in the mix. And shit, Manny, the Feds only work big drug cases, then try to work their way up the food chain. And you know who's at the top and they didn't get there by being voted Mr. Personality. If anybody had the *huevos* to knock off an undercover cop, it's one of those guys."

"I know. I'm working on it. But listen." Munoz held up a palm for patience. "The reason my man couldn't tell me was because Horgan was under investigation."

Earl stared in surprise. "That's interesting. What for?"

"He wouldn't tell me. But it had something to do with his cases."

"Very interesting. I'll draft a subpoena for Horgan's Federal case files. Can I use what your man told you?"

"No, this was just between us. But I didn't think the State courts had any jurisdiction over the Feds."

"Yeah, yeah," Earl said. "I know. They don't. But let's get them into court. Maybe we can pry something out of them."

"Worth a try."

Earl wrote a note on his legal pad, then put down the pen and looked at Munoz. "So what do you make of the DA's stuff?"

"A confession to a jailhouse snitch? Sweet Jesus, Bobby. How stupid is Seabrooke? What's he doing bearing his soul to this Snyder asshole? Besides, I thought he was housed in High Power, isolated from everybody. What's he doing in Torrance?"

"He *is* in High Power. It says in the report they sent him on a dry run to Torrance by mistake. I warned him, but more than that, Seabrooke is not the type to be chatting up a guy like Snyder. Believe me, he never even talked to this guy." Earl paused and grimaced, as if trying to convince himself of the truth of his own words and failing. "You know how it is in a high profile case. It's inevitable that a snitch is gonna' pop up."

"Well, the snitch sure has a lot of details, that's what worries me. Usually these snitches just come up with 'he told me he did it.' But here, he's got Horgan surprising our man, who panicked and starts blasting. The snitch even has the location and the gun, a twenty-two, which ain't real common, and that our man didn't even take time to get the money. That's a lot of information, who else would he get it from?"

Earl sat grimly silent.

"He's even got Seabrooke calling home."

"Yeah, I know," Earl said. "They found a cellphone dropped at the scene, with the last call to an out of service number that was just one digit off from his home number. Like he panicked and dialed the wrong number."

"One of those throw-away phones you buy on the street. Registered to Mr. Nobody," Munoz said.

"God damn, I hate snitches. Give me a lying cop any day. At least they think they're doing it for the right reasons." Earl stared off in disgust. "Anyway, you're right. The details kill us. We've got to find out where he got them. They haven't even appeared in the paper, as yet. See if you can get a copy of all Snyder's visitation slips, see who he's been talking to."

Munoz wrote in his notebook.

"The DA obviously cut Snyder some kind of a deal," Earl said. "I'll make a discovery request to Jim Jessup for any benefits they dangled in front of Snyder. According to Snyder's rap sheets, he has a case pending. Armed robbery with great bodily injury. With his record that's a third strike. Which means they'll weld his cell door shut and burn his paperwork. Go see if you can get the reports without a subpoena, no need to tip the DA to everything we're doing."

"I'm still owed some favors over at record keeping," Munoz said.

"I'll look at the court file. I want to talk to Snyder's lawyer. See what he's willing to tell me." Earl paused in thought. "Yeah, and I'll check with the PD, they keep a file on snitches. See if Snyder is a regular at playing the system."

"You might want to check for civilian complaints against Horgan. He's the type that would have a jacket," Munoz said. "On the other hand, it's doubtful that anyone with the balls to drop a cop would waste time filing a complaint with the Department."

"I'll file the motion anyway, you never know. What about canvassing the shops in the area? Maybe somebody saw someone going into the restaurant that night. Those Chinese seem to always be working."

Munoz made a note. "I'll have to do it around midnight. See who's around. Who needs to sleep, anyway?"

"So, what do you make of this girl, Crystal, says she's Horgan's girlfriend." Earl searched his notes. "Crystal Robinson, has a bit of a record herself. Probably a hype. Says she and Horgan argued and he left her place around midnight. The police recovered Horgan's cellphone, and the last call he received was from her. Probably trying to make up. She says she didn't know where he went. He didn't come back that night."

"You know," Munoz said, "when some of these guys go undercover they end up going native. Really get into the life. Shack up with whores and junkies, even do a little chipping. So with a guy like Horgan it wouldn't surprise me."

"Yeah, the tox screen from the coroner shows he was smoking a bit of the ganja, with traces of coke."

"So maybe she is his girlfriend. Birds of a feather," Munoz said.

"We'll see. I'll try and get an interview with her." Earl paused in thought. "We're scheduled for our first appearance in front of Judge Jefferson next week. I'll file that motion for Horgan's personnel package and see how he rules. That should give me a read on Jefferson. Then maybe I'll bring up getting a walk-through of Horgan's place. I just have this feeling. I need a better understanding of who this guy really was."

Munoz heaved himself up and went to say goodbye to Martha. Earl got some phone calls out of the way and headed out of his office.

"I know it's a foolish question," Martha said. "But did you check your emails?"

Earl stared at her with the look of a condemned man.

"I'll take that silence for a 'no.'" Her look of bafflement was tempered by a slight grin. When Earl first moved in, she had assumed, because of his age, he would be tech savvy. His subsequent performance had quickly disabused her of that notion, and ever since she had been monitoring his emails. "Your co-counsel on the Duncan case emailed you a draft of a motion he wants you to edit. He needs to file it today."

Earl looked at her as if he had been offered a choice between a blindfold or a hood before facing a firing squad. When he was growing up in San Cabrero, there had been no computers in his parent's modest home. In college and law school he had persisted in taking notes by hand and typing his papers. Now he struggled to catch up.

Earl stepped back into his office. Hal, his computer, sat complacently on a side table. But Earl was not fooled. He knew this would be a contest - one in which only Hal knew the rules. Would Hal be content this time in just obstinately refusing a simple command, or would he feel the need to wipe away hours of work as effortlessly as an eraser across a chalkboard. Earl took a deep breath and approached cautiously.

An hour later an explosion of ear-piercing curses erupted from Earl's office. Martha rushed in. Earl stood with the computer raised above his head as if poised to launch it out the window. "I knew it. I knew it," he shouted in a sputtering rage. "He did it again. He ate every damn thing I'd written."

"Bobby," Martha said sternly. "Put the computer down."

Earl stared back in a daze, as if he didn't recognize her, then he clamped his eyes firmly shut and heaved a sigh. He placed the computer back on his desk and collapsed into his chair. "I'm sorry, Martha. But God damn it. The son of a bitch does it every time."

"Don't worry. You probably just pushed the wrong button. Go get a cup of coffee. I'll get it back."

"I'm sorry, Martha," Earl said sheepishly. "But...."

"Hush. Get your coffee."

By the time Earl returned, Martha had repaired the damage, as she had on so many other occasions, and she sent him on his way. She had learned there were some things she just couldn't change. But one thing was certain. She would be getting some flowers tomorrow.

CHAPTER 10

In an orchestra, the musicians tune their instruments to a single note from the oboe. In a courtroom, the staff members adjust their attitude to the tone set by the judge. If the judge respects the lawyers, the staff will likewise. If the judge views defense lawyers as obstacles on the road to justice, the staff will treat them accordingly. The atmosphere in the courtroom of Judge Fredrick Jefferson was calm and dignified.

Earl walked over to the clerk and handed her a business card, which she stapled to the file. The clerk's desk was notable for the absence of the normal collection of pet photographs, bobble head dolls and fake flowers. The clerk was a primly dressed middle-aged woman with smooth cocoa-colored skin that matched the mahogany sheen of the judge's bench. "Good morning, Mr. Earl," she said with a polite smile. "Mr. Jessup and Ms. Price have already checked in. We received your motions and the judge has them in chambers."

Earl thanked her and headed toward Jessup, who was at his usual post against the jury box. Samantha stood beside him reading some papers.

There were no other lawyers in court, which meant their case was the only one on the Monday calendar. Several reporters sat among the usual court watchers, but fewer than in the previous crowd. The DA must have tipped them off that not much would be happening today.

"Jim," Earl said. "Sam." He nodded and smiled.

"Bobby," Sam said, "I don't believe you've met Detective Tanner. He's in charge of the investigation." She turned aside, and Jack Tanner rose from his seat in the jury box. Earl stepped forward and stuck out his hand. "Bobby Earl," he said. Tanner took his hand in a tight grip and started to apply pressure. Earl locked eyes with Tanner and squeezed back. The years of working on the roads for his father had left Earl with a grip like a walnut cracker. Neither changed expression, but finally Tanner released his hand.

"You know, Counselor," Tanner said, "you could save us all a lot of trouble."

"How's that, Detective?"

"Just leave me alone with your client for a few minutes." Tanner slid his hands into his pants pockets, pushing back his suit coat to reveal his shoulder holster.

Earl gave Tanner an amused look and turned away. Thinking in stereotypes had always struck Earl as lazy, an easy way to misjudge people and make missteps. To consider Tanner just another macho bully would be a mistake. Earl had seen something else in Tanner's cold, hard stare. He had the dispassionate eyes of a wolf looking for the most vulnerable prey. Tanner was a true hunter of men. No quarter would be given in this fight.

Sensing the tension, Sam spoke up. "Bobby, any problems with the discovery?"

"Actually, there was," he replied in mock seriousness.

"And what was that?" she asked with a grin, anticipating one of his attempts at humor.

"You left out something."

"And what was that?"

"All the evidence that points to innocence," he said.

"You noticed that, did you?" she smiled.

Earl liked to disparage his chances to prosecutors, portraying any defense as a mere exercise in futility, hoping to engender the over-confidence that might sap the energy needed to nail shut all the doors and answer all the questions. Anything for an edge.

"There is one thing, though. I'd like the address and phone number of that witness of yours, what's her name?" Earl said, feigning forgetfulness. "You know, the woman who was with Horgan that night?"

"Crystal Robinson," Sam said.

"That's right," Earl replied.

Samantha studied Earl for a moment, as if trying to see behind his words. "You know she won't talk to you."

"Maybe, but I'd like to hear that from her."

"She has security concerns, so I can't give you her address." Earl started to speak, but Sam held up a hand. "But I'll tell you what." She looked over at Jessup who had been making a point of appearing to ignore the conversation. He shrugged his shoulders, deferring to her. "I'll set up an interview for you, in my office."

"I'd prefer to interview her alone."

"Now I'm hurt, Bobby, I thought you enjoyed my company," Sam said playfully.

Earl smiled. "How about next Monday, at 10:00? You provide the coffee."

"See you then," she said.

Earl walked away wondering who was playing whom. The bailiff let him into the lockup area. Seabrooke was the only inmate in the holding cell. As they stood facing each other through the bars, Earl explained what to expect in court and promised to visit Seabrooke in the jail. The door to the courtroom opened, and the bailiff interrupted them to say the judge was "taking the bench."

Judge Jefferson, his back as straight as it had been in his days at the police academy, walked unhurriedly onto the bench, holding the case file in one hand. His close-cropped hair was a grizzled grey, but his brown skin was surprisingly unwrinkled. He settled himself comfortably in his chair and carefully arranged papers on the bench before looking up at the courtroom. "Good morning. I see the Seabrooke case has been sent here for trial."

The lawyers stepped forward and identified themselves. Jessup, sensing something different in this court's atmosphere, left the jury box rail and, along with Samantha, stood at the counsel table.

"Before bringing out the defendant, I have requests from some news outlets for photographic coverage of today's session," the judge said. "I don't know enough about the possible effect that might have on any eventual trial of this case, so that request will be denied for now. We'll take it up again when we consider the pretrial motions."

Jessup accepted this ruling without comment, sensing argument would be futile.

"There is also a joint request from several news media to televise the trial. Assuming there is a trial. I'll take that up later, as well. At which time I'll hear from counsel, of course, since I'm sure you all will have something to say on this subject." The judge looked at the lawyers with an understanding smile. "Good. Let's bring out the defendant." He nodded at the bailiff. "Why don't you all take a seat and we'll deal with these motions Mr. Earl filed."

When Seabrooke joined Earl at the counsel table, there was no need to ask that his chains be removed. He didn't have any.

"Good morning Mr. Seabrooke," the judge said. "We have been dealing with requests from the media to take photographs of you during this hearing. I've postponed a decision on that to a later date. That was why you didn't join us earlier."

"Thank you for telling me," Seabrooke said.

Earl was surprised and elated by this exchange. For a judge to speak respectfully to a defendant as if he were a human being, rather than ignore him like a piece of furniture, sent a strong signal to a jury on how they should view the defendant. It told them the defendant was one of "us," rather than one of "them." The "them" who did not deserve the protection of our laws or any consideration of a possible outcome other than guilt.

"Mr. Earl has a motion to keep the Grand Jury transcript sealed," the judge said. "What's the People's position?"

"The People oppose," Jessup said from his seat. In most courts that was all that was needed to be said in order to produce the judicial rubber stamp.

Jefferson stared at him for a moment, then gave an amused smile. "Stand up, Mr. Jessup. You are a fine figure of a man and should welcome the chance to be on your feet when you address the Court." Jessup pushed himself upright, buttoned his coat and stood like a chastened school boy. "Now, educate me, Mr. Jessup. Since both sides already have the transcript, how does releasing it to the public help this case?"

"Because the public has a right to know what goes on in our courts. So they can have confidence that the judicial process is open and fair," Jessup said.

"If openness was the issue," the judge said, "it's curious the People would choose to proceed by a secret Grand Jury rather than a Preliminary Hearing in open court. My concern is protecting a fair trial. What if some of this evidence turns out to be inadmissible at trial?" The judge arched his eyebrows at Jessup. "Once it's out there I might have trouble getting an unbiased jury." He paused, but Jessup didn't respond to this unaccustomed opposition from the bench. Earl was starting to realize why Judge McKeene had sent the prosecutors here. "No, Mr. Jessup," Jefferson continued. "I think we'll leave the transcript sealed and let the public learn about the case in court."

Jessup sank back into his chair with a sullen expression.

"Now, Mr. Earl." Bobby quickly stood. "This motion to get the records from the police department for citizen complaints against Officer Horgan."

"Yes, your Honor," Earl said.

"I've read your declaration explaining why you think these complaints might be relevant. It's a clever argument, but I don't see it." With a playful smile, he cocked his head at Earl "You're not alleging self-defense in this case, are you?"

"Since my client didn't shoot Officer Horgan, such a defense wouldn't be appropriate, your Honor," Earl said with a straight face.

"I didn't think so," the judge said. "I'm going to deny it for now. If you come up with something more, we'll revisit it. Anything further?"

"There is, your Honor," Earl said. "A defense request for access to Officer Horgan's residence. The prosecution considered the house of some importance because a search warrant was executed and scientific tests were conducted at the location."

"I assume the defense has copies of all those reports," the judge said. "So an on-site inspection seems awfully tangential to me." The judge turned to Jessup. "Is anyone living there now? I'm reluctant to disturb the family's privacy under these circumstances."

"I don't know, your Honor," Jessup said as he partially rose and sank back down again.

"Well," Jefferson said slowly, shaking his head.

"If I can assist the Court." Sam's voice caught everyone by surprise.

"I'd welcome it, Ms. Price," Jefferson said with a kindly smile.

"I'm more familiar with this aspect of the case than Mr. Jessup. At present the house is unoccupied."

"I see," said Jefferson. "Do you see any problem with a supervised inspection by the defense?"

Sam glanced down at Jessup, who stared straight ahead with a petulant expression. "No, your Honor," she said in a clear voice.

"All right, so ordered. How is discovery proceeding? I don't want this case to drag on over discovery disputes."

"We have additional material for Mr. Earl today," Jessup said, getting to his feet, glancing at Sam to sit down. "We don't anticipate any problems."

"Good, I'll see you all back here for pretrial motions in three weeks and we'll pick a trial date."

After the judge retired into chambers, the lawyers stood at the counsel table gathering up their papers. Sam told Jessup she would see him back in the office and left. Earl touched Seabrooke on the shoulder and nodded goodbye. Still looking down at his papers, he said, "Jim, I haven't gotten a reply to my discovery request for the deal you cut with Jake Snyder, your snitch."

"Yeah, I wanted to save paper. There was no deal."

Earl stopped what he was doing and turned an incredulous face to Jessup. "No deal?"

Jessup continued to stuff papers in his briefcase. "That's right," he said. "No deal."

"So your snitch is just doing his civic duty as a good citizen."

Jessup shut his briefcase, shrugged his shoulders and gave Earl a "so-sue-me" look.

"Is that the way he sees it, Jim?"

"Ask him. But you'll have to ask him on the stand. He's represented, so you can't interview him without his lawyer's permission." Jessup gave Earl a smug look. "You may have a little trouble with that."

"Who's his lawyer?"

"Phil Cummings," Jessup said over his shoulder as he headed for the courtroom doors. "Good luck."

Earl knew Phil Cummings, a journeyman lawyer who hung around the courthouse waiting for judges to appoint him on indigent clients. Perhaps they should have a chat.

In the hallway outside the courtroom, reporters huddled around Rocky Cavalli, the DA, politely listening. No shouted questions or thrusting microphones. It looked more like a cocktail party than a news conference. TV cameramen stood at a distance, cameras resting on the marble floor, calmly waiting for their promised footage.

As Earl pushed through the courtroom doors, he could hear Cavalli's clear, confident voice. "I cannot comment on the particulars of the case, because the judge has denied us the right to inform the public. But I can assure you that my office will make every effort to see that this gag order is lifted. I understand the vital role the press plays in informing the public about how their courts are functioning. And this case is exactly the type of case the public needs to follow, because the murder of a decorated police officer is a crime against us all. So it is of the utmost importance that this prosecution be handled in an open and transparent manner. Only the unfettered scrutiny of the press can assure the public that in the end justice was done."

A few reporters hastily peeled off the pack and caught up with Earl, though they were obviously anxious to get back. He knew he was being punished by the media for not returning their phone calls and refusing interviews. In a united front they were imposing what in their world was considered the ultimate penalty – they refused to mention his name in print or on television.

"Why do you think the DA disqualified McKeene?" asked a young man in a corduroy jacket and bleached blue jeans.

"You'll have to ask him," Earl said.

"What do you think of Jefferson's rulings today?"

"They seemed even-handed and fair."

The reporters smirked at Earl and turned abruptly to rejoin the huddle around the District Attorney. As they walked rapidly away, Earl heard one remark, "I told you the asshole wouldn't say anything."

When Earl reached his car in the underground parking structure, he heard footsteps and instinctively turned to face the approaching stranger.

"Mr. Earl, I'm Richard Walker, LAPD. You got a minute? There's some things you should know."

Earl recognized the name. "You're the safe-cracker."

"That's one way to describe it." Walker hesitated. "You and I don't know each other, but I checked you out. They say you can be trusted. You play it straight."

"Yeah, it's a hard habit to break."

"So I'd like your word that this conversation never happened. You know the Department rules against me talking with a defense lawyer."

"No sleeping with the enemy," Earl said as he studied Walker. "All right, Sergeant." Earl dropped his briefcase and leaned back against the car.

"To start with, in a strange way, Sydney Seabrooke and I know each other. When I run into him, we talk one professional to another. He's a first rate safe man, one of the few people I can really talk shop with, like a respected rival who plays for the other team."

Earl nodded; he knew the feeling. There were DAs he respected as worthy opponents with whom he would, on occasion, share a drink, but whom he would never call a friend.

"Don't get me wrong. Your man is a thief. A first rate thief, but still a thief. I've been after him for years, and when I bust him, which I will, he's gonna do time." Walker fixed Earl with a hard stare to confirm there were no misunderstandings. "But that's sort of what I wanted you to know. Sydney takes other people's property, he's not a killer."

"That's an opinion that isn't widely shared, Sergeant."

Walker smirked. "Sydney's a coward. About ten years back, he hit this large supermarket after a big cash holiday weekend. He's working on the safe when the manager unexpectedly shows up. The manager's so scared he wets himself. Never could make an ID. Sydney just runs. No tough guy stuff. Sydney's a chicken shit."

"Why are you telling me this, Sergeant?"

"Because I'm convinced that Sydney did not shoot that officer." Walker paused. "Look, I don't expect you to understand."

"Is that because I'm a defense lawyer?"

"That's not what I said," Walker shot back. "I don't expect people to see things the way I do. That's really not a concern of mine. But this situation here, even with a guy like Seabrooke, is just not right. There's no way he's good for this. They should be looking for the guy who really did this."

"Well, I'll do my best," Earl said and leaned down for his briefcase.

"Wait a minute. You're missing the point."

"And what *is* the point, Sergeant?" Earl said as he straightened up with his briefcase in hand.

Walker looked him straight in the eye. "If you ask me on the stand about Sydney, I'll tell the truth."

Earl stared back at Walker, taking his measure. "You saying what I think you're saying?"

"You know the Department will not allow cops to appear as character witnesses for defendants. But if I'm already on the stand for the DA and you ask about Seabrooke's character, I can testify. They can't stop me."

"How about the markings on his tools?"

"Those are legit. My partner and I did them ourselves." He gave Earl an ironic smile. "I said I'd tell the truth."

They stared at each other in silence. After a moment, Earl dropped his briefcase again and reached out his hand. "Sergeant Walker, it's a pleasure to meet you."

That night Earl sank back into his familiar place on the couch and turned on the TV. Henceforth climbed up beside him and flopped down, anticipating the usual bowl of popcorn that accompanied every sports telecast. However, tonight's fare was not a ball game. All week the Channel 5 news readers had been hyping that *The People's Voice* would devote this week's entire show to "the never-before-told details of the Officer Horgan tragedy, as seen through the eyes of those who knew him best." Earl figured it was only fair that he should know at least as much as any future juror. On cue, The Thumb's face filled the screen to deliver the "teaser" about the upcoming show before viewers changed channels. During the commercial, Bobby went to the kitchen for a beer while Henceforth daintily scratched his floppy ears with a hind paw.

When Bobby returned, he saw the face of a lantern jawed man on the screen, the Marlboro man in a police captain's uniform. Seated across from him, Glass leaned forward in a show of sympathy, speaking in a Barbara Walters tone of sincerity. "Captain, I would like to extend my personal sympathies for the loss of your son, Officer Horgan. And the gratitude of us all for his service."

Captain Horgan nodded.

"Captain, I understand your son's service was part of a long family tradition?"

"He was the fourth generation of our family to serve in the Department," Horgan said in a clipped tone, obviously uncomfortable.

"Perhaps, Captain, you could share with us what type of police officer your son was?"

Captain Horgan cleared his throat. "Terry was a credit to the Department. He served with distinction and embodied what is expected from our officers. He always made me very proud."

"Thank you Captain, I know this is difficult for you," Glass said, moving on. Childhood photos of Officer Horgan appeared on screen, while Glass' disembodied voice pried family details from the reluctant Captain. Photos of young Terry on his bike, in his Little League uniform, the high school football hero and prom king, the college years playing football for UCLA.

Glass thanked his guest, then he turned and introduced a segment he had filmed earlier in the week. Glass appeared wearing a tan suit and pale green shirt with matching tie, looking out of place in his soft leather shoes standing on the grass of a football field. He held a microphone toward a heavy set man dressed in a sweatshirt and gym shorts.

"Coach Tilson, you were Terry Horgan's running back coach at UCLA."

"That's right. He was a gifted athlete. Strong, fast, good pair of hands. He played real well for us. Alternated with Tyshon Brewer, until his injury."

"People tell me, Coach Tilson, that Terry was well liked by his teammates and coaches."

"He was a real favorite with his teammates, a real team leader. Until that injury. He blew out his knee. Afterwards he sort of went inside himself." The coach hesitated. "He was real coachable, except for one bad habit."

Glass hesitated until he seemed to remember the power of editing. "And what was that?"

The coach smiled. "Well, he could pop through a hole in the line real good. But when he got in the back field, instead of eating up the yards he would go looking for a defensive back. He loved to hit the little suckers." The coach laughed. "He would actually veer off to get one. Hurt his yardage. Couldn't break him of it."

"Could he have played at the professional level?"

The coach thought for a moment. "Before the injury, he might have had a shot on special teams, where you need that kamikaze attitude. I always thought he would become a coach. But he always said he wanted to be a cop. Called it the family business."

"Thanks, Coach, and good luck with the season."

Earl felt a sinking sensation. He knew the presumption of innocence was a legal fiction. Most jurors assumed anyone sitting in the defendant's chair must be guilty. Why else would he be there? Earl could deal with that. That was what trials were for. But a trial was fought on two different, but parallel, planes. On the surface, the jurors watched the battle over the facts, each side trying to persuade the jurors that their version was the true one. But underneath, a morality play was unfolding. A struggle to shape the emotional prism through which the jurors viewed the testimony and which image of the defendant would prevail. A jury with a sympathetic view of the defendant as just "one of us" could interpret the same testimony as a probable explanation rather than an outrageous lie. The opposite view could turn a solid alibi into an obvious conspiracy. Starting behind on the law was one thing, but having the jurors step into the courtroom on a crusade to avenge the murder of Saint Horgan was a hurdle too high. Earl got up to get another beer. Henceforth sniffed at himself as if to see whether that accounted for the absence of popcorn.

When Earl returned, Glass was speaking to a sturdy looking man dressed in a brown suit with a white button down dress shirt and a look that said "law enforcement." The man stared warily at Glass as if worried about saying the wrong thing, like a cop who had spent too much time on the witness stand.

"Special agent Kellog, you were Terry Horgan's partner when he was assigned to the Federal task force on drug enforcement. What was that experience like?"

Kellog paused, choosing his words. "Officer Horgan was on loan to the Bureau from LAPD. We weren't partners in the normal sense; I was more his contact person. He worked undercover, deep undercover and preferred to work on his own. He was responsible for breaking up some major drug operations. He had this extensive network of informants, to whom he was extremely loyal, always guarding their identities. He wouldn't even reveal their identities to us. He said it was safer for them and for him to work it that way. We made some very big busts based on his work."

"Sounds like dangerous work," Glass said, urging him on.

"It was dangerous, but Terry never seemed to mind. As he put it, he liked working without a net."

Glass thanked his guest, then he swiveled around in his chair to face District Attorney Rocky Cavalli. Seated next to Cavalli was a young woman who looked in her late twenties, with long, limp black hair, dressed in a stiff white blouse. A small gold cross was suspended on a chain around her thin neck. Her dark eyes stared ahead without expression. Earl figured most people would consider her attractive, but sad. To Earl she looked burned out, as if a fire had once raged inside her, leaving her empty, like a ravaged tree still standing but hollow inside. Earl knew he was looking at Crystal Robinson.

"We welcome back a frequent guest, the District Attorney of Los Angeles County, Rocky Cavalli. It's a pleasure to have you with us again," Glass said. "And this is Crystal Robinson, longtime companion of Officer Horgan. Welcome to *The People's Voice*." Glass and Cavalli chatted on in dramatic terms about a life cut short, while Crystal contributed nods and short phrases of agreement. One of her comments caught Earl's attention. "Terry was different from other people. He did what he wanted to do, not what other people wanted or thought was OK." She darted a quick look at the DA. "I mean, he always did what he thought was right."

A commercial came on, and Earl picked up the remote. There was only so much of this sanctification he could stand. He stroked Henceforth, who had lost patience and was snoring with his eyes only half shut. He was about to turn off the TV when a photo of Seabrooke filled the screen as Glass announced his weekly feature, The Inside Story. "I understand that this Seabrooke guy has only been indicted, not convicted and under our system is presumed innocent. That's all well and good. But *The People's Voice* knows the Inside Story. The fact is, he has already confessed to murdering Officer Horgan. That's right, confessed."

Earl dropped the remote. He was stunned. He felt like he had as a boy when his father would suddenly slap the back of his head. How could this happen? This was the very reason he had the Grand Jury transcript sealed from the public and any potential jurors. To most people, if they heard that someone had confessed, that was all they needed. Case closed. By the time they heard that the source of this so-called confession was some jail house snitch with a suitcase of reasons to lie, they were no longer listening.

Earl stared at the screen, his mind clouded with anger. How could he get to Glass? Go on his show and intone about the sanctity of a fair trial for the man everyone thought had killed a police officer? The Thumb would love those odds. What was the old saw about not getting into a pissing contest with a skunk? He longed for the rough justice of the rugby pitch where the response to a cheap shot was delivered swiftly and in kind.

Counseling himself to tamp down his anger, he felt his mind come back into focus. There was Glass introducing his panel of lawyer experts, who were supposed to tell people what to think. The three wise men sat at a long table with their name cards prominently displayed. Earl recognized the man on the right, with slicked-back dark hair and toothy grin, as a former prosecutor of questionable ethics; the one in the middle projected a professorial air with a goatee and bow tie; while the third, in a dark blue tailored suit, had the polished look of a white collar crime attorney from a large firm that specialized in making deals.

"Arthur Leone," Glass said, addressing the man on the left. "As a former prosecutor, tell us what we can expect from the defense in this case."

"This is a tough one," Leone intoned solemnly. "Under California law, any killing that occurs while someone is committing a felony, such as this burglary, is automatically a first degree murder and qualifies for the death penalty. It doesn't matter how the death occurs."

The man with the goatee and bow tie jumped in. "That's why the defense shouldn't fight guilt. Remember, there are two phases to the trial. First there's the trial to decide if he's guilty, then a trial to decide if he gets death. The defendant is going to fall on a first degree homicide, so the defense attorney should save his credibility with the jury for the penalty trial. If he argues his client didn't do it during the guilt trial, the jury won't believe anything he says when they get to penalty. So he should hang back until the penalty trial, then he can argue his client was surprised and just reacted or it was an accident or whatever and try and save his life."

"So whatever works," Glass asked, "no matter what really happened?"

The white collar crime expert answered. "Nobody knows what happened except Seabrooke and he'll never testify. So." He shrugged. "Whatever works."

Earl turned off the television.

CHAPTER 11

Earl dropped onto a metal chair in the attorney visiting room, then he pulled out a legal pad and gazed around. It was Friday night, yet a dozen lawyers were hunched forward talking with their inmate clients, producing a solid din of sound that swallowed up any individual conversation. He settled in for the usual wait, but business must have been slow; Seabrooke appeared in only 45 minutes. Seabrooke was a ludicrous sight with his slight frame, hobbling in shackles between two large escorts, as if he constituted a clear and present danger to every living police officer. After the deputies cuffed him to the table and left, Seabrooke searched Earl's face for some recognition of what he was subjected to.

"I'm sorry you have to go through that," Earl said. "But there's nothing that can be done. No judge wants to get involved with security inside the jail."

Seabrooke closed his eyes briefly and nodded.

"There are some things we need to talk about," Earl said, reaching down into his briefcase. He held up a mug shot of Jake Snyder, the snitch. "Do you recognize this guy?"

Seabrooke stared for a moment, then turned to Earl with a puzzled expression. "No. Why?"

"You sure?"

"Of course I'm sure, what's this all about?"

"Were you ever transported to the Torrance courthouse?" Earl asked.

"Yes. I sat in the lock-up all day. Some clerical error. Very annoying. Anyway," Seabrooke said in an irritated voice, "what are you getting at?"

Earl leaned back. He was afraid of this. "This is Jake Snyder," he said, holding up the photograph again and then tossing it in disgust onto the table. "Snyder says that you two were in the Torrance lock-up together and you explained to him how you killed the cop."

Seabrooke looked at him in disbelief. "That's ridiculous. Why would I do that? Even if it were true, I don't even know this man."

Seabrooke turned away. After a pause he turned back and said in a dismissive tone, "This is obviously a lie. No one is going to believe this."

"It's not that easy," Earl said. "He's got some details that are troubling."

"What details?"

"He says that after the shooting you made a phone call to your wife and the police found a cellphone at the scene. They pulled up the last number called."

"I don't even own a cellphone. Those records are too easily accessed."

"This was one of those 'throw aways,' not registered to anyone," Earl said.

Seabrooke sat silently shaking his head as if in disbelief. Finally, he looked up. "What number was called?"

Earl dug out a binder from his brief case and flipped through some pages. "626–381-8201."

"That's not my number," Seabrooke said. "My number is 331, not 381."

"Excellent," Earl said. But it wasn't excellent. He knew the DA would argue that Seabrooke panicked and dialed the wrong number. It was close enough. But he would save that discussion for another time.

"You had me worried for a minute," Seabrooke said with a smile of relief. Earl started to pack up his papers, but Seabrooke held up a hand. "Before you go, there's something I should tell you." Earl stopped. This was never a welcome opening. Earl sank back onto his chair.

"It didn't happen exactly as I told you," Seabrooke said uneasily.

Earl made an effort not to show his apprehension. "I see," he said. "What did happen?"

Seabrooke studied Earl's face for any sign of an impending backlash. "When I heard someone at the door I did try to gather up my tools and get out of there," he said defensively. "But I didn't have enough time. I couldn't make it to the back door without being seen, so I ducked into the kitchen."

"Go on," Earl said. He didn't like where this was going.

"There was an alley door in the kitchen, but I would have made a lot of noise getting it open. So I just hid there. Remember, I didn't know who that safe belonged to, but I figured it wasn't some Chinese cook. I could hear someone pacing around out there. Then the front door opened, and I heard someone else come in."

"How many people came in?"

"I don't know. I'm pretty sure I only heard two voices, but I was hiding in the kitchen, and couldn't hear clearly."

"What were they talking about?"

"I couldn't tell," Seabrooke said, shaking his head in frustration. "But they were arguing and I think I heard something about money."

Of course, Earl thought, the universal lubricant for greed and evil. "Did it sound like a dope deal gone bad? You hear any dope talk, kilos, smack, anything?"

"I'm sorry," Seabrooke said, shaking his head. "After a couple minutes it got quiet and then I heard a shot. It sounded like a cannon. Then another and another."

Earl stared off, turning it over in his mind. There were a lot of possibilities but no answers. All it did, for sure, was put Seabrooke there when Horgan had been shot. That fact couldn't exactly be called helpful. "Then what happened?" he asked.

"I was frightened. I mean really frightened. I wanted to get out of there but I didn't know if anyone was still there. I couldn't hear anything, but I waited to be sure. My heart was beating so loudly I was afraid someone would hear. Finally, I grabbed my gear and got the hell out of there, through the back door."

"Did you see anyone?"

He shook his head. "I glanced in the office and saw someone lying on the floor. I thought I was going to have a heart attack."

"Did you go in there? Did you see anything?"

Seabrooke looked pleadingly at Earl. "You must be joking."

Earl sat quietly for a moment. "I'm glad you told me."

"To be honest, I was afraid to in the beginning. I figured you wouldn't believe me and think I was guilty, so you wouldn't put much effort into defending me."

Earl gave him a wry smile. "It doesn't work that way with me." But Earl knew it would work exactly that way with a jury. An argument that a phantom killer did it while Seabrooke was in the next room wasn't the most favored tactic in the defense playbook.

Earl signaled the deputy at the desk to call for Seabrooke's escort. While they waited, they spoke about Seabrooke's jail conditions. Earl noticed that Seabrooke was a bit gamey, which probably meant he was afraid to go into the jail shower, taking to heart the old admonition against bending over to pick up the soap. To spare Seabrooke embarrassment, Earl explained that a deputy escort to the shower was a needed precaution to keep him away from snitches. He promised to arrange it. Seabrooke seemed grateful.

As Seabrooke hobbled away, Earl put in another visitation slip. There was another shut-in he needed to see.

While he waited, Earl re-read the Seabrooke reports he had brought. Still no answers. He began pacing around the Attorney room. It was 6:00 p.m. He knew the deputies changed shifts at 7:00 p.m., which meant everything shut down, no inmate movement for an hour while they did a headcount. At least Phillipe's, home of the Original French-Dipped Sandwich, was only two blocks away, if he was forced to leave and return later. He had a fondness for the joint. Sawdust on the floor, long communal tables with doctors from General Hospital and lawyers from the courthouse hunkered down alongside plumbers and janitors. No white tablecloths imposing conformity and order. It reminded him of the raucous mix that had greeted him at Berkeley.

His thoughts were interrupted by the familiar jail chimes, the clink and rattle of chains. A large Hispanic man with a shaved head shuffled into the room surrounded by four deputies. When he saw Earl, he smiled and lifted his heavily manacled hands in greeting. The guards pretended not to notice. He slowly lowered himself onto the stool opposite Earl, as if testing its support. The guards ran his chains through the table's metal eyelets, then fumbled to close the handcuffs around his thick wrists. A pattern of prison ink tattoos circled his neck and disappeared down into his blue denim shirt collar, giving a hint of the full canvas that must cover his thick chest and back.

His history was written in tattoos, like the rings of a tree. A journey into "La Vida Loca," the crazy life. It started with "Baby Frog Town" when he was jumped into his first gang. An inked teardrop near one eye told of his time at the California Youth Prison. The "187" recorded his first murder. "Mi Familia," etched on his neck, was the final entry, the last stop.

"So, Chuey, what took you so long? I've been waiting here for over an hour," Earl said good-naturedly, as if this was a social engagement.

"Oh, man, these fools." The big man nodded his head toward his retreating escorts. "They show up at my cell with a two-man escort." He smirked in disgust. "Shit, like I'm some kinda fuckin' punk. Two-man escort, my ass. Show me some respect. I'm a four-man escort. They know that." He shook his head. "They expect me to go to the joint with a jacket for a two-man escort. No fucking way. I told the motherfuckers to get me my four man escort or they can lick my hairy balls." He wrinkled his brow in disbelief. "So we had a bit of a delay." He laughed.

"I understand." Earl smiled.

"Anyway, it's good to see you, bro. I still owe you for what you did for my sister's kid, Little Cholito."

"Happy to do it. Your sister is a very nice woman."

"She came to see me," the big man said in surprise. "She still works for that same punk ass judge in Pasadena and Little Cholito is a college boy. Can you believe it?"

"He's a good kid. Your sister did a good job."

"Yeah, well, we'll see. But she tells me you still won't take any money."

"She can't afford what I charge, Chuey. So I'd rather do it as a favor."

"I can afford it. I still run things from in here and I'll still run things when I get to the joint. I'll send over a package."

"Thanks for the offer, but I'll tell you what, do me a favor and we'll call it even," Earl said.

"Name it, bro."

"You still run your cell block, right?"

Chuey gave Earl a puzzled look, like he suddenly realized that Earl had Alzheimer's. "Run my cellblock? I'm the shot caller for Mi Familia in here. No green light on a hit goes out unless I sign off. I run the dope. I pick the trustees. I run my own store. Even the pigs don't fuck with me, because I take care of their discipline problems when somebody needs a lesson."

Earl looked at the big man's fists and tried to imagine them as teaching tools. Earl held up his hands. "Sorry. No disrespect intended."

Chuey nodded, accepting the apology.

"I checked the booking log," Earl said. "You've got a guy on your row named Jake Snyder."

"Jake The Snake," Chuey said promptly.

"He's a witness in one of my cases."

"That the cop killer case?"

Chuey leaned forward and in a hushed tone asked, "You want something to happen to him?"

"No, no. Just find out about him. Like who comes to see him, who he calls, who's his connect on the outside, that kind of thing."

"Now it makes sense." Chuey nodded sagely. "They pulled The Snake off the row one day. Comes back and says they needed another paddy for a line-up. A few days later this asshole guard comes by, fucking with me about how if I'm supposed to be running my cell block, how come Snyder got phone time without my OK."

"I thought everybody had access to the phones," Earl said.

"Yeah, pay phones and you got to call collect. But the guards can tape those calls and there's this recording that says the call is coming from the jail. He was talking about a private phone."

"You mean like one of the office phones?" Earl asked.

Chuey nodded slowly with a knowing grin.

"What's the guard's name?" Earl continued.

"Lucas, at least that's what's on his name plate. But The Snake's not with me anymore. They probably moved him to the snitch tank with the other cheese eaters."

Earl nodded as he thought about the implications. A phone with an outside line meant access to outside information. But from whom? None of the details in Jake Snyder's story were public knowledge. He didn't like where this was heading, but he would have to sort it out later.

"Before they moved him was he tight with his cellies, get visitors, mail, anything?"

"Nobody trusted him, nobody liked him. The only guy who hung with him was this young dude, named Emilio, probably because Emelio wasn't all there." Chuey tapped a forefinger against his temple. "The kid was a fairy, so I didn't have nothin' to do with him, but I did talk to him once. He said his mother worked the crops up around Watsonville. When he was a baby she probably had to take him with her into the fields. A lot of them used to do that."

Chuey looked away.

He left it unsaid, but Earl knew what he meant. He had seen it before. The women nestled their babies in a furrow so they could be near them as they worked. It was a snug fit, almost like a crib, except they forgot about the sun. The heat from the sun would slowly bring the baby's brain fluid to a boil. Not a good first step on the climb out of poverty.

"Was this Emilio maybe Snyder's girlfriend or something?"

"Nah. Not likely. The kid had some kinda protection on the outside. Supposed to be some real bad dude. That was the word anyway. Snyder was too chicken-shit to rub up against that."

"If Snyder's out of reach, maybe you can help me with something else. There's this Chinese guy, Henry Lee, runs a restaurant in Chinatown named Looh Fung. He may be into something. I need to know if he's a player or just a civilian."

"I'll let you know. Should be easy. We got this hookup now with that chink gang, the Wa Ching." He gave Earl a knowing look. "You should have taken the money, bro." He grinned as if he had gotten the better of the deal.

CHAPTER 12

The traffic on a Monday morning on the Santa Monica freeway was easy to predict - it would be a parking lot. Earl expected this and left home early in order to arrive downtown at the DA's offices on time.

Samantha Price's office, however, was not what he expected. Women prosecutors usually felt the need for their offices to project a starker image – more like the lair of a cold but efficient soldier in the war against crime with only Health Department rules preventing them from mounting the stuffed heads of the guilty on the walls.

But Sam's office was personal. On one wall was a framed photograph of her college lacrosse team. A small refrigerator sat in the corner with a pot of coffee brewing on top. Her desk was littered with stacks of papers. The wall behind was noticeable for its absence of framed law degrees, just a taped-up child's drawing of a smiling woman with her back to a black robed figure behind a brown box. At the bottom, in block printing, "AUNTIE SAM IS A LAWYER."

"Well Auntie Sam," Earl said from the doorway, "how's the coffee in this joint?" He laid a bag of breakfast rolls on a stack of papers on the desk.

"See for yourself, Uncle Bobby," Sam grinned, motioning with a cup in her hand. She sat at her desk in an expensive green leather chair that was clearly not county issue, wearing black slacks and a blue pullover sweater. Her long legs were crossed comfortably on top of the desk. She reached for the bag of rolls and buried her face in the open top. "Smells good," she said, "you bake them?"

"I tried, but I got dog hairs in the batter."

"That wouldn't be a problem if you had a sweet girl like Beauty." She picked up a framed photo of a scraggly toothed black mutt having a very bad hair day. Earl stepped behind the desk and peered over her shoulder. He could smell the fresh scent of her hair and noticed the tilt of her lips as she smiled. His eyes followed the graceful curve of her neck, which led to a sprinkle of faint freckles on her chest and the promise of generous breasts. He stepped back to move away from where his thoughts were headed.

"No disrespect," Earl said, "but I think you need an intervention before you name your next dog."

"Oh," she moaned, peering at the photo. "Look at those eyes." She set the frame down next to a photograph of a blond young woman with a radiant smile, holding a little girl in a scotch plaid dress and black Mary Jane shoes.

"The budding artiste, I assume." Earl nodded toward the photograph.

"My sister Karen and her daughter Rachel." She stared at the photograph with an affectionate smile. "My sister's greatest fear is that Rachel will grow up and look like me." Earl tipped his head and frowned a question. "See, my sister was always a great beauty and I was, well, me. I remember one Sunday after church we went to the Biltmore Hotel to meet my grandmother for tea. I was about twelve, and Karen was thirteen or fourteen, but she was already stunning. As we walked by the bar, I heard a man say to his buddy, 'would you look at that, already gorgeous.' 'Yeah,' his buddy said, 'I hope the sister's smart.'" She looked at Earl, then tipped back in her chair and let out a deep throated laugh.

Earl joined her with a smile. "You know of course drinking in the afternoon is one of the leading causes of early onset blindness." She laughed again.

Earl poured a cup of coffee and sat down in a chair opposite. "So where is our TV star?"

"You saw her on Glass's show, did you?" she asked.

Earl nodded slowly, fixing her with a meaningful stare.

"I know, I know," she said. "But, it wasn't my call. Rocky needs the coverage and Glass is not somebody you want to piss off."

"Of that I'm painfully aware. How did he come up with this supposed confession?"

"That I do not know. You have my word on it," she said firmly. "We don't need any cheap shots to win this case."

He could not help himself, he believed her. But as they walked down the hall there was a little voice in the back of his head that kept asking if maybe there was something clouding his judgment about her.

The conference room had a long library style table and nothing on the government grey walls except the official framed photograph of Rocky Cavalli. Crystal Robinson, her white blouse no longer crisp, sat on the far side of the table. Jack Tanner sat on her right, his suit coat hung neatly on the next chair, his shirt sleeves rolled up to reveal his dark-haired forearms. On Crystal's other side was an attractive young Hispanic woman, with high cheek bones, beaked nose and lustrous black hair.

"You know Detective Tanner," Sam said as they entered the room. "This is Crystal Robinson and Marjalita Campos, the victim counselor." No one looked up. The silence was icy.

Earl was familiar with the work of victim counselors. As county employees, their ostensible job was to inform victims of their legal rights, protect them from harassment and explain court procedures. In reality, they functioned as the prosecutor's surrogate, cautioning against cooperating with the defense, coaching on how to testify, how to act, and what to wear in court. They passed on the subtle messages and instructions that a prosecutor could not pass on, not without losing his ticket.

Sam took the chair at the head of the table, an empty chair away from the others. Earl sat across from Crystal.

"Counselor," Tanner said in a take-charge voice. "I've explained to Ms. Robinson that it is completely up to her whether she wants to talk to you or not. She understands that she is under no legal obligation to talk to you, but she can if she so chooses. It's her decision." Tanner turned and looked at Crystal for confirmation. "She has decided that she does not want to be interviewed, so I'm sorry you wasted your...."

"Slow up a minute there, chief," Earl interrupted. There was something about the way he said it that silenced Tanner. Earl turned to look at Crystal. "Ms. Robinson, I'm Bobby Earl. I represent Mr. Seabrooke."

"I don't want to talk," Crystal blurted out.

"That's fine," Earl said calmly. "That's your choice. But there is another part to this that maybe Detective Tanner didn't tell you about."

"Counselor," Tanner said, glaring at Earl, who kept looking at Crystal. "Maybe you need to get your ears checked."

"Both of you calm down," Sam said. "Let's hear what Mr. Earl has to say, then Crystal can decide." Tanner bit his lip.

"You are not the only one with rights here, Crystal," Earl continued as if there had been no interruption. "Mr. Seabrooke and I also have a right. If you decide not to answer any questions, we have the right to tell the jury that. What do you think a jury would make of that? They might think you had something to hide or that you were not exactly an independent witness, just somebody who would only say what helped the prosecution. Either way it would probably take a little of the shine off."

Crystal's eyes clouded in doubt. She turned and looked for guidance to Tanner, then to Sam who was studying Earl like a poker player appraising an opponent who was raising the bet. After a pause, still staring at Earl, Sam said, "Maybe Crystal would like to answer a few questions. Let's take them one at a time." Tanner looked wide-eyed at Sam as if her sanity had come into question.

Earl nodded and reached into his briefcase. He pushed a police report across the table to Crystal. "This is what the police said you told them when they first interviewed you. Is it correct?"

Crystal turned to Tanner who gave a nod. "Yes," she said.

"You want to read it first? Have you ever read it?"

Crystal narrowed her eyes and stared ahead. Earl picked up the report. "It says here you were Horgan's girlfriend. You had an argument that night and he left your apartment around midnight." Earl looked up. "What were you arguing about?"

"I don't remember. Just stuff."

"You called him later that night. What did you talk about?"

"I just called to say I was sorry about the argument."

"You know where he was going? Did he say he was meeting someone?" Earl asked.

"I don't know anything about that."

"Did he ever talk to you about his work?"

"No," she said.

"Did you expect him to come back to your place that night?"

"He always did," she said, with a strange hint of bitterness.

"What was he doing with a safe in that Chinese restaurant?"

"Not a clue."

"But you knew he kept money in that safe," he said, pinning her with a hard stare.

After a pause, she wet her lips and swallowed. "He mentioned something about it."

"You know where the money in the safe came from?"

"Nope."

"You know the combination?"

"Are you kidding?"

Sam held up her hand to Crystal. "I think she has answered your questions on that subject. Anything else?"

"Just a couple. How did you meet Horgan?"

"I don't remember," Crystal said.

"Judging from your rap sheet, I'm guessing you met him as Officer Horgan, undercover narc. Is that how it happened?"

Crystal darted a look at Sam, who folded her legal pad and stood up. "Well, we're getting a little far afield here. So I guess we're finished. Don't you think so, Crystal?"

"Yes," she said, staring daggers at Earl.

Earl sat studying Crystal, accepting that Sam had pulled the plug. These interviews were always a gamble. There was no right answer about whether to push for an interview with a hostile prosecution witness. Usually there was little to gain from a witness determined to play dumb. At least if they refused to talk he could mount his self-righteous high horse in front of the jury and rail about obstructing the search for truth. But in this case, the gamble had paid off. He had learned something, or at least he thought he had. He had long ago learned to trust his gut instincts and his instincts were telling him Crystal Robinson knew a lot more about the money in the safe. But what his gut was not telling him was how that fit into anything.

It was a short drive from the Courthouse to the Men's Central Jail. Earl easily found a parking place in the lot next to the jail. He hoped the sparsely filled lot meant the visiting room would be empty. But as he entered the Attorney's visiting room he realized he would have no such luck. The low steady drone of huddled conversations filled the room. A couple of lawyers raised a hand at Earl in greeting and returned to their clients. A full room meant a long wait. Luckily he had brought some files he could review. An hour and a half later, Chuey appeared, this time with a five-man escort.

Earl sat down.

"What is this? Creeping inflation?" he asked.

Chuey looked puzzled until Earl pointed his chin in the direction of the escorts. "Oh," Chuey smiled. "They said I'd been disruptive." He slowly pronounced the word in sections. "Maybe I should 'bitch slap' the motherfuckers. See what they call that."

Chuey looked down the row to the inmate chained two stools away. "Hey, Gato, how's the Crip killer?" The man nodded glumly.

"Gato?" Earl asked. "What, like a cat, he's got nine lives?"

"No, man. He just pulled nine life sentences. He grabs the chain for Pelican Bay tomorrow"

Earl grimaced. "So what's up with our Chinese friend?" he asked.

"Right to business, eh bro?"

"Like they say, the inmate count waits for no man."

Chuey glanced at the clock, then turned back with a knowing look. "Seems your man Henry Lee had a few specials on his menu."

"I thought so," Earl said.

"He ran a wire transfer out of his restaurant."

It was Earl's turn to look puzzled.

"I thought you were this hot shit lawyer that knew everything." Earl shrugged. Chuey pretended disbelief, but seemed to enjoy being able to explain something to Earl. "Let's say you're a dope dealer and you're making good money. This is a problem, because all your money is in cash. You go to put it in the bank, they got to report it and bank transfers leave a paper trail. You try to buy a house with it, and the fucking escrow people won't take cash anymore. Try taking more than ten big out of the country and get caught, you go to the slam and they keep your money."

"I thought cash was king in this economy."

"Not if you're a dope dealer. So that's where the wire transfer comes in. You go to your friend Lee with a suitcase of cash. He's got a 'connect' overseas. They set up a telephone call. You have a man with the connect on the other end. Lee verifies he has the cash sitting in front of him and the connect then hands over the same amount to your man who deposits it in one of them secret banks."

"Numbered Swiss accounts," Earl said.

"Right, and of course Lee takes a healthy cut for services."

"What does Lee do with the cash?"

"He launders it through his restaurants."

"How did you find this out?"

"Don't worry, counselor. It's solid, Lee pays the Wa Ching gang a 'morbida' for protecting his restaurants. I got it from their shot caller." He held up a hand. "No names."

"So does their 'little bite' include the wire?"

"No, and the Wa Ching was really pissed about it. They got the restaurant protection but that was it. Lee said he already had insurance or an insurance man or some shit for the wire business. I didn't push it because I didn't want us to get pulled into it. Some brother was supposedly the insurance man and we got enough shit kicking off with the Bloods right now. We don't need another beef. But this brother must be one bad motherfucker if Wa Ching won't fuck with him." Chuey gave a smile of professional respect.

Earl leaned back to think. The police report of Lee's interview mentioned that Horgan had been getting a cut from the restaurant based on a deal between the grandfathers. That kind of ancestor worship had never felt right to him. This made more sense. Horgan probably let other cops know he used the restaurant to set up undercover buys, which would give cover to the comings and goings of dope dealers and turn the restaurant into a kind of safe zone. Other narcs would be leery of showing too much interest in the place for fear of exposing Horgan.

Earl considered the possibilities. A deal with Henry Lee might account for the money in the safe. Maybe Horgan got greedy and wanted a bigger cut. Maybe he threatened to blow up the whole operation. Maybe, maybe, maybe. More questions with no answers.

"Thanks, Chuey."

"No problem, bro. Just tell my sister we're even."

***

Earl returned to his office and grudgingly performed some routine tasks on his other cases, then went home to think about what he had learned. It seemed that whatever he uncovered about Seabrooke's case, it never fit with anything else. It was as if he were collecting pieces to totally different puzzles. He needed to clear his head. He needed a run on the beach.

The ocean was choppy, and the grey sky seemed to hover like a low ceiling. A cold wind off the water blew in random gusts as if unable to make up its mind. Earl's bare feet pounded on the hard, wet sand as he ran along the surf line, shore birds scurried out of his path on toothpick legs. Suddenly an uninvited memory pushed its way into his thoughts and refused to leave. It was about another grey day, on another beach. One with his father.

He must have been about seven when his father unexpectedly took him to the beach near their home in San Cabrero. It was a cold grey morning with wisps of fog still in the air. They drove, as usual, without speaking and parked the pickup in the sand on the side of the road. The wind bent the sea grass on the dunes, which rose high above the road so he couldn't see the ocean. But he could hear it. The waves sounded angry as they slammed loudly onto the sand. His father pulled a short flat board from the bed of the truck and fastened fishing weights around it. From a burlap bag he lifted a dead fish and nailed it flat on the board.

They walked in silence over the dunes to the water. The wind was damp and icy. He felt chilled in his Pendleton shirt and jeans. He worried that he would get wet sand in his school shoes and that his mother would be angry. At the water's edge his father heaved the board into the sea, but the waves pushed it back. On his third try the board landed beyond the waves. "Now watch," his father commanded.

The board floated just under the surface, pulled down by the weights, but buoyed by the wood. Down the beach a line of pelicans sailed toward them, as if in formation, staying just under the crest of a wave. As they passed, one suddenly peeled off and shot straight upward, then turned like a swimmer touching the wall and dove back down, gracefully folding its long wings and straightening out, like an arrow falling from the sky.

Bobby had seen pelicans do this before. Each time a great bird would slice into the water, almost without a ripple, to emerge with a fish tail wriggling out of the side of its beak, water cascading from its pouch, tossing its head back to swallow. But not this time. When the bird hit the board the water erupted violently as the bird thrashed awkwardly about, churning up the water, clumsily beating with its powerful wings. Soon it stopped struggling and floated quietly on the rolling sea, its lower beak hanging awkwardly in the water, like a ship's broken mast. Bobby imagined he could see the bird's bloodshot eyes staring at him, as if asking for an explanation.

"See," his father shouted, pulling Bobby around to face him. "That's what life is. Things are never what they seem. People are never what they seem. Never what you hope they are." He paused for Bobby to dutifully recite that he understood. Bobby knew what he was supposed to say, but something in him refused. His silent stare provoked his father to shake him until his head flopped violently about. "You remember this or you'll end up like that stupid fucking bird."

Earl came out of his reverie. Looking back, he never knew if his father meant to impart some worldly wisdom, lessons presumably learned in his asphalt resurfacing business, or to confess his own unhappiness and disappointment with life. Earl gazed out over the waves. Suddenly the wind off the ocean was cold. It was time to turn for home.

CHAPTER 13

Earl sat drumming his fingers on his mahogany desk top, waiting for Munoz to maneuver his bulk into a client chair, carefully, as if it might give way. It was like watching a semi truck backing into a parking space between two Ferraris. Normally this would amuse Earl, but today he was anxious. If he was going to convince a jury, then he needed a narrative, a story that explained things. Any good trial lawyer was really only a salesman. He was selling a story. So what was his story?

Earl quickly told Munoz what he had learned from Chuey and Crystal. Manny seemed particularly intrigued by the fact that Lee, the restaurant owner, had access to some "muscle," and he complimented Earl on getting Crystal to admit she knew Horgan kept money in the safe. "So, that's my end, Manny. Now, surprise me."

The big man pulled out his pocket notebook as his face squinted an apology. "Not much, Bobby, but we'll get there." This was not what Earl wanted to hear, but he did not voice his concerns. Panic was contagious. Seabrooke was due back in front of Judge Jefferson in ten days to set a trial date, and Earl was afraid Jefferson would jam him with an early one. Earl could hear the clock ticking, which was why they were in the office at 8:00 a.m. on a Thursday morning.

"I served the subpoena on the Feds for Horgan's case files," Munoz said. "They at least showed me some respect by waiting until my back was turned to toss it in the trash can. They said the State Courts had no jurisdiction over them, which in Fed talk means go fuck yourself."

"We'll see about that, Manny."

"The jail's another story. I told them I wanted to pull the visiting slips on our snitch. The Sergeant in charge of legal affairs couldn't be more accommodating. Like I was dating his ugly sister. So he walks me to this storage room, opens the door and says 'knock yourself out.' The place is floor to ceiling cardboard boxes filled with visiting slips. No order, no record. They just bundle each day's worth and throw them in a box. Every three years they throw them all out."

"There's nothing on the computer? I thought they had this new computer system?" Earl asked incredulously.

"They do, but they just switched over and so far they only keep track of inmate visitors if a prosecutor requests it."

"Manny, I need to know who visited this guy. How am I going to explain the details he puts in Seabrooke's mouth? Maybe the cops fed them to him. I don't trust Tanner. But that's a long shot, and we couldn't prove it anyway. So I need those slips."

"Don't worry, you'll get them. I spoke to my niece. She's going to a community college and could use the money. I worked it out with the jail. They'll let her sit in there a couple hours a day and go through the boxes."

"A couple hours a day? Manny, how long is this going to take?"

"Bobby, there's thousands of slips in there. Remember, there's two visiting rooms, the civilian's and the attorney's. Who knows, maybe she'll get lucky."

Earl shut his eyes. When was he going to catch a break in this case?

"But I did pull those court files you wanted and made copies." He passed over an accordion file labeled Crystal Robinson. "Bunch of misdemeanor hype shit and a felony sale. About what you'd expect."

Earl leafed through the folder, planning to study it later.

"The snitch's files make more interesting reading. He has a couple of priors, but for some reason he never did any serious time on them." He passed over another file bulging with papers. "One thing is clear, though; this is one nasty little motherfucker. You should have some fun with him on the stand."

Earl thumbed through the files glumly. "Unfortunately that's not how it works. In court I'm not allowed to ask what he actually did in these cases, just whether he was convicted of a certain felony crime, like robbery with bodily injury. The jury never hears the juicy stuff."

"That's too bad. In one of his prior cases he pistol-whipped this woman because she was shaking too bad to open the till." Munoz shook his head. "You know when I started out, armed robbers were the gentlemen of the profession. None of this cowboy stuff. The last thing they wanted was trouble, get the money and get out. When they got caught, they did their time, no whining, considered it the cost of doing business. Hell, they were even polite."

Earl smiled at what passed for nostalgia in their strange world. "The good old days, before ball players were jacked up on steroids and had to get paid to sign a kid's autograph."

"So where is Snyder's case now?"

"He pled. He's waiting to be sentenced."

"He pled to all three counts?" Earl asked incredulously. "Including the strikes?"

"Not only that, but they added one that had been filed against some other guy and he pled to that too."

Earl flipped through the files until he pulled one out. "Emilio Chavez. Armed robbery."

"That's the one," Munoz said.

"Wait a minute. Emilio, Emilio." Earl searched his memory. "That sounds like the kid that Chuey said was tight with Snyder before they moved him."

"Maybe Snyder figured that since he's going up anyway, adding another case won't make much difference, so he might as well get a little night candy." Munoz winked.

"Or Snyder's worried the DA will find it later and piss backwards on him. Maybe he's just being sure whatever deal he makes covers everything that's out there."

Earl turned to a police report in the Emilio Chavez file and began reading. "This was a grocery store hold-up. That's not Snyder's MO. And it says here they've got a positive ID from a woman customer. A mother with her kid, no less. Why would a DA agree to swallow this and cut Chavez loose?"

Munoz smiled. "And look who represents him."

Earl glanced at the front of the file. "Tommy Margolin? That's a switch."

"Bit of a comedown from big time dope cases to a chicken shit grocery store robbery, huh?"

Tommy Margolin was one of the biggest dope lawyers in town. He usually represented somebody low down on the organization chart, but his very substantial fees came from the top and that was where his loyalty lay. His job was not to represent the poor peon who got caught, it was to insure the peon did not cooperate with the prosecution in exchange for a lighter sentence. Cooperating would mean turning on the boss, the one who paid Tommy's fee. The prosecution was always told his clients had no interest in cooperating and they always did more time than they had to.

This schizophrenic loyalty was one good reason Earl never got into the dope lawyer club. He preferred a nice clean murder any day. But what was Margolin doing representing this kid in the first place? Emilio must be some king pin's lame nephew, too thick to work in the family business, or else Margolin had been short lunch money one day.

***

Earl pulled to the curb of a tree-lined street in San Marino and shut off his engine He sat and listened to the chatter of birds in the graceful maple tree in Horgan's front yard. The classic California bungalow, undoubtedly inherited from his grandfather, sat silently in the shade. Some shingles were missing on the wood-shake roof and an upstairs window shutter hung at an angle from a missing hinge. In the flower beds next to the house, red azaleas peeked out from among the weeds. The lawn was a parched tan. The once proud house seemed almost ashamed of its condition, like a faded society matron reduced to wearing a shabby dress.

Earl felt a sense of anticipation as he opened the front door. Most defense lawyers focused on the prosecution case, looking for a weakness. That was important, of course, but playing defense was not Earl's style. He needed his own story, not the DA's. He understood what the conventional wisdom would have advised. Always Follow the Money. But Earl's gut told him something different. His instinct told him the key to this case was Horgan. The real Horgan behind that uniform, the one somebody wanted dead. Seeing how Horgan had lived might be a window into that life.

Normally such a journey would be troubling to Earl. He tried to avoid learning too much about victims. Empathy might sand off his edge and that was never good for his clients. There were enough people to carry the empathy load. In this case, however, he suspected that any feelings that were aroused for Terry Horgan were not going to be the softer kind.

"Hello, Counselor, come on in." Sergeant Wilson walked into the living room from the kitchen carrying a bag of potato chips and a can of beer. His bulbous red nose had flowered into what Earl's grandmother had called a whiskey blossom. A faded tee shirt stretched to cover his beer belly but left a gap of stomach showing.

"Wilson, you get all the tough assignments."

"Yeah." He held up the pilfered potato chips. "Combat pay for babysitting your ass." Around the Department he was known as Wrong Door Wilson, for his unfortunate habit of confusing addresses on search warrants and kicking in the doors of innocent neighbors. Wilson rarely recognized his mistake until after his team had "tossed" the house, ripped open mattresses, broken dishes and dumped out all the drawers, meting out the usual search warrant punishment. Recognizing this proclivity,

Wilson carried a stack of business cards obtained from officers in adjacent police agencies. He would hand one of these pilfered cards to the outraged occupants with assurances of full compensation and encourage them to call in the morning.

Wilson flopped onto the living room couch and dug into the potato chips. "You know the rules, lookie but no takie," he mumbled.

The heavy overstuffed furniture looked original. The fabric had faded with time, except for a section on each of the arms where crocheted doilies had probably rested. A dark wooden bookcase sat next to a fireplace of rounded river rock. The stones above the mouth were black with soot. This was not the house that Earl had expected. Horgan might have slept here, but he never lived here.

On top of the bookcase, a half dozen silver framed photographs of stern-faced men stared out from under shiny-visored caps. Each one in uniform, each chest thick with rows of citation bars. The Horgan clan, LAPD royalty stretching back to the days when Los Angeles had street cars. Moving along the gallery of photos, Earl felt like a general passing in review. Fittingly, the now familiar photo of Terry Horgan was at the end of the line.

The adjoining room had probably served as a parlor. Wilson heaved a sigh as he hoisted himself upright and followed Earl. This room looked more like what Earl had imagined. Two Easy Boy recliners faced a large flat screen television. A sand-colored modern couch against the wall had enough stains to pass for a Jackson Pollock print. On the coffee table a glossy magazine cover featured a bare-breasted beauty straddling a block of ice. Her sultry gaze was wasted on the empty pizza box lying opposite, its lid gaping open. An assortment of beer cans, crushed in a show of manly strength, dotted the table like collapsed top hats.

At the far end of the room a heavy-legged wooden desk was positioned under the only windows, which were hidden behind heavy green curtains. On the corner of the desk was a video with a picture of a well-developed, pig-tailed young woman in a school girl uniform, licking a popsicle. "Wilson," Earl said, holding up the video. "I need to take a look at this video to see if there's anything on it that might be useful."

"Be my guest," Wilson said, not paying attention, leaning against the door frame. "But whatever it is, it stays here."

The picture that filled the TV screen was shot at such close range that it was difficult to identify exactly which body parts were gyrating. This did not seem to be a problem, however, for Wilson. Dropping into a recliner he said over his shoulder, "Good choice, Counselor."

With Wilson occupied, Earl moved back to the desk. The moans and groans coming from the TV seemed more comical than erotic, but judging from the back of Wilson's head he seemed transfixed. On a table next to the desk was another group of framed photographs. Horgan in his glory days. A solo shot in a new UCLA football uniform, no helmet, ball tucked under his arm, posing like the runner on the Heisman Trophy. Horgan in a tee shirt, seated at a table cluttered with beer bottles, arm around Crystal Robinson, surrounded by grinning young men and women, stooping to be included in the picture. Earl studied the healthy young faces. Attractive, clear-eyed, svelte women and well-built young men with fashionable stubble. What did they see when they looked at Horgan? What was Earl missing?

Earl quietly slid open the desk's middle drawer and found a jumble of credit card receipts, take-out menus and match books from various restaurants and bars. The graveyard of a thousand bachelor nights. The detritus in the other drawers was equally unhelpful.

He picked up Horgan's football photo, a college pre-season publicity shot. Earl remembered those days. Standing on the baseball field in the pleasantly warm sun, with the sweet smell of newly cut grass, the crisp feel of a newly pressed uniform, dreams of the new season with all its promise before him, certain that this was the year he would be a starter. But it was never to be. The coach loved heavy lumber, the long ball hitters, not a tactician behind the plate. After all these years, Earl was amazed that this sense of failure still seemed fresh. No matter how often he repeated the old mantra, "it was only a game," he remained unconvinced.

Turning back to the table, but still caught in the memory of that old regret, he set down the photograph more forcibly than he intended. Horgan's photo slipped down inside the frame, cutting off his legs. Earl picked up the frame and unfastened the back, intending to center the photo, when another photo fell out. Earl glanced at Wilson, whose attention was still focused on the never-ending coupling.

Earl stared at the fallen photo in surprise. There was Horgan sitting on the trunk of an old sports car, proudly grinning into the camera, his arm firmly around the slim shoulders of a grim- faced Tommy Margolin, the dope lawyer. Talk about an odd couple. What were Horgan and Margolin doing together? It seemed incongruous. Then he saw it. The driver's door of the car stood open and the inside panel had been dislodged. Stuffed behind the panel was a wall of tightly wedged packages wrapped in plastic. Earl suspected they were not next year's

Christmas presents. A newspaper was prominently displayed, fixing the date.

It still made no sense. The size and wrapping suggested the packages were kilos of heroin. If Margolin had been busted, Earl would have heard about it. And why didn't they bust Margolin if he was transporting drugs? To a cop, busting a defense lawyer ranked ahead of sex on any pleasure scale. But more than that, it made no sense that Margolin would drive around with a load of dope when there were desperately poor Mexicans, aptly referred to as "mules," who would take the risk for pathetically little money. Earl neither liked nor respected Margolin, but he did not think he was stupid.

Earl slipped the photograph into his pocket and returned the frame to its proper place. The rest of the house revealed little about Terry Horgan, the person. It was as if he had lived in his grandfather's time capsule, feeling afraid or unworthy to change anything except one small corner.

As he was leaving, he shouted a "thanks" at Wilson, who grunted a reply, his attention still riveted on the video. Back in his car, Earl dialed Munoz on his cellphone. He pulled out the photo and squinted to read the license plate on the car. There was no answer so he left a message to check out the registered owner. He needed some facts before he talked to Margolin.

Marjalita Campos stood at a clothing rack and lifted up a blue silk blouse to the afternoon light. She knew the colors that worked for her, but choosing clothes for this skinny white chick was difficult. This was a part of her job as a victim counselor that she normally enjoyed; it was a treat to buy clothes and not to have to look at the price tags. Too bad the clothes had to be right for court and TV. Annie's Boutique – Smart and Chic had some good stuff, but Marjalita would have preferred to shop on Melrose Avenue in West Hollywood. But the DAs were always complaining that "the clothes have to be appropriate, Marjalita. What a jury would expect." It had been months before she understood the look they wanted. It had to be a little snappier than a nun, more like what a girl would wear to meet her boyfriend's parents for the first time.

Jessup had explained to her that he was going to call Crystal as a witness and that she had to "look right" or it would "reflect badly" on Officer Horgan, whatever that meant. The well-groomed salesgirl stood patiently, order book in hand. Marjalita had been here before, so the girl knew there would be a sale and who was paying the bill. Marjalita pulled out a long sleeved white blouse and held it next to a blue wool jacket and skirt she had already set aside. "Crystal, why don't you try this on? It might look good on you."

Crystal sat silently against the wall, lost in her own thoughts. She hated clothing stores. Her mother used to take her shopping, but only in the children's section. Even when she was eleven or twelve she was still trying on frilly pinafores. These were for those special occasions when they would play dress-up. Her mother would fix her hair in pigtails, layer on mascara and rouge her cheeks.

Each stranger who came for dress-up was always introduced as her "uncle." It was always the same. She would parade around for a while under his cold leering stare. Then her mother would "have to leave to run an errand" and would not return until after her "uncle" had left. Crystal would hear her mother bang against the wall as she drunkenly maneuvered down the hall. She would crawl into bed with Crystal, blubbering about what a "good girl" Crystal was, promising she would never have to see her "uncle" again. Until, that is, the inevitable next "uncle" came.

Marjalita touched her shoulder. Startled, Crystal looked up. Marjalita smiled and laid some clothes on her lap. Crystal rose from her chair and obediently carried the clothes into a changing cubicle and closed the curtain. Marjalita stood just outside, trying to think of small talk with which she could engage Crystal. She knew the importance of establishing a relationship with those under her care. Normally that was not a problem, but it was with Crystal. At first, Marjalita thought it was just a natural quietness or reserve on her part. But now she realized it ran deeper. It was a complete indifference to personal connections. In dealing with people, Crystal had nailed shut the door on her own feelings and dismissed any effort by others to offer up theirs. It was not just that she did not trust offers of friendship. She acted as if she were incapable of even recognizing that such overtures were being made. As if she lived on the surface of life. Whatever the reason for this wall between them, Marjalita was through trying to figure it out. This was just one cold white bitch.

"So, Crystal, what do you think?" Marjalita peered through the small gap in the curtain. Crystal was taking off the blouse. Marjalita saw that her thin forearms were streaked with a network of black lines, as if some medical technician had used a crayon to map her veins. She knew these were the "track" marks from a thousand injections using needles sterilized over an open flame. Ghost trails of soot embedded in her skin. Marjalita had expected this. The DA had cautioned her about Crystal's drug history and emphasized the need for long sleeved tops. What she did not expect was on Crystal's back - small round, angry scars, like random red polka dots on her pale white skin. These were not injection marks. Marjalita had seen them once before on a small child. They were burn marks from cigarettes, and they did not get there from smoking in bed. Her quick mind started to imagine a sizzling sound and the smell of burnt flesh, so she spoke up to interrupt her thoughts. "We'll take the blouse, don't you agree Crystal?"

It was late afternoon in East LA and still uncomfortably warm. The woman seated on the park bench would have liked to arrive here earlier, but what with getting her husband off to work, feeding the little one and tidying up, the time just slipped away. Even so, the park was empty this time of day, so little Aaron had the sandbox to himself. He played well by himself for a two-year-old, and she could relax. She reached into the pocket of his baby stroller and took out her magazine. Charlie made fun of her if she looked at it at home, but she enjoyed reading about the celebrities.

She heaved a contented sigh. Finally, things were back to normal. After the robbery at Mr. Gararow's market, there had been all that fuss, all those police with their questions and photographs. They even got upset with her when she said she wasn't scared. How could she be? The boy with the gun seemed so little. He was the one who looked scared. And he had such beautiful eyes. It was a shame. Oh well. She opened her magazine.

A thick-set black man, who looked to be in his late thirties, sauntered toward her. She paid no notice until he stopped and was standing over her. There was an ashy tint to his broad face that robbed his skin of any sheen. He had sleepy eyes, filled with a cold confidence, as if he had seen it all before and knew what was going to happen. His thigh length black leather coat stretched to cover his barrel chest and thick arms. Deon Hawkins gave a cold smile that never reached his eyes. "Mrs. Wolensky?" he asked in a soft voice.

"Yes," she said, and glanced around to see if anyone was nearby.

"There's a little somethin' we needs to talk about." He sat down next to her, adjusted his coat to his large frame and stared straight ahead at the sandbox. Deon Hawkins had never understood sandboxes. Growing up in the projects, he had done whatever was needed to climb out of the dirt and filth he was born into. Why would someone make their kid play in it?

"You got a nice boy there," he said, still staring ahead.

"Well, thanks, but we were just leaving," she said nervously and started to rise.

Without turning to face her, he casually closed a large hand around her forearm and seemingly without an effort made her arm go numb. "Sit a spell," he said.

"Please, you're hurting . . . "

"Just hush up and listen," he said calmly. "I ain't gonna hurt you." To any passerby they would have just seemed like two people enjoying the afternoon sun. "You went and made a mistake the other day. See you picked out a friend of mind for the police and said he robbed that store. You mighta' thought my friend Emelio was the one, but you was wrong. It happens, I understand," he said in that calm, quiet voice that seemed at odds with his size. With his free hand, he took a small can of lighter fluid from a jacket pocket. "When you 'splain this here mistake to the police, they'll understand too." He began to methodically pour the lighter fluid on the baby stroller, as if he were basting a turkey. When he finished, he turned for the first time and looked into her terrified eyes. "You understand what I'm sayin', don't you, Mrs. Wolensky?" He released her arm and took out a pack of cigarettes, tapped the pack on his hand and slowly pulled one out with his mouth. He offered her the pack with a questioning look. He shrugged when she didn't respond and put away the pack. Then he pulled out a lighter and thumbed a flame to life.

"Oh, God," she stammered.

He lit his cigarette, inhaled deeply and slowly blew smoke toward the stroller. After a few moments, he stood up, tugged at his jacket and turned to stare down at her. "You don't wanna see me again, now do ya', Mrs. Wolensky?"

"Oh, please, I don't want any trouble."

"Then we ain't gonna have any. S'long as you understand you made a mistake."

"I will, I did, uh, whatever you say."

"Good. So let's forget we ever had this little talk. Okay?"

"Yes, yes, of course."

Hawkins turned and walked slowly away, trailing smoke. He never looked back.

CHAPTER 14

When Earl got to the courthouse that Monday morning, Judge McKeene's clerk spotted him in the hallway and told him the judge would like to see him. McKeene was seated at his desk when Earl was ushered in. He waved to a chair across the desk. "I understand you're due back in court in a week. So how are things progressing with the case?" he asked. "Although I'm not on the case anymore, I promised you'd have what you needed, and I'm just checking to make sure that's being done."

"No complaints judge, thanks for checking," Earl said, wondering where this was headed. If Judge McKeene was concerned about the defense getting a fair shake and a level playing field, it would constitute a historic first.

McKeene pursed his lips and turned to look out the window. The sky was a smoggy grey. "I met Horgan, you know," he said.

"Really?" Earl asked, genuinely interested.

"Yes. He was on loan to a Federal task force then. I forget why he was here, probably something to do with one of his old LAPD cases, but we got to talking about his work over there. I thought it was permissible to discuss it because they were all Federal cases and would stay across the street. None were going to end up before me." He looked at Earl to confirm his ethical standards.

"Of course," Earl said, leaving his true opinion unspoken.

"He struck me as a very brave young man. He was investigating the Castro Brothers. Very powerful people. Very dangerous people, I'm told." McKeene paused for a sign of recognition from Earl.

"Aren't they the ones who own that shopping complex in East LA?"

"El Gran Mercado. Dozens of shops and markets that cater to the Hispanic community."

"But I thought Horgan was with the Drug Enforcement Task Force?"

"He was. He said something about suspecting they were major marijuana distributors." McKeene looked at Earl with a puzzled expression. "But I'm sure the People have given you all this information in discovery."

"I'll go back and check my files." Earl knew there was nothing in the reports about this.

"I just assumed you knew all this. Perhaps we shouldn't have discussed it." McKeene rose from his chair. "Well, I'm glad things are going well. Good luck." Earl rose and left the judge's chambers, closing the door behind him. He knew the judge was aware that discussing the case without the prosecutor present was clearly improper. What Earl did not know was why McKeene was telling him all this.

Back at his office, Martha directed him to go through his emails. A young colleague, Saul Pransky, was asking whether he could trust the word of a certain DA. He had attached the DA's email assuring Saul a crucial piece of evidence had never left the evidence locker, concluding that there was no need to call a string of witnesses to testify it had not been exposed to other evidence or tampered with.

Earl knew the DA and did not trust him. He wrote Saul that the DA probably had a problem with his case he was trying to cover up, and that if Saul ever shook hands with the DA he should count his finger afterward to see if he still had them all.

Earl was reluctant to push reply out of a fear that Hal would take it upon himself to send his message back to that DA. So he scrolled down his directory to the S's and sent a new email to Saul.

A few minutes later Martha buzzed him. "Did you send an email to a DA named Samantha Price?

"You've gotta be kidding," Earl said despairingly. He turned and looked at Hal sitting quietly on his side table. "That was way out of line, Hal," he hissed between clenched teeth.

"I'm sure you can explain it to her," Martha said. "She's on the line."

Earl reluctantly picked up the phone.

"You know," Sam said, struggling to control her laughter. "When I played field hockey, there were certain statements made by opposing players that our coach called bulletin board material. Something to fire up the troops."

"I've heard something about that," Earl said, but to him it was no laughing matter. It had taken him years to earn the grudging respect of the DA's Office, He had a reputation of fighting hard, but fair. However, a publicized attack on the integrity of one of their own would force them to circle the wagons in support and punish Earl. He normally wouldn't care, except that, in reality, it was his clients who would be punished, not Earl.

Harsher plea deals, longer sentences. That was something he did care about.

Sam continued. "When you look for someone's email address, it's probably a good idea to check more than the first letter."

"Yeah, somebody could end up sending an email to the wrong person."

"Unofficially, if I had gotten such an email, I would have probably agreed with it. But officially, I never received such an email. Somehow it must have gotten deleted and sent to the recycle bin. Which for a tech wizard like you, does not mean it was converted into paper for your sports section."

Earl was silent for a moment. "Thank you, Sam," he said seriously. "And thanks for not making me ask."

"Don't know what you're talking about. Besides I have to go deal with some spam, which by the way, is not a culinary dish."

"Understood. And thanks again." He hung up and leaned back in his chair with a grin on his face.

Earl drew the curtains to block out the late afternoon sun. He had left the office early and was sitting on his couch watching a baseball game on television. Earlier that afternoon, after returning to the office from his audience with Judge McKeene, he had diligently returned each of the phone calls that Martha had ordered him to answer and then turned once again to the Seabrooke binders. But the words all seemed to blend together into a solid blank wall, with no way to climb over it. He needed a break, so he headed home.

To Earl, listening to the soothing voice of Vin Scully describe a Dodger road game was what a Bach violin sonata must be to other people. A scoreless pitchers' duel was unfolding, his favorite. An accordion file marked "Crystal Robinson" lay next to him and a large bowl of popcorn was on his lap. At his feet, Henceforth sat on the rug staring up at him with intense concentration. Between handfuls stuffed into his own mouth, he would toss a few kernels in Henceforth's direction. The big dog showed surprising agility in catching them in midair, snapping his jaws shut like a shark and immediately resuming his focused stare.

The only time, other than in the pursuit of popcorn, that Henceforth had shown such passion was when the neighbor's German Shepherd had squared off with him. On that morning, Earl had opened the front door to get the newspaper, only to find Butch from next door lifting his leg on it. Earl yelled at the dog, who promptly growled at him and began barking menacingly. Apparently this violated the ancient code that dictated that respect be accorded He Who Feeds Me. Henceforth bolted out the door and bull-rushed the Shepherd, sending him sprawling on his back. Henceforth stood over him, teeth bared, until the other dog gave some subtle sign of submission, known only to dogs, and limped away. When the neighbor came to complain that Henceforth was a neighborhood menace, the big dog shoved his nose into the man's crotch asking to be petted. The neighbor left in a huff.

Between innings, Earl would pull a case folder from the file and make notes on a legal pad. The cases were arranged chronologically, a history of Crystal's descent into addiction and depravity marked by the usual arrests along the way. Driving juiced on pills, under the influence of heroin, possessing a hype kit, the typical signposts on a road to personal destruction. None of it was particularly helpful; it was about what Earl had expected and exactly why he had brought this file home. If he just sat and watched the game, he would have felt guilty about not working on the case. So this necessary but unproductive task eased his conscience and let him enjoy the game.

At the top of the sixth inning, Earl picked up the last Crystal Robinson file. Now this was more like it. A sales case. A conviction for selling drugs was a felony and something he could bring out in front of the jury. Not much, but it might reflect on Horgan and his choice of bedmates. It never hurt to dirty up the victim a little. Earl flipped to the arrest report. Crystal had been scooped up during a raid on a basement dope lab, the place where pure heroin was diluted, hopefully with an innocuous substance like baby powder rather than battery acid. The more times a dealer could cut the heroin, the more he increased the profits, but make it too weak and the customers would go elsewhere. So a tester was needed, just like in the wine industry, someone with a discriminating palate or arm, as the case might be. Crystal told the police that was her role, just a guinea pig, not a pusher.

Earl picked up the court docket sheet. All Earl needed was to verify that Crystal had pled to the felony. Even a tester was part of the conspiracy to sell drugs, so this was a slam dunk, as a man once said. Earl stared at the last line of the docket sheet thinking for a moment that he must have picked up the wrong sheet. Right name, right case number, wrong last entry, just one word, "Dismissed." It made no sense. Maybe a lighter sentence or even a referral to drug rehab, but an outright dismissal, no way.

He looked up at the television, but paid no attention to what was on the screen. Only one explanation seemed to fit. She must have turned snitch, prepared to testify against her co-defendants and anyone else she knew. A snitch trumped a convicted felon as an unsavory companion for a police officer.

Earl reached for the phone and punched in the number of Harry Lesser, a public defender he knew. "Harry, who loves you?" he asked, when Lesser picked up.

"If this is Bobby Earl, you are not the one." Harry Lesser had a reputation for pushing the ethical envelope, sometimes off the table. Once, on a hopeless case, he had typed up a phony defense investigator's report that stated the defendant had an iron clad alibi. Just before the trial was to commence, Harry left the report out on counsel table while he stepped out of the courtroom. As he expected, the legal protection surrounding the document did not prevent the DA from surreptitiously reading it and offering Harry's client a sweet deal upon his return.

"Come on, Harry, who laughs at your lame jokes?"

"That just proves you have poor taste. Besides you fucked me in our last trial."

"That's not true, Harry. I told you to ask for a separate trial for your man."

"Yeah, well, the judge didn't give it to me, did he? And you rammed it so far up my guy's ass he probably stood up the whole ride to the joint."

"Harry, I told you before we started that I was going to lay it off on your guy. Hell, you would have done the same thing if you were in my place."

"Maybe," he said reluctantly. "So what do you want?"

"Just to hear your voice, Harry."

"Yeah, and I look like Brad Pitt."

"Okay, okay, I need a favor."

"Really, Bobby. I'm shocked."

"I need you to go to the office computer file on snitches and check out a name for me. I know you guys keep it up to date so you can conflict off all the hard cases and go home early."

"Very funny. What's the name? I'll do it, but you owe me one. And as the Godfather would have said, someday I will call on you."

"Crystal Robinson - that's Crystal without an H - and thanks." Earl could hear the click of computer keys. He realized this would take a while because the file was a hodgepodge of the different types of these termites who ate away at the integrity of the judicial system. There were those who, when indicted, won the race to the prosecutor's door to offer to testify against their friends for a deal; the professional informants who made a living selling tips, some of which might actually be true; and those who set up people by suggesting an attractive crime so they would have something to trade. After a few minutes Harry returned to the line. "Nothing. Zippo"

"You're kidding? You keep the file under the name they use in court, right Harry?"

"A snitch by any other name would not smell the same."

"Thanks, Harry." Earl hung up and sat in silence. It was not that the answer to this question was so important, it was just that he did not like loose ends. Henceforth who had been waiting patiently for another handout, gave up and issued a pitiful whine. Earl tossed him some popcorn. In the court system, there were certain givens you could count on. Policemen lied about the legal reasons for searches, judges would give harsher sentences if the press was watching and prosecutors did not dismiss solid cases.

Earl picked up the case folder, looking for the name of the lawyer who represented Crystal when the case was dismissed. He smiled. Written next to "Represented by" was the name George Kennedy, Public Defender. Earl picked up the phone and tossed more popcorn to Henceforth.

"George, it's Bobby Earl, I want you to take a trip down Memory Lane."

"Not too far back, I hope. I did some bad shit back in the day."

"Not too far. Two years. You represented a Crystal Robinson on a sales case that got dismissed. I was curious why."

"Cause' I'm one bad-ass defense lawyer, that's why."

"Yeah, George, I know, but what about this particular case?" There was a silence on the other end. "Do you even remember the case, George?"

"Two years ago? I don't even remember who I was fucking two years ago. Once that case file hits the closed box I push delete on my computer-like mind."

"I understand," Earl chuckled. "Do me a favor, Big Blue. Pull the file and see if it jogs that hard disk memory of yours. No rush. It's not that big a deal."

"For you, my man, of course. I'll call you back."

Earl returned to the game. By the eighth inning the game was still scoreless, but the manager was apparently not satisfied. He called for another pitching change. The phone rang as the TV announcer was explaining that the new pitcher was their "closer," who always pitched the last two innings.

"I do remember the case now," Kennedy said, "but you know what, I still don't know why they dismissed. The DA just came in and said they were going to punt."

"You ask why, George?"

"You kidding, Bobby? I was just happy to get rid of another case. I got out of there as fast as I could, before he changed his mind."

"You think you could ask?"

"I think so, we get along pretty good. The DA is pissed at his supervisor, so it's a common enemy unites kind-of-thing. But I've got to pick the right time."

"I understand. Thanks, George."

On the south side of downtown, past the Traffic Court on Hill Street and the sweat shops of the Garment District, but before you reach the imposing brick and limestone buildings of the USC campus and their neighbor, the historic Los Angeles Coliseum, there is an area called Tenement Square. Four square blocks of shabby apartment buildings, their rooms are crammed with the families of recent immigrants, over which the city has ceded its housing authority to the care of slum landlords.

On a deserted side street, shrouded in the predawn darkness, an old Buick with dented fenders and a layer of dirt, sat parked at the curb. It was the type of car that went unnoticed, which was exactly what it was meant to be. A large black man was sprawled on the front seat, his leather coat stretched tightly over his thick shoulders. He reminded himself again that the chink at the Looh Fung Restaurant had said he thought this guy was sort of the leader and that he worked the swing shift. Which meant he should get off work around 4:00 a.m. So there was nothing to do but wait. That was okay. It was part of the job and Deon Hawkins was good at his job.

He liked doing these little jobs for the chink. They paid good and were usually easy. Like this one. The chink wanted all these tenants out of his building so he could do some sort of real estate deal. But he didn't want to hassle with evictions and being drug into court by some 'poor peoples' lawyer. Somebody might start asking questions. The wrong kinda questions.

He stared out the windshield at the tenement building next to the curb. The outside fire-escape latticed down the front, bleeding rust onto the bricks; cardboard had been used to replace broken window panes and dirty sheets were nailed up for curtains. A wooden sign over the entrance read "Hill Street Manor." Hawkins' lips curled into a sneer. Some rich white bitch musta' come up with that shit, he thought. And she probably didn't even think it was funny. Like the mothafucka' who named the projects where he grew up – Knickerson Gardens. More like The Crack Gardens. Or The Roach Castle. Yeah, that's it, like that ad on TV.

Suddenly, Hawkins sat up. A Hispanic man had appeared around the corner. He was wearing a sweat shirt dabbed with paint smears and was carrying a small Styrofoam cooler. He looked to Hawkins to be in his thirties with the squat square build and bowed legs of an Andean Indian.

Hawkins got out of the car. He walked onto the sidewalk and leaned back against the front fender with folded arms. "José," he called, when the man got near.

The man stopped and stared warily at Hawkins, then glanced quickly up and down the street.

"It's okay," Hawkins said. "I just want to talk to you."

"What for? Do I know you?" the man asked with a clipped Spanish accent.

"Mr. Lee, he sent me. You know, the guy what owns them restaurants. He says you been causin' a fuss."

"Mr. Lee," the man spat out the name. "We pay rent, he do nothing. No plumbing. No heat. A fucking 'rata' bit my kid." He paused as if to gather courage. "Fuck Mr. Lee and fuck his restaurantes. We all decide." He waved his arm at the building. "No more fucking rent. That lady abogada at the Center, she say what he does is not right."

"Well, that's the thing, José. Mr. Lee, he don't give a shit about the rent."

The man stared in puzzlement.

Hawkins pushed off the car and walked slowly toward the man. "See what you and the rest of them folks got to do is move out."

"Move out?" the man said in astonishment. "I got *familia*."

The man backed up as Hawkins advanced. When he bumped up against the building, he glanced quickly about, then dropped his cooler and braced himself as if for a fight.

"Don't get all scared like," Hawkins said, holding out his upraised palms. When Hawkins got close, he towered over the frightened man. In a flash, Hawkins smashed a fist into the man's face. His head snapped back and thudded against the brick wall. The man collapsed onto the pavement like a puppet with its strings cut. Hawkins grabbed one leg and effortlessly pulled the unconscious body across the sidewalk and into the gutter. He flipped the man onto his stomach and positioned his mouth on the edge of the curb.

Hawkins stepped back as if to admire his work, then raised one shoe and stomped down hard on the back of the man's head. Teeth clattered on the pavement like a box of spilled Chicklets. He stood back and studied the man, then used the toe of one shoe to roll him onto his back. He leaned down and slapped the man into semi-consciousness.

"Listen to me, you dumb motherfucker," Hawkins hissed.

The man pushed out a moan.

"When I come back, all you folks gonna be gone." He slapped the man again. "You got that? Cause' if you ain't, next time it's gonna get ugly."

Hawkins straightened up and calmly shrugged his shoulders, adjusting his jacket. He got back in his car and thought for a moment. He decided not to run over the man's legs. That would only delay things. He put the car in gear and drove slowly into the night.

It had been a successful Friday morning for Bobby Earl. A judge had given him a continuance on one of his defenseless cases. A small victory in a strategy of delay that he hoped would eventually result in a clearance sale price for the case. In the hall outside the courtroom a family of Hispanics stood huddled around a grey-haired woman who was sitting on a bench quietly crying. A young woman knelt down and put an arm around her shoulders while the men shifted their weight from foot to foot in an awkward silence. People walked by without a glance, either oblivious in their self-absorption or inured to such anguish by careers immersed in daily suffering. Earl could not tell whether the group was the family of a defendant who the judge had just dropped into a cement hole, or the family of a victim who had been led on by the false promise that this day would bring closure. It was the same either way, two sides of the same sad coin.

Farther down the hall, he stopped to hold a courtroom door open for a young woman struggling to exit while pushing an older man in a wheelchair. The man had a sun-wrinkled face and long blond hair pulled back in a ponytail. A beaded necklace lay on top of his embroidered denim work shirt. He looked like a museum piece from the Haight Ashbury flower power days. He and the young woman made a mismatched pair. She was beautiful.

She smiled in gratitude as they passed and headed for the elevator. He was five strides down the hall before it hit him. This was one of the beaming young women in the photograph with Horgan. Earl had a talent for remembering faces. It probably came from studying the faces of potential jurors for any hint of their true character. Whoever said that by middle age you had the face you had earned was right. You could tell a lot about jurors and how they might vote from a downturned mouth or a pair of dull eyes.

He turned to catch up with her, only to see the elevator doors close behind the pair. Just as well, he thought; what was she going to tell him, that Horgan knew how to get down and party? As he continued down the hall, a little voice in the back of his mind started to murmur. Earl believed in luck, fate, whatever you wanted to call it. The little voice said if chance put this woman in his path, don't ignore it.

He retraced his steps back to that courtroom. The sign on the door said Civil Department, Law and Motion. Earl asked the clerk for the file of the woman pushing the wheelchair. The clerk laughed and heaved a court file masquerading as a telephone book onto the counter. He carried the file to the counsel table.

The original entry on the file had been made six years before, bringing to mind the Dickens tale of *Jarndyce v. Jarndyce*, the lawsuit that never ended. This was a civil lawsuit to return property that the County had seized. There was no need to check the docket to know that Mr. Thompson, the old man in the wheel chair, was acting as his own lawyer. This was apparent from the documents he filed with phrases such as "Nazi storm troopers," and "a man's home is his castle."

Earl flipped to the front of the file in search of the facts. Mr. Thompson, it seemed, owned a horse ranch on the bluffs overlooking the ocean in Malibu. Apparently he was putting his horse manure to good use by growing a dozen marijuana plants in a greenhouse behind the stables. LAPD swooped in with a search warrant, and that's when it got ugly. The police said they thought Thompson reached for a gun; he said he was picking up his cat to protect her. He was shot and paralyzed. The jury believed the cops.

After the criminal case was concluded, the county started civil forfeiture proceedings. California law allowed the State to take any land that had been used to commit a drug crime. In Thompson's case it seemed like a harsh response, given the relatively small amount of dope, until Earl saw the appraisal report on the property. There was a decent amount of money at stake. Seizing property had become a major source of income for police departments, because once the forfeiture was final, the property could be sold at auction, and the arresting police agency was entitled by statute to a hefty portion of the proceeds.

Earl was about to close the file when he saw a copy of the the search warrant affidavit , the sworn statement that was supposed to explain to the judge why the cops suspected illegal drugs were there and why a search was justified. When he got to the last page a bell went off inside his head. The officer who had signed the affidavit and led the search team was Terrence Michael Horgan. And the young woman pushing Thompson's wheelchair was probably the old man's daughter. But what was Thompson's daughter doing photographed in Horgan's crowd. Earl reached for his cell to call Munoz. He needed some answers.

It was past midnight. The dented Buick sat alone in the deserted parking lot of a small strip mall. Most people would have described its geographical location in proximity to Olvera Street, the tourist attraction lined with stalls of "authentic" Mexican trinkets, or the historic old Union Station with its Mission Revival architecture and travertine marble floors. Both were just two blocks away. But the more pertinent landmark was right across the street, the Men's Central Jail.

Emilio Chavez opened the passenger door and slid onto the front seat next to the driver. "Boy, thanks, Deon," he said excitedly. "I hated it in there. No TV, nothing. And the people were so mean." The big man behind the steering wheel was silent. Emilio studied him and became subdued. "I'm sorry, Deon. I'm really, really sorry."

In the glow of the jail's floodlights, Deon Hawkins stared straight ahead at the low brick wall lining the strip-mall parking area. The bricks on the edge of the driveway entrance were broken and missing. On the wall was scribbled "Give me liberty or give me Meth," just above "Stiff Meat Stevie dropped a dime on me."

"Don't be mad at me, Dee. I hate it when you're mad at me."

"It's okay," Hawkins said and gently patted the younger man's hand. Emilio was twenty years old but could pass for sixteen, with large soft eyes, long glossy black hair and a wide, full mouth. His white tank top was stretched tightly over his lean, unmuscled chest.

"I just wanted to show you that I could do something on my own. I thought the grocery store would be easy. I guess I didn't think so good."

"I know," Hawkins said, slowly nodding. "But we can't go jackin' people no more. I told you that."

"I know. It was stupid." Emilio looked down at his hands.

"We're into insurance now. We got to stay neutral. What if that store was paying protection, or if that woman had got shot and was some Vato's old lady."

"I know," Emilio said, his eyes downcast. "I fucked up."

"If somethin' kicked off, then where'd we be? We'd be taking sides, settling our own scores." Hawkins pursed his lips. "Then we got no more business."

Emilio sat silently, studying his hands as if they held the answer. Hawkins stared at Emilio. He was so beautiful, like one of those angel statues outside that church off Avalon Boulevard. Hawkins remembered the night he first picked up Emilio. He was turning tricks on Sunset Boulevard. He looked so small and defenseless, without a stray dog's chance of surviving. The streets would have sucked the life out of him, then spit what was left into the gutter.

Hawkins had always sealed himself off behind a wall of hate that prevented him from seeing people and feeling what they felt. He only knew a faceless rage that smoldered inside him. But when he saw Emilio for the first time, his wall crumbled. Something welled up inside him that he had never felt before. It both frightened and excited him all at once. For the first time in his life, the idea of protecting someone, being responsible for someone, pulled at Hawkins. They had been together ever since.

Nobody ever took care of Hawkins growing up in the notorious Knickerson Gardens projects. His crackhead mother called him Little Dee because of his size and told him he was "born 'growed up' and could take care of his own self." After a while he realized he had a talent, a very valuable talent – he was the last guy you ever wanted to fuck with. The street said Little Dee just plain didn't care, he didn't care about himself or anybody else. Maybe he was born that way or maybe the street beat it out of him, but either way, he became the guy you called at midnight. His reputation was such that all it took to settle a dispute between drug dealers was for one of them to say, "Okay, asshole, this is the last time I talk to you. Either we sort this out or the next voice you'll hear will be Little Dee's."

Hawkins reached across the front seat and pulled Emilio to his chest and enveloped him in his thick arms. "I'll be good, Dee," Emelio muttered. "You just wait and see."

"I knows you will," Hawkins said as he smoothed Emilio's hair. "They leave you alone in there?"

Emilio looked up into the big man's face. "Course they did. Once I told em' about you and me, nobody messed with me. Everybody knows you, Dee." He smiled and snuggled back down.

"Let's go get a burger at Tommy's," Hawkins said. "You'd like that, wouldn't you?"

CHAPTER 15

Earl pulled into the underground parking structure next to the courthouse, and drove down to the third floor. Not being in trial, he did not have to worry about being seen by jurors, so he had driven his other car, the one he affectionately called Old Blue. It was his first indulgence when he started to make money. A pale blue, 1971 Mercedes Benz convertible with glove leather seats. At first he had been self-conscious, like an older man with a too-young wife. But he just kept reminding himself that he had earned this car. He maneuvered into his favorite parking slot between two pillars that protected his car doors from those who drove by Braille. He got out and ran his hand over the fenders as over the coat of a fine race horse.

It had been only three weeks since he last appeared on the Seabrooke case, but despite the demands of his other cases he had filed all his motions on time. Walking up the stairs, he reviewed in his mind the arguments he planned to make. With each step he took, his briefcase nudged his leg, weighed down by the paper war his motions had ignited.

On the sidewalk, he looked over at the courthouse. Cement squares framed the windows, giving it the look of a large egg crate. Its unimaginative architecture had none of the character of the old Hall of Justice it had replaced. No sense of seriousness or fear. Facing the courthouse across a parking lot, like a patriarch at the head of the table, sat a monumental Deco structure covering an entire city block. Above its crested balconies, chiseled in gigantic letters on its granite wall was "The Times." He glanced at the newspaper's large illuminated clock which said 8:15. Enough of this, he had better hustle.

When he reached Department 102 and opened the courtroom door he was met by the clamor of a dozen indistinguishable conversations. The courtroom was packed. A group of lawyers whom Earl did not recognize were huddled around Jessup. They were undoubtedly there in response to his motions. The reporters in the front rows of the public section turned when he entered, whispered to each other, then turned back around. He was pleased to see he was as popular as ever.

As he maneuvered through the crowded aisle, he saw Thomas Glass, host of the TV show *The People's Voice,* seated inside the rail.

Glass turned with an amused look and nodded at Earl. The Thumb did not seem overly concerned about Earl's motion to hold him in contempt for broadcasting Seabrooke's sealed confession. Earl flashed a grin in return and headed toward the courtroom's lockup to explain to Seabrooke why he had filed all these motions that he expected to lose. Sometimes you had to fight a few losing battles in order to set up a victory. But when he described this strategy, Seabrooke did not seem to understand.

The bailiff called for order as the door of the judge's chambers opened. The room quieted and people jostled for a seat as in a game of musical chairs. Judge Jefferson called the case and Seabrooke was brought out to sit next to Earl. The judge shuffled through a pile of papers on the bench and slid out a small stack.

"Good morning. Let's take up your first motion, Mr. Earl." The judge slid some papers off the top of the pile. "As I understand it, you have subpoenaed the Federal Drug Enforcement Agency for the reports on the investigations in which Officer Horgan was involved."

"That's correct, your Honor. These reports may well point to a possible suspect in his murder. If Officer Horgan was dealing with high level narcotics traffickers, which I believe he was, then he was involved with some very dangerous people who might be the real perpetrators of this murder. I need the reports to show that – "

A short, athletic-looking young man in a pinstripe suit stepped forward. "Jason Bentley, Assistant United Sates Attorney, representing the Government."

"Mr. Earl, I've read your papers and the Government's opposition. The law seems pretty clear. As a State Court, I have no power to compel the federal government to comply with your subpoena unless they voluntarily want to cooperate. Apparently that's not the case." The judge looked at the US Attorney, who slowly shook his head.

"There is another avenue," Earl said. "If the District Attorney's Office would request the reports, I am sure the Federal Government would comply."

"That might change things, Your Honor," the US Attorney said. "But we have received no such request."

"Mr. Jessup?" the judge inquired.

"We have no intention of making such a request," Jessup said.

"Well, Mr. Earl, whether it's fair or not, that's where it sits. Your request for Officer Horgan's investigative reports is denied."

"Now, Mr. Earl, let's take up your next motion. You state that the alleged confession by your client, contained in the sealed Grand Jury transcript, was broadcast to the public on the *The People's Voice* on

Channel 5. As a consequence, you want me to order Mr. Glass to reveal the source of this information and if he refuses to hold him in contempt of court."

A distinguished-looking man in a tailored grey pinstripe suit and tasseled loafers stepped forward. With an apparently practiced gesture, he swept off his designer eye glasses with a manicured hand. "Robert Arnold, your honor, of Arnold and Hutchins, representing Mr. Glass."

"Good morning, Mr. Arnold."

"This matter is easily disposed of your Honor. Mr. Glass does not intend to reveal his source and as we pointed out in our court papers, under the California Shield Law, a television journalist has immunity for refusing to disclose the source of any information communicated to the public. By the initiative process, the voters of California even incorporated this protection into the State's Constitution. This Court simply lacks the authority to punish Mr. Glass for refusing to reveal his source."

The judge looked at Earl. "That does appear to be the law, Mr. Earl."

"However," Earl said, "you do have the authority to protect Mr. Seabrooke from future prejudicial statements and leaks from the prosecutor's office. This is a case that should be tried in the courtroom, not on television or in the press. I'm requesting that the Court issue a restraining order against the parties not to publicly discuss any of the facts of the case, release any documents, offer any opinion concerning the strength of the case or make statements about Mr. Seabrooke's guilt or innocence."

Jessup jumped to his feet. "Judge, I haven't received any notice of this request."

The judge's lips curled slightly in amusement. "Mr. Jessup, it is obvious that you're a man who's quick on his feet." There was a slight titter from the onlookers. "I'm sure you can articulate your position without spending a week in the library, that is if people use the library anymore."

Jessup looked down at Sam, then back up again. "Judge, the District Attorney's Office is the People's lawyer and it only proper that we inform them about the People's business and how it is being conducted. It's important that Mr. Cavalli, as an elected official, be able to explain to the public through the press how he is conducting his office."

"I agree with you. I have no intention of interfering with the press. In fact, I intend to set aside front row seats for the press, so they can attend every day of the trial and learn the facts firsthand. But I do intend to control the parties to this litigation and make sure that any accused who appears before me receives a fair trial." He swept the room with a challenging look. "The motion is granted." The judge looked at Earl. "And the order applies to all parties, Mr. Earl, including you." Earl nodded. This was what he was after all along. The defense never won a duel with the prosecution in the press.

"Now," the judge said, "with regard to the question of television coverage of the trial, I'm inclined to grant it in some form, but I want to hear your views, so we will take that up at the pretrial hearing. Which brings us to the selection of a trial date. I have given this some thought and I think, given the interest in the case, we should resolve this sooner rather than later. We'll start jury selection two months from today."

Earl had expected to get jammed with an early trial date. But, two months! That was not a lot of time for a case like this, particularly one for which he had yet to find a defense. But he knew it was hopeless to argue with Jefferson. Not having a trial date had made it easy to avoid any thoughts of failure. The luxury of time always held out the hope that something would turn up. Now there was a deadline. Fear started to grip him. He berated himself for needing to take a case like this and was angry that if he lost he would now have an innocent man on his conscience.

Earl left the courtroom, took the elevator up to the ninth floor and entered a door marked "Attorney Lounge." It should have read "Defense Lawyer Lounge," because no prosecutor ever set foot inside. This was the defense lawyers' sanctuary, where they could speak freely among their colleagues without worrying about being overheard by jurors or clerks. It was here that grievances were aired about the inanity of some judge, the dishonesty of a particular prosecutor or the general frustration of swimming against the tide of moral righteousness. It was understood that what was confided in this room, stayed in this room.

The sound of boisterous laughter engulfed him as he pushed open the door. The room was full. Lawyers sprawled on couches and easy chairs or hunched over tables cluttered with documents and food containers. Several people called his name and urged him to join them. A tall, heavily built woman left her seat to give him a hug and thank him for helping her on a case. Earl begged off the invitations, explaining that he had to meet his investigator, and sat at a small table against a window.

Earl was watching an attractive young woman in tight slacks maneuver through the room when a voice beside him said, "That'll get your soldier to salute." Earl turned to find Munoz staring at the retreating woman. "But chasing tail is not going to keep that hound of yours fed," Munoz chuckled.

"You're right." Earl pulled out a chair. "You want something to eat?" He pushed a half-sandwich across the table.

"No way. I'm going to El Tepeyac for a giant Hollenbeck burrito. If you can eat the whole thing, it's free." The big man patted his sizable stomach. "It's like found money."

"We have a trial date. Two months." Munoz widened his eyes in surprise. "So I hope you've been doing something besides trying to bankrupt that restaurant?"

"A little something. I found that woman you asked about."

"The daughter of the wheelchair hippie? The one in the photo with Horgan?"

"The same," Munoz said. "Delight Thompson." He flipped open his little notebook. "She works at the Equestrian Center exercising horses. Lives with her old man. No record and a bit of a looker judging from her DMV photo." He slid a photocopy across the table.

Earl recognized the face. The same shy smile and blue eyes. "You know, Manny, there's got to be something going on with her. Horgan led a raid on her old man's ranch, who gets shot and crippled in the process. So what in the hell is she doing in that group photo I saw at Horgan's house, flashing her porcelain brights like one of his party girls?"

"Maybe she wanted to fuck him to death."

Earl gave Munoz a disapproving stare. "Cute, Manny." He pushed the photocopy back across the table. "Go use your inestimable charm on her and see what you can find out." Earl paused. "What about that photo of Tommy Margolin, Mr. Big Time Dope Lawyer? What's he doing posing with Horgan and a carload of dope?"

"That's interesting. The car had been seized in a dope bust a while back and later put up for auction at one of those State sales. Margolin bought it, the same day as the date on the photo."

"So how does Margolin fit in all this?" Earl asked.

"It's an old ploy. The cops found the dope when they first inventoried the car. They left it in there when it was put up for auction thinking the drug dealer would take a chance it wasn't discovered and send somebody to buy the car. Enter Margolin. Then the cops stop the car and nail the driver."

"Okay, he's busted with dope in the car and no charges are filed? They must have done something, they're not going to let that slide by."

"I'm with you," Munoz said. "The name of the game is to flip the driver. Get him to give up the dealer. So I figured if Margolin rolled, the cops would have gotten a search warrant for the location where he was taking the car. So I go check downtown where they file all the search warrants and I find it based on the date."

"So what did it say?"

"That's the thing. I got no idea. It's sealed."

"It's been ordered sealed?" Earl asked in astonishment. "What's so secret that nobody can read it? It's a search warrant for Christ's sake."

"When I was with LAPD, the only time we asked a judge to do that was when we got the warrant based on a tip from a real hot informant and we wanted to keep his identity confidential."

Earl sat thinking for a moment. "Maybe attorney Margolin and I should have a little chat."

Manny Munoz spoke to one of the grooms in Spanish and was told he could find Delight Thompson at the jumping ring. Enjoying the warmth of the afternoon sun, he followed the dirt path as directed, past a white-fenced corral where sleek, well-fed horses stood in the shade swishing their tails at flies. Wooden jumping hurdles sat idle inside the enclosure. Munoz breathed in the dry smell of horse dung and let his mind drift back to his childhood in Mexico. In his village, people owned either donkeys or mules, working animals that plowed the fields and carried the produce. But not his father. He owned a horse – El Rey, a huge animal, twenty hands at the shoulder and so strong only his father could ride him. As the top man at the nearby plywood factory, his father was the acknowledged leader of their little village, just as Manny's grandfather had been the top man before him. Every Sunday after Church, his father would mount El Rey and ride through the village talking to the people, hearing their complaints, settling disputes, deciding what should be done in the village. When his father returned home, Manny got to brush and currycomb the large stallion, who would stand quietly, head held aloft, ignoring the village children who gathered to watch and whisper in admiration.

Manny's thoughts returned to the present when he reached the last enclosure, where a young woman wearing a protective helmet and jeans was circling the ring on a Chestnut mare. She sat the horse well, straight-backed, reins held tautly to maintain the pace at a steady cantor. She turned the horse toward a high wooden jump. As they approached, she leaned forward over the horse's neck and urged her over the wooden crossbar. After clearing the rail, she pounded the horse on the shoulder and spoke words of approval. Munoz folded his arms over the corral fence and grinned. "Nicely done," he called.

The woman reined the horse in and looked over at Munoz. "You must be Manny. You called me," she said.

"And you must be Miss Thompson. Nice to meet you," he said.

She rode over to the ring's gate, dismounted and led her horse through. She took off her helmet and tossed her long blond hair free.

"Nice horse," he said, patting the mare on the rump. "She's a bit on the small side though, isn't she?"

"Yeah." She rubbed the mare's soft muzzle, looking into her large eyes. "But she's got a soft mouth and is a real sweetie. Aren't you Diamond?" The horse tossed her head. "I'm training her for the owner. I wish she were mine." She put a small carrot on her palm and held it up to the horse's mouth, where it quickly disappeared. "But you didn't come here to talk horses. Walk with me. I need to cool her down."

Munoz fell in stride with her. "I appreciate you taking the time to see me."

"No problem. So you work for the guy who shot Horgan?"

"Well, the guy who is accused of it."

"As far as I'm concerned they should give your guy a medal. He did the world a favor." She looked over at Munoz. "Unless, of course, we happen to run short of assholes."

"I understand," Munoz said. "You must have gone through a lot with your father."

"You have no idea what that man did to my father." She gave Munoz a challenging look. "My father was a sweet, gentle man. An old hippie. Peace, love and all that. He smoked some weed with his friends and boarded horses. That was pretty much it. He never hurt a soul."

"You said 'was'. He's still alive, isn't he? You two live together, right?"

"The father I knew is gone. He's a shell. He is totally consumed by a lawsuit to get his ranch back. That's all he talks about. There's no room left in our apartment because of all the stacks of papers, files and books. He sits all day at my computer writing letters. Or else researching these petitions he writes to the court."

"I'm sorry," Munoz said. "I'm genuinely sorry. It must be tough." They walked on in silence. After a minute, she turned to him. "So how did you find me, anyway?"

"Officer Horgan had a photo in his house. You were in the group."

She gave a begrudging smile. "Of course. My alter ego, Tiffany the party girl."

"We sort of wondered. Given what he did to your father."

"That's why I was there. I hated that man. I never knew I could hate like that." She seemed to drift off somewhere, no longer talking to Munoz. "I wanted him to suffer. I mean really suffer. So I had this plan. I found out where they hung out and started going there. Pretty soon I was part of the group. Horgan was a player, so I dropped a few hints. It was easy."

"What about his girlfriend, Crystal? I thought they were going together?"

She gave him a skeptical frown. "He treated her like a dog. 'Come, sit, stay,' and she took it, for whatever good it did her. It was clear by then to everyone that she had reached her expiration date with him. He was going to toss her out. That was the way he was. He used women. It was only a matter of time and she knew it."

"So what was your plan?"

"He invited me to his house one night. His playpen, as he called it. I figured I'd go there, then call the police and say he raped me. I already had bruises from a fall when a horse refused a jump, so all I had to do was rip my clothes and bang my face into a wall."

"That might have been tough to make stick if they found out about his connection to your father. That's a pretty good motive to lie or to do a lot of things."

She searched Munoz's face. "I didn't kill the son of a bitch, if that's what you're thinking. Not that I didn't think about it. But I wanted him to suffer. Even if he eventually beat the case, in the meantime I would drag him through the dirt. Let him see what it felt like."

"So what happened?"

"I went to his house. Actually, it was the night he got killed. How's that for timing?" She gave Munoz a quizzical look. "But when I got to the door, I hear him arguing with some guy inside. So I go back to my truck to wait for this guy to leave. But pretty soon they both come out and take off. So I left."

"Did they drive off together?"

"No, they each got in their own car."

"What did this other guy look like?"

"Oh, I don't know," she said. "Sort of an average looking guy." She thought for a moment and suddenly stopped walking. The horse shook her head, impatient to get back to the stable and more carrots. "But you know, I saw him later."

"Where was that?"

"On television. They said he was Horgan's partner or something. Some kind of Federal Agent."

CHAPTER 16

Sitting hunched over the counter at Jimmy's Diner, Earl poured sugar into his coffee mug. It was 8:00 p.m., the "in-between time," when the dinner crowd had left and it was too early for the night owls. Behind the counter, Jimmy was scraping grease off the grill. His long white apron had enough stains to serve as a color chart of the day's menu. Earl ordered a burger with fries and, pointing to Jimmy's apron, asked for some red, yellow and green "on the side."

Jimmy's Diner had a television on the wall behind the counter to keep the late night customers company. Earl looked over at the screen. Thomas Glass sat behind his studio desk, introducing a segment of his program called "The Whole Truth." Glass stared stern-faced into the camera, striking a pose of righteous indignation.

"Defending your right to know what your courts are really up to is never easy and today was no exception. To learn the truth behind any story, this reporter must promise my sources that their identities will never be revealed. Without this assurance they would never provide the information that you need to know. Today a defense lawyer tried to force me to break that trust. This lawyer, Bobby Earl, represents the man who murdered Officer Horgan. Excuse me, I forgot to say 'allegedly.'" He drew out the word as if it tasted bad. "He threatened to put me in jail if I didn't reveal my sources. Well," he gave a knowing smile, "you know how far that got him." The off-camera studio audience applauded. "But he was able to push the judge into issuing a gag order. That's right. Your prosecutor, doing your business, is forbidden to tell you about the case. I wonder what Mr. Earl is afraid of?" The camera moved in for a close-up. "Mr. Earl, why don't you want us to hear the truth?"

Earl turned away. "Hey, Jimmy, turn that thing off. I want to keep my food down."

The plain steel and glass building seemed like a chaperone at the prom amid the nighttime flash and dazzle of Sunset Boulevard. A building thrown together on the cheap, hoping to take advantage of a glamorous address. Above the entrance, in large gold letters, a sign read, "The

Margolin Law Building." Earl took the elevator up to the third floor. The waiting room was empty.

The door at the end of the room opened and a man walked out. He wore a blue work shirt with "Vito" sewn above the pocket and had a disgruntled expression on his face. He stared straight ahead as he passed. Stenciled on the back of the shirt was "A-1 Reliable Towing." Earl knew Margolin took in personal injury cases as a sideline to his criminal practice. Margolin must be paying off his 'cappers,' the people who steered cases his way for a cut of the client's settlement. Strictly illegal but rarely prosecuted.

The door opened again. Tommy Margolin was in the doorway in a linen sports coat, pink polo shirt and pressed jeans. His thinning hair was dyed shoe-polish black. A thick gold necklace nestled in his graying chest hair. "Bobby. Good to see you. Come in."

It was a large wood-paneled room. Margolin took a seat behind a massive carved mahogany desk, without a paper or book on its polished surface. On the wall behind him was an oil painting of the great man himself. "You want a drink or anything?" Margolin gestured toward a glass-front cabinet. Leaning against the wall next to it was a granite-block of a black man in a thigh-length black leather jacket, with a diamond stud winking from his left ear. "Oh, this is Mr. Deon Hawkins. I was just paying some referral fees and . . . "

Earl interrupted him. "Is that what they call them these days?"

Margolin smiled. "Come now, Bobby. Custom of the trade and all that. Everyone does it." He waited in vain for Earl to agree, then plowed on. "Anyway, there are certain negotiations involved, as you might imagine. So Mr. Hawkins is here to maintain civility. Sort of an insurance policy against any unpleasantness."

Earl looked at Hawkins, who stood sleepy-eyed, silently staring back. Earl said nothing as he sized up the ominous figure. There was something unnerving in Hawkins' unblinking stare. Something feral. As if he had lived apart for too long, beyond any rules.

Margolin broke the silence. "And, of course, many of these sources prefer to be paid in cash, so I try to accommodate them. It's probably unnecessary, but Mr. Hawkins also provides a certain degree of security."

"I'm sure he does." Earl looked at Hawkins, who slowly nodded in affirmation.

Margolin turned to Hawkins. "Well, I guess that does it for this evening, Mr. Hawkins. Thank you for your services."

Hawkins' gaze slowly shifted from Earl to Margolin and then back again. With a slight smile, he pushed himself away from the wall and stood adjusting his jacket. Then he turned and walked slowly out of the room, shutting the door behind him.

"A strange man," Margolin said. "But very reliable. A client recommended him." He walked over to the cabinet and poured himself a drink. "You're sure?" he asked, gesturing with his glass. Earl shook his head.

"I hear you're representing somebody on a robbery beef," Earl said. "Not exactly your specialty. What gives?"

Margolin cocked his head as if at a loss for Earl's meaning. After a beat he nodded his head in comprehension. "Oh, the Chavez kid. I'm just doing a favor. Emilio is a special friend of Mr. Hawkins. Never hurts to build good will." He stepped back to his desk. "So what's all this about a photograph?" he asked casually as he sat back down.

Earl took out a copy of the photograph of Margolin and Horgan on the car stuffed with dope and slid it across the clean surface of the desk. Margolin turned it with the edge of his glass as if afraid to touch it. He squinted at it with a puzzled expression. "What's this supposed to be?"

"Let's not play games, Tommy."

"Who's playing games? Anybody can fake a photograph. Where'd you have it done, anyway?" He pushed the photo back at Earl. "You should have had Photoshop pose me fucking a goat. More interesting."

Earl fixed him with a hard stare. "There are two ways this can go, Tommy. One way is for you to explain this on the witness stand, where I can show that you bought that car at a police auction. I have the records. The police confiscated the car in some drug bust. I figure, they find the dope, but leave it alone to see who would come calling, maybe lead them to Mr. Big. You show up. Horgan doesn't make you for a car enthusiast, so he figures he's got a twofer. He busts you and you get diarrhea of the mouth. You give up whoever you're doing this for. Then Horgan gets a search warrant for this Mr. Big based on a tip from a confidential reliable informant. So when I get my judge to unseal that warrant, I bet the name I find on there will be yours."

"Wait a minute, pal. You can't just toss that kind of shit around. I represent some very big people. Very dangerous people. You are way out of your league here. Accusations like that can get somebody hurt. Permanently hurt."

"Seems like a good reason," Earl said, "to try it the other way. Why don't you just tell me what happened."

Margolin stared at Earl, his mouth curved in disgust. He swallowed his drink in one gulp and went to the cabinet for another. When he sat back down, he heaved a sigh and looked away. "All right," he said with a tone of resignation. "I had this client. A very important client." He shot a glance at Earl to see if he understood. "He told me the car had sentimental value to him and asked me to go buy it. He obviously couldn't appear at a police auction. When Horgan stopped me I had no idea the dope was there. Horgan set me up."

Earl raised an eyebrow and gave him a skeptical look. "Go on," he said.

"Look, I knew I could beat the case, but it would take time and money and be bad for my reputation." Earl stifled a smile. "So Horgan told me if I just delivered the car as promised, he would forget the whole thing and keep my name out of it."

"You know, Tommy, I thought we had an understanding. I thought you were going to be straight."

"I am. That's what happened," Margolin insisted.

"I'm having a hard time buying Horgan as a catch and release kind of guy. If he had you on the hook, I sort of doubt he would have just let you go." Earl paused, waiting for a reply.

"Well, that's what happened."

"Let me tell you the way I see it. Once you delivered that car, Horgan owned you. If he circulated that photo, it wouldn't have taken a Sherlock Holmes to figure out you set somebody up and my guess is that particular somebody probably had issues with his anger management. So the question is, what did Horgan want from you?" Earl gave him a cheerless smile. "How am I doing so far?"

"You've got all the answers, you tell me."

"It wasn't money or you would have just paid it. Besides Horgan was probably afraid you would set him up, wear a wire or something. That leaves just one thing. He wanted information. Information from your clients. So you fed him tips based on confidential conversations with your clients about their drug business and that's how Horgan made all those busts. He just never named you as his informant."

Margolin twisted his face into a smirk. "Let me ask you something. If your little fairy tale is true, and I am not saying it is, what harm would there have been? If Horgan got some inside information and took some scumbags off the street, where's the loss? We're not talking about Joe Citizen here."

"The only trouble, Tommy, was that you actually pretend to be a lawyer."

"You know, Bobby, I hope that halo of yours doesn't get too tight."

"There is one thing, though, that I wonder about. What was it like living each day with Horgan holding that secret over your head? Knowing what would happen to you if Horgan got careless and let it slip that you were snitching-off your clients. Wondering what he would do now that he was being transferred and didn't need you anymore. I bet you weren't real broken up when you heard he died."

"I had nothing to do with that!" Margolin shouted.

"Have it your own way, Tommy." Earl stood and turned toward the door.

"Wait a minute. What about the photo. Let's talk. What do you want for it?"

"You still don't get it, do you? I've got a client, Tommy. Your problems are your problems."

"You better think about what you're doing, Earl," Margolin said in a loud voice. "Somebody could get hurt here and it ain't gonna be me." Earl kept walking. "I got friends, you know." Earl shut the door behind him.

When he was on the sidewalk he pulled out his cellphone. If there was one thing he hated it was trying to explain anything as 'just a coincidence.' It was usually just lazy thinking, because things were rarely just a coincidence. When Margolin described Hawkins as an insurance policy it jogged his memory. Hadn't Chuey told him that Lee, the Chinese restaurant owner, used an 'insurance man' as security for his wire business? Earl left a message for Munoz to go see Chuey at the jail and find out if the insurance man that Lee was using sounded like Deon Hawkins. He reminded Munoz to use his name and to say he was asking for a personal favor. That would cost him, but if the Wa Ching and Mi Familia were not currently shanking each other, Chuey could find out if Mr. Hawkins had another client.

Sam hated coming to the jail. Escorted to a small room that reeked of the smell of disinfectant, with not a sign of human habitation, she sat down at a small government-issue metal table and reviewed her notes. To keep informants safe from inmate justice, every interview had to be conducted in this cement box, away from prying eyes. Jessup had designated Jake Snyder as her witness or, as he so quaintly put it, "the scumbag's yours. I hate dealing with snitches." The trial was two months away, but Sam figured Snyder would require an extra scrubbing before he was fit for the witness box.

The metal door creaked open, and Snyder stepped inside. He stopped when he saw Sam, momentarily confused. "Who are you? Where's Jessup?"

"I'm Deputy District Attorney Price. I'll be trying the Seabrooke case with Mr. Jessup. You'll be my witness, so please take a seat."

"Well hot damn, this must be my lucky day." Snyder sat down across the table from her. His lips parted in a leer.

Sam slid a paper in front of him. "This is a report of the statement you made about your conversation with Seabrooke. Read it, please."

"I've only read this thing about a dozen times already."

"Read it again."

He narrowed his eyes. "Sure, whatever you say." He stared blankly at the paper for a minute, then looked up.

"So what else can you tell me that's not in there?" Sam said.

"That's pretty much it."

Sam fixed him with a stare. "Mr. Snyder...."

"Jake, call me Jake," he smiled.

"Mr. Snyder," Sam repeated. "When you testify, there is this little thing called cross-examination...."

"Hell, I know that," he interrupted. "That 'little ol' never mind.' Shoot, don't you worry about it. I can handle that."

Sam was reminded of what an old DA had told her about preparing witnesses. "With snitches, there's never enough sandpaper." Sam gave him an incredulous look. "Mr. Snyder, the man who will be questioning you is Bobby Earl. He happens to be a very good lawyer. So let's go over some things."

Snyder leaned back and studied Sam. "This is your first big case, ain't it?"

"I've tried plenty of cases, Mr. Snyder. Don't worry about that." She looked down at her notes. "For example, why, out of all the people in that holding cell, did Seabrooke pick you to confide in?"

"I've just got one of those faces, I guess. People trust me."

Sam heaved a frustrated sigh. "That is what I'm talking about. That answer is never going to fly."

"How come? Let's take you and me, for instance."

"Let's not," she said with a humorless smile.

"No, listen. We're going to be working together, right? So we have to trust each other."

"I'm not following you, Mr. Snyder."

Snyder rose and picked up his chair. "I'll explain it to you," he said as he moved to her side of the table and sat down facing her. "You're a young DA trying to make it. This big time case is your ticket. It could set you up. And I'm your star witness. As a matter of fact, without me, you ain't got no case." Snyder paused and let his eyes roam over Sam's body, before returning his gaze to meet her cold stare. "So if you need me to testify a certain way, just tell me. I trust you, I'll do it. And if I need certain things, you'll make sure I get them, because you trust me. That way we both make out." He rubbed a hand slowly down his thigh, extending it toward her.

Sam's eyes, full of rage, glared into his. She slammed her fist down hard on his forearm and in a flash grabbed his hand in a thumb hold. Snyder yelped, but was immobilized in her grip. She leaned her face into his. "Listen to me, you piece of human refuse. What you are going to do is testify and testify truthfully. Because if you don't, I will personally see to it that you are dropped in a hole for that robbery case of yours that is so deep, they will have to pump air down to you. Do we understand each other?" She gave his thumb some extra pressure.

"Jesus Christ," he exclaimed. "Yes. Yes."

"Now get your ass on your side of the table and let's go over your testimony." She released him.

Snyder jumped up holding his hand. "For Christ sake, I was only kidding around. You about broke my fucking thumb."

Sam opened her notebook and stared down at the page. Without looking up, she pointed to the other side of the table.

CHAPTER 17

"You got five minutes," Agent Kellog said, his jaw tensed in anger. He glared down at Earl and Munoz crammed together on one side of a booth in Jimmy's Diner. It was 3:00 in the afternoon and the place was nearly empty.

"Grab a seat," Earl said, gesturing across the table to the empty vinyl bench. "You want some coffee?"

"You gotta be kidding," Kellog said in disgust. Millie, the waitress, approached with a smile, but he waved her away. She gave Earl a quizzical look and left.

Munoz had told Earl about his interview with Delight Thompson, in which she said she was outside Horgan's house the night of the murder and heard him arguing with his partner just before he drove off. Most interesting of all was that there was not a single word of this in the LAPD interview of Agent Kellog.

Earl sat silently, locking eyes with Kellog. It had taken only a brief reference over the phone to a certain argument with Horgan to set up this meeting, so Earl understood why Kellog looked like he wanted to punch somebody, and Earl had a pretty good idea who that might be.

"Listen," Munoz said. "We're not looking to bust your balls. We just want a little information."

Kellog turned his angry eyes on Munoz. "Do you think I give a flying fuck what you want?"

"Oh, but I think you do," Earl said quietly. Kellog turned to him with a wary look. "See, we know Horgan was the subject of an internal Bureau investigation. And we have a witness who puts you at Horgan's the night he was killed, heard you arguing and saw you both leave at the same time."

"Look," Munoz put in. "I spent thirty years with the LAPD. So you and I both know how this works. You're Horgan's partner, so in an internal investigation, the Bureau is going to interview you first. They'll do that before they ever talk with Horgan to see if you know anything. And they are going to tell you not to talk to Horgan about it, so they can spring it on him." Munoz waited for a response, but Kellog just stared back at him. "On top of that, you didn't tell the LAPD you saw Horgan that night. You know what assholes those investigators are. They would probably figure you were over there so you two could get your stories straight. And not cooperating with a murder investigation? Well." Munoz shrugged his shoulders.

Kellog slowly shook his head. "How do you guys sleep at night?"

"Not very well," Earl said. "I'm representing a guy who may be innocent. So get off your high horse and tell us what the investigation was about and what you were doing over there. Then we can all get the fuck out of here."

Kellog ran a hand over his face as he thought. After a minute he spoke in a monotone, as if the words were being pulled out of him. He turned to Munoz. "It's just like it is for you guys on the State side. To make a case, we need to grab the bad guys with the dope. To do that we need a warrant."

"You can't just knock on the door and ask to come in," Munoz said sympathetically.

Kellog gave him a begrudging nod. "Just like you, to get our probable cause for a judge to sign off on the warrant, we use informants. Now you guys use snitches who have already caught a case. You cut them a deal, dismiss their case, shorten their time, whatever. That's their payoff."

It was Munoz's turn to nod in agreement. Kellog sighed and continued. "But on the Fed side, we can use, like, professionals. You know, free agents for hire. We pay them. They go out and try to make cases. They're not in trouble, they don't have a case or anything like that. And they sure don't do it out of a sense of civic duty. They do it for money. How much depends on the deal they make with the agent who's running them. Some get so much per bust, others so much a month."

"And, of course, under that arrangement, they would have no reason to lie," Earl said in mock sincerity.

Kellog smirked. "So Horgan had this informant. He gave us some big tips. I mean quality stuff. Locations of stash houses; where big buys were going down; couriers to follow. Nothing minor league. I didn't even know who it was. It was his big secret. He was the only one who could have any contact. I thought it was weird, but he said the informant wanted it that way. So, what the hell, the less contact I have with snitches the better."

"So why the investigation?" Earl asked.

"The deal Horgan had made was that the informant got a percentage of any cash we seized and we made a lot of big busts together. We seized a lot of cash, so that percentage amounted to some serious money. The Bureau just wasn't sure that it all ended up going to the informant."

"They thought Horgan was taking a cut," Earl said. Kellog reluctantly nodded. "So who was the informant?"

"I swear to God I have no idea."

"You're telling us," Earl said skeptically, "that the informant never got named in a warrant or testified in court?"

"Come on. You know we don't have to name a confidential informant unless they know something that could help the defense. Horgan made sure that never happened. There was never a name in the reports, just a 'CI' told us whatever. Enough to justify the search, nothing more."

"What about a judge asking to question the informant himself to see if there was something more that wasn't in the report?"

"That only happened a couple times. It was done in chambers and Horgan handled it."

"So what were you doing over at Horgan's?" Earl asked.

"I get called into the OPR." He glanced at Earl. "The Office of Public Responsibility," he explained. "They start questioning me as if I had something to do with Horgan's little scam. I've been with the Bureau for ten years. Those kind of questions can ruin a career. Even if you get cleared, you still got a stink on you. So I was pissed."

"So you went to talk to him."

Agent Kellog nodded reluctantly. "I knew I shouldn't have. I was told not to. But I was pissed. Horgan had to know this would involve me. What kind of an asshole would drag his partner into this kind of shit?"

"Some partner," Munoz said. "So what did he say?"

"Oh, he denied it, of course. So we got into it. Pretty heated. Luckily his cellphone rang or I don't know what I might have done."

"Who called?" Earl asked.

"I don't know, he just said he had to go. He said we would talk in the morning. Promised he could straighten it all out." Kellog scoffed. "So we left." He pursed his lips. "That was it."

"One last thing," Earl said. "What about the Castro brothers?"

"What about them?"

"You and Horgan were investigating them, I understand."

"Who wasn't? The word on the street was they were big pot distributors. Supposedly they had a connection with some cartel down south."

"Rough crowd," Munoz noted.

"Horgan said he had a new informant, one who was going to get us on the inside of the Castro organization. Give us 'intel' on the higher-ups, so we could nail them. But it never went anywhere. The Castros are so insulated, so many layers between them and the street, it's almost impossible to work your way up the chain unless you have somebody on the inside. All you get are bottom fish. Not worth it." Kellog looked from Earl to Munoz and back again. "That it?" When Earl nodded, he bolted for the door.

Earl slid around to the now vacant side of the booth and called Millie over for a refill on his coffee. Munoz said he was going to check on one of the cases that Snyder, the snitch, had pled guilty to. Something didn't smell right to him. Earl sat thinking, staring into his coffee cup. At least this answered where the money in the safe had come from. It was the cash that was supposed to have been paid to Horgan's "informant" as a fee for tipping them off. A percentage of all the drug money they seized each time. But if Kellog was telling the truth, and that was a big if, who was Horgan going to meet?

It felt strange to Manny Munoz to have to park in the visitor's lot of Parker Center after all those years as a fixture in the old building. The headquarters of the LAPD sat right behind City Hall, as if a reminder of the power the Department wielded in the city. It was known on the street as the Glass House because of its 1950's steel and glass construction. Manny thought the name an ironic choice, given the Department's policy against transparency in its decision making and its paranoia over news leaks.

He checked in with the officer at the desk and took the elevator up to the third floor, then followed the painted yellow line on the linoleum floor to a door marked Robbery Homicide and stopped. No matter how many times he had come here, it had never felt like he was coming to "work." What his father and grandfather had done was work. He thought of his childhood in Mexico. There had been a plywood factory near his village. Not very modern, it ran on hand labor, but it employed all the men of his village. The top job at the factory was the "loader," the man who picked up the sheets of plywood and loaded them onto the trucks. The loader had to be able to lift three sheets at a time, lean them against his shoulder and walk, bent sideways, to the truck. Trip after trip, day after day. The job went to the strongest man in the village. He was paid the most and was the village's most respected man. He was the one who spoke for the men to the Patron. His father had been the loader.

His grandfather had been the loader before him. Now his grandfather shuffled with a cane, bent low to one side, like a tree shaped by the wind. His back had eventually given out, like the loader before him; the same fate that awaited his father. To the Patron it was simple arithmetic - the cost of buying a fork lift was greater than just continuing to replace the loader when he broke down.

Manny's father knew his future. It had sat across the table from him each morning when Manny's grandfather had his breakfast. When the village midwife, the "comadrona," said his wife was pregnant with a boy, Manny's father sent her to "El Norte" with her brother, so his son would be born an American citizen. She returned with Manny. Now Manny sent money home each month because his father's future had caught up with him.

Munoz pushed open the door. The large room was a loud and busy place, crammed with a dozen old wooden desks all littered with Styrofoam cups and stacks of paper. Men and women shouted across the room in friendly banter while colleagues, each with a finger in one ear, tried to speak on the phone. Coats were perched on the backs of chairs while men in rolled-up shirt sleeves and shoulder harnessed semi-automatics sat writing reports. In Munoz's day he had carried a four-inch 38-caliber Smith and Wesson. Now the new recruits were being issued 40-caliber Glocks. An ugly weapon in his opinion, but you had to match fire power with the fire power of the street.

This room had once been Munoz's fiefdom. Head of Robbery Homicide, the Chief Honcho, El Jefe. He had been as comfortable in this room as in his own living room. The old feelings flooded back, the camaraderie, the sense of belonging, the bond of "us against them," the bone-deep thrill of a manhunt. And, of course, drinks afterwards at the Code Seven, too hyped-up from the chase to go home, surrounded by their own kind, the only ones who understood. His gaze drifted over the room and confirmed what he already knew. His time was past. There was not a single face he recognized.

Someone directed him to the corner desk, where a lean young man with a crew cut and a Glock in his holster sat reading a document. "Detective Duncan, I'm Manny Munoz."

Duncan looked up and gave him a cool greeting. "Yeah, Captain Hicks said I should talk to you."

"Harry and I go back a long way," Munoz said.

"He said you were okay, even though you've gone over to the other side, working for a cop killer. I guess you've got your reasons."

Munoz held his tongue and stopped himself from clenching his fists. "I understand you have the Emilio Chavez case."

"Had, is more like it," Duncan said.

"How so?" Munoz asked.

"The DA dismissed it. Some other asshole copped to it and my eyeball witness pissed backwards on me." Munoz made a face as if surprised. "I think Chavez's boyfriend got to her."

"Who's that?"

"Deon Hawkins. One very bad dude."

Munoz went on full alert. There was that name again. "What do you know about him?"

"Not much. He has a big rep on the street. Came out of Knickerson Gardens, but never got into the gang thing. We know he's good for a lot of bad shit. Killings, jacks, the whole nine yards. We've arrested him on several capers but never been able to make it stick."

Munoz nodded and thought to himself that Detective Duncan was wrong about one thing. He did know something about Hawkins. The fact that he came out of Knickerson Gardens told you a lot. Originally built for the families of World War II vets, Knickerson Gardens had once been a community. Single-story duplexes with trimmed front lawns and well-tended flower beds. But not any longer. It was now the most dangerous public housing project in the city. For any kid growing up there, a walk to school meant passing junkies nodding off in doorways, the night's harvest of dead bodies sprawled on the grass and the smoldering ruins of burned out cars. Casualties of the drug wars. If they got to school, they were greeted by rows of names painted on the side of the gym. Not to be mistaken for an academic honor roll, they were the names of classmates who had been murdered in the Gardens. Even an LAPD patrol car was required to radio the station before entering. "We're going in," was all that need be said. In twenty minutes, if they did not radio that they had made it out, a SWAT team was sent in. Any kid who grew up there without the protection of a gang was one tough kid and maybe a little crazy.

"So if Emilio had a boyfriend, how come he wasn't in the soft tank? I understand he was in general population. Isn't that where he met the guy that copped to his case?"

"Who's gonna mess with him in the county jail?" Duncan said. "Hawkins is a known quantity on the street. Now, if his sweetheart had hit the joint, well, that woulda' been a different story. Those lifers in State Prison don't give a shit. He would have been somebody's girlfriend."

"Sounds like this Deon has some serious street cred."

"Even the dope dealers use him on heavy deals. When the dope and the money come together in one place for the exchange, that's when shit can happen. Rip-offs, killings, whatever. So both sides hire Hawkins to police it. If either side does something stupid, he's the one they have to answer to. He's an equal opportunity nightmare. A stone cold killer."

Earl had been lying in bed in a half-asleep dream state when the phone rang. He had been reliving a day back when he was a teenager, working on his father's road crew, laying asphalt in the summer heat, covered in sweat and grime. If you looked in the distance, the heat waves off the road made the images dance. It was the day his father stopped slapping him. During that day's lunch break, he had been sitting in the shade of the dump truck with the Mexican crew talking about their favorite "luchadore" and which of the Mexican wrestlers had the best mask. His father was bent over the machinery of their old roller, trying to coax the great hulk into one more pass, and quickly approaching his customary boiling point. He angrily called over his shoulder for Bobby to bring him the sledgehammer. The Mexicans fell into an uncomfortable silence and lowered their gazes as if embarrassed to witness the expected scene. When Señor Earl was in one of his moods, there were few situations in which Bobby was not found to have committed some transgression.

Ramón, a heavyset man with a sweat-stained bandana knotted on his head, looked over at Bobby. "Go on," he said, grinning slyly. "Show him, mijo."

The ten-pound sledgehammer lay in the dust. Bobby knelt down and picked up the end of the handle, leaving the hammer head resting on the ground. He rose and straightened his arm, the resting hammer aligned perfectly. Slowly he raised his arm, keeping both his arm and the hammer's handle straight out from his body until they were parallel to the ground.

"Hey, Señor Earl," Ramón called. "Bobby's got the sledge." The Mexicans tried to muffle their laughter at the expression on his father's face. Bobby flipped the sledge in the air and caught it by the hammer end. He smiled to himself, never looking at his father. There was no need.

The phone rang again. Earl groped across the bed to reach it. Henceforth, as usual, had jumped onto the bed during the night and was now occupying most of it. The big dog never opened his eyes as Earl clambered over him. He lay on his side as if comatose, legs stiffly extended, refusing to move. His only response was a low grumble at being so rudely disturbed.

"Hello," Earl mumbled into the receiver as he looked at the clock. 8:00 a.m. He had overslept.

"Bobby, it's Martha. You should come to the office." Her voice sounded tense.

"What's wrong, Martha?"

"Somebody broke in last night. I called the police, but you need to be here."

"On my way." It was the first time he had ever heard Martha without her 'captain on the bridge' command voice.

He pulled on pants and a shirt and drove hurriedly to the office. When he walked in, a police officer was sitting next to Martha's desk filling out a form. "Oh, Bobby," she said with relief. "They climbed in Mr. McManis' window. I told that man to keep that window locked. I'm so mad I could spit."

"It's okay, Martha."

"He wants to know what's missing," she said, nodding at the officer. "I can't even tell." She sounded flustered, not in control. It was easy to forget her age.

"Don't worry. I'll check." He opened his office door and surveyed the room. It seemed remarkably untouched. He felt relieved to see his old slot machine in its place, then indignant that it had not been deemed worthy enough to steal. He ran his eyes over the notebooks lining the shelves. No gaps, nothing appeared missing. Sitting at his desk, he rummaged through the drawers and his stacks of papers. All seemed accounted for. He was leaning back in his chair when he saw it. Hal, his computer, was missing. After all their battles, he was surprised to feel a genuine sense of loss. As if a respected enemy had fallen.

"Martha, could you come here for a minute?" She appeared immediately. "It seems they took my computer. What else is missing?"

"Your computer?" She seemed calmer. "How's that for irony?"

"I know, I know. I should take a class. Now, what else is missing?

"Well, as far as we can tell, they took Mr. McManis' cigars and his bottle of Scotch, which is a good thing as far as I'm concerned. And a roll of stamps that was on my desk. That's about it. They must have been scared off."

"You're probably right," he said as she left the room. There was no harm in trying to reassure her, but he was certain they got exactly what they came for, it just did not happen to be what they wanted. Earl could think of several people who would be more than interested in knowing his trial strategy, previewing his defense, learning who he had interviewed, what witnesses he really planned to call, what areas he planned to probe in cross-examination. That information could answer a lot of questions for a lot of people. That was why taking his computer made sense. That is, it would if he worked like most lawyers. He glanced over at the notebooks with their pages of handwritten notes. Sometimes it paid to be old school.

CHAPTER 18

"When your case comes up, believe me, you will get my full attention. But now, it's somebody else's turn." Earl had been on the phone for fifteen minutes, patiently explaining to a frustrated client why his case had to wait behind Seabrooke's, when Martha buzzed. Earl put the client on hold.

"That nice young policeman has gone and there is someone on the line who will only identify himself as 'the most handsome lawyer in town.'"

Earl chuckled. Grabbing any excuse to stop the client's whining, Earl said he had to go and punched the other line. "Handsome George Kennedy, I presume."

"Who else could it be," Kennedy replied.

"What's going on, George?"

"Well, you asked me to check on why that Crystal Robinson case was dismissed."

"You able to find out anything?"

"Hey, does Pinocchio have a wooden asshole? Of course I did. Seems it was a cop who stepped up. He wanted Crystal out to work as his informant."

"Who was the cop?" Earl asked.

"Does the name Terrence Horgan mean anything?"

"You gotta be kidding."

"I thought you'd be interested."

"Thanks, George. Thanks a lot."

"For you, my man, of course, because I know you would do the same for me." Earl knew this meant he owed him and could expect Kennedy to collect.

Earl tipped back in his chair and tried to figure where this news might lead him. Horgan must have gotten Crystal out of jail so he could "front" her as his informant. The one who got a generous percentage of any drug cash they seized as a result of her alleged tips. He undoubtedly promised to split the proceeds, then convinced her to leave it all at the restaurant for safe keeping.

The problem was that Crystal was also Horgan's girlfriend. A police officer sleeping with his informant could put a whole lot of prosecutions in jeopardy. Not to mention putting a few careers on the line if anyone asked who was minding the store while Horgan was playing this little charade. No wonder Horgan wanted to keep his informant secret. His real source was probably Tommy Margolin, the dope lawyer, ratting on his own clients, but Horgan couldn't say that to the judge, it would raise too many legal problems and word of it would have quickly leaked out. So he used Crystal's name when necessary. Lying to a judge that your bedmate was the reliable, independent source in order to get a search warrant sounded a lot like perjury. And a bad search warrant meant you could not use the dope you found as evidence in court. No dope, no case. No wonder Agent Kellog was a bit upset. If this ever came out there were bound to be questions about where Horgan's partner fit in. It was a question Earl was asking himself.

A knock on the door jarred him out of his thoughts. He looked up to see Munoz filling the door frame. "You working on the over-and-under line for tonight's game?" Munoz asked.

"That would probably be a better use of my time." Earl gestured to the piles of papers on his desk. "There's just a month left before trial and I've got nothing."

"Well, I brought you something." Munoz held up two manila envelopes. "That niece of mine is something else. She went through every fucking visiting slip for the entire year. Here are the slips for every visitor that snitch has had since the day of the Horgan killing." Munoz tossed one of the envelopes onto the desk.

Earl tore it open, hoping for a clue as to where Jake 'The Snake' Snyder had learned the details about the killing that made his story about Seabrooke's confession so credible. Earl knew the prosecution would show that Snyder had no access to outside sources of information about the case. No television or newspapers were allowed in the jail and all phone calls from inside were monitored. That just left visitors as a possible source. Without any other origin for Snyder's details about the crime, the prosecution would argue the only way Snyder could have learned of them was from the killer – Sydney Seabrooke.

Earl pulled out a thin stack of white forms. "Probation officer, cop," he recited as he flipped through the stack. "Detective Tanner, Jessup, cop, cop." He dropped the papers on the desk. "This is it? No girlfriend, no old hype buddy, nobody who could have slipped him the stuff on the tube or in the newspapers?"

"Sorry, Bobby. But she was really thorough, believe me. Here." He tossed Earl the second envelope. "She even copied the slips for the visits he had before the killing. Said she knew they wouldn't be helpful, but she wanted to show you how careful she was."

Earl pushed the envelope aside. "Okay, okay, I know she did a good job." He ran a hand through his hair. "I'm just disappointed, that's all. Now I'm left arguing that the cops must have fed him the facts. You know how far that's gonna get me."

"Yeah, I know. Since they stopped letting newspapers into the jail and started listening in on the pay phones, it doesn't leave much."

"I shouldn't be surprised. That seems to be the way this case goes." Earl pushed away from the desk. "Come on, I'll buy you a beer. We can bring each other up to speed, if speed is the right word for our pace."

"That may take more than a single beer," Munoz said.

"I certainly hope so," Earl replied.

Two beers with Munoz led to dinner at El Tepeyac and more talk about the case. Afterwards, instead of heading home, Earl drove north on the 405 Freeway over the hills euphemistically called the Santa Monica Mountains. His thoughts were racing but kept stumbling over the same hurdle. How could he explain the details in the snitch's story? No visitors. No newspapers. Where did he get them? And Jessup had told him that the DA's office had not even given Snyder a deal. He needed something or Snyder was going to punch Seabrooke's ticket for Death Row. That was why Earl was driving to this storefront law office in the San Fernando Valley.

It was late, but the lights were still on. An earlier phone call had insured that. Stepping through the glass-paneled front door, Earl was surprised at the cramped quarters. No waiting room, no secretary, one room. Phil Cummings sat stiffly at his desk, staring warily at Bobby Earl. Behind the desk, mounted on the wall was a large silvery fish, its mouth gaping open. Under it was printed, "He couldn't keep his mouth shut either."

"You represent Jake Snyder, don't you, Phil?" Earl said as he sat down.

"Yeah, I got appointed to handle his case," Cummings said.

"So what's going on with the case?" Earl asked.

"We made a deal, and he's just waiting to be sentenced."

Earl was not surprised. This was the fate of most of the lawyer's clients. Cummings rarely went to trial, which was the primary reason the judges liked him. "And when will that be?" Earl asked.

"We don't have a date yet for sentencing."

"I guess that will depend on how he testifies against my man."

"Look, Bobby, I know you don't like snitches. But don't blame me. Snyder set this up himself, I just negotiated the deal. What else was I supposed to do? He's my client."

"So how exactly did he arrange this miraculous piece of good fortune?"

"Bobby," Cummings pleaded. "You know I can't tell you that. It's privileged. Attorney/client and all that."

"Not exactly, Phil. You may not be able to repeat what your client told you, but that does not cover your little chats with the cops and the DA."

"Oh, I don't know, Bobby." Cummings pushed back from the desk as if it were suddenly hot to the touch.

"Well, I do know. I had the attorney visiting slips pulled. There is one for you and the DA to visit Snyder a couple of weeks after the Horgan homicide, which, according to the reports, was when he first laid out Seabrooke's alleged cop-out. Funny thing though, Phil, there's not a single visiting slip for you between the time of the homicide and when you went hand in hand with Jessup."

"So what? I don't understand."

"I'll explain it to you. Jessup is not the kind of DA who is going to interview a snitch cold. He would want somebody to do some spade work first, sort of smooth out the rough spots, so when he interviews the snitch the report reads like a script."

"Yeah, so?"

"So that means a detective talked with Snyder first and he talked to him without his lawyer there."

A light finally went off behind Cummings' eyes. "Now wait a minute, Bobby."

"And I am sure this detective checked with you first and got your okay. And I bet if I ask him on the stand he'll say so and have the notes to prove it." Earl paused to let this sink in. "Not exactly by the book, was it? It might even make some judges think twice about putting defendants in your care."

"Come on, you know how it is. I've got a lot of cases. I can't run down to the jail every time some client calls."

"So tell me who did."

Cummings pushed papers around on his desk in frustration, picked up a pen before tossing it aside. He fixed Earl with a brief stare, then looked down at his desk. "Okay. I got a call."

"Who from?"

"The detective on Snyder's case, a Sergeant Brown. He tells me Snyder wants to talk to him, says Snyder has some information." He glanced up at Earl. "So I said go ahead, just don't talk to him about his case. I figured Snyder was toast anyway, so if he knew something they might cut him a deal."

"Then what happened?"

"Nothing. I didn't hear anything."

"Which means whatever Snyder was selling they weren't buying."

"Probably. So then I got a couple more calls. Another one from Brown, and then one from some detective named Tanner or Taylor or something. The detective on your case. After that last visit I got a call from Jessup and you know the rest."

"So what kind of deal did you make?"

"Okay, okay," he said in resignation. "There's nothing on paper, but Jessup told me I could trust him. Jessup wanted Snyder to be able to say on the stand that no promises were made for his testimony."

"So he looks like a good citizen just doing his part," Earl said.

"I did tell Jessup how dangerous it would be for Snyder to hit the joint with a snitch jacket, but Jessup said not to worry about it. He promised to speak up for Snyder at sentencing. We're in front of Judge Cameron, and you know he's sort of a rubber stamp for the DA, so I figured it was okay."

"So Snyder gets a pass?"

Cummings shrugged. "You figure it out."

The large black man always made Henry Lee uncomfortable. There was something about the way he just sat there, staring with those eyes, never saying a word, waiting for Lee to speak. Lee's father had warned him about dealing with the "heigui," the black devils. They were unreliable and untrustworthy, the kind of people who made mistakes that you had to pay for. But this Hawkins was different. A client had first brought him in as security on a big money transfer. Lee had tried him out on a problem he had with a client who had given him some counterfeit money for a wire transfer. The matter was settled the next day. After that he had always used Hawkins as security and for any other task that required his particular talents.

It was late, and the darkened restaurant was deserted. The only light in the office was from a small desk lamp. Lee stared out of the dim shadows at the black man across his neatly arranged desk. A small ivory Buddha sat meditating under a cone of light from the desk lamp. Lee picked up the carving and slowly rubbed its smooth contours between his palms. He was thinking how his father had always admonished him never to keep all his business in one place. That was why he paid the Wa Ching to protect his restaurant and hired Hawkins for the wire transfers. As his stockbroker preached, he was diversified. It had worked out well. Until now. Now there was a problem. He put down the carving and lit a cigarette.

"Mr. Hawkins. I hear people are talking about you."

"What's that supposed to mean?"

"People ask questions. Checking up on you. What is that all about?"

"How the fuck would I know? Who's telling you this?"

"Reliable people."

The big man smiled to himself. "You mean the Wa Ching?"

"Among others."

"You believe them Wa Ching?" he smirked. "They just want your business."

"That's a reasonable assumption. I would normally agree with you, Mr. Hawkins, except for one thing." Lee lifted a paper off his desk. "I have been subpoenaed to appear in court on the Officer Horgan killing."

"So what? You own the place where it went down. That's all."

"But that is not all, Mr. Hawkins. People are also asking about you, and that makes me nervous. It makes me think that someone believes they're connected." He waited for Hawkins to absorb this. "It is the nail that sticks up that gets hit, Mr. Hawkins. It appears you have brought us to the attention of the authorities."

"So who's askin' about me?"

"Some people working on the Seabrooke case. The same ones who subpoenaed me." He lifted the paper. "Seabrooke's people."

Hawkins looked silently at the paper.

"I think we have a problem," Lee said. "Don't you?"

They sat in silence as Lee waited to see how the black man would respond. Lee drew on his cigarette and slowly blew smoke into the shadows. There was another saying he knew, but decided it was best left unsaid. 'It is a wise dog that scratches his own fleas.'

CHAPTER 19

Earl was in the courthouse early because George Kennedy had called in his favor for the information on Crystal Robinson. Kennedy was putting on a judge trial in front of Julius "The Just" for a comedy discount and needed an appreciative audience to cue the old bastard when to laugh.

Earl was familiar with this stepchild of the judicial system. Decades on the bench had had its effect on Judge Julius Vinson. Too many defendants had stood before him, with too many canned pleas for mercy. Only the names seemed to change. Any milk of human kindness in his small glass had long since curdled. Now nothing could divert him from his self-appointed task of doling out the harshest, most punitive sentences in the courthouse. Most lawyers would rather face a tax audit than stand next to a client in his courtroom. But this long, numbing process had produced one interesting byproduct in the judge. Since he no longer recognized the humanity of those before him, their only interest was as a source of amusement. Thus, the comedy discount. If Julius found a defendant or his case comical, he would discount his normal sentence. The bigger the laugh, the greater the discount.

Earl stepped into the courtroom and took a seat in the front row. He nodded to Kennedy, who flashed him a smile. Kennedy rose from his seat inside the rail. "We're ready on the Marvin Green matter, your Honor." A thin, wiry man on the bench, with narrow bird-like shoulders and a receding chin, peered down at him with a mischievous grin. "Is this the case we discussed?"

"It is, your Honor."

"You know the rules, counsel."

"I do, your Honor."

"Very well, bring out the defendant. Miss Jacobs, take the waivers."

The metal door on the courtroom lock-up swung open. A young black man ducked his head under the door frame and entered the courtroom. To say he was tall would be an understatement. Marvin Green must have been close to 6' 10" and thin as a pipe cleaner. When he sat down at the counsel table he looked like an adult perched at a children's tea party.

The DA speed-read the required jury waivers, sounding as inaudible as a public address announcement at the airport. Each time his lawyer nodded at him, Marvin dutifully said "yes," clearly not understanding a word. A square-built Korean man took the witness stand, and the DA quickly established he had been robbed by the defendant. Kennedy stood up.

"Mr. Park, you own a small neighborhood market?"

"Yes. Many year."

"Did Mr. Green ever come in there?"

"Marvin, he come all time. Since he boy. He live on block."

"What happened this day, Mr. Park?"

"Well, he come my store. He have paper bag on head. Two holes for eye. He point gun and say he want my money."

"And what did you say?"

"I say, Marvin, what you do?"

"And what did Marvin say?"

"He say 'It's not me'."

The court staff started to giggle. Earl let out a healthy guffaw. Kennedy stood transfixed, eyes fixed on the judge, like a ballplayer watching a hit down the line to see if it landed fair or foul. Slowly, the judge's thin lips parted in an appreciative smile. Kennedy sat down.

Three floors above Judge Vinson's courtroom, the air in his office felt lifeless to Rocky Cavalli, like someone had already breathed all the oxygen out of it. He shed his coat and loosened his tie. He had just returned from a League of Women Voters luncheon, where he explained his Three Strikes policy and trolled for votes. He hated it.

There was a perfunctory knock on the door before Phil Ruzzi, his campaign manager, pushed it open. "I thought we should take the temperature on the Seabrooke case," Ruzzi said. "It goes to trial in a few weeks. Your girl said you had some time, so I scheduled a meeting." Cavalli rolled his eyes and flopped down into his chair. "It'll be quick," Ruzzi said. "I just don't want this to go south and come back to bite us in the ass."

"Stop calling her my girl. She's my Assistant. Aren't you supposed to know about those things?" Cavalli asked with irritation.

"Sorry, bad habit."

Cavalli sat brooding for a moment, then looked up. "Did you find out anything about what we discussed? You know, on the defense side of Seabrooke."

"I sent somebody to his office."

Cavalli held up his hands. "Jesus fucking Christ," he said in exasperation. "I told you I did not want to know anything about your end of it." He glared at Ruzzi. "Are you brain dead today?"

Ruzzi ignored the jibe. "I searched what they brought back and there is nothing there."

"Nothing? What do you mean, nothing?"

"I'm telling you there was nothing on his computer about Seabrooke."

Cavalli shook his head in disgust. "Okay. Enough. Get them in here."

Ruzzi stepped to the door, and Jim Jessup and Samantha walked in, followed by Bob Bishop, the Chief of Trials. They settled into chairs around the conference table and waited. Cavalli hunched forward, elbows on the desk, and stared silently across the room at them. He moved his gaze from one face to the next, finally coming to rest on Jessup. "So, are you going to win this case?"

Jessup seemed taken aback. "Yeah, sure, I think so."

"You think so?" Cavalli said. "You better. We got an opening in the Lancaster office. Make a nice long drive every morning. What do you know about the defense? What's he gonna do?"

Bishop stepped in to rescue Jessup. "We've just exchanged discovery. There's nobody really on his witness list. We don't think he's planning to put on an affirmative defense."

"You think that's good?" Cavalli asked sarcastically. "I don't. I don't think so at all. This guy Earl is no chump. I've heard his name around. He's not just going to mail it in. If he's not putting on a defense, then he must think there's a hole in our case. Is there?"

"There's no hole," Bishop said. "He's not putting on a defense, because there is no defense. The defendant is a career safe-cracker who panicked when Horgan walked in on him." He held up his hand and counted off his fingers. "We have the safe drilled by a professional. A tool at the scene we can trace back to the defendant. A cellphone he dropped there trying to call his home number. And a jailhouse 'cop-out.' A good one, with details. So we're in good shape."

"We better be." Cavalli's gaze fell on Samantha. "You're not saying anything. What do you think?"

Samantha glanced at Bishop, then met Cavalli's stare. "I think Mr. Bishop is right on the facts of the case. All we need to worry about is the sideshow stuff."

"What stuff?" Cavalli asked.

"The things that could start a jury thinking, making up their own story rather than following the evidence."

"Stop dancing around. What stuff?"

"Stuff like what is Horgan doing in a Chinese restaurant at midnight with a safe full of money. The owner of the restaurant is on the defense witness list and will testify it was Horgan's safe. Plus, Bobby – I mean Mr. Earl – has already tried to get Horgan's Federal cases, so he is probably going to plant the idea of other suspects. Slip in the idea that Horgan was working undercover, that drug dealers are dangerous people. Talk about drug rip-offs and what would happen if Horgan's cover got blown. That kind of thing. Raise the possibility of another shooter."

"So can we keep that shit out? Who's doing the motions?"

"I am," Samantha said.

Cavalli looked at Bishop. "If that shit comes in, the jury's going to start thinking dirty cop and killer drug dealers and start writing a movie script. Who else can we put on the motions?"

Bishop glanced at Samantha. "We don't need anybody else."

Cavalli stared at Bishop for a beat before turning back to Samantha. "Anything else?"

"There is one thing," Samantha said. "Earl has this lawyer on his list. Thomas Margolin. His only connection to the case is that he represents a guy who was originally charged with one of the robberies that our cop-out witness now says he's good for. We dismissed the case against Margolin's man."

"So where is he going with that?" Cavalli asked.

Samantha shrugged. "I don't really know. Maybe Earl put him on the list just to throw us off and waste our time."

"I used to do that." Cavalli smiled at the memory, then turned back to Bishop. "So what kind of a deal did we give our snitch?"

Bishop nodded at Jessup. "I gave his lawyer the nod. Nothing on paper. We'll see how the snitch testifies and then decide. But he can testify he wasn't bought."

Wouldn't that be nice? Cavalli thought. He had sold a piece of himself for every rung of the ladder he had climbed. "All right, keep me informed." He turned in his chair to stare out the window. It was a nice view from the top floor.

"I don't care. I would rather get the death penalty than spend the rest of my life in a concrete box."

Earl stared across the table at Seabrooke. The interview room was quiet. It was late. The deputy at the desk yawned and stretched, looking as though he wished Earl would finish and leave. Seabrooke's defiant stand was the sort of challenge Earl had heard before from defendants. Earl had just broached the subject of preparing for the possibility of a penalty trial. This always came as a cold dose of reality to someone on the other side of that table, one they did not want to face. A conviction on this murder charge automatically sentenced him to spend the rest of his life in prison, without the possibility of parole. But that didn't change the fact that a second trial would immediately start, before the same jury, to decide whether he got the death penalty. Only this time they would be hearing about Seabrooke the person, his life, the good, bad or ugly. And this was where the problem came in. For Earl to prepare for that, Seabrooke had to talk about himself, his upbringing, how he came to be sitting on the other side of this table.

The one thing that most men facing the death penalty had in common was a refusal to talk about their childhood. Most of them had committed a murder of such exceptional savagery that they were considered the "worst of the worst," unredeemable human waste. The truth was that people capable of such depravity didn't just wake up one morning and decide to go off the rails. Such a mind was usually shaped by a childhood filled with the same level of cruelty and sadism that characterized their own crime; a childhood of such callous brutality that it killed something deep inside them, some part of their humanity. So it was not surprising they did not want to parade such painful and humiliating memories before twelve strangers in the hope of winning the consolation prize of a life in prison without any hope of ever being released.

But Seabrooke's reluctance was different. He had not crawled out of such a pit. His reluctance was the result of a calculation. Why drop his shield of arrogance if the odds were slim and the benefits illusory?

"Sydney, listen to me," Earl said. "I'm not telling you I expect to lose the case. I'm saying there are certain practical advantages to talking about your past. First, there may be something in your background that might help us beat the case. Maybe not, but let me decide that. But more importantly, let's say the judge makes a terrible legal ruling, just plain wrong, or the prosecutors pull some dirty trick. We can appeal and ask for a new trial. If the jury gives you life without parole, we get two chances on appeal. First, we go the Court of Appeals and if we win there, that's it. We get a new trial. The DA can't appeal from that. If we don't win there, we can ask the State Supreme Court to take a look at it. If you get the death penalty, our appeal goes straight to the State Supreme Court. So, we double our chances on appeal by winning in the penalty trial."

Seabrooke stared hard into Earl's eyes. The wheels were turning.

Earl, of course, was lying. But he did not mind doing it if it was for a client's benefit. He knew the chance of any appellate court reversing the trial of a cop-killer was about the same as his were of being asked to manage the Dodgers. If the judge or prosecutor stepped all over the rules, the appellate courts had a painless way of dealing with it. They acknowledged that a mistake had been made, but concluded that it was only a "harmless error." A mistake that they were somehow able to determine in hindsight had not affected the outcome. Case closed.

But this realization did not change Earl's calculation. Giving up was not in his playbook. If they went into a penalty trial, and he was down to begging for Seabrooke's life, he at least wanted to have something to beg with.

"All right," Seabrooke said. "Why not? What do you want to know?"

"Well, you had mentioned you were estranged from your father. What was that about?"

Seabrooke's eyes bored into Earl's. Then he breathed deep and gathered himself as if he were about to plunge into icy water. "My mother and father divorced when I was quite young. I didn't see much of my father. Hardly at all, actually. I was sent to a boarding school where I did well academically. Not much of a challenge, really, so I was accepted at several universities.

"Why choose Princeton?" Earl asked to keep him talking.

"My father was a theoretical mathematician. Not an eminent one, but respected. Theoretical mathematics is a young man's game; they don't even award the Fields Medal to anyone over forty. My father was well past his prime and had settled in as head of the Math Department at Princeton. Tuition there was waived for children of the faculty, so my attending was a purely economic decision."

"Your father still must have been proud. Getting into Princeton is no mean feat."

"He was at first," Seabrooke said with an ironic smile. "I had a particular aptitude for mathematics, described by some as a gift, so I declared my major in his department as a freshman. The class work was easy enough, but there was one problem. I had no money. At least not the kind of money that would allow me to keep company with classmates of a certain station." He gave Earl a look to see if he understood. "You know, those with the breeding that comes from old money."

Earl nodded, suppressing any remark about advantages that the children of the rich "earned" by the mere fact of being born.

"So I developed an arrangement with some of the upper classmen in the department. They paid me to do their math assignments. We all profited and the math they were doing was more interesting than what we were assigned in my classes. Then finals came. One of my customers was in my father's class. On the final my father had added a bonus question which they could take home to try and solve. I still remember it - prove the special case of Fermat's last theorem. I worked on it for a while and then it just came to me. It was a beautiful proof, very elegant."

"So, I guess you did have a gift," Earl said.

Seabrooke shrugged. "A difficulty arose because this particular student had done quite poorly on the final, so when he handed in the proof, my father was naturally incredulous. When confronted about it, the senior quickly confessed, but claimed that I was the principal instigator." Seabrooke raised his eyebrows at Earl to see if he appreciated the predictability of such betrayals. "My father was furious. But it's interesting, it was not so much because I was dishonest, but rather that I cared more about the money than about the honor of having solved the problem. Plus, that I would now have a shadow over any career I might undertake in mathematics."

"So what happened?"

"I was called before the Honor Board. My father testified. He said that if they showed me any leniency it would reflect badly upon him. He was concerned that people would assume he had exercised undue influence." Seabrooke gave Earl a cheerless smile. "I think he was worried about his career. So he urged that I be expelled. Which I was."

They sat in silence for a moment. "Let me ask you something," Earl said. "Did it ever occur to you that your father might have been jealous of you? That you had a gift that he never had?"

Seabrooke looked bewildered, then an amused smile spread across his face. "I never thought of that," he said.

"You know, Sydney, my grandmother was an unsentimental woman and she had these sayings she would toss around. When I complained to her about the unfairness of some of my father's actions, she used to say, 'you can pick your friends and you can pick your nose, but you can't pick your parents." There was an uncomfortable silence, and then for the first time Earl heard Seabrooke laugh.

"But why give up mathematics?" Earl asked. "I'm sure you could have gotten into some other college and gone on to teach somewhere."

"And spend my four score and ten tutoring second-rate minds, only to end up a hollow husk like my father? No thank you."

"All right. Then why a safecracker?"

Seabrooke gave him an indulgent smile. "The money, dear boy. The money."

Back in his cell, Seabrooke lay with arms folded behind his head, staring at the stained mattress of the empty bunk above him. For him the most punishing part of his confinement was not the loss of freedom, but the solitude that forced him to dwell among his own thoughts. Exploring this interior frightened him. It would never lead to some dazzling enlightenment, like Darwin conceiving the theory of evolution, it would simply be a journey filled with pain, ending in disappointment.

This was why he resented Earl's prying questions. Now his mind wouldn't let them go. He knew it hadn't been the money that had drawn him to his strange profession. That was just a convenient answer. Even in this computer age, he realized there were still places for his gift in the financial world, spotting price differentials in the option markets or between convertible bonds and the company's stock price.

If one had choices it was never just the money that made you cross over to the other side. But he didn't feel obligated to explain himself so others could pass judgment on his choices. Why should he tell anyone about the pride he felt at being the best at what he did, one of the elite few who had mastered this demanding craft; the satisfaction he felt at solving the puzzle of an intricate locking mechanism; the exhilaration that came from defying all the rules; the thrill and excitement of the game. Just knowing he would never live a shriveled-up life like his father.

The smell of "pruno" suddenly cut through the customary stench of caged bodies, interrupting his thoughts. Someone's bootleg alcohol must be ready for "uncasking." That is, a plastic bag of fermenting fruit was being removed from its hiding place inside a toilet. Not exactly nectar of the gods. He sat up. Anything to stop this useless musing. Perhaps this batch would prove to be the elusive "Pruno Classico." As they say, "When in Rome."

CHAPTER 20

It was 6:30, and the morning sun was an orange glow above the rooftops. In Earl's neighbor's elm tree a family of little finches was chirping excitedly. It was going to be a hot day. Earl stood barefoot on his front porch, dressed in jeans and a tee-shirt. He bent over to pick up the morning paper and received a gentle prod in the rear end from Henceforth. A hint that it was breakfast time.

Earl sat down on the front steps and opened the paper. On page three was a reminder that the Seabrooke trial would start in one week. Two months had flown by, and he was still without a clear strategy. For the first time, the immediacy of the case hit him. It was no longer a future prospect with time for things to develop. A surge of anxiety flooded through him. If he lost this case, he would spend the rest of his career labeled as the guy who lost the Seabrooke case and a lifetime haunted by his failure to save an innocent man. Henceforth settled beside him and pawed his hand to indicate that a rub was in order. Earl obliged, telling himself that this fear was just his ordinary pretrial ritual of doubt and worry. Once the trial started he would settle down. He was almost convinced. Almost.

He lifted his face to the warmth of the rising sun. Across the street an old, puke yellow, dented Buick was parked at the curb. He had never seen it before. It was not exactly the ride of choice in this neighborhood. The sun's glare on the dusty window obscured the interior, but Earl thought he saw someone inside. Suddenly he felt uneasy, without knowing exactly why. It was not like him to be on edge. True, there were some people who were not very pleased with him right now. Munoz had finished serving the defense trial subpoenas, and Earl's voicemail was filled with heated messages. Margolin and Lee were both threatening; one fuming and direct, the other cold and subtle. Agent Kellog had called him a "major" asshole. Delight Thompson never called. After a moment he scoffed at himself for being paranoid. Probably just somebody in that beat-up car sleeping off a good drunk. He went back inside and shut the door.

After breakfast, he and Henceforth walked into the bedroom. Henceforth climbed wearily onto the bed for a nap. Apparently it had been an exhausting morning for him, what with eating breakfast and getting a rub. Earl knelt down and felt under the bed. He ran his hand over the familiar curve of his old wooden baseball bat. He stood up and chuckled at himself, both for being concerned and for the primitive nature of his home protection system. He got dressed and headed to the office.

When he walked in, Martha was focused on the morning's crossword puzzle. She spoke to him without looking up. "You got some more motions from the DA on Seabrooke. I guess they want to paper you to death. And there's a package for you."

Earl stepped into his office and sank into his chair. Martha, as always, had arranged his mail neatly on his desk. He flipped through the letters that contained the usual invitations to fundraisers for judges up for reelection, all sponsored by local law firms. Those got tossed into the wastebasket. Earl knew he should play the game because judges kept track of their contributors. But it always seemed so blatant, like it was expected. He resented it.

The legal briefs from the DA were more attempts at keeping out any evidence that might be helpful to the defense. Sam was writing their motions, and he had been impressed. They were well-researched and written in a clean, straightforward style. Earl could appreciate good lawyering, even if it made his job more difficult, and she was certainly doing that. He set them aside for later when he would read them upstairs in the library, where he could concentrate uninterrupted and check the appellate cases she was relying on.

Next he turned to the package, a large brown envelope with no return address. A thin stack of papers slid out. On top was a copy of a standard FBI 302 form, used to report investigation activities. At the bottom of the typed page was the name of the person reporting. Officer Terrence Horgan.

Earl quickly began reading. Horgan was reporting a conversation with an unidentified confidential informant, or CI, at an undisclosed location.

> The CI identified Juan and Rafael Castro as the sole owners and operators of El Gran Mercado, a large supermarket complex located in East Los Angeles. The CI reports that for the past several years the Castro brothers have been a major distributor and seller of marijuana in the greater Los Angeles area. They are the Los

Angeles connection for a Mexican drug cartel operating out of Michoacán. The transport vehicles of El Gran Mercado are used to smuggle large quantities of marijuana from Mexico across the border, concealed among the containers of vegetables and fruits. The marijuana is stored in El Gran Mercado warehouses. It is delivered to a network of smaller distributors and sellers by the El Mercado delivery trucks.

The CI reports that the Castro brothers have strong political ties to Los Angeles District Attorney Carmine Cavalli, who has actively discouraged local police agencies from investigating the Castro brothers' operation.

The CI is considered highly reliable and has suggested certain lines of investigation which the reporting officer intends to follow.

The next few pages were copies of a document issued by the LA County Election Commission on the last county-wide election in which all the candidates were required to identify the contributors to their campaigns. Earl turned to the District Attorney race and Cavalli's contributors. The names were listed in descending order by the amount of their donations. The top two names for Cavalli were Juan and Rafael Castro.

This, at least, explained why Judge McKeene had made a point of telling him that Horgan was investigating the Castro brothers. It also seemed clear that McKeene was the CI in Horgan's report. Earl smiled to himself. He had to admire McKeene's cunning. Everyone knew McKeene wanted to run against Cavalli for DA, which was why he had wanted to keep the Seabrooke case with all its media coverage. To get his name known. He had appointed Earl as someone he perceived as a bomb thrower, unafraid to take on the DA.

McKeene undoubtedly knew he could never publicly accuse Cavalli of protecting the Castros without hard evidence. It would have sounded like a groundless smear tactic and inevitably led to a backlash against him. But in a high publicity case, as the trial judge, if the defense lawyer brought up the Castro brothers as possible suspects, McKeene could have pushed his agenda while looking as if he were merely attempting to insure a fair trial. McKeene had been counting on Earl to ask for a court order that the DA reveal any reports concerning the Castros, arguing that Horgan might have put himself in danger trying to penetrate their organization. When the DA could not produce these nonexistent reports, McKeene would act shocked and then the contributors list would mysteriously surface. The unsubstantiated allegation of a cover-up would be widely reported and some of the mud would stick.

It was a clever plan, Earl thought, except McKeene had apparently forgotten there was a wild card in the deck. Cavalli could disqualify McKeene and force him off the case, which he promptly had done. That was how they ended up in front of Judge Jefferson. But Earl could not fault McKeene for a lack of persistence. Without even presiding over the case, McKeene was still trying to work his scheme. The only problem was that going after Cavalli did not help Earl's client. Throwing dirt at the DA did not make the Castro brothers suspects in Horgan's murder. Cavalli had several not so likable qualities, but protecting drug dealers was not one of them.

The Castros' campaign contributions probably had more to do with Cavalli's campaign promises than anything else. In the last election Cavalli had gone after the sitting DA for allowing the medical marijuana dispensaries to operate freely, anywhere in the city. Cavalli ran a TV ad expressing his alarm that "there are more marijuana dispensaries in Los Angeles than Starbucks," followed by images of dispensaries next to churches and schools. Cavalli promised to shut them down. No wonder the Castro brothers contributed to his campaign. If they were moving marijuana, it just made good business sense to eliminate the competition.

Smearing the DA might get Earl some attention but it would not create a defense for Seabrooke. To make a case against the Castro brothers as suspects in Horgan's killing, he needed some facts. And those he did not have. Besides, he hated being used. McKeene apparently assumed that Earl would so relish a moment in the spotlight he would jump at the chance. Judge McKeene was going to be sorely disappointed. He would have to find another messenger boy.

But that did not mean Earl was going to take his eye off the Castro brothers. He had tried to get the Feds to turn over Horgan's investigation reports, to see who Horgan was investigating. But the almighty Feds had refused to cooperate. He needed to find another way. One he had never tried before.

* * * *

Jimmy's Diner was just starting to fill up with the after-work crowd. Samantha Price slid onto the red vinyl bench opposite Earl. She had her hair pulled back and was wearing court attire, a dark blue suit and white blouse. But even this understated outfit couldn't conceal her shapely figure. Earl had to remind himself to stick to business.

Sam gave him a grin. "So what's the big secret, Agent X?"

"I wanted to expand your culinary palette. Only half the menu here is actually garnished with ptomaine."

Millie approached and offered Sam coffee. "You bet," she said and noticed Millie's rhinestone name tag. "I had a cousin named Margaret that we called Millie. Pretty name."

"Thanks. It was my Gran's name." As she turned away she gave Earl an approving look and a wink.

"So what's up? I have to say your phone call piqued my curiosity."

Earl removed some papers from his inside jacket pocket and slid them across the table. It was the Horgan report that had been dropped on Earl in which a "confidential informant" described the Castro Brother's drug operation and DA Cavalli's supposed cover-up in exchange for their political contributions.

Sam arched her eyebrows in mock surprise and began to read. After a moment she glanced up at Earl with a serious face, then continued reading. When she finished, she pushed the pages slowly back to him, then folded her arms and gave him a wary look. "So why are you showing me this? And where in the hell did you get it?"

"It was in a package delivered to my office. No return address. I have a good idea who sent it and it wasn't to help Seabrooke."

"So what do you plan to do with it?"

"That's the problem. What if Horgan followed up on this tip and started investigating the Castro Brothers. Maybe he got too close and made himself a problem. From their reputation on the street, they seem to have this annoying habit of eliminating their problems in the same simple way. Permanently. I don't think they would have hesitated to remove such a problem just because it happened to be a cop. Which would give me another suspect in Horgan's murder besides ol' Sydney. That would help my case. You know that."

"Sure. You need to put somebody else in the frame besides your man."

"I have a duty to my client to try and pursue that. What I don't have is a reason to throw mud at Cavalli if it doesn't help my client." He gave Sam a look to see if she understood. "Don't get me wrong. I don't like Cavalli. I think he is an unprincipled bully who lacks the judgment needed for that office."

"He speaks very highly of you, as well," Sam said.

"You know I tried to get Horgan's reports from the Feds, and you saw how that went," Earl said, and Sam nodded. "So that is my dilemma. I can't just ignore this." Earl tapped a finger on the pages lying on the table. "But I need more than just this one report. I need to find out if Horgan did follow up and started investigating the Castros. If he did there will be other reports."

"Okay," Sam said.

"Now, one way to get those reports would be for me to parade into court waving this report and demand the DA pressure the Feds to turn over Horgan's investigation file. But that would broadcast these allegations that Cavalli was covering-up for the Castros, which would raise a shit storm."

"So where do I fit in?"

"I thought about going to Bob Bishop as Chief of Trials," Earl said. "He's a decent enough guy. And ask him to make an informal request to the Feds. But he would have to tell Cavalli about the report and then I could never trust any answer I got."

"You can trust Bishop. He is an incredibly ethical man."

"I know that, but Cavalli is not. Cavalli would take the decision away from Bishop and handle it himself."

"So we're back to me," Sam said.

"I'm sorry, but I don't see any other way. I feel I can trust you. I don't know why, I just do."

"Well, thanks. That puts you in very exclusive company, because in the office I'm on the 'bleeding heart' watch list. Every deal I make is scrutinized to make sure I don't give away the store." She smiled glumly then gestured toward the report. "So what, exactly, am I supposed to do about that?"

"Look, I know this isn't in either of our playbooks. But let me suggest something. You could go to that US Attorney who appeared in court. Tell him you have a problem. You've got a defense lawyer who is trying to prop up all kinds of straw men as possible shooters. One of the candidates is the Castros and he seems to have an inside source feeding him information. You are swamped with work chasing down these red herrings, so it would help if you could cross somebody off the list. All you need to know is if Horgan was investigating the Castros. You don't need to know any details, you don't need to see anything, just whether there are any reports. If not, it would save you wasting a lot of time on smoke screens."

"And what if the US Attorney just lies to me and says there are no reports?"

"Then I'll know, because I've got this one." Earl tapped the pages.

"And if there are reports, what then?"

Earl pursed his lips. "I'll have to come up with a Plan B."

"Just remind me again, why I should do this? When I last checked, helping the defense was not part of my job description."

"I know. You're right. All I can say is that I want to try this case and, yeah, I want to win it. And I know you do too. But I want a trial, a real trial, not a tabloid circus. I don't want to be known as the guy whose trial strategy was to carry somebody else's slop bucket. And I don't think you want the whole trial to be about defending Cavalli's reputation, rather than prosecuting Seabrooke. Which is exactly what Cavalli would make Jessup do." Earl stared deep into Sam's eyes. "Look, maybe I'm way off base here. I wouldn't blame you for telling me to go pound sand."

Sam stared off across the room. After a minute she turned back to Earl. "I'll think about it."

"Fair enough," Earl said.

"Now tell me," she said, reaching for a menu. "What's the chef's specialty?"

Back at his office with Munoz, Earl sat struggling with his emotions. He prided himself on staying calm under pressure. But this was different. He was not just worried, he was scared, plain scared of failure. He was about to start the biggest trial of his life on Monday, and he still had no defense. Sure, he had ways to attack the prosecution case, but in a cop killing that was never going to be good enough. When it came to reasonable doubt, juries used a sliding scale. The more serious the crime, the less proof required. With a cop killing there was no such thing as a reasonable doubt, you had to convince them the defendant was innocent.

"Come on, Bobby," Munoz said. "We've been there before. You'll pull it out. Something will turn up." Munoz had brought the donuts, and they were on their second cup of coffee.

"Manny, I'm telling you this son of a bitch may be innocent. That's a whole different ball game. I can't go in there hoping for a break.

Hell, you know how that will end. I'll be up at San Quentin watching him get strapped onto the gurney."

"I know. It eats at you."

"I need something. Anything, so I can go on the offensive. I need to put somebody else in that chair besides Seabrooke."

"So let's go over it again," Munoz said. "Maybe we missed something."

"All right," Earl agreed without conviction. He flipped open a three-ring binder and began to turn the handwritten pages.

Munoz put down his coffee cup and opened his small notebook. "What about Tommy Margolin? Nothing like offering up a lawyer as the bad guy," he said with a grin.

"He's a possible. He certainly had a motive. Horgan was holding what amounted to a death sentence over his head. Margolin represents some major players. Like Jaime Cervantes, head of the Michoacán Cartel. If Horgan had ever let slip that Margolin was snitching on them, the best he could have hoped for was a quick bullet. Maybe he was tired of living with that hanging over his head?"

"And there was the rumor Horgan was facing a Federal investigation," Munoz added. "If Margolin heard about it, he was probably worried about what might come out."

"Plus he had the means to do it."

"Yeah, Mr. Hawkins," Munoz nodded. "So we got motive, means and opportunity."

"But like I told you, under California law I need something else before the judge will even let the jury hear any of this. I need some fact that actually ties Margolin to the crime, like a fingerprint, an eyeball ID, a statement, something. And that we do not have. In lawyer-speak, it's called the rule of third party culpability."

Munoz turned back to his notebook. "How about Lee, the restaurant owner with the wire transfer business?"

"I don't know," Earl said. "What's his motive? Horgan gave him a perfect cover for his business."

"Maybe Horgan got greedy and wanted a bigger piece than the five points Lee said he was getting. Remember, in his interview Lee said they were renegotiating. Maybe Lee decided to go for a deep discount. Like six feet deep." Munoz grinned.

"More likely, Lee might have seen Horgan as a danger. If Lee heard about the investigation, he might have been concerned that if Horgan took a fall he would offer up Lee for a better deal."

"And remember, I told you, Chuey said Lee used Hawkins as security," Munoz said, arching his eyebrows.

"Yeah, I remember, but I've got the same problem. I need something to tie him to the shooting."

"It was in his damned restaurant," Munoz said excitedly.

"I know. I know. It's something. That's why he was subpoenaed. I'm just not sure how much I can prove about his wire business." Earl continued to turn pages. "What about the daughter of that wheelchair hippie?"

"Delight Thompson," Munoz said. "Well, she had one hell of a motive, seeing as how Horgan put her old man in a wheelchair."

"Who says she didn't just follow Horgan that night and do him at the restaurant? Maybe she's the one who called him to set up a meeting," Earl suggested.

"It's possible. She really hated the son of a bitch and she's plenty tough enough to do it. And I gave up a long time ago trying to figure out who was lying."

"Maybe I can do something with her on the stand."

Munoz studied his little notebook. "Why are we stretching for this? If I had to put money on it, I'd go with the Castro brothers. If they're connected to one of those drug cartels like that report says and they thought Horgan was getting too close, do you think they would hesitate to off a cop? They're piling up body bags like cord wood down there, cops, politicians, judges, whoever. To them dropping a nosey LA cop would be like scratching their ass."

"I'm working on that angle. Waiting to hear."

"Okay, what about Agent Kellog? I never did like those Feds. What if he was in on the scam and was afraid Horgan would give him up? Eliminate Horgan, eliminate the threat, and what better place than right next to the money? Then it looks like it's all on Horgan."

"Your girlfriend Delight does put Kellog with Horgan that night. So he is definitely on the table, probably our best shot, in fact," Earl said.

"So there's one for sure. And what about Horgan's girlfriend, Crystal? You said she knew about the money. Horgan was probably claiming she was the informant, rather than having to name Margolin. Maybe they argued over money or she just got scared about the investigation. Besides, Delight said Horgan was going to dump her, so what did she have to lose?"

"Yeah, but when the jury sees her, that's going to be a hard sell. She just doesn't look like she's got the *huevos*."

"Okay," Munoz concurred. "But with that lineup, something is bound to break your way. It's got to."

"I hope so, but let's not overlook a few little details. Before I can put somebody else in Seabrooke's chair I have to explain a few things to the jury, like the drilled safe, the tool they can trace to our man, the cop-out and that cellphone."

"That cellphone hurts. It does look like he tried to call home. But you said Seabrooke denies that it's his. You think he's lying?"

"Maybe," Earl said. "But why just about that? He admitted he was there." Earl paused in thought. "It's almost like the cellphone was planted, but why? I don't see the cops doing it. Too risky, too many people. And Aradano, the bondsman, was the one who sent him to the restaurant to do the job. Why set Seabrooke up when it could blow back on you?"

Munoz daintily lifted a donut from the box and shoved half into his mouth. "You want to go over it again?" he mumbled.

The sun slanted through the wooden shutters of Earl's office window, tracing bars of light on his desk. It was late Friday afternoon, and he was still sifting through the Seabrooke binders in a vain attempt to see something new. There was a knock at the door and Martha stepped in, shutting the door behind her. "There's a man here to see you," she said. "And he doesn't have an appointment."

"The nerve," Earl said. "Doesn't he know how important I am? Why, I've actually been on television."

"Yes, I know, your lordship. But listen, I don't like the looks of this one."

"Martha, you don't like the looks of any of my clients. What's his name?"

"Deon Hawkins. *Mister* Deon Hawkins, as he put it."

Earl felt a jolt of apprehension. This was both unexpected and unwelcome, to say the least. He shut his binders. "Show him in, Martha, but leave the door open."

She made a disapproving face and left. In a moment the door opened, and Hawkins filled the doorway. He took his time slowly gazing around the room, then shut the door behind himself.

"Mr. Hawkins," Earl said, keeping his seat.

Hawkins nodded and sat down in one of the client chairs. He stared silently at Earl with a bemused expression, as if enjoying a private joke.

After a minute, Earl broke the silence. "You just looking for a place to rest or have you got something you want to say?"

Hawkins' smile broadened. "I like that about you. You got some brass." He paused. "For a little man."

"That's good to know. I'll put it on my résumé. So, is that it?"

The smile slowly melted off Hawkins' face. "I wish it was, Mr. Earl. I truly do. But you been tracking dog shit in my house." He fixed Earl with a hard stare. "Now what would you do if somebody spread dog shit all over your living room?"

"You know, I'm not up on my Zen master allusions, you better spell it out for me."

"Ya' see, I got this little business. I keep bad things from happenin' to certain peoples. I sorta protects them, like puttin' a roof over 'em. And you been messin' with that."

"How is that?"

"Well, you been threatenin' to make people go to court. People who don't want to go to court. Threatenin' to talk about stuff that ought not to be talked about. You understand now?"

"I'm getting the drift."

"See, it's simple. You just go on and try that little ol' case of yours and leave my people out of it. Then we all square."

"And why should I do that?"

"Cause' it's healthier that way. Less things to worry yourself about. See I could even protect *you* from bad things. You got that nice house over in Venice and that nice car. And lord forbid, you might break a leg or somethin' and couldn't go runnin' on the beach with that mangy ol' dog of yours."

"You threatening me, Mr. Hawkins?"

"Threatenin'? I didn't hear no threats. You hear a threat?"

"Well, I'll tell you. This little talk has been about as much of a good thing as I can stand. So you just go back and tell Margolin or Lee or whoever else sent you, that if it will help my client, their ass is going on the witness stand."

Hawkins gave Earl a bone-chilling stare. "I am truly sorry to hear that. Here I was thinkin' you was a smart man, Mr. Earl. I guess I was wrong. You enjoy the rest of your day. What's left of it." The big man rose, adjusted his long leather jacket and walked slowly out of the room. He left the door open.

A minute later, Martha came in. "I don't like that man, Bobby. He scares me."

"He scares me too, Martha. I hope that's all he does."

CHAPTER 21

At 5:30 a.m., it was still dark outside, but Earl figured he might as well get up. He had spent the night in a vain attempt to sleep, while his mind wrestled with thoughts and fears about the case. The trial was scheduled to start today.

After a shower and shave, he opened his closet. His suits were divided into two opposing fashion camps. On the left were his custom-tailored suits of English worsted wools, cashmere blends and Italian linen with knife-edge creases. Hanging on the rack above were dress shirts of 250-thread Egyptian and Sea Island cotton, in all the colors and hues of an artist's palette. These were the clothes he wore for brief court appearances, initial client interviews or to impress women. Having spent his college and law school years in a sweatshirt and jeans, he was pleasantly surprised to discover a genuine fondness for fine clothes.

On the right hung the suits he only wore during jury trials. Off-the-rack wool suits in slightly different shades of dark blue and grey. Serious, solid, no-nonsense suits. Above them hung identical white button-down collar shirts, like a sales rack at Sears. A pair of black wing-tip shoes, which he had polished and buffed to a spit shine last night, sat ready on the floor.

His lucky tee-shirt was on a hook, with its reprint of the stripe-suited convict pictured on the Monopoly "Get Out of Jail Free" game card. Under it was printed "A reasonable doubt for a reasonable price." He had first worn it when he found he was out of clean undershirts and had to start a trial. The success of that trial had made wearing it a pretrial ritual. It was just like in college – back then, before every baseball game, he had to listen to John Fogerty sing *Centerfield* with the fitting lyric "Put me in coach, I'm ready to play."

He dressed and stood adjusting his regimental striped tie in the closet mirror. No gold cufflinks or matching silk pocket handkerchief for his jury. That might have worked for somebody else, but not for Bobby Earl. He was more Jimmy Stewart than Johnny Cochrane.

Jurors, like everyone else, viewed people through a screen of prejudices and opinions that colored their judgments. Some might be influenced by the suit he wore or who he talked to in the hallway or where he went to lunch. The assumptions that could be drawn were as varied as the lives of the jurors. For that very reason Earl hoped to start each trial as a blank slate. He wanted the jurors' impression of him to be based solely on what happened within the four walls of the courtroom, so during trial he had lunch each day downstairs in the Attorney's Lounge and never socialized in the hallway.

He turned from the mirror. On the bed, Henceforth was snoring peacefully. He was not used to Earl's morning routine starting so early. Suddenly he boisterously broke wind and the loud report startled him awake. He immediately looked around for the culprit. Earl gently patted his head, reassuring him that the danger was past. Henceforth nuzzled Earl's pillow into the proper shape and settled back down. Earl sighed, wishing he could do the same, but the long-anticipated day had arrived. It was Monday. Show time.

Rather than take the freeway, he headed east on Venice Boulevard. Sitting in bumper to bumper freeway traffic would have given him too much time to think. The challenge offered by the competitive street commuters jockeying for any small advantage would keep his mind occupied. When he reached downtown, he turned on 3rd Street and pulled into Louis' garage. It was a bit of a walk to the courthouse, but far enough away so no juror was likely to see his car. Who knew what they might think of Old Blue?

Up ahead, television trucks sat smugly in the middle of the sidewalk as pedestrians squeezed by, brushing up against the courthouse wall. The drivers and cameramen huddled at the curb holding Starbucks coffee cups, talking expansively and looking about with expressions of entitlement. At least Earl knew what he could expect upstairs.

In the courtroom, Judge Jefferson sat silently on the bench, his grizzled grey head bent over a stack of papers. There was an air of anticipation in the crowded room. The wooden benches creaked as people shifted impatiently, talking in hushed tones to their neighbors, waiting for the start of proceedings. Earl sat beside Seabrooke at the counsel table, staring up at the judge. Seabrooke was wearing the conservative grey suit and dark tie that Earl had arranged to be brought to the court. Earl figured that Seabrooke at fifty was too old and the case too serious to try for the softer look of a shirt and sweater.

Earl could sense Seabrooke's agitation. Who could blame him? Earl was nervous himself. Further down the table, to his right, Samantha and Jim Jessup occupied the prosecutor's traditional seats next to the jury box. Sam looked eager to begin, like a thoroughbred in the starting gate. A small gold pin of a dog shone on her blue suit jacket. She turned and shot Earl a grin, not a challenging look, more like that of a kid who had studied hard for an exam and was looking forward to the chance to show it. Beside her, Jessup wore his usual glum face and trademark grey suit.

Earl turned to reassure Seabrooke, then surveyed the courtroom. On the chairs inside the rail, Rocky Cavalli and his deputies sat among several well-tailored lawyers, undoubtedly from big civil firms. Behind them, taped to the end of the first two rows of the public sector, a small hand-printed sign read "Press." The reporters sat there, whispering among themselves under the disapproving glare of the bailiff. Across the aisle, the first row was a solid wall of uniformed LAPD officers, jammed together in a show of solidarity for their fallen comrade and a none-too-subtle reminder to the jury to do the right thing. The rest of the courtroom was filled with a collection of the curious.

"Good morning," the judge said. "Let's start with this request from several media outlets to televise the proceedings. That request is joined in by the prosecution and opposed by the defense. Let me see if I understand your respective positions. Your view, Mr. Jessup, is that by televising the trial, the public will have the opportunity to see that their judicial business is conducted fairly and impartially. And Mr. Earl, you argue that the mere fact of knowing they are on television will affect how witnesses testify and cause the jurors to be swayed by concern over the public's opinion about their verdict."

The judge paused and kneaded his chin in thought. After a moment he stared resolutely at the audience. "I agree with the prosecution that the public has a right to know that justice is meted out in their courtrooms. That's my job and the public has a right to know if that is being done. That's where the press comes in. Their service is one of the cornerstones of our democratic system. That is why I have reserved the first two rows of this courtroom for the press so they can report directly about what transpires here."

"But television coverage poses a different question. Particularly when the entire trial will not be shown, just those portions considered to be good television. Luckily, wiser heads than mine have considered this. No Federal court in the country permits television coverage of its trials. Even the Justices of the Supreme Court of the United States, who only hear lawyers' arguments, do not allow cameras in their courtroom." The judge paused. "On balance, it is probably best that I follow the lead of these distinguished brethren, so I am denying the petition to permit television coverage."

Earl sat quietly, with no triumphant smile, no visible reaction at all. He knew it was important not to give this judge the impression that he felt it was his argument that had carried the day. Jefferson was a judge who made his own calls and it would have been a mistake to act as if he had influenced the decision. Jefferson would promptly have disabused Earl of that notion and probably at a cost. Earl was not going to make his client pay that price.

But Earl was impressed. Jefferson was a sly old fox. He managed to give the impression that news reporters were so welcome in his court that one expected them to be offered a seat next to him on the bench, and that his decision banning cameras seemed to have been forced on him by the United States Supreme Court. It was well-played.

"Let's deal with these other motions," the judge said. "Mr. Earl has a motion here to bar Los Angeles Police Officers from this courtroom. What do the People think about that?"

Earl rose to his feet, anxious to point out he only objected to their presence in uniform. The judge held up his hand. "I'll hear from the People, Mr. Earl," he said. Earl sat back down.

"Your Honor, the People strongly object," Samantha said in a clear voice. "This is a public courtroom and these officers should not be treated like second class citizens. They have all the same rights as any other citizen. It would be an affront to their service, in this of all cases, not to allow them to see justice done."

Earl got to his feet, but the judge once again motioned him to sit. "I agree with you, Ms. Price. I served in the Department for ten years and wore that uniform with pride. These officers are owed our gratitude and respect for their service. They are welcome in this court any day." He nodded to the row of black uniforms. "But in this particular case, it would probably be best if they left their uniforms at home. We wouldn't want the public to think they were still on duty and sitting here at the taxpayer's expense, rather than out patrolling our streets. That will be the order."

Earl smiled to himself at the way the judge had ruled in his favor but made it look like he was concerned about the officers. Samantha stood. "But, your Honor." The judge raised his eyebrows and fixed her with a firm stare. "That is the ruling, Ms. Price." He waited for Sam to sit back down. "Now, the People have a motion to exclude the results of the Coroner's toxicology tests."

"Your Honor," Earl said. "The blood tests detected that Horgan had ingested both marijuana and cocaine shortly before he was shot, and the jury should know that."

"I don't see why," the judge said. "Unless you can show me how his state of sobriety somehow contributed to the shooting." The judge held up another sheaf of papers. "That seems to be the same issue with the money found in the safe. I can see why it would be a reason to break into the safe, but how is it a reason for the shooting? Allowing the jurors to hear this will inevitably lead them to speculate about the source of the money without any evidence of where it came from. Until you can come up with some connection, I'm going to exclude it."

Earl had expected these rulings but they still hurt. The whole complexion of the case turned on what the jury thought of Horgan. Was he a Medal of Valor winner cut down in the line of duty or was he a dirty cop who got shot while he was loaded? If the jury was just going to see a white-washed version of Horgan, this case just got a lot harder.

"Now, Mr. Earl, what about this motion of yours to prevent the People from referring to Officer Horgan as a Medal of Valor winner. Such an honor seems an integral part of who he was."

"It well may be, but Officer Horgan's character is not an issue in this trial. Evidence of a victim's character is not admissible to prove his conduct on a particular occasion and nobody is questioning Officer Horgan's courage. Given the court's ruling that the money in the safe is to be excluded, it seems Officer Horgan's character will appear untainted before the jury and not in need of further burnishing."

"Well, Ms. Price, it sounds like he has me there. You can't have it both ways. If he can't bring up the money in the safe, it seems Officer Horgan's character is off the table."

"We'll submit the motion, your Honor," she said, quitting while she was ahead

The judge continued. "On the question of character evidence, the defense has a motion here to exclude mention of Mr. Seabrooke's criminal career, which for brevity we'll refer to as a professional safe-cracker. How is that relevant, Ms. Price?"

"It's relevant on the issue of identity. The People will introduce evidence that the manner with which this safe was attacked was extremely sophisticated, so much so that only someone of the defendant's level of expertise could have accomplished it."

"There is just one problem with that theory of admissibility," Earl said. "It is directly at odds with the state of the law. For such conduct to be admissible the act must be so identical as to almost amount to a fingerprint. The technique utilized must be one that only Mr. Seabrooke was capable of using."

"Do you have such evidence, Ms. Price?" Jefferson asked. "Is this a one-of-a-kind type of break-in?"

"I can't make that representation to the Court. But the available pool of candidates for this type of a job is very limited."

"Well, that's not good enough, so I will exclude mention of his career as a safe-cracker until you come up with something more definitive."

"Now, Ms. Price," the judge went on. "You have a motion here to prevent the defense from offering evidence that other people might have had a motive to kill Officer Horgan. What's that all about?"

"Yes, your Honor. Mr. Earl has several people on his witness list who are unconnected to the events of this homicide. It is our belief that he intends to try to present evidence that these other individuals may have had a motive to harm Officer Horgan. Under California law it is not enough to merely show that some other person might have had a reason to harm Officer Horgan. There must be facts that connect that person to the actual commission of the crime, a murder weapon, a fingerprint, an eyewitness. Something besides the rather unremarkable fact that somebody held a grudge against a particular police officer. So perhaps the defense could inform the Court if there is any such connecting evidence?"

"That is the law, Mr. Earl," the judge said. "Do you have such evidence?"

Earl stared back at the judge, his jaw set in frustration. "Not at the moment, your Honor. We're still investigating."

"All right," the judge said, gathering up his papers. "I will reserve ruling on this motion until we get to the defense." Jefferson stood up. "We'll take the lunch break. I'll see you all back here at 1:30."

Seabrooke sat silently beside him. Earl could sense his dejection. During a trial, Earl often forgot about his client. It was as if his client's presence was merely his ticket into the game, like the buy-in for a high stakes poker match. Once it started, the trial was all that mattered; the client became almost a stage prop. Winning the trial was what Earl cared about and what the client was desperate for, but this singular focus made for a lonely ride for the client. Earl glanced at Seabrooke, who was staring vacantly ahead with a look of resignation.

"Did you understand the judge's rulings?" Earl asked.

"Most assuredly," Seabrooke said. "We're going to lose."

"What are you talking about? This isn't even the first round. Just a bunch of jockeying by the lawyers."

Seabrooke did not respond.

"Listen to me," Earl said. "I'll tell you what will lose this case. If you keep looking like you've already been convicted."

Seabrooke turned to him with an ironic smile. "Looking for excuses already, are we?"

Earl locked eyes with him. "I did not take this case in order to lose it. I'll take care of my end, but you damn well better hold up yours. They are bringing in a group of prospective jurors this afternoon to see who can sit through a five-week trial. Every one of them is going to be looking at you, sizing you up, deciding if you look like the kind of person who could have done this. So snap out of it. Look alert, pay attention, like this is finally your chance to prove you did not do this." Seabrooke stared at him thoughtfully. "And they will be watching how we are together. Whether we get along, whether I seem concerned about you. So I may put my arm around you, touch you on the shoulder. Get used to it. And never argue with me in front of the jury. There may be times you disagree with what I'm doing, how I'm handling the case. That's fine. But wait until we're back in the lock-up. Then we'll talk about it." Earl paused, waiting for a response.

"All right," Seabrooke nodded. "I understand."

"And not just with me." Earl glanced over at the bailiff seated at his desk, bent over paperwork. "They'll want to know what the bailiff thinks of you. He represents the voice of law enforcement in here. If he acts relaxed around you, they'll figure he doesn't think you're dangerous. His name is Jeremiah Davis. Mr. Davis to you. So don't give him any trouble and treat him with respect." Seabrooke nodded.

Earl stood up. "I'll see you after lunch."

Earl sprawled on the sofa. It had been a long day. After the lunch recess they started the process of selecting a jury by sorting through the jury pool to determine whether serving for several weeks would constitute a hardship for anyone. A legal hardship, not just a pain in the ass. The judge had moved through the individual excuses with the speed of a cattle auctioneer. But the imagination and ingenuity exhibited by people trying to avoid their civic duty was truly impressive. The only excuse that seemed to sell with Jefferson was if their employer refused to pay them during jury service.

The one light moment for Earl in the tedious process had been the response from an employee of the local television station. The same station that carried the *The People's Voice*, whose news coverage was devoted to crime stories and their resulting court proceedings. The station would not pay their employees if they served on a jury. Not one day.

By the end of the process there were about one hundred stalwarts left. Earl shifted his gaze to a pair of cardboard boxes sitting by the front door. They were filled with the lengthy questionnaires that each prospective juror had been required to fill out at the end of the day. Each side had a copy of the answers and the judge had given the lawyers three days off to study them. But not tonight. He would start fresh in the morning.

Henceforth climbed onto the couch and flopped on his back, exposing his sizable belly in case anyone wanted to give it a rub. Earl obliged. It was amusing to see the big dog bare his teeth in what passed for a smile of contentment. With his other hand, Earl picked up the remote and clicked on the television. It was time for the *The People's Voice*. He might as well see what the jurors were watching. The judge had ordered the jurors to avoid any press or television coverage of the trial, but Earl suspected that, for more than a few, the temptation would prove too great.

"Good evening," Glass began as the camera moved in tighter. "The trial of Sydney Seabrooke, the man charged with the cold-blooded murder of Medal of Valor winner Officer Terrence Horgan, started today amid some controversy. We will be following it closely."

The picture shifted to footage of the DA's earlier press conference. Cavalli stood at a podium, flanked by the State and national flags, explaining why he had urged the judge to televise the trial. Apparently TV coverage was necessary because the Court's gag order prevented him from discussing the facts of the case, which left television as the only way for the public to learn if justice was being done in their courts. Earl noticed that each and every time Cavalli mentioned Horgan's name it was prefaced by "Medal of Valor winner," until one would think it was his first name.

Glass returned to the screen for the feature he called the Inside Story. "It seems the judge assigned to the Seabrooke case does not feel we should know what goes on in our criminal courts. This jurist will not even allow a single hidden camera inside the courtroom to televise the trial. This public scrutiny would not cost the taxpayers one penny. The only cost is that now you won't be able to see what's going on in your own courtroom." A picture of a smiling Judge Jefferson was flashed on the screen. "But you are not alone. Judge Jefferson doesn't even want the jury to see all the facts in the case. He decided today that the jury could not be told that Officer Horgan was using cocaine and marijuana the night he was killed or that there was two hundred and fifty thousand dollars in the safe where he was shot." Glass paused with a disgusted look. "Now can somebody explain to me why we can't trust the jurors with that information?"

Earl sat up straight. This was not one he had seen coming. He would have expected Glass to be reluctant to piss off such an important inside source as the DA's office. The Thumb had either just bought himself a ticket to reporter Siberia, or else he had something on Cavalli and it must be pretty juicy. Either way, now Earl was hoping that all the jurors were watching. Whoever said that cases should be tried in the courtroom and not on television?

A commercial came on and when Glass returned he was with his panel of experts. "Well, Don Leone," he said with familiar jocularity, in a nod to Arthur Leone's Italian roots. "As a former prosecutor, please tell us what we learned from today's proceedings?"

"Quite a bit actually," said the man Earl recognized the frequent pontificator on the show. "The prosecution has a very solid case that will put the defendant at the scene the night of the shooting. We know Seabrooke was a professional safe-cracker and it's clear he was there that night to break into the restaurant's safe. That means the only hope for the defense is to show somebody else was responsible for this killing."

"Can he possibly do that?" Glass asked.

"Apparently not. The prosecution very cleverly anticipated that would be his move. So they challenged the defense to disclose whether or not they had any evidence linking someone else to the killing. Seabrooke's lawyer admitted today there was none."

"Where does that leave Seabrooke?"

"With a jury you never want to say there isn't a chance. But in this one, the prosecution case looks as close to a sure thing as you can get."

Earl clicked off the television. He needed a beer and a good night's sleep.

CHAPTER 22

The morning sun coming through the kitchen window framed a square of light on the floor. Henceforth was loudly lapping water from his dish. Earl sat at the kitchen table in a tee shirt and sweat pants. He had gotten up at sunrise and gone for a run on the beach. Now it was time to get down to work. When the case resumed, they would start the process of "death qualifying" the jurors by talking to each one about what they were prepared to do if they found Seabrooke guilty, even though they hadn't heard any evidence in the case. To Earl this process always seemed backwards. It reminded him of the Red Queen in *Alice in Wonderland*. "First the execution, then the trial."

He reached into a cardboard box, and pulled out the first of the questionnaires. The US Supreme Court had decided that the only people who could sit on a jury in a capital case were people who were willing to impose the death penalty. If a person did not believe in it and was unwilling to sentence someone to death they were automatically disqualified. So Earl first turned to page 5. The heading read Death Penalty. There was no reason for Earl to read an entire questionnaire if someone did not pass the litmus test. Even those persons who qualified and supported the death penalty but expressed some slight reservation would never make it because the prosecution would use one of their challenges to excuse them. With 25 challenges, a smart prosecutor could pretty well clear the board of any but the strongest death penalty enthusiasts. Leaving the defense facing the ultimate stacked deck.

Earl pushed the first questionnaire to the corner of the table. This juror had given a thoughtful but equivocal answer about the death penalty. His questionnaire would be the start of the "why bother" pile. Earl continued to work his way through the questionnaires, making four separate piles as he read. In the first stack were the questionnaires of those jurors he felt he did not want on the jury; in the second were those he thought he probably would want, in the third pile were those about whom he was undecided, and in the fourth those who had shown any reluctance to impose the death penalty. On each questionnaire he placed a number corresponding to its particular stack, which he would later replace with a numerical favorability ranking once he had seen and talked to each of the prospective jurors.

These three categories dictated how he would approach questioning the jurors in each group. With those he did not want, he would just go through the motions, hoping the prosecution would mistakenly excuse them and save him one of his precious challenges. With those he did want on the jury he would just ask them routine questions and try not to expose their true leanings to the prosecution. With the undecided group, he would ask more probing questions in order to get a sense of who they were.

By mid-afternoon he had worked his way deep into the first box of questionnaires. He rose from his chair, stretched and took a plate with crumbs from his peanut and jelly sandwich to the sink. He pulled a questionnaire he had tabbed and picked up the wall phone. On the second ring a voice answered.

"Samantha Price, Deputy District Attorney."

"This is Bobby Earl, beleaguered defense counsel."

"You calling to throw in the towel?"

"That comes later. But I am calling to help you out."

"Let me guess. You want to donate one of your snappy suits to Jessup."

"It would never fit him in the shoulders."

"Whoa, big fella. That's my partner in crime you're talking about. Or, as one of your clients would more elegantly put it, that's my crimee.'"

"Actually, I called to give you a heads-up on a good juror for you," Earl said.

"I can't wait to hear this one."

"Take a look at juror number 30. He says he's a strong supporter of the death penalty, but he would refuse to give it if the defendant was acting in self-defense."

Sam gave a full throated laugh. "You're right. That's my kind of guy."

"Just trying to help."

"Well one good turn deserves another. I checked with that US Attorney. He says Horgan only filed one report about the Castro brothers. He wouldn't give me a copy, but he described it. It sounded like the one you showed me."

"You believe him, Sam?"

"I sorta do. Why would he tell me about one if he was going to stonewall it?"

To Earl this sounded like both good and bad news. It was bad because if there was only the one report, there wasn't enough evidence for him to make a convincing argument that the Castros were the ones responsible for Horgan's killing. It was good news because he wouldn't have to be a pawn in Judge McKeene's political game by smearing Cavalli with allegations of a cover-up to enhance McKeene's chances of being elected District Attorney. Such a maneuver wouldn't have helped Earl's client and would have made him feel more like a sleaze merchant than a trial lawyer.

"Thanks, Sam. I appreciate you doing this."

"Yeah, well, that's the only break I'm going to cut you, big fella."

"I know that. Wouldn't want it any other way. But thanks." He paused; he wanted to continue to talk to her but didn't know what to say. "Well, pleasant reading."

"You too, Bobby."

Martha Sullivan opened the back door and called, "Thomas. Breakfast Mister Thomas." She peered into the morning darkness. It was too early for the sun, but not for Mister Thomas. The old alley cat was usually waiting in the bushes by this time. She still remembered the first time they met. She had gotten up at 5:00 a.m., as usual, so she could read the paper, get in her swim, and still arrive at the office before Bobby and Mr. McManis. She had heard the trash cans rattling in the back yard and, when she went to investigate, Thomas poked his head out of her garbage can. He looked like a cartoon. One eye was missing, an ear had been chewed off, and his matted coat was the color of dirty dish water. To Martha, his expression seemed to say "You should see the other guy." She had started to laugh.

Martha had never considered herself an easy touch, so when she started leaving food out for him on the back steps she told herself it was merely a practical solution to keep him out of the trash. It took a year of coaxing to get him to step inside the kitchen, which she justified to herself as an experiment in behavior modification. Grooming him was just a way of protecting her furniture from shedding cat hairs. That was five years ago.

But this morning she was irritated with him. She did not like any deviation in her closely scripted routine. Thomas had seemed his old self last night. As usual, they had dinner together, then Thomas sat in her lap as she watched the evening news. Afterwards, Thomas had gone out for his nightly prowl, and she had gotten into bed with her book.

She called his name once more, then slowly shook her head. This tardiness would not do. She would have to have a word with Mister Thomas. She turned and walked to the front of the house to get her morning paper with her beloved crossword puzzle.

She opened the front door and scanned the front porch, hoping the paper had not been tossed into her flower beds. As she stepped forward in the dark, her head bumped into something. Startled, she looked up. She was staring into the face of Mister Thomas. He was swinging gently from the porch light, a thin cord tied around his neck. His body was charred. He had been set on fire. He looked so thin and scrawny without his hair. A note was nailed into his blackened chest. A red stream trailed down the page from the blood-smeared letters. "I WAS NOSEY." She opened her mouth to scream, but no sound came.

Earl was stepping out of his office just as Martha pushed through the back door. It was Thursday; he had spent two days at home with the questionnaires and he needed a change of scenery. "Martha Sullivan," Earl said with a smile. "This is a first. Me getting to the office before you."

Martha walked purposefully to the closet, avoiding eye contact, hung up her coat and went silently to her desk. She slid over a stack of papers from one side of the desk and stared dully at it. Her eyes were red from crying.

Earl stepped toward her. "Martha, what's wrong?"

She clamped her eyes shut as she fought for control. After a moment she took a deep breath, opened her eyes wide, and exhaled. "There was an incident," she said. "But it's over and I'd rather not talk about it."

Earl sat down in the chair next to the desk. "Martha, please tell me what happened."

She turned and looked at him, then back down at the desk. "It's nothing, really. I had this little friend." She darted a look at Earl. "I mean, this cat. He was killed this morning."

"I'm so sorry Martha. How did it happen?"

She looked at Earl, and her face finally yielded to the pain. She buried her face in her hands. In a choked voice she gasped out, "They set him on fire."

"They what? My God." He put a hand on her shoulder. After a minute she looked up and collected herself. "He was a tough little guy, who'd been through a lot. He deserved better."

Earl glanced away, not knowing what to say.

"The ignorant bastards even put a note on little Thomas, but were too damn stupid to even get it right."

"What do you mean, Martha?"

"They wanted to say 'curiosity killed the cat' but it came out 'I was nosey.' The cowardly bastards."

Earl was stunned. This was not a message meant for Martha. Someone wanted Earl to back off. And if he had to guess, that someone was Deon Hawkins. He must have figured that threatening Earl directly was probably not the most effective move. And he was right. If running a risk was necessary for him to do his job, that was a call he was willing to make. That is, when it was only his ass on the line. But if his actions were putting someone else in danger, particularly somebody like Martha, that was a whole different matter. Now he had a problem. How did he choose between Martha's safety and his duty to his client? His efforts were obviously making someone nervous, which could only mean that he was doing something right. If he only knew what.

"Martha," he said. "You know what you need? A little break in the routine."

"Don't be ridiculous," she said, recovering her old command voice.

"You haven't been to see your sister and her kids since last Christmas."

"And I'll see them this coming Christmas."

"Do this for me, Martha. You know I never know what to get you for Christmas. Please. I'll book the flight."

She stared back at him for a moment. "This is about your case, isn't it?"

"I think it might be."

"I don't like being run off like this."

"I know."

"At the same time, I don't want to be a distraction. I know how you get when you're in trial." She heaved a sigh. "Who'll take care of the office?"

"We'll bring in a temp to answer the phones." She gave him a startled look.

"I promise she won't touch your files, and we'll just send the typing out while you're gone."

"All right, if you think it best."

"I'll call Manny. He can drive you home so you can pack."

With Martha's safety accounted for, Earl's thoughts turned to himself. How long would someone like Hawkins be content with issuing mere threats? Earl suddenly felt a chill.

"Bobby, Martha made me promise. So let's not argue about it." After getting Martha packed and to the airport, Munoz had returned to the office. Resting on the desk between them was a snub-nosed revolver, shoved snugly into a worn leather holster. "I'm supposed to call her tonight," Munoz continued. "If you don't take it, she said she'll be on the next plane back."

Earl gave Munoz an annoyed look. He hated guns. Most of all he hated handguns. He had a rifle as a boy and knew how to use it. But a handgun was good for only one thing, and it wasn't deer hunting.

"Look, Bobby. I know you think you can handle yourself in rough situations. And I'm sure you can. But Martha told me that Deon Hawkins paid you a visit. That makes it a whole different ball game. He's not about a few cracked ribs or chipped teeth. He's only called in for a final solution." He fixed Earl with a stare. "Listen to me. This is one scary motherfucker." He slid the gun toward Earl.

Earl reluctantly nodded. "All right," he said quietly.

On Friday, everyone returned to the packed courtroom to commence qualifying jurors to sit on a capital case. The judge questioned each juror because it was his decision whether or not they passed. After five days, the judge had winnowed the jury pool down to 78 death qualified jurors, who had either not figured out how to get excused or did not want to be. The final step was the "voir dire" of the jurors. Twelve jurors would be put in the box and both sides had a chance to ask each a few questions. Then each side had the right to excuse some of the jurors; no reason need be stated for such challenges, no questions asked. First one side, then the other, back and forth like a tennis match, until both sides said they accepted the group of jurors who were currently sitting or until they exhausted their 25 challenges. If one side accepted the jury when their turn came but the other side then excused a juror, the process continued anew.

This was where the game began in earnest. A chess match limited to 25 moves. Each side determined to sweep the board of the other's favorite jurors and finish with a "fair" jury that would vote their way. The clerk had randomly arranged a list of the jurors in numerical order from 1 to 78. This ranking was the order in which each juror would be called to the box, so when a juror was excused, each side would know who the replacement would be.

Sitting at the counsel table, waiting for court to start, Earl arranged his questionnaires in the same order as the juror list. The jurors sat in the public section, talking among themselves, old friends by now, seasoned veterans who had survived the first cut. Earl stretched his neck muscles. He was tired. It had been hard work during the qualification phase, thinking of the right questions, carefully choosing his words, showing respect for opposing opinions, always aware the jurors in the audience were listening. But this was no time to let up, selecting the right jury was critical, absolutely critical.

Earl looked around the room. Jessup and Sam were huddled at their table with a middle-aged woman, who wore large dangling earrings and a bulky knit sweater. Probably their professional jury consultant. She had undoubtedly read the jurors' questionnaires and was here to study them when they hit the box.

Earl did not use traditional jury consultants. He preferred to trust his own judgement. In his experience, there was no ideal defense juror. Just his type of juror. All defense lawyers had a particular type of juror with whom they were comfortable. A juror who might be receptive to the courtroom style of another attorney, would not necessarily be amenable to Earl's approach. For Earl, picking jurors was based on a gut feeling, more than anything else. He wanted jurors he felt comfortable with. Jurors he could talk to and who would listen. Still, Earl did have his own consultant, of sorts, one who could give him insights that he could not get from the questionnaires or voir dire. Rudy Pasquelly, a used car salesman and former client. Rudy made a living sizing people up, figuring out what line to pitch them. Earl used Rudy as another set of eyes to study the jurors when he could not. Rudy sat in the back of the room, blending in. Watching and listening. During a recess, he would sit in the hallway to see who talked to whom, what they talked about, who was a loner, what book someone was reading, who was unafraid to go out shopping on Broadway, all the little details that said a lot.

Judge Jefferson took the bench and the first twelve names on the list were called to the jury box. Most people would say, if asked, that a jury consisted of twelve people. Unfortunately, that was not Earl's experience. In reality, three, or at most four, jurors decided most cases. They were the ones with strong opinions, who would lead the deliberations and argue for their point of view. The rest would just go along out of timidity or lack of interest. For Earl, jury selection really boiled down to a process of "de-selection." It was not so much about picking the jurors he wanted as avoiding the jurors he did not want. He never hoped for a perfect jury, just one without a prosecution bully in the jury room.

After both sides had questioned the first twelve, they started to make their challenges to individual jurors. First Earl, then Jessup. Back and forth like chess players exchanging pieces. As each juror was excused the next on the list was called from the audience to fill the vacant seat. By the afternoon Earl had used seventeen of his challenges, and Jessup had used only fourteen. This disparity arose because on three occasions Jessup had accepted the jury when it was his turn to challenge, but Earl had exercised a challenge and excused a juror. If Earl had also accepted the jury, the people sitting in the box would have been sworn in as the jury.

Earl looked over at the faces in the jury box. There were still two jurors sitting there that he just could not live with. He scanned the roster of upcoming jurors. Beside each name he had written a favorability rating. The next five jurors on the list to be called he had ranked as strong prosecution jurors. He was entering a desert. He had seen this wasteland when he had conducted a mock selection the night before, guessing who Jessup might kick off and where they might end up. He never thought they would get here.

If Earl had to use a challenge on the two unacceptable jurors in the box and on each of the five upcoming prosecution jurors, he would be left with only one remaining challenge of his original 25. A silver bullet, which he might as well use on himself. In a war of attrition, with each side picking off the jurors they felt would favor their opponent, to run out of ammunition would be fatal. If they continued to alternate challenges Earl would exhaust his 25 and Jessup would still have at least three and maybe more if he accepted the jury when Earl was forced to use a challenge to excuse a pro-prosecution juror. Jessup could then use his remaining challenges to pick the jury he wanted while Earl sat by and watched.

There was only one way to erase this disparity. Earl had to accept the jury when his turn came even though there were pro-prosecution jurors in the box and hope Jessup did not accept the jury at that point. If Earl could accept the jury on enough occasions when Jessup continued to excuse jurors he could draw even with Jessup on the number of challenges they each had. But it was a gamble. If Jessup accepted on any of those occasions when he also accepted, Earl would end up staring into those unwanted faces the entire trial, the ones who had decided Seabrooke's fate the minute they heard the charges.

By 4:00 p.m., Earl had passed twice and Jessup had continued to challenge. Earl looked at the panel and tried to convince himself that juror Number 3, the insurance adjustor, was really not as bad as he thought. But he couldn't do it. Number 3 was a guilty vote waiting to happen. He rose to accept the jury, trying hard to sound relaxed. When he sat back down he glanced at Jessup out of the corner of his eye. Jessup was studying him like a card player trying to read his opponent's face. Earl's chest felt tight, his breathing was shallow. Jessup stood up. Earl closed his eyes. "The People wish to thank and excuse juror Number 5." Earl exhaled the breath he had been holding. A sense of relief washed over him like a warm shower. He had made it across.

In the next thirty minutes, they had a jury. It was one he could live with. They chose three alternate jurors in case something happened to any of the regulars. The judge recessed until the next Monday, telling the jury they would begin with opening statements. Earl felt drained, his sweat-dampened shirt clung to his back. As he watched the jurors leave the courtroom he had a sinking feeling, like buyer's remorse, that he had guessed wrong. He stopped himself. This was the familiar second-guessing he always went through. He was just tired. Earl gave Seabrooke an encouraging word, gathered his papers and left the courtroom.

CHAPTER 23

"You have been summoned here to judge the act of a coward," Jessup said as he began his opening statement. He gripped the podium in a stance of barely controlled anger. His gaze passed from one juror to the next as he stared deep into their eyes. "On the night of June 3rd, Officer Terrence Michael Horgan was protecting this community as a police officer in the Los Angeles Police Department. By 2:00 a.m. the next morning he was dead. Murdered in cold blood. Gunned down as he stood defenseless. And the man who committed this cowardly act is sitting in this courtroom." He pointed an accusing finger at Seabrooke. "Right over there. And the reason Officer Horgan's young life had to be extinguished? The reason he had to die? Because he dared to interrupt Mr. Seabrooke when he was in the midst of stealing someone else's property."

The jurors shifted their attention to Seabrooke, who stared straight ahead as Earl had instructed him. Earl wore an expression of polite indifference, as if he had heard all this before. "You have been selected to determine his guilt. Fortunately, your task should prove to be simple, because the People's case against Mr. Seabrooke is quite strong. In fact, it's overwhelming."

Earl knew he could object. Opening statements were supposed to be an opportunity for each side to summarize their evidence, to merely give a preview of what was coming. It was not a chance to argue the strength of the case or issue a call for vengeance. Such tactics were not allowed. But Earl did not want to start off the case by objecting. It would give the impression he was afraid of the facts.

Jessup began to list the prosecution witnesses and what they would testify to: a safe had been professionally drilled; a tool left at the scene could be traced back to Seabrooke; a cellphone at the scene had been used in an unsuccessful attempt to call Seabrooke's house; and finally his confession to a fellow inmate that contained facts only the murderer could have known. Jessup concluded by asking the jury for "the only verdict possible in the face of this evidence. Guilty. Guilty of murder in the first degree." He sat back down, joining Sam and Detective Tanner at the prosecutor's table. Tanner gave him an approving nod.

Earl had to admit, Jessup had done a good job. He had marshaled the facts into a compelling case for conviction, and he certainly had the facts to do it. The courtroom was unnaturally still, as if suddenly forced into a somber mood. Jessup had hurled each fact at Earl like a challenge, daring him to explain it, and now every eye in the room was on him. Judge Jefferson tilted his head toward Earl and arched an eyebrow into a question. His lips were slightly raised in a bemused smile, as if questioning the wisdom of Earl saying anything after the case Jessup had just made. "Mr. Earl?" he asked.

Earl had worked on an opening over the weekend. But it had been a struggle. He had no story to tell, no answers to give. He couldn't promise what he couldn't deliver or Jessup would beat him senseless with it in final argument. Earl rose slowly and faced the jurors.

"The prosecutor just gave you a list of the witnesses he plans to call for the prosecution." Earl spoke calmly, evenly, as if Jessup had merely read a list of names, not a crushing litany of evidence. "He did a good job, very thorough. Except he was wrong about one thing. He called them prosecution witnesses. That's not exactly right. The prosecution gets to call these witnesses because the prosecution puts on its case first. Remember, we discussed this in voir dire, how the prosecution has to prove its case and prove it beyond a reasonable doubt. We don't have to prove Mr. Seabrooke innocent, they have to try to prove him guilty. That is our system. That is the law."

Earl's gaze drifted among the jurors. Jessup's opening statement had hurt, but they were still making eye contact. They were still willing to listen. In fact, juror Number 5 was nodding at him as if to say she remembered the lesson.

"These witnesses are not prosecution witnesses; they are just witnesses. Nobody owns them. They don't belong to one side or the other. If the prosecution didn't call some of them, we would. There is an old saying that there are two sides to every story. We intend to tell our side of the story, and we'll do it through the witnesses that the prosecution is going to call. So when you hear their testimony, don't think it is just there to support the prosecutor's case. You must decide what it is that the testimony proves and not just assume it helps the side who called the witness."

Earl returned to his seat knowing he had not delivered much of an opening. It was difficult to give a preview of your defense when you didn't have one. But at least he had gotten up and spoken, given the impression he had something to offer. He glanced over at the jury. There were no apparent looks of disbelief at his charade of an opening statement. Juror Number 5 even turned to her seat-mate with a bright look of anticipation as if she expected a real contest. Detective Tanner leaned forward into Earl's view and smirked to let Earl know he wasn't fooled.

As the investigating officer, Tanner was the only witness who was allowed to sit in court and listen to the testimony of all the other witnesses.

When they had all returned from the noon recess, the judge said, "Call your first."

Predictably, Jessup elected to start with the crime scene. Nothing set the right tone like an afternoon spent looking at photos of a lifeless body and talking about death. "The People call Detective Jack Tanner," Jessup announced. Tanner stepped forward carrying a large poster board which he mounted against the wall next to the witness box. On the board was a scale diagram of the restaurant. In the room marked "Office," the desk and safe were indicated and small boxes were labeled "Tool" and "Cell phone." The outline of a sprawled body was drawn next to the desk, like the chalk marks at the crime scene.

With a few preliminary questions, Jessup had Tanner describe the location where the shooting took place and the evidence that was recovered. "When you recovered the cellphone, were you able to determine the last number that was called?"

"Yes, we were. It was 626-381-8201."

"Were you able to determine whose phone number that was?"

"It's not in service, but it is only one digit off the number at the defendant's house."

"So if someone panicked they might have misdialed?"

"Objection," Earl said. "I'm sure Sergeant Tanner is qualified to offer many opinions on many subjects, but that isn't one of them."

"Sustained," Jefferson said.

Jessup then moved on to the real purpose of Tanner's testimony, the introduction of one glossy print after another of Horgan's dead body. Tanner described each photo, which was then passed among the jurors. Colored shots of Horgan with his lifeless eyes staring straight into the camera; the burned cloth of his shirt circling the gunshot holes; a bright red lake of blood pooling around his head like a halo; his crumpled body with its limbs thrown unnaturally askew.

Earl had urged the judge to exclude the photographs as too inflammatory, particularly since there was no dispute about the cause of death. But the judge had fallen back on the old saw that "the prosecution had a right to prove its case."

When it came time to cross-examine, Earl merely wanted to put an end to this grisly focus. "No questions," he said absently, not looking up from his notebook, as if nothing of importance had been discussed. Tanner was excused, but remained seated in the witness box. He fixed Earl with a disgusted look, as if disappointed in Earl for failing to duel with him on the stand.

The judge recessed for the day, and the room came noisily to life as everyone stood and headed toward the door, talking and laughing from pent-up energy.

Rocky Cavalli sat looking out his window, his back to the people taking their seats around the conference table. He liked this time of day. The sun was setting, silhouetting the skyscrapers in shadow. Soon the windows of these buildings would be lit up, turning them into glittering towers. Downtown seemed like a different city at night.

"So how did it go today?" Cavalli asked as he turned to face the table. Jessup and Sam sat in the center, flanked by Bob Bishop and Phil Ruzzi who was slouched in a chair off to the side.

"It couldn't have gone much better," Bishop said. "Hell, Earl gave sort of a noncommittal opening and then didn't even ask a question on cross." He turned for affirmation to Jessup. "Going according to plan, I'd say."

"The pretrial rulings went our way," Jessup said. "That took a lot of his stuff off the table. From the sound of his opening, I'd say we were in pretty good shape."

"How's our coverage?" Cavalli asked.

"It's been very favorable," Ruzzi said. "Any criticism seems to be focused on the judge, which is fine. In fact, we should probably think about another press conference in a day or two. If the case is going well, we need to make sure you own it."

Cavalli sat expressionless, letting his gaze drift over the group until it settled on Sam. "You waiting for someone to congratulate you on the motions?"

"They were pretty straightforward, honestly," she replied. "I don't think the judge had much of a choice."

"So you agree with all these rosy assessments, or are they just blowing smoke up my ass?"

Sam pursed her lips. "I think the case is going well. The only thing we have to worry about is some holdout hanging up the jury."

"Why bring that up?" Cavalli asked. He turned to Jessup. "You let some nut job on the jury?"

"It's a good jury," Jessup said. "I like them. Sam is just a little worried about this one juror, but she'll come around."

"Who's the juror?" Cavalli stared at Sam.

"Juror Number 5. I've been watching the jury," Sam said. "They are all paying attention. It's just that this one juror seems to be a bit too attentive to Bobby Earl. She nods at him and smiles, like she's following his lead."

"What is it? She got hot pants for him or something?"

"Hardly," Sam frowned. "It's not that. She just seems to like him." She paused in thought. "Actually, it's more than that. She seems to trust him."

Cavalli sat silently, tapping his pen on the desk like a metronome in time with his thoughts. "All right, keep me informed. Good luck tomorrow." They all stood, anxious to leave. "Ruzzi," Cavalli said. "Stay a minute, there's something we should discuss."

***

By the time Earl settled onto his couch and turned on the television, Thomas Glass was already talking with his panel of experts about the case. "So Don Leone, what did you make of the opening statements today?"

"Very interesting. It actually gave us a preview of what to expect in this case. I thought the District Attorney, Jim Jessup, did an excellent job. He laid out the prosecution case in a convincing way, which was not surprising since it seems they have a pretty solid case. And he had that good prosecutorial tone, a little angry."

"What about the defense?"

"Not much there, really. And that is pretty much what we can expect, I think, from here on out. As far as I'm concerned the defense made a mistake to even give one. He had nothing to say, so he should have waived it. All he accomplished was to let us know he was shooting blanks."

The commentator next to Leone was new to the panel. "I disagree," he said, removing his round-framed glasses. "The defense had to say something. He just didn't want to commit himself. So he gave what an old lawyer once described to me as 'a dead branch opening'. So named because birds like to perch on dead branches, so they can take off in any direction."

Glass looked dumbfounded, as if the lawyer had suddenly decided to speak in Urdu. Earl sensed he would not be seeing this lawyer on the panel again any time soon. Glass turned back to Leone. "How about those photographs? Awfully graphic, weren't they?"

"Well, death is not pretty," Leone said. "Besides, prosecutors love demonstrative evidence. Photos, charts, murder weapons, anything they can hold up and show to the jury. It seems to give credibility to their case if they have something tangible. And it all goes back into the jury room during deliberations to remind them of the prosecution case."

They broke for a commercial. Earl leaned back and closed his eyes, telling himself that murder trials always seemed rough in the beginning. Glass came back on with his segment called the "Inside Story."

"Your reporter has just learned of a rather disturbing circumstance. Sources close to the Seabrooke trial tell me the defense has in its possession evidence that apparently it's afraid to present on Seabrooke's behalf. It seems the evidence might cause some political embarrassment for the District Attorney's Office. Apparently, Bobby Earl, the defense lawyer, doesn't want to risk being kicked out of the Old Boys' Club where favors are traded. By the way, you can rest assured that this reporter will never be invited into that chummy group."

Earl was stunned. What in the hell was Glass talking about? Then it hit him. The Castro Brothers. Judge McKeene must have grown impatient with Earl and gone to the bullpen for a more willing pitcher. If McKeene was going to run for DA against Cavalli he needed an issue for the voters and nothing sold like corruption. But in order to stay on the moral high ground, McKeene needed Earl to trot out the Horgan report with its unsubstantiated allegation of a cover-up by Cavalli in exchange for campaign donations. Now, it seemed, McKeene had enlisted Glass in an effort to pressure Earl into using the report.

"Now don't get me wrong. Whatever this evidence is, I think the case against this Seabrooke guy sounds open and shut. I just don't want him whining on appeal that his lawyer dropped the ball and he didn't get a fair trial, forcing us to go through this all over again."

Earl clicked off the television. He had taken enough hits for one day. He stepped into the kitchen, and took the telephone off the hook. He needed to sleep, not play 'no comment' with reporters all night.

CHAPTER 24

Seated at the counsel table, Bobby Earl surveyed the courtroom. It was the second day of trial. Next to the witness stand a Styrofoam manikin was propped up like a sentry. To Earl, this signaled that Jessup's next witness would be the coroner, Peter Nakamura. Around the courthouse, the manikin was referred to as General Custer because of the coroner's practice of thrusting wooden shafts into it to demonstrate the path of bullets. At the end of his testimony the manikin would look like Custer after the Battle of the Little Big Horn.

Nakamura was noted among forensic experts for his discovery that the drug level in a completely decomposed corpse could be calculated from the fly maggots feasting on the remains. Apparently the little creatures got loaded in direct proportion to the drug level in their host. Nakamura's enthusiasm for these types of subjects was why prosecutors always scheduled his appearance first thing in the morning, rather than just after lunch.

Nakamura settled into the witness box and assumed a well-practiced look of impartiality. Jessup walked him through his credentials and his not-surprising conclusion that the cause of Officer Horgan's death was the three bullet holes in his chest. This was followed by some poking and prodding of General Custer, and then Jessup turned to the coroner's real contribution: the autopsy photos. Glossy 8 by 10s of Horgan's pale naked body laid out on a white porcelain slab, which had been scanned into Jessup's computer, now appeared on a TV screen that had been wheeled into the courtroom. Nakamura explained that there were no bruises on the body to suggest there had been a struggle and, in fact, the path of one of the bullets demonstrated that Officer Horgan had his arms raised as if to surrender.

"Your witness, Mr. Earl," Jefferson said.

"Doctor Nakamura," Earl began, rising from his chair. "I see from your report that you were able to determine the caliber of the weapon used in the shooting."

"I was. I recovered one of the slugs, which had come to rest in the left lung. From its weight, it was determined to be a .22 caliber bullet."

"You determined that by actually weighing the slug itself?"

"Yes, each caliber of weapon uses a different size bullet, which we can determine by weighing the slug, if one is recovered."

"Now, a .22 caliber is not a particularly powerful gun, is it?"

"I'm not an expert on firearms," Nakamura said, turning with a humble smile to the jurors. "But it's common knowledge that a .22 is the smallest of the handguns."

"The way you describe it, Officer Horgan was standing with his hands up when he was shot."

"That is my opinion."

"It almost sounds like he was deliberately executed."

Nakamura looked puzzled, then darted a look at Jessup. "That is one way to describe it."

"So did it surprise you that the killer used a .22, rather than a larger caliber gun?"

"Not at all. I have performed a number of autopsies during my career on victims who were similarly situated."

"When you say similarly situated, you mean 'professional hits,' where a person was specifically targeted and killed."

"Objection," Jessup said, finally realizing where Earl was headed. "That calls for speculation."

"Sustained," Jefferson said.

"Well, have you had cases where, in forming your opinion, you were provided information by the police that a victim had been specifically targeted and a .22 was the murder weapon?"

"Same objection," Jessup said.

"Overruled. He can answer," Jefferson said.

"Yes," Nakamura said.

"Can you tell us why a .22 might be the weapon of choice of such a killer?"

Nakamura looked at Jessup and heaved a sigh. "Ironically, it's because it is a small caliber. With a powerful weapon, the shot might pass right through the body without hitting a vital organ. If the slug strikes a bone or muscle mass, it just tears through it and keeps going. But a .22 isn't powerful enough to do that. Once a slug hits something, like a rib bone, it will ricochet and tumble around inside the body like a pin ball, slicing through organs and blood vessels until it comes to rest. The damage can be enormous."

"Thank you, Doctor." As Earl took his seat he casually glanced down the table to the prosecutor's end. Detective Tanner was speaking to Jenson in hushed tones. Jenson stared straight ahead, then turned his face away from the jury and brusquely said something under his breath to

Tanner, who turned aside clenching his jaw and staring angrily into the distance.

"Call your next," Jefferson said.

Sam stood up. "Call Sergeant Richard Walker to the stand." Earl was surprised that Jenson was letting her participate. He had kept her on the sidelines for so long her face could have been on a milk carton.

Walker sat stiffly in the witness box with his hands folded before him. He seemed out of place in a suit and tie, even one that probably came from a Sears and Roebuck catalog. Sam took him through his credentials as an expert locksmith and deftly slipped in that he learned his trade serving his country in Viet Nam. She quickly moved on to the crime scene and the tool that was found there. A photograph of the borescope lying on the office floor was held up and displayed to the jury. Walker explained how he had originally obtained the scope from Seabrooke during a routine auto stop several years ago and had secretly marked it with his initials before returning it so it could be identified if it happened to turn up at a future crime scene. A photo of the enlarged markings was passed among the jurors.

Earl had argued in an earlier hearing that since a previous Court had ruled the seizure of Seabrooke's borescope had been illegal, the tool should be excluded. But Jefferson found there was nothing illegal about marking the scope, and it was recovered this time because it had apparently been left behind.

"Did you determine how entry was made to the restaurant?" Sam asked.

"I did. The back door lock had been picked."

"Could you explain that to us?"

Walker showed the jury two thin metal rods with hooks at the end and explained how they could be inserted into locks to manipulate the tumblers.

"How did you come to the conclusion the lock was picked rather than just opened with a key?"

"I removed the lock and took it to the LAPD crime lab where I sawed it in half, then examined the inner chamber where the tumblers are located." Walker turned to the jury like a teacher warming to his subject. "Lock parts are typically made of soft metal, brass in this case, while the pick tool is usually made of hardened steel. So if a pick is scraped across a tumbler it will leave a mark."

"How is that type of mark different from the mark a key might make?"

"It's the location. You look for marks in areas that are inaccessible to the biting surface of a key." Walker held up an enlarged photo of the sawed half of the lock and pointed out some scratches. "These thin scrapes across the inside corrosion are not marks a key would produce."

"Did you examine the safe at that location?"

"I did," Walker said.

"And what did you determine?"

"That the safe had been professionally drilled in an attempt to gain entry." A photo of the drill hole was circulated among the jurors.

"When you say professionally drilled, what do you mean by that?"

"A small hole had been drilled in the back of the safe for this scope to be inserted." He held up the scope. "This would allow one to view the lock through the keyhole of the metal box covering the mechanism. The tumblers could then be seen and the dial turned to open the safe."

"But why do you say professionally drilled?"

"Because the entry point had to be precisely calculated, there was absolutely no room for error. This is extremely difficult because the location and size of the box protecting the locking mechanism from being viewed in this manner is a closely guarded secret. To make this drill as accurately as it was done, necessitates a thorough knowledge of every type and make of safe and the ability to make the mathematical calculations necessary to hit the exact location of the keyhole on this particular model. Only an expert with a real gift could have done this."

"You have spoken privately with Mr. Seabrooke, have you not, about the locksmith trade?'

"On several occasions."

"Based upon those conversations, would you consider him to be a master locksmith?"

"One of the very best."

"Now, was an entry made into this safe?" Sam asked.

"I can't say for certain. The safe's defenses had been defeated. All that remained was to merely dial one more number in the combination, which would have been quite simple using the scope. But, apparently this was not done."

"So it appeared he was interrupted?"

"I would think so. The safe's contents appeared to be intact."

"Thank you, Sergeant," Sam said as she returned to her seat.

"Mr. Earl?" Jefferson said.

Earl had hoped that, despite the judge's ruling, Walker might let slip a mention of the two hundred and fifty thousand dollars in cash in the safe, but on reflection he was not surprised. Walker was a man who played by the rules. Earl was about to see whether that code applied to both sides. But first he wanted to test the waters.

"Sergeant Walker, you told us about this scope and how it could be used," Earl said. "Is this an unusual item or one in fairly wide use?"

"It's a common tool that every competent locksmith would have in his tool kit," Walker said.

"So there are dozens of these in circulation?"

"I would say that's right."

"Is this the type of tool which might be traded or sold among locksmiths?"

"Yes, there is a fairly active market for used tools. You just have to look in the trade journals or go to eBay."

"Well, would it be fair to say that the last time you knew that Mr. Seabrooke had possession of this tool was two years ago, and you have no knowledge about what might have happened to it since then?"

"That's correct."

"And with regard to the restaurant's back door, you are of the opinion that the lock was picked?"

"I am."

"But you cannot determine, can you, when that occurred?"

"I cannot."

"So someone could have picked or attempted to pick this particular lock a year or more ago and left these marks?"

"That is certainly possible."

Earl stepped back to the counsel table and pretended to consult his notes, giving himself time to think. So far, so good, he thought. But now he was about to toss Walker a big fat one, right down the middle of the plate, the type of question you never asked a cop. If Walker wanted to hurt Seabrooke, he could give this one a ride out of the park. He had told Earl he would tell the truth. Now Earl was about to find out which version of the truth Walker was talking about.

"Sergeant Walker, you have been familiar with Mr. Seabrooke for a number of years, have you not?"

"You might say we're old acquaintances."

"You have spoken to him on a number of occasions and heard his reputation discussed among your colleagues?"

"I have."

"In your opinion, Sergeant, what is Mr. Seabrooke's reputation for violence?" Earl asked and held his breath.

"Mr. Seabrooke has a reputation as a very nonviolent individual. Timid is probably a better description. He is someone who has a reputation for going out of his way to avoid any kind of violent confrontation."

"Have you ever known Mr. Seabrooke to carry a gun or weapon of any kind?"

"Never."

Thank you, Sergeant."

Sam was on her feet. "May we approach?"

Jefferson nodded. The lawyers all walked to the side of the judge's bench, where they huddled together leaning toward the judge.

"You are one daring young man," Jefferson said to Earl with a bemused smile.

"Or plain foolish," Jessup said. "That's why I didn't object. This opens the door on Seabrooke's character."

Jefferson gave him a look. "Let me hear from Ms. Price, it's her witness."

"It does seem to challenge the Court's earlier ruling excluding any mention of Mr. Seabrooke's long career as a professional safe-cracker," Sam said.

"Not exactly, judge," Earl said. "The evidence code permits me to limit character evidence to reputation for a particular character trait. Which I did. I only asked about violence. This does not open the door to other character traits, such as honesty. If the People have evidence of acts of violence by my client, these, of course, would be admissible. But that's it."

Jefferson turned and picked up a book from his side table. He leafed to a section and sat reading. After a minute he closed the book. "I think Mr. Earl has the best of it on this one. Have you got any evidence of violence by Seabrooke?"

"Not at this time." Sam looked at Earl. "This caught us a little by surprise."

"I understand," Jefferson said. "If you come up with any, I'll let you put it on, but evidence of his career as a thief is still off limits. Now, if you don't have anything else, we'll recess for the evening."

"I have a few words for Sergeant Walker," Jessup said. "But I'll do that in my office."

Earl returned to his seat beside Seabrooke and waited for the jurors to gather their belongings and leave the courtroom. "You owe Walker one hell of a thank you," Earl said.

"I wasn't surprised," Seabrooke said. "He's a very honest man. A bit too rigid, perhaps, but honest."

Earl stood up, but Seabrooke remained seated. "Is any of this making a difference?" he asked as if to himself.

Unfortunately, Earl knew the answer to this one. Simply put, no. Oh, he probably made himself look good, tap dancing around, winning a few concessions. But in the end, there was still a big goose egg on the scoreboard. That opening he kept hoping for had not materialized. "We're doing fine Sydney," he said.

Seabrooke stood and gave Earl a humorless smile. "You may be a good lawyer, Bobby Earl, but you're a pathetic liar." He turned and joined the bailiff at the door to the lock-up. Before leaving, he turned back. "It's ironic really, when you think about it. After all the crimes I have actually committed, for which I have never been punished, that it should end like this. Paying for something I didn't do. It's rather a ham-handed way to balance the books, wouldn't you say?" He turned without waiting for an answer, and the door clanked shut.

"It was the craziest, most unexpected thing I've ever seen in a court of law," the man with a goatee and bow tie said across the table to a smiling Thomas Glass. In Earl's darkened front room, the only light was from the television. The Thumb's program had become a nightly ritual for Earl, a dose of self-flagellation after his microwave dinner.

"There he was with a gift from the judge," the goatee said. "The prosecution was blocked from parading in all Seabrooke's victims, then along comes this 'defense lawyer'," the goatee made quotation signs with his fingers, "and proceeds to just throw it all away. Asking about Seabrooke's character puts his whole past in play. It opens the door to anything the prosecution can dig up. And believe me they will find things." He rolled his eyes. "When I was a prosecutor, I would have sent a car to pick up this kinda lawyer to make sure he didn't miss court."

Glass chuckled. "As the saying goes, other than that, Mrs. Lincoln, how did the rest of the evening go?"

"It was a good day for the prosecution. They set the scene and got right to the photographs of the killing, which is necessary to make this tragedy real for the jury. Let them see what they're dealing with. Then they laid out a very compelling circumstantial case for conviction, which is going to be extremely difficult for the defense to explain away." Earl got up from the couch as the goatee began to list on his fingers the all-too-familiar pieces of prosecution evidence. "All in all," he concluded, "round one for the prosecution."

Earl clicked off the television.

CHAPTER 25

"So what's going on?" Earl asked. He was standing with Jeremiah Davis, the bailiff, waiting for the jury to be summoned into the courtroom. It was a position he liked to assume each morning, so they would see him in a friendly conversation with a symbol of law enforcement. What better way to show he was one of them? But this morning, there was a different feeling in the courtroom, one he did not recognize.

"The judge got a phone call," Davis said. "He'll tell you about it."

The judge took the bench without the jury and called the lawyers up to the side bar. "My clerk received a phone call yesterday after we recessed," the judge said to the lawyers. "I thought it best not to discuss it in open court to avoid the media. The caller did not identify himself, but said he was connected to the publishing business. He told Mrs. Fremont that one of our jurors was shopping around a book proposal on the case."

"Ms. Price received the same call, your Honor," Jessup said. "This has caused a great deal of concern in my office. Any book worth publishing would depend on the jury reaching a guilty verdict. This would create a conflict for the juror and might result in a reversal on appeal. Out of a sense of fairness, the People feel the best course is not to take any chances. We should just replace the juror with one of the alternates."

"What did the caller say, Ms. Price?"

"Essentially what you described, judge," Sam said. "He refused to give his name or any details that could be verified."

"Would someone please tell me which juror we're talking about," Earl said.

"Juror Number 5," Sam said.

How convenient," Earl said, aware of the juror's attentiveness.

"Will both sides stipulate that I can talk to her in chambers, with the court reporter, but without counsel?" the judge asked.

"Of course," Sam said, as Jessup was about to object.

"I'll stipulate," Earl said. "I just hope this attention doesn't make her self-conscious about her position and force her to take a back seat during deliberations."

"I understand," the judge said, then sent the bailiff into the jury room to summon Juror Number 5. As she walked toward the judge's chambers she gave Earl a concerned look. He returned a reassuring smile.

Fifteen minutes later the juror walked back to the jury room without making eye contact with anyone. The judge returned to the bench. "The juror emphatically denied the report. Given its anonymous nature and the lack of verifiable details, I see no reason to alter the jury's composition." He turned to the bailiff. "Mr. Davis, would you bring in the jury, please. And remind them we only have a half day today because of my meeting, and there is no court on Friday, so the lawyers can attend to their other cases."

"Don't worry, judge," the bailiff said with a grin. "Friday off. They're not likely to forget that."

"Do you have some short witnesses, Mr. Jessup, to take us up to the noon break?"

Jessup gave a curt nod, sulking about the ruling. He turned to Sam and gestured toward the courtroom door. Apparently it would fall to her to fill the time. Sam went to summon Deputy Torres from the hallway.

Torres slid into the witness box and squared his shoulders. With his standard-issue buzz cut and clear-eyed stare, he looked like a recruiting poster. He even spoke with the clipped delivery he had learned in the academy. He explained that he currently worked in inmate transportation, but that his four-year tenure in the jail made him familiar with most of its workings. Sam established that inmates in the jail had no access to newspapers, radio or television as a source of information from the outside. Even visitors were separated by a Plexiglass window and had to speak over phones that the deputies monitored. As for an inmate like Jake Snyder, once he was designated a prosecution witness, he was transferred to a special cell block and all his visits and telephone calls were routinely tape recorded.

"Moving to a different subject, Deputy Torres, did you bring the transportation records for Mr. Seabrooke and Mr. Snyder?"

"Yes, Ma'am."

"Do those records indicate whether they were ever transported together?"

The deputy looked down at a paper in front of him. "They were both bused together on the same day in August from Central Jail to the Torrance courthouse."

"Did Mr. Seabrooke have a court appearance that day?"

"No ma'am. It seems to have been a clerical error. It happens sometimes."

"Thank you, deputy."

During this testimony, Earl had strolled over to the courtroom drinking fountain in an effort to demonstrate the unimportance of this testimony.

"Mr. Earl?" the judge asked.

"Excuse me, your Honor," Earl said, as if he had not been following the testimony. "No questions."

The last witness for the day was Theodore Willingham, the bailiff in the Torrance courtroom where Snyder had been scheduled to appear. He explained how the courthouse lock-up consisted of a single large cell in the basement where all those in custody were kept together until they were brought up to their respective courtrooms.

"Do you have the court list for the day Mr. Snyder was to appear in the Torrance court?"

"Yes, ma'am."

"Does Mr. Seabrooke's name appear on that list?"

"No ma'am. But, he and Snyder were on the same bus. It was probably a clerical error."

"So Mr. Seabrooke and Mr. Snyder would have spent the morning together in the basement lock-up?" Sam asked.

"Not just the morning. Torrance is the last stop for the east county Sheriff's bus. They pick up our bodies at the end of the day."

Earl had fought the temptation all evening, but at 9:00 p.m. he succumbed. Dropping onto the couch, he clicked on the television. He was bone tired and this weekend was sure to be spent grinding through his case notebooks, so he had hoped to spend a mindless evening watching the sports channel. But he could not stop himself.

"We had a short day, today," Glass said.

The man across the desk had a thick neck and a jaw that jutted out like the prow of a ship. His grey crew-cut was as thick as a newly mowed lawn. Earl recognized Kenneth Barnes, former Federal prosecutor and would-be political candidate in search of a race he could win.

"Short but sweet," Barnes said. "The prosecution opened with the Napoleon on Elba gambit. An excellent move."

"For those of us not up on our history, why don't you put that so we regular folks can understand."

"The prosecution has an informant to whom Seabrooke confessed. A fellow named Snyder. Juries don't like informants, don't trust them. To be believable, an informant needs details that that could only have come from the murderer. So the prosecution has to show his conversation with Seabrooke was the only place he could have learned about them. They need to prove he was cut off from any other source for that information, like he was isolated on an island. Napoleon on Elba."

"Were they able to do that?"

"It sure sounded that way. Unless the defense comes up with something, that confession is going to be a killer." Barnes grinned impishly. "No pun intended."

"On a different note, there seemed to be concern today about one of the jurors. The judge talked to her alone in chambers. What have you heard?"

"Not much. Everything was at the side bar where we couldn't hear, and there's this gag order so the lawyers can't tell us. But this type of situation sometimes arises if someone has tried to tamper with a juror."

"What does that mean? Tamper with a juror."

"All the lawyers are strictly forbidden to have any contact with the jurors. This avoids anyone trying to influence a juror in some way."

"You mean like bribing them? Buying their vote?"

"That is always a possibility, but of course, we're just guessing here."

"Well, it would only take one juror to frustrate justice and prevent a verdict. I certainly hope the authorities are on the alert for that danger."

Earl stopped himself from throwing the remote at the screen and contented himself with a string of expletives. Henceforth looked up, startled out of his nap, and whined an apology just in case he had unknowingly transgressed. Earl reached down and patted him gently. "What do you say we get out Old Blue and go for a drive? I need to clear my head."

For Earl, Friday had been a day of racing from one courthouse to another, in order to explain that since he was in trial, his other cases would have to be postponed. Only one of the judges had difficulty grasping the concept that the entire judicial system did not actually revolve around his courtroom.

By Sunday, he had spent most of the weekend in his office, scouring every page of every notebook lining his shelves, unable to shake the feeling that he was just going through the motions in court, like an actor reading his lines, unable to change the script.

Earl picked up his coffee cup and walked down the hall to the office coffee machine. Back at his desk, he sat thinking, cradling the cup in his hands. He hated this case, hated Jessup for his smugness; he was even starting to hate the jury. He was going to lose this case. It was no longer about his reputation or his pathetic need for acclaim. Now it was about losing a case for an innocent man. He had actually tried to convince himself that Seabrooke was in fact guilty. There was certainly plenty of evidence for that, and it would have made things much easier. But he just couldn't do it. In his gut he knew otherwise.

This was getting him nowhere but down. He drained his coffee cup and pulled open a bottom drawer to stash the cup. In the drawer was a manila envelope which he did not recognize. He picked it up, then he remembered. Snyder's visitor slips before the Horgan killing. What information could someone have passed to Snyder about a murder before it even happened? He was about to toss the envelope back in the drawer when his compulsiveness stopped him. What the hell, you never knew.

He tore open the envelope and four white slips slid onto the desk. The first two bore the name of "Johnny Aradano" on the visitor's line, written in childlike block letters. The bondsman must have been out trolling for business. Aradano was known to check the jail booking register for new inmates whom he would call out to negotiate with about posting their bail. The slips were dated a week apart. They must have agreed on a price during the first visit and Aradano returned a week later to see if Snyder had raised the money. Apparently not. Snyder was still inside.

The next form was for a "Bianca Taylor." Probably a girlfriend of Snyder's or somebody he tried to put the touch on for bail money. The last slip was for a "Tareesha Rollins." The name meant nothing to Earl

Earl dropped the slips back into the envelope and closed the drawer. Another dead end. He picked up his briefcase and began stuffing in the notebooks for tomorrow's court session. Last Thursday Jessup had told the judge he intended to call Crystal Robinson on Monday and wanted Earl cautioned not to bring up her misdemeanor drug convictions. Earl was painfully aware that these were inadmissible, leaving nothing to tarnish the image of the grieving girlfriend, but he resented Jessup rubbing his nose in it. He grabbed Crystal's notebook off the shelf and headed for the back door, wondering if Jessup would dress her like a nun or a cheerleader.

Something kept faintly buzzing in the back of his mind. Then it hit him. He hurried back to his office, dropped Crystal's notebook onto the desk and whipped through the pages until he came to the section marked "Criminal Record." There was a box on her last arrest report marked "Aliases." He ran his finger down the list of names and stopped.

There it was, "Bianca Taylor." Crystal had visited Jake Snyder two weeks before the Horgan killing, using an old alias. Easy enough to do; you could buy a phony ID on any street corner downtown. But why?

He pulled out all the visiting slips and arranged them in chronological order. First Crystal had visited Snyder, then Aradano had visited him, followed by this Tareesha woman and finally Aradano again. Five days later Horgan lay dead in a Chinese restaurant. Earl stared at the row of forms. This was his opening, he could feel it. He told himself to stay calm and think. It was here, he just had to find it. He needed a beer, and he needed to think. It was crunch time.

At home, he sat on his back steps in the cool of the late afternoon. The sun was low; light flickered through the trees. A half-empty beer bottle stood to his left, next to an open can of peanuts. Henceforth squatted on his other side, resting his front legs on the step below. This was where Earl did his best thinking.

He kept turning the pieces around in his mind, trying to find the pattern that made them fit as a whole. It was there, he was sure of it. But how? He took a swig from his beer and crunched a few peanuts and gave a handful to Henceforth. His thoughts whirled, as he tried to squeeze the facts into one frame after another, only to find something that refused to fit. Gazing up at the sky, he watched a pelican gracefully sail homeward with outstretched wings. He remembered his father's cruel lesson when he was a child and the memory of that broken bird. What had his father shouted? "Things are never what they seem. People are never what they seem."

Then it was suddenly there, as if a thick fog had lifted. All the weight of worry and doubt seemed to fall away in a rush of relief. He felt jubilant, like a prisoner unexpectedly released. At last he knew what to do, no more dancing around. Maybe he couldn't carry it off, but at least now he had a fighting chance. He felt strong and confident. At last this was going to be a trial, a real trial. He had squared the circle.

CHAPTER 26

"Call Crystal Robinson," Jessup said.

Crystal sat inside the rail next to her handler. Marjalita patted her hand and gave her a reassuring smile. She rose and walked toward the witness stand already holding a handkerchief. Dressed primly in a white blouse under a blue linen jacket and skirt, she could have been a suburban soccer mom, except that her hollow-eyed stare seemed haunted, not sleepless from PTA overload.

"You and Officer Horgan had a romantic relationship, did you not?" Jessup asked.

"We did."

"Had there been talk of marriage?"

"Things hadn't gotten that far," Crystal said with a shy smile.

Jessup had her testify in detail about her shock and grief when she heard of Horgan's death. She covered her eyes with the handkerchief and asked for a glass of water.

"On the night of his death, you two had planned to spend the night at your place, is that right?"

"Yes, but we had an argument, and Terry left."

"So this was unexpected?"

"Absolutely."

"Were you aware of any plans Officer Horgan had that night, other than with you?"

"None at all. If we hadn't argued," she said with a catch in her throat, "he would never have left and then ..." She dabbed at her eyes.

"He never mentioned an appointment or anything about going to that restaurant?"

"No, nothing. He was supposed to be with me."

"Thank you, Ms. Robinson." Jessup gave Earl a smug look and sat down.

Earl admired her performance, emotional but understated. Jessup must have prepared her. The testimony fit perfectly into the prosecution theory that Horgan went to the restaurant unexpectedly and stumbled on a robbery in progress. Seabrooke panicked and shot him. Polishing Horgan's memory with a few tears didn't hurt either.

Earl stood up. "May we have a conference in chambers, your Honor?"

The judge gave him a puzzled look. "Is that necessary?"

"It is."

Once in chambers, the lawyers remained standing, facing the judge at his desk. Earl gripped the top of the high-backed visitor chair in front of him. Next to him, Jessup stood with his arms crossed, looking impatient. Ever diligent, Sam held a legal pad ready to jot notes.

"Judge," Earl said. "I'd like to revisit the Court's ruling on Ms. Robinson's criminal record."

"We've already been over that," Jessup said.

"Do you have anything new that would make her record relevant?" the judge asked.

"I do. As we know, Ms. Robinson was arrested and charged with the sale of heroin. That case was dismissed. The officer who arranged that dismissal was Officer Horgan."

"Excuse me," Jessup said, turning to Earl. "Where did this come from? I don't suppose it's too much to ask if you have any proof of this?"

"Just order up the DA's file on the case. It's right in there."

"Can you do that, Mr. Jessup?" the judge asked.

Jessup stared sullenly at Earl for a moment before turning to the judge. "There's no need," he said quietly.

"You mean it's true?" the judge said. "You knew about this?"

Jessup nodded. "But," he said, "I still don't see how it's relevant."

"Horgan was on loan to a Federal narcotics task force," Earl explained. "He got Crystal out so she could work for him as an informant. The Feds pay their snitches. In cash. It's just not a coincidence that a large amount of cash was in that safe and that Crystal has admitted she knew about it. I think she had more than a passing interest in that money. I just want the opportunity to explore that with her."

"This is just one big fishing expedition," Jessup said. "None of this proves anything."

"Well," the judge said. "Mr. Earl has built up a credibility account with me, so I'm going to let him draw on it for this one." His gaze shifted and he locked eyes with Earl. "But this better go somewhere. If you end up overdrawn, there's going to be more than a little fine to pay."

"I'll need a minute with the witness," Jessup said. "She's been told her record was not going to come up."

"I'd rather get her cold, judge," Earl said.

"Take a minute," the judge said to Jessup. "It will avoid confusion."

Back in the courtroom, Jessup and Sam huddled with Crystal. Earl knew Jessup was telling her what questions to expect and the things she should not try to deny. Now came the challenge of cross-examination. Earl had a story he wanted to tell, but he had to tell it through people who were determined not to help. The art was to get them to say what they were determined not to say. It would be so much easier if he could write the lines which the witnesses would repeat. It was at times like this that he envied prosecutors like Jessup.

Back on the stand, Earl led Crystal through the dismissal of her case, which she had been schooled to admit.

"In exchange for getting your case dismissed, you went to work for Officer Horgan as an informant, correct?"

"I wanted to stop the drugs. They were ruining lives. So I was happy to give him a few tips," Crystal said.

"It was a little more than a few tips, wasn't it? You were named as his confidential informant on several search warrants."

"I don't know much about the legal stuff."

"But you knew you were getting paid for your information? You were supposed to get part of any drug money that was recovered."

"I never received any of that," she said adamantly.

"That may be. But you were supposed to get that money weren't you?"

"Oh," she said with a grimace. "Terry said something about that, but I never received any."

"In some of those arrests, a huge amount of cash was recovered, wasn't it? So your cut would have been quite sizable."

"I suppose so."

"Officer Horgan was being transferred back to the LAPD, wasn't he?"

"He mentioned it."

"Which meant he wouldn't need your services any longer."

Crystal shrugged. "I guess so."

"You also knew that Horgan had a safe at that restaurant with a lot of money in it."

Crystal looked at Jessup, then glared back at Earl. "That's right, Counsel."

"So let's summarize where we're at. Does the following sound correct? You worked for Horgan as an informant. He was supposed to pay you a portion of the drug money recovered. You never received it. And you knew Horgan had cash in a safe at the restaurant. Is that right so far?"

"I guess so."

"Now, most people in your situation would probably have thought that it was their money in that safe. Is that what you figured?"

"Objection!" Jessup shouted. "Is this some kind of guessing game?"

"I don't know if guessing is a legal objection," the judge said. "But if it is, it's overruled."

"I never thought about it," she said.

"You thought enough to go see a friend about it, didn't you?" Earl asked.

"I don't know what you're talking about."

"You went to visit Jake Snyder at the County Jail, didn't you?"

"That name's not familiar."

"How about Bianca Taylor? That is one of your aliases isn't it?"

"You tell me."

Earl took a page from a notebook on his table, showed it to Jessup, then placed it on the witness stand. "You gave that name as one of your aliases when you were arrested on the sales case." He pointed at the box on the arrest report.

"Yeah, so what?"

"So let's be very clear here. Your testimony is that you never visited Jake Snyder at the Men's County Jail."

Crystal stared warily at Earl. "That's what I said."

Earl stepped back to his table and picked up a visitor's slip. He walked over and showed it to Jessup.

"Objection, we weren't provided with a copy of this in discovery."

"Your Honor," Earl said. "This is cross-examination. I didn't call this witness. I'm under no obligation to preview my cross with the prosecution. Besides, you can refresh a witness' recollection with just about anything."

"Overruled," the judge said.

Earl walked up to the witness stand and laid the form before her. "Take a look at this, Ms. Robinson, and tell us if you want to change your testimony."

Crystal shifted back in her chair as if the paper were contaminated. Her eyes darted around the room as if she were looking for an escape. "Oh, yeah, that's right," she said. "I must of forgot."

"Visiting the jail, using an alias, is not something someone easily forgets, Ms. Robinson. Let's be honest here. You were lying when you denied visiting Snyder, weren't you?"

"Objection, he's badgering the witness," Jessup said.

"Overruled. You may answer."

Crystal fixed Earl with an icy stare. "I guess," she said.

It ran through Earl's mind that on television this was where the lawyer was supposed to turn to the jury and slowly say "you guess?" But he never pulled that sort of stunt. He had learned it was a mistake to automatically assume a jury was with you. You had to let them come to their own conclusion, not make it for them. Then you could build on it. Not before.

"No guess about it. You lied, didn't you?"

"Okay," she said defiantly. "Yes."

"But what I'd like to know is what was so important about that visit that you used an alias and then lied under oath to keep it a secret?"

She looked in desperation at Jenson, then up at the judge. "Look," she said in a pleading voice. "He was somebody I knew in the old days. I was just ashamed to admit it. I just went to see if I could help him get straight. Is that so bad?"

"Actually, I think you went for another reason. You went to him for help. Horgan was leaving you behind, and you wanted your money. Snyder had made a profession out of robbing people, so you figured he would know how to get it."

"Objection!" Jessup shouted. "Who is testifying here? That's not a question."

"Overruled, for now," the judge said.

"You're crazy," she snapped. "Those are your words, not mine."

Earl stepped back to the table and looked down at a notebook. "Now, the police recovered Officer Horgan's cellphone and it showed that you were the last person to call him, you're aware of that?"

"That's what I've been told." She glared at him.

"When you met with Jake Snyder, didn't he tell you he would help, and that all you had to do was get Officer Horgan to that restaurant on that exact date and time?"

"That's a lie. We had an argument, I wanted to apologize."

"There was no argument, was there, Crystal? You called and threatened to expose him for keeping the payments unless he met you at the restaurant and gave you your cut."

"That's bullshit."

"Objection!" Jessup shouted. "This is ridiculous. He's just making statements. This isn't cross-examination."

"Ms. Robinson," the judge said. "Watch your language. I gather your answer is a denial?"

"Yes, sir." She turned to the jury. "I never wanted Terry to get hurt."

"That's enough," the judge said. "I assume you are through, Mr. Earl?" He gave Earl a look that turned his question into an order.

"Yes, your Honor."

"We'll take a short recess."

As Earl sat down, Seabrooke leaned over. "When did you learn about that visit? Why didn't you tell me? This is quite helpful, isn't it?"

"I don't know yet," Earl said. "Go with Mr. Davis. We'll talk later. I need to think about the next witness." Seabrooke turned and left without voicing his customary pessimism. Apparently the examination had won Earl some newfound respect from his client.

He leaned back in his chair and folded his hands behind his head. This was more like it, he thought. At the end of the table, Jessup spoke furiously to Detective Tanner who jumped up and left the courtroom. Tanner was undoubtedly on his way to the jail to check on Snyder's visitors. Good luck with that, Earl chuckled. Manny's niece had carefully followed the jailor's instructions and returned everything back where she found it. Which meant it would be days before Jessup got anything.

Jessup strode up to Earl, who remained seated, slowly rocking and staring ahead. "You plan on playing hide-the-ball with any of our other witnesses?" Jessup snapped. "We gave you our documents, I foolishly assumed you would do the same."

Earl swiveled in his chair and looked hard at Jessup. "Jim, I gave you everything you were legally entitled to. If you put on a liar, you've got to expect a few surprises."

"So it's a one-way street, is that it? We give and you don't."

"Look, you called her, I didn't. If it was my witness, of course you're entitled to any documents, but not when it's cross-examination."

"So no professional courtesy? No heads up?"

"What, so you can prep your witnesses in advance? Now why should I do that, Jim? Here's a novel idea, how about telling your witnesses to testify truthfully?"

"Okay, you want to play it that way," Jessup said. His eyes were slits. "You're a real cheap shot artist, you know that?"

"It's called cross-examination, Jimbo."

Jessup turned and joined Sam, who was talking excitedly with Crystal. Earl studied Crystal, thinking the last thing she said was probably the most truthful. She never did want Terry hurt.

The recess over, Earl watched the jury file into the box, chatting and joking. At least they were having a good time. Jessup was on his feet.

"Call Sergeant Brown." The burly Sergeant entered and sat down, placing a case folder on the shelf of the witness stand and settling in. His red tie must have been new, Earl thought, because there was not one food stain on it. Under Jessup's guidance, Brown identified himself as the investigator on Jake Snyder's robbery cases. He explained that a week after the murder, Snyder summoned him to the jail and told him about the Seabrooke confession. Brown insisted he had not provided Snyder with any details of the murder and that the first account Snyder gave to him was consistent with the later ones he gave to the prosecution.

"Sergeant Brown," Earl began his cross-examination. "The visit you just told us about with Jake Snyder wasn't the first time you met with him, was it?"

"Let me check my log," Brown said in a helpful tone and opened the case folder. "I don't see another entry here, so it must have been."

"Maybe I can help you out. You know Phil Cummings, don't you? Mr. Snyder's lawyer?" Earl thought back to his visit with the storefront lawyer with his court appointed cases and a wall mounted fish that warned clients to keep their mouths shut.

"I do."

"If I told you he said that in early June you called him about Mr. Snyder, would that jog your memory?"

Brown looked up at the ceiling. "I probably spoke to him at some point about Snyder. It was my case."

"If Phil Cummings said you asked for permission to speak with Snyder alone, would that be correct?"

Brown looked down at Jessup, then back at Earl. "You know, I think you're right. Must have forgotten. I was sorta busy around then." He turned and gave a knowing smile to the jury.

"And the reason you visited was because Snyder wanted to snitch on somebody to get a deal on his cases."

"Gosh, I don't really remember."

"Well, there was no other reason for you to talk to him, was there? You promised Cummings you would not talk about his case, so why else go down there?"

"When you put it that way, you're probably right."

"So what did Snyder offer?"

"I don't honestly recall."

"Come now, sergeant. He offered to give you information about a corrupt police officer, didn't he? That's not something you're likely to forget."

"Objection, where's this headed?" Jessup asked heatedly. "Some kind of backdoor character assassination?"

"Mr. Earl, you had best be proceeding in good faith here," the judge said sternly.

"I am, your Honor," Earl said, wishing he were as confident as he sounded. This was all a hunch, based on the fact that Crystal had visited Snyder earlier. She would undoubtedly have told Snyder about Horgan's scam in which he used her as his supposed informant and allocated a portion of the drug money they recovered as her fee for allegedly providing the information. The fact that Horgan was keeping the money in a restaurant safe was the carrot to get Snyder's help. To somebody like Snyder, Crystal and Horgan were no more than commodities to be sold. The only question was how much he could get for them. The trick now for Earl was to get Sergeant Brown to admit that Snyder offered to give him information about a crooked cop in exchange for a deal on his cases. But all Earl had was a bluff.

"Snyder was shopping this around, wasn't he? Looking for a deal. He talked to you about it, but you weren't the only one. He talked to others. He wanted to see what price he could get. Isn't that right?"

The threat of other witnesses raised the possibility of being caught in a lie. Brown swallowed and cleared his throat. "He might have mentioned something about that. But the officer wasn't even in our department."

"It had to do with a Federal task force, didn't it?"

"Something like that."

"So you told him no deal, right? That information wasn't good enough to trade for all his cases."

"I probably didn't believe him."

"A good solid citizen like Jake Snyder? You didn't believe him?"

"Objection, the sergeant's opinion is irrelevant," Jessup said in a disgusted tone.

"Sustained," the judge said.

"So, you told Snyder he had to come up with something else, something bigger, if he wanted out from under his cases."

"I don't remember what I said, but I didn't pass it on."

"Then you got another call from Snyder asking you to come down again, didn't you?"

"Yeah, when he told me about Seabrooke."

"No, before that. You called his lawyer again and went down to see him a second time."

Brown stared at Earl, calculating. "Yeah, I think so," he said.

"And Snyder asked you for a favor, didn't he?"

"I don't know what you mean."

"He asked if you could arrange for him to have access to a telephone."

"All the inmates have access to the phones."

"Not the public phones. A private line, one the jailers couldn't listen in on."

"I'm not following you."

Earl walked back to his table and flipped open a notebook and stared at his notes of his talk with Chuey. He placed his hand on the page and stared at Brown, like a chess player about to checkmate an unsuspecting opponent and enjoying the moment. He held up a paper as if reading from it. "Isn't it true that you arranged for a Deputy Lucas to escort Snyder from cellblock B to a private phone?"

Brown grimaced. Earl knew what he was thinking. Was this case worth risking his pension for? Brown tossed his head as if in resignation. "Snitches are always asking for something. I probably authorized it so he could call his family."

"Or anybody else," Earl said pointedly.

"I suppose. Ask him."

"With an outside line he could call other courts, Detective bureaus, jail transportation, just about anybody. Couldn't he?"

"It's a phone. You figure it out."

Earl dropped his briefcase at his front door and pulled out his keys. He was tired, but a good tired. The case had gone well today. But tomorrow would be the test. He unlocked the front door and Henceforth was there to greet him, tap dancing with his nails on the hardwood floor.

Earl turned back to pick up his briefcase when he heard a voice. "You just couldn't leave it be, could you," the voice said. Earl looked up, startled. Deon Hawkins stepped into the light. In his right hand was a gun. It was pointed at Earl. "Why don't we just step inside, counselor," he said, gesturing with the pistol. Earl froze. He knew if he left the lighted porch and went into the dark house, there was only one way this was going to end.

He darted a look down at his briefcase. He had foolishly stuffed Munoz's gun inside in order to carry it into the house. Days of concentrating on the case had lulled him into dropping his guard.

Suddenly he heard a deep guttural growl behind him and a large body hurtled past. Henceforth launched himself through the air at the big man. All seventy pounds of animal fury slammed into Hawkins' chest and they both toppled in a heap onto the lawn. Henceforth was on top, snarling and snapping, but Hawkins held the dog away with both his massive hands around the dog's throat. The big man rolled onto his side, then heaved Henceforth back toward Earl. The dog landed hard against the edge of the cement steps and let out a whelp of pain. Slowly, Henceforth struggled to his feet and stood unsteadily snarling at Hawkins with bared teeth.

Hawkins was on his feet, looking wildly about the lawn. He had lost the gun. The street light threw a glint off something lying on the grass, halfway between the two men. Hawkins locked eyes with Earl. They had both seen it. Hawkins lunged first and reached the gun. Earl leaped off the steps as Hawkins rose up with the gun. Earl swung his right leg with all the power that years of rugby had built. His foot connected with Hawkins' hand and the gun flew into the darkness. Hawkins yelled in pain and grabbed his hand. He turned and looked at Earl with cold rage. He slowly stalked toward him, his arms spread, as if yearning to crush something.

"Hey," someone shouted from next door. "Did that damned dog bite you? I been telling that young man it would come to this." Hawkins looked over his shoulder, then back at Earl. "This ain't over." He pulled a small flashlight from his leather jacket and frantically began to search the ground. Earl scooped up Henceforth and dove inside the house, kicking the door shut behind him. He lay on the floor, in the dark, holding Henceforth until he heard the scream of tires as a car sped away.

Earl sat up. Henceforth lay on his side, panting heavily. He reached out and patted him. The dog whimpered when Earl touched his side. Earl realized his ribs must be broken. "You need a vet, big fella.'" He stared into the darkness. "And somebody else is badly in need of a major ass kicking."

CHAPTER 27

After leaving Henceforth with the vet, Earl had spent the night at a rundown motel. He was tired. Motels were good for one thing in his view and it wasn't sleeping. He had not called the police. The prospect of spending most of the night repeating his tale to a string of cops relishing the fact that a defense lawyer was asking them for help, did not exactly appeal to him. Besides, it would have been a waste of time. Without a scratch on him and no witness, it was his word against Hawkins'. The neighbor did not see what happened and would only want to point the finger at poor Henceforth. He needed to keep his focus on the case. He had something else planned for Mr. Hawkins.

That morning, Earl was waiting in the hallway when Jeremiah Davis opened the doors to the courtroom. He sank down heavily into his chair at the counsel table and drank deeply from the coffee container he had brought from the snack bar. Lots of sugar, he needed the energy. People were arriving and filling the benches. Word must have spread. The case was no longer just a walk through.

Johnny Aradano, the bondsman, arrived, glad-handing and passing out his card, spinning his jokes like a Tibetan prayer wheel. He had dressed for the occasion with a red silk shirt unbuttoned to his chest, a gold chain looped around his neck and a pinky ring with a red stone the size of a paperweight. Earl smiled, he could not have asked for more.

Tanner stood talking to Jessup who was leaning back against the jury box, arms folded, staring down at the floor. Tanner held out his arms, palms raised, and shrugged his shoulders. He must be delivering the news on Snyder's visitor records, Earl thought. Sam stood at their table turning the pages in a folder. She called Earl over.

"You sleep in that shirt or are you trying for the sympathy vote as the overworked defense lawyer?"

"It's long story," Earl said. "What's up?"

"This is my big day. Jessup has given me the awesome task of proving your man was on the street at the time of the murder," Sam said facetiously. "You want to stipulate that Aradano had bailed him out?"

"I wouldn't dream of robbing you of your big chance. It's like when Lou Gehrig subbed for Wally Pipp. It was supposed to be just for that day, but he was never out of the lineup after that."

Sam looked at him askance. "You just want to see if I can deal with Mr. 'Jokeathon.'"

"We all have our burdens," Earl grinned.

She handed him the folder. "This is Aradano's bail file. We had a little trouble getting Mr. Aradano to respond to our subpoenas. That's why you didn't get a copy in discovery. I won't introduce it if you've got a problem."

"Let me have a look at it." He took the folder back to his table. Flipping past the surety forms, he focused on the handwritten information sheet which Aradano had scrawled out on Seabrooke. After finally deciphering it, he opened one of his notebooks and turned to a police report. Placing a finger on a line in each document, he looked back and forth comparing. Then he casually closed the folder and walked back to Sam.

"I don't care," Earl said. "Go ahead and use it."

"Now you've got me worried," she said. "After your little surprises yesterday, nothing seems safe anymore." Earl gave her a self-deprecating smile and went back to his chair.

"The People call Johnny Aradano," Sam said.

Aradano settled into the witness chair and turned to the judge. "Good morning, your Honor. Good to see you again." The judge ignored him.

Sam marched Aradano through his testimony, not allowing him an opportunity to play the clown. He explained how he posted bail for Mr. Seabrooke, who was then released from the County Jail on June 1st and remained free until his arrest on June 4th.

"So on June 3rd, the night Officer Horgan was murdered, Mr. Seabrooke was no longer incarcerated?" Sam asked.

"No, ma'am. You see...."

"And there were no conditions on his bail?" she asked, interrupting Aradano. "He was free to come and go as he pleased?"

"You bet, I...."

"There was nothing that you are aware of that would have prevented Mr. Seabrooke from being at that restaurant on the night of the killing?"

"Looks that way," Aradano said, turning to the jury.

"Thank you, Mr. Aradano."

Earl let Sam get away with her last question. Jessup had made sure to keep her on the sidelines, so when she finally got in the game a little theatrics were understandable.

Earl stood and began his cross-examination. "Mr. Aradano," he said. "You're in the business of posting bail for a fee. So tell us what you charged Mr. Seabrooke for that service."

"Nothin'. I did it as a favor."

"That was very generous of you. Had you known Mr. Seabrooke long?"

"Nah, it was a favor for a friend."

"Who was that?"

"I don't remember. I like to help people. I do a lot of favors." He turned to the jury for approval.

"Actually, you got Mr. Seabrooke out of jail so he could do a job for you, didn't you?"

"A job? Whata' ya' talkin' about? I already got somebody to wash my car." There was a giggle in the audience and Aradano flashed a smile.

"Before you posted Mr. Seabrooke's bail you went down to the jail and visited Jake Snyder, didn't you?"

"I visit lots of people in the jail. I'm a bondsman, remember? Comes with the territory."

"I understand," Earl said, and he picked up a visitor's form from his table. He showed Sam the slip. She stared at it and gave a "here we go again" sigh. Earl turned back to Aradano. "Looking at this slip, I see you visited Jake Snyder on May 23rd, about ten days before Officer Horgan was killed."

"Sure, to see if he could scratch together the coin for bail."

"And while you were there he told you about a safe at a certain Chinese restaurant with lots of cash in it, didn't he?"

"Man, I thought I was supposed to be the one who was punch drunk. You must be smokin' somethin.'" Several people laughed, and Aradano grinned.

"It was after visiting Snyder that you called out Mr. Seabrooke, an expert locksmith. Then you posted bail for him, a perfect stranger, free of charge. Is that about it?"

"You got the slip, you figure it out."

"After that, you returned to talk with Snyder," Earl picked up another small form. "You visited Snyder again on June 2nd, the day after Mr. Seabrooke was released."

"A'course. To see if he had the money," Aradano said in a mocking tone. "You got nothin' better to do than read these 'call outs'?"

Earl ignored the jibe. "When you met with Snyder he asked for the contact number for the man you selected for the job, didn't he?"

"I told you. There wasn't no job." He turned to the jury and rolled his eyes.

"You have your file up there. Read us the phone number you have written down for Mr. Seabrooke."

"What's a' matter? You can't read or somethin'?"

"Do us a favor. Your handwriting is a little difficult to decipher."

Aradano heaved a sigh and opened the folder, sullenly turning the pages. "You want me to tell you Seabrooke's number?"

"Please. Just read the telephone number you have for him."

"626-381-8201."

Earl stepped to the counsel table and lifted a notebook that lay open. He looked at the page. "That's funny. That's the same number that was dialed on the cellphone that was left at the restaurant. Except, that's not Seabrooke's number, is it? In fact, it's nobody's. It's a non-working number."

"That's the one he gave me."

"Look again at your scribbling. You sure that's 381 and not 331?"

Aradano studied his writing. "Oh, you're right. I never was no good in school."

"But if you had given what you thought was Seabrooke's home number to Snyder when you visited him, you would have made the same mistake you made when you read it to us the first time. And if Snyder passed it on to someone, it would have been that same wrong number, the one punched into the cellphone left on the floor. Pretty big coincidence, isn't it?"

"Objection," Sam said. "The document speaks for itself. The numbers are the numbers."

"The jury will have the file, along with the other exhibits, in the jury room. They can decide," the judge said. 'We'll take our noon recess."

In the courthouse holding-cells down on the sixth floor, the deputies were passing out baloney sandwiches and apples. Sergeant Tanner walked down the aisle between the cells, careful not to let his suit coat brush against the bars. At the end of the row, in a cell by himself, he found Jake Snyder sitting on the cement bench, grinding his initials into the wall with a paper clip. On his wrist was a red plastic band, labeling him a "keep away." Like all informants, he was transported separately, housed separately, fed separately, all to keep him safely away from the other inmates.

Tanner stood silently watching Snyder as if seeing him for the first time, wondering why anyone would want to record his name in this particular guest book. Snyder sensed his presence. "Sergeant Tanner. Come to wish me luck? Won't need it. I'm gonna do good, you'll see."

Tanner nodded knowingly and curled a finger for Snyder to come to him. Snyder walked over and leaned close, gripping the bars with both hands. Tanner locked eyes with him as he casually reached through the bars and gathered a handful of Snyder's shirt collar in his fist. He pulled Snyder slowly toward him until Snyder's face was squeezed in a vice grip between the bars. Snyder's eyes were wide with fear and bewilderment. "Sergeant Tanner, Jesus please, what'd I do?"

"What did you do?" Tanner said calmly. "Why nothing, Jake. It's what you didn't do."

"Jesus fucking Christ, Sergeant. I didn't do nothin'."

"Oh, but you did, Jake. You had some visitors, didn't you? Visitors you didn't tell me about."

Snyder clamped his eyes shut. "You're killing me Sarge." Tanner released his grip and Snyder staggered back, pressing his hands to his face.

"Listen to me, Jake," Tanner shouted. Snyder dropped his hands and stood breathing hard, staring warily at Tanner.

"Did you have a visit from Crystal Robinson?" Tanner asked angrily.

Snyder froze. "No way. I don't even know the bitch," he pleaded.

Tanner stood silently, working hard to subdue his impulse to crush Snyder's windpipe. What mattered now was the case, he told himself. And not just any case, a cop killing. Sure, Horgan might have got a little bent, but he was still a cop. Fucking civilians had no idea what it did to you to wade through the city's human garbage every day. So bad cop, good cop, whatever, Horgan was one of theirs and nobody gets away with killing a cop. Everyone knew that. That message was what helped keep you alive on the street. It might make some punk hesitate before pulling the trigger; it's what gave you that little extra edge that could mean survival.

Tanner stared at Snyder. The thought that all this hinged on the pathetic creature standing before him made his gut burn, like he had swallowed battery acid. He took a deep breath. "All right," he said in a controlled voice. "You're going on the stand right after lunch. So there's some things you gotta know." Snyder stood straightening his shirt and nodding at Tanner that he understood. Tanner knew that coaching a witness was against the rules, and writing a script for him was called suborning perjury. But losing this case would send a message to the street that maybe you could get away with killing a cop. He could not let that happen.

"People have already testified. They admitted certain things. So don't look like an asshole trying to deny them." Snyder nodded, alert now, his attitude all business. "Crystal said she visited you. Said she was a friend from the old days, wanted to get you straight."

Snyder slowly shook his head in disappointment. "Okay, I got it," he said.

"You told Sergeant Brown about a dirty cop, no names." Snyder opened his mouth to protest. Tanner held up his hand. "Just listen," he said firmly.

"Okay, okay," Snyder said in submission.

"Brown told you no deal, then he arranged for you to use an outside phone line. It was probably to call your family, but you decide." Snyder heaved a frustrated sigh and rolled his eyes. "Concentrate, Jake. You can do this. Aradano said he saw you twice about posting your bail. But you never asked about Seabrooke. Got that?"

"Yeah, yeah," Snyder said thoughtfully.

"This asshole defense lawyer has your visitor slips, so be careful."

"I can do it," Snyder said.

"You better, because if you fuck up this case, as God is my witness, I will personally find the biggest, baddest booty buster in the joint for your cell mate, so every night you can look forward to polishing his Johnson."

After the recess, Sam called Jake Snyder to the witness stand. He was still dressed in jail blues. Sam had made no attempt to sugar-coat who he was - a jail house snitch. It was a nice move, Earl thought. She was being honest with the jury; they would like that. Sam led Snyder straight to his tale of the confession. The jail, he explained, had gotten those bound for court up at 5:00 a.m., as usual, and on a bus, so they arrived hours early at the Torrance court. Snyder just happened to find himself sitting next to Seabrooke on a cement bench in the basement lock-up. They got to talking. Seabrooke was frightened and with a little prodding by Snyder, the confession poured out.

"He said he was there to crack the safe," Snyder recited. "He figured after the weekend there'd be a lot of cash in it."

"So what stopped him?" Sam asked.

"He said this guy showed up. He didn't hear him come in and all of a sudden he was right there. Seabrooke panicked and shot him. He never even knew he was a cop."

"Where did he get the gun?"

"He said he carried it for backup. More for show than anything. It was just a little ol' .22."

"Then what did he do?"

"He said he freaked out and tried to call his wife but he couldn't get through."

"What then?"

"He said he just grabbed what he could of his stuff and ...." Snyder hesitated and looked up at the judge coyly. "I don't know if I'm supposed to use this word?"

"If that was what you heard, you can repeat it," the judge said.

"He said he got the fuck out of there as fast as he could."

"What happened to the gun?"

"He said they'd never find it 'cause he throwed it down a storm drain."

"Now, why do you suppose the defendant told you all that?" Sam asked.

"I got no idea. I guess he was just one scared fella and needed to tell somebody. He kept saying over and over, he didn't know the guy was a cop."

"Have you been promised anything by me or anyone else in the District Attorney's Office for your testimony here today?"

"No ma'am, not a thing."

Sam moved on then to Snyder's criminal record and had him recite all his felony convictions. Earl was not surprised she would bring out the toxic material before Earl could raise it on cross. It made her look honest and took the sting out of learning Snyder was no rookie. It would be old news by the time Earl got to it.

Earl's admiration for Sam's examination turned to concern when she began to lead Snyder through the visitors he had before the homicide. Earl had counted on Snyder staying true to form and lying about them. He looked down the table and gave Tanner a hard stare. The expression on Tanner's face, as if he were trying hard to disappear, confirmed his suspicions.

Snyder answered Sam's questions about his visitors as if they were non-events in his busy social life. Yes, Crystal was an old friend who was always trying to save him. Yes, he had heard something about a dishonest cop and tried to pass the information on to Sergeant Brown, who had been kind enough to let him use a phone to call his family. No, Aradano didn't tell him anything about Seabrooke, but Snyder did try to get Aradano to post his bail.

Sam sat down. Jessup gave her a grudging nod of approval. Snyder had done well and judging by the cocky glint in his eye, he knew it. Snyder's confidence on the stand had steadily grown under Sam's steady questioning. Now he turned to face Earl with all the assurance of an actor answering a curtain call. Earl sat for a minute, not getting to his feet. His mind was racing. This called for a change in strategy.

"Mr. Earl, do you have any questions?" the judge asked.

"A few, your Honor," he said with a smile. "Maybe just a few." He stood at his table, staring down at his papers. There is a tone with each witness that needed to be set with the first note. The proper pitch. Snyder needed to be treated like the creature he was.

"You were telling us about your felony convictions," Earl finally said. "The list of people you robbed at gunpoint. You know, the people who work for a living. Among them were the people at the El Terasco Market, is that right?"

"Sounds right," Snyder said matter-of-factly.

"Where is that market, by the way?"

Snyder's eyes lost focus for a moment. "You know, I don't rightly recollect."

"How many check stands did it have, how many clerks and customers?"

"You know, I wasn't real together back then, so I couldn't really tell you."

"No idea about a place you're supposed to have robbed?"

"Sorry." Snyder shrugged.

"Objection," Sam said. "The facts of the convictions aren't admissible or relevant."

"Sustained," Jefferson said.

"Someone else was originally charged with that robbery, weren't they? In fact, a witness to the robbery had actually identified this other person, isn't that right?"

"Yeah, a kid named Emilio."

"So why did you plead guilty to it?"

"Cause' I did it." Snyder made a face as if the answer were obvious.

"Quite a charitable gesture on your part."

"Well, I met the kid in jail. Nice kid, but a little slow, you know what I mean. Sorta an idgit', really. And soft. No way he was gonna make it in the joint. I felt sorry for him."

"You must have gotten to know him quite well. So you talked, spent time together?"

"Yeah, we hung out, not much else to do in there."

"Then he must have told you about his friend, Deon Hawkins."

"Objection," Sam said. "This is all irrelevant."

"Mr. Earl," the judge said. "I assume you are headed somewhere with this."

"I'm trying, judge."

"Well, step on the gas," Jefferson said.

"Did Emilio tell you about Deon Hawkins?"

"I don't recollect," Snyder said.

"The most important person in his life and you're telling us he never mentioned him?"

Snyder hesitated. "Hawkins, Hawkins. Yeah, I remember now. I think they was butt buddies, if you know what I mean." Snyder grinned slyly.

"So you must have heard about Hawkins' reputation. He is known as a very dangerous man, isn't he?"

"People in jail are always puffing up their feathers. I don't pay no mind to that kind a' talk."

Earl paused a moment, as if in thought. "You know, Mr. Snyder, there's one thing I don't get. With all due respect, you don't strike me as somebody who would take on another felony case, a strike in fact, without getting something for it."

"Objection," Sam said. "That's a statement, not a question. I thought this was supposed to be cross-examination."

"Sustained," Jefferson said.

"Well, let me put it this way. You're getting something for testifying here today, aren't you?"

"You know, I don't really know for sure. I figure my testifying here is the right thing to do, with a cop getting killed and all. But if it helps me down the line, you won't see me complaining."

"Come on, Mr. Snyder. It's not about doing the right thing, now is it? Let's call it by its real name. You're a jailhouse snitch and the only reason you're testifying is to help yourself. When this case is done and it comes time for you to be sentenced, you expect to hear a friendly word to the judge from that side of the table." Earl gestured toward Jessup. "Isn't that right?"

"Look, I heard what I heard. If that lightens my load, I ain't about to jump my traces. But that don't change what I heard none."

"What about Emilio's case? Didn't you get something for riding his beef?"

"What could a kid like Emilio do for me?"

"You may be right about Emilio, but his friend Hawkins is a different matter."

"Man, you sound like them salesmen fellas on TV that keep telling me I gotta get something."

"But you did need something. You had all these cases, all those strikes. You were looking at spending the rest of your life in prison. So you met with Detective Brown and tried to cut a deal in exchange for information about a corrupt cop. But Brown turned you down and said you needed something better than that."

"Yeah, we been over this."

"So, that's where Hawkins comes in, isn't it?"

"Look, I don't know what you're getting at. I never even laid eyes on this Hawkins guy."

"You ever meet a woman named Tareesha Rollins?"

"No, I never did. Where do you come up with all this stuff?"

"That *is* strange, Mr. Snyder, because she came to visit you at the men's Central Jail." Earl picked up a visitor's form and showed it to Sam. He walked over to the witness box and placed it in front of Snyder.

"Yeah, I see it. I must have known her by her street name or something."

Earl stepped back to his table. There was one thing he knew. You could always count on the law of unintended consequences to come into play. You just never knew how. Now he was grateful that Tanner had warned Snyder about the visitor's slips. Snyder's fear of getting caught in a lie just might enable Earl to pull this off. Earl reached down and picked up another visitation form, except this was one he had written himself during the lunch recess. He studied the bogus form, then turned back to Snyder.

"In fact, Emilio had a visit from Mr. Hawkins at the very same time as your visit with Tareesha Rollins, didn't he?" Earl held up the form as if it were proof, as irrefutable as simple arithmetic.

Snyder stared hard at Earl before speaking. "I think, one day, Emilio and me did have a visit at the same time."

"It's something you would remember because according to that slip," Earl pointed to the form on the witness stand, "you and Emilio sat next to each other during your visits." Earl locked eyes with Snyder, not letting him look away, as if challenging him to dare disagree.

"Yeah, I remember something like that."

Earl quietly took a deep breath, then slowly exhaled. He tucked the bogus form out of sight under a notebook. Snyder had fallen for it. He had him in a box. Now it was time to slow down and polish the trap door so the jury would see it coming.

Earl walked up to the witness stand and showed Snyder the booking photo of Hawkins. "This is the man who was visiting Emilio, isn't it?"

"Looks sorta like him. But I wasn't paying no attention."

"You've been to the jail visiting room enough to help us get an idea of what it's like. It's a large room, correct? Lots of people, lots of noise? Kids running around. People coming in and going out. Getting up and sitting down."

"Yeah, it's a zoo."

"You sit side by side on fixed stools, with inmates and visitors separated by Plexiglas, speaking to each other through phones."

"Right, no contact visits."

"You're not supposed to switch seats and visit somebody else, are you? But the deputies can't watch everybody, right? So it happens."

"I suppose."

"So if Hawkins brought this Rollins woman to act as your visitor when he was visiting Emilio, then switched seats with her, you two could have had a cozy little chat."

Sam jumped to her feet. "Objection, this is pure conjecture."

"Your Honor," Earl said. "I'm merely asking Mr. Snyder as an expert on the procedures in the visiting room for his opinion."

"That is certainly a novel approach," Jefferson said. "But given his record, he probably is an expert, so I'll permit it." He turned to Snyder. "You can answer."

"You'd get hammered if they caught you switching," Snyder said.

"But it's possible."

"Yeah, but what you're forgetting is them deputies listen in on the phones. So why go to all that bother? You can't say nothin' private."

"You could write on a piece of paper and hold it up to the glass, couldn't you? Between that and a few words, I would imagine you could get a lot said, don't you think?"

"How do I know? I ain't never done that."

"So you say, Mr. Snyder. So you say. I have nothing further."

Sam jumped to her feet and led Snyder through a recital of denials, No, he had no involvement with Hawkins. No, nobody promised him a deal in exchange for his testimony. Snyder concluded with a repeat performance of Seabrooke's confession, and Sam returned to her seat.

Jessup stood up. He buttoned his coat and solemnly announced, "The People rest, your Honor."

The judge turned to the jury. "That concludes the People's case. I am going to consult with counsel at the side bar about scheduling, so you can talk among yourselves, if you wish."

At the bench, the judge asked Earl if he intended to put on a defense. "I've only got one witness, judge. Detective Duncan, to impeach Snyder on the robbery case that Hawkins' friend, Emilio Chavez, was originally charged with, but that Snyder eventually pled to. I don't think Snyder committed that robbery, but pled to it in order to get something from Hawkins."

"We object, your Honor," Jessup said. "He's not on the witness list. Besides this is all irrelevant, a sideshow. I feel like I'm watching *Law and Order*."

"Judge, I didn't know that Snyder would admit meeting with Hawkins until today," Earl said.

"It's a stretch, but I'll allow it. After the detective, you intend to rest?"

"Yes, your Honor."

"What," Jessup said facetiously to Earl. "We don't get to hear a fairy tale from your client?"

"We've already heard enough fairy tales for one day, don't you think?"

"All right, gentlemen," the judge said. "We'll take the defense witness tomorrow morning, then move right into final arguments. See you tomorrow."

Earl returned to his chair. Exhaustion swept over him. Even the realization that the trial was nearing its end was no relief; it just meant a verdict was coming. He watched the jury as they retreated into the jury room only to scurry out with their coats and the empty bags they used to haul provisions into their little "club room." The bailiff had told him they appeared to be anticipating a long haul, because they were outfitting it with a coffee maker, sodas and enough pastries for a county fair bakeoff. They walked out, chatting like old friends. Earl studied their faces. Togetherness was not exactly what you wanted to see if you were looking for the contentiousness that might produce a hung jury. Earl wondered if they had followed any of his cross-examination. Were they still listening, or had they already made up their minds?

A quiet fell over the empty courtroom. The clerk went back into the judge's chambers carrying an armful of files. At his desk, the bailiff was filling out his paperwork, letting Earl have a minute with his client. Earl turned to Seabrooke, who was staring into the distance, grave-faced, thinking. In a tired voice, Earl explained that the DAs had finished their case, and tomorrow he would call an LAPD detective as their only witness.

Seabrooke did not respond, continuing to stare off as if he had not heard. Slowly he turned to face Earl. "I want to testify," he said.

Earl slowly drew in a deep breath, thinking this was one thing he didn't need right now. He tried to keep the irritation out of his voice. "Sydney, we've been over this. That is not a good idea."

"That's your opinion. This is my life. I have a right to testify, and that's what I want to do. I don't need your permission."

"You're right, Sydney," Earl said, tight-lipped. "You don't. It's your right. So let's go back in the lock-up and discuss this."

The bailiff placed Seabrooke in the court's holding cell, then slid a plastic chair across the cement floor to Earl as he closed the courtroom door behind himself. Earl placed the chair next to the cell bars so when Seabrooke sat on the cement bench inside they would be at eye level. Seabrooke sat down, but he refused to look at Earl, choosing to lean forward and stare at the floor, lips clamped shut in defiance.

"Sydney, I know you're scared. Believe me, I understand. And I know it's frustrating having to sit there, not able to say anything in your own defense." Earl paused. "Look, right now the jury probably figures you're the one who broke in there and that you tried to crack the safe. Okay, we can live with that. But there's a chance they might also believe you got scared off when Horgan arrived, and you fled. The last thing we need is for you to get up there and tell them you were actually there when Horgan was shot, but you didn't do it. Some mystery man did it."

"That's not what I'm going to say." Seabrooke continued to stare at the floor.

"What are you talking about?" Earl asked.

Seabrooke sat up straight and turned to face Earl. "I'm going to testify that when I heard Horgan at the front door, I ran out the back. I waited out front for him to leave so I could go back in and finish the job. While I was hiding out there, I saw a man enter and heard several gunshots. So I panicked and went home."

Earl stared at him. "But that's not true, Sydney."

"So what? Everyone else is lying."

"That may be so. But I can't let you do that."

"What have you got to do with it?"

"It's perjury. I can't be a party to that."

"Oh, please," Seabrooke mocked. "You represent people you know are guilty and you try to get them off. Who are you kidding?"

Earl sat thinking. How could he explain this to Seabrooke? If a client told Earl a story that was about as convincing as a fairy tale, insisting it was the gospel, that was one thing. If that client refused to follow Earl's advice and insisted on telling the jury this bedtime story, that was his decision. Earl's job was to be his lawyer, not his judge. It was for the jury to determine if he was "testilying." But if a client told him he was planning to lie when he testified, that was different. For Earl to go along with that made him a part of it. As much as he wanted to win, there was a line he wouldn't cross. It was like stealing the catcher's signs in baseball. If your teammate got on second base and could see how the catcher signaled for a particular pitch, that was baseball. If you put a guy in the center field stands with binoculars, that was cheating.

"Sydney, listen to me. I won't do that."

Seabrooke gripped the cell bars in both fists, his face flushed with anger. "I have a right to testify. You can't stop me. Why are you being like this?"

"Calm down, Sydney. You're right. You can get on the witness stand."

"Thank you," Seabrooke said and sagged back against the cement wall, as if drained by this battle of wills.

"But that doesn't mean I have to help you. I will tell the judge you want to testify, but that I won't be asking you any questions. So you can sit up there and tell your story, but I won't be saying anything." Seabrooke looked at him in dismay. "So what do you think the jury will make of that?" Earl asked calmly.

"You know damn well what they will think. You might as well tell them I'm lying. You can't do that."

"Not only can I, but believe me, I will."

"But I didn't do this. I did not kill that man. You're supposed to help me." He leaned forward and put his face in his hands. "I don't believe this."

"I *am* trying to help you. If you only knew how much I'm trying to help you."

CHAPTER 28

After Earl left the courthouse, he drove the surface streets through downtown, stopping several times to backtrack, making certain he wasn't followed. After Hawkins' social call he was taking no chances. First he needed to finish the case, then he would deal with Hawkins. He called Munoz on his cellphone to make certain that Detective Duncan would be in court tomorrow morning. Maybe through Duncan, he could slip in Hawkins' reputation.

After circling the block, he pulled into the parking lot at Jimmy's Diner. He walked inside, then he settled in a back booth. He lifted the notebooks from his briefcase, lined them up and reached for a new legal pad of yellow paper. Then he called the vet. Henceforth was doing fine. Millie brought him a cup of coffee and left without speaking. She was used to Earl's routine. The Diner was where he constructed all his final arguments. Somehow it helped to have life around him.

Over the next three hours he filled page after handwritten page with the outline of his argument. He always kept the pad on the podium during his argument, but he rarely referred to it. To Earl, reading from notes distanced you from your own words, as if you were disavowing any emotional investment in them. Such an argument never sounded heartfelt. He wanted the jury to know he was laying it out there, that he was taking this personally and they had better as well.

He looked at his notes. He was pushing all his chips in on this one. He was stepping outside his role and asking the jury to trust him. It was the only chance.

By the time he reached his motel it was nearly midnight. He had deliberately selected one in a seedy neighborhood. Stepping from his car, he could hear the motel's red neon sign sputtering. Some of the tubes had burned out and it now advertised the anonymity of a "notel." A lone hooker, in a dress the size of a postage stamp, stood at the bus stop. She cocked a hip and gave Earl the eye. "Not tonight," he called with a smile. He locked his briefcase in the trunk. He was tired and needed to sleep.

He climbed the stairs to the walkway that ran along the second story carrying a change of clothes in his left hand and Munoz's holstered gun in the other. At the door to his room, he clamped the gun under his left arm and put the key in the lock. He slowly pushed open the door. He felt certain he had not been followed, but he wasn't about to bet his life on it. The light from the street spilled through the open door onto the stained carpet. Something moved in the shadows. Earl flung himself onto the floor as a shot thundered in the small room. His gun was jarred free and disappeared in a tangle of clothes.

Earl scrambled back onto the walkway. He sprang to his feet and sprinted for the stairs. Another shot exploded behind him. A bullet ripped into the stucco wall beside him, gouging a path until it shattered a window. He bounded down the staircase, two steps at a time, and leaped for the landing below. He crumpled on impact and somersaulted up against the railing. There was a stabbing pain in his right ankle. He hobbled down the next flight of stairs, frantic at the slow pace. When he reached the pavement, he pressed his back up against the building and listened. Above, he could hear running footsteps pounding down the walkway, heading his way. It was Hawkins, it had to be. But whoever it was, one thing was clear. Someone was trying to kill him. The thought was chilling. His mind felt frozen with fear. He had to get out of here, but where?

To his right, he saw an alley that ran behind the motel, and he limped toward it. Each step sent a jolt of pain up his leg. He reached the corner of the building and ducked around it. A shot tore off a chunk of the corner. Again he could hear running footsteps. Frantically he looked up and down the alley for somewhere to hide. Across the alley was an open door, hung with a curtain. There was a light from inside. He heaved himself off the back wall and propelled himself toward the doorway. The narrow alley suddenly seemed impossibly wide. It was taking forever to cross. At last he reached the doorway and plunged through the curtain. The cement floor inside was wet and slick and his leather soles started to slide. His feet went out from under him and he landed hard on his back. A shot tore through the curtain and rattled off the cooking pots hanging from the ceiling above him. He was in the kitchen of a restaurant.

He scrambled to right himself. But his right ankle buckled and he fell forward onto the floor. Looking up, he saw a young Chicano holding a mop, his eyes wide with astonishment. "Shut the door!" Earl shouted. "Shut the door." The boy didn't move, as frozen as a statue. "*Cuerra la puerta. El hombre afuera nos matera.*" The boy leaped forward, slamming the metal door shut. Something solid rammed into it. Earl lay on the wet floor, breathing hard. A distant police siren was growing louder. He closed his eyes and laid his cheek against the cold wet cement, glad to taste the soapy water, glad to be alive.

Earl sat at the counsel table. His eyes burned from lack of sleep, and his head was throbbing. Last night he had sat through a series of police interviews. He never mentioned Hawkins. After raising his name in court that day, it would have sounded contrived. After answering the detectives' questions with a mantra of "I don't know," he limped to a drugstore for tape and aspirin. He had spent enough time in athletic training rooms to know how to tape up his ankle, and that would have to do for now. In the night's last remaining hours, back in the motel room, he had tried to sleep, but he had only shifted from one position to another in search of relief from the pain. Medication was not an option, he needed a clear head.

The courtroom was filling up. There was a buzz of excitement in the din of conversation. Jessup and Sam stood at the rail, chatting with a cheering section of DAs in the front row. Behind them was a group of Public Defenders who had come to hear Earl's final argument. George Kennedy's pale raspberry suit stood out among the somber grey of his colleagues. He flashed Earl a thumbs up. A few private defense lawyers were scattered about, pretending they were not there to learn from Earl, but just for diversion. The press was poised on the end of each aisle, positioned to get out quickly. The cops were in the back, all dressed in their 'civies,' drilling Earl and Seabrooke with looks of contempt.

Munoz caught his eye and nodded. Late last night, Earl had called him again to make sure his witness would appear and ended up telling him what happened. Manny had insisted on driving him to court, and Earl suspected he had spent the night in the motel parking lot, watching his room. When they arrived this morning, Manny stowed his service revolver in the glove compartment. Court security frowned on people packing handguns, but judging from the look in Manny's eyes, he didn't need one.

Earl turned to the front of the courtroom and shut his eyes. He needed to control his emotions. He was angry, very angry. It was not just about what had happened. Certainly it had been scary, terrifying in fact, that someone had actually tried to kill him. It enraged him that someone had just arbitrarily decided his life should end. But it was doubly galling because it had happened the night before his final argument. There were no "redo's" for final arguments. This was the only time he would get to talk to the jury, really talk to them and try to persuade them. The one chance he had to speak for Seabrooke. He had to be at his best. He owed Seabrooke that, he owed himself that. He did not want to look back on this case and feel that he had not given his all to defend an innocent man. He could not let last night distract him, derail his concentration. He shut his eyes tighter and willed himself to retreat into that place inside where he shut out the world, the core where he was alone, where he felt strong. He must focus, that would be his revenge.

When the judge took the bench, Earl called Detective Duncan as his witness. He quickly established that Duncan had been the investigator on the robbery with which Emilio Chavez had originally been charged. The robbery Snyder was now claiming was his. When Jessup objected, Earl explained that he was calling Duncan to impeach Snyder, to prove he had lied about committing that robbery. What Earl really wanted was to slip in Duncan's opinion of Deon Hawkins.

It proved surprisingly easy to draw Duncan out about Hawkins, almost as if he had been waiting for this chance to tell people. There was none of the normal amnesia that officers suffer when summoned to assist the defense. With every question about the robbery at the El Terasco Market and the witness who changed her mind, Duncan would veer off on a tangent about Hawkins. Duncan spoke with conviction about Hawkins' reputation as a dangerous and violent man, a predator whom even seasoned officers feared. Duncan identified a mug shot of Hawkins in which he looked like everyone's worse nightmare. Jessup kept popping up objecting to the testimony, trying to signal to Duncan that he was hurting the prosecution, but like a runaway train he hurtled right through the warning lights. Duncan's frustration over Hawkins' continued presence on "his streets" came pouring out in the form of anecdotes and rumors, all of which the judge instructed the jury to ignore, as if it were possible to un-ring a bell. With a sidelong glance at the jury, Earl could tell they had heard enough. None of them would be inviting Hawkins home to dinner any time soon. Earl sat down and Jessup passed on cross-examination. The judge announced a short recess.

When they resumed, the judge invited Jessup to address the jury. In a dry, businesslike manner, Jessup explained the law to them. He put up a power-point point presentation on the portable TV screen that listed the legal requirements of burglary and the next, those for felony murder. Pointing to the screen, he explained how any killing during the course of a burglary was automatically first degree murder and qualified for the death penalty. After this short course on the law, he moved on to the circumstances that tied Seabrooke to the crime. A new image on the screen itemized Seabrooke's tool, the cellphone call and, of course, the confession. Jessup did not apologize for Snyder, but joined the jury in their presumed discomfort over relying on someone of Snyder's character for a decision like this. He told them that, luckily, the truth of the confession did not rest on Snyder's word alone, but rather in the details of the story. Details, he emphasized, that only the murderer could know.

Jessup sat down without a concluding emotional flourish, no call for Horgan to be avenged, no plea to protect society. There would be time for that. The rules allowed Jessup a second argument after Earl had finished. One to which Earl could not reply. Jessup had the ultimate final word.

"We'll take a short recess," the judge said. "Then we'll hear from the defense." Earl stayed in his seat when Davis, the bailiff, put Seabrooke back in the lock-up. Seabrooke no longer asked questions or showed much interest in the proceedings. The pressure was taking its toll. It had reduced him to a fixture, a piece of furniture that merely needed to be in its place for the trial to go on.

Tanner was suddenly standing over Earl. "I heard you had a little trouble last night," he said.

"A bit," Earl replied, not looking at him.

"I can't imagine who would be pissed at a guy like you," Tanner said with a bemused smile. "Like they say, must be some kinda Karma."

Earl looked up at him. "What's this, a little pregame trash talking? Save it, you're not very good at it." He swiveled his chair to look out at the onlookers, ignoring Tanner who returned to his seat. Earl noticed that the police officers in the audience had left their seats in the back and assembled on the front benches on his side of the room. Earl was familiar with this prosecution tactic where supporters were placed in the jury's sight line behind the defense lawyer. During final argument, when the jury looked at Earl, they would also be staring into the faces of the cops. From that position, the officers could give a soundless response to Earl's argument by making animated facial expressions of derision and disbelief. By registering this disapproval, like a negative applause meter, they hoped to at least distract the jurors, if not influence their reaction to Earl's words.

When Judge Jefferson returned, before the jury was brought in, Earl expressed his concern about the audience. Jefferson's steely gaze swept over the room. "This is a court of law," he said firmly. "This is not *American Idol*. There is no audience participation. The basis of the rule of law is that decisions such as this are insulated from outside influences." He searched the room for any sign of dissent. "What's more, this is my courtroom. And I will not tolerate it. If I detect the slightest display of approval or disapproval for either side during these arguments, that person will promptly find themselves a guest of the county." Jefferson turned to his bailiff. "Mr. Davis, you be my second set of eyes."

Davis put his hands on his hips and surveyed the audience. "Yes sir, your Honor."

"Now, bring in the jury, Mr. Davis, and we'll proceed with the arguments."

The jury filed in, and the judge nodded at Earl to begin. Earl walked with a firm step over to the jury rail, consciously ignoring the pain in his ankle. He stood silently looking at one face and then the next. "Mr. Seabrooke is a thief," he said matter-of-factly. "He broke into that restaurant in order to open that safe and steal its contents. You should find him guilty of burglary." The collective intake of breath was almost audible. Several jurors snuck a wide-eyed glance at their companions.

"But that doesn't make him a murderer," Earl continued. "In fact, I hope to show you that he is totally innocent of that crime." Behind him, he could hear benches creaking as people stirred in the audience. "By telling you this, Mr. Seabrooke and I are putting our trust in you. Trusting that you remember you are judges, and as judges must apply the law wherever it leads you. That you will obey your oaths and apply the protections of those laws to whoever sits before you.

"So let's talk about those laws and then we'll talk about the facts. The facts that show Mr. Seabrooke is innocent of the murder of Officer Horgan." Earl stepped over to the blackboard where he had hung several poster-size blow-ups of certain jury instructions. Flipping over each page for the jury to read, he explained the language and meaning of the Law of Reasonable Doubt, the Presumption of Innocence and the Prosecutor's Burden of Proof. He paused when he reached the instruction labeled Circumstantial Evidence. "This is a case that rests on circumstantial evidence, that is, the type of facts which require you to interpret what they prove. Facts which might mean different things, lead you to different conclusions. For example, if a fire alarm goes off at school, it could mean there's really a fire. Then again, it could be a routine fire drill. Or maybe it's just some kids playing a prank. Because there are different ways to look at this type of evidence, it is subject to a special law. That law says if there are two reasonable interpretations of this type of evidence, one that points to innocence and one to guilt, you are required to adopt the one that points to innocence. That is the law." He paused as if acknowledging a consensus. "So let's look at those facts the prosecutor put on his board, the ones he says can only be explained by Mr. Seabrooke's guilt. Because if there is another way to look at those facts, another reasonable explanation that indicates he is innocent, the law says you must find Mr. Seabrooke not guilty. Let me show you that way.

"First, let me tell you a story, because I think it has some application here. When I was growing up, my uncle had a pack of hound dogs he used for hunting. I was ten years old when he gave me my first dog, a puppy. The only condition was that I had to go hunting with him. One night we drove out to the forest in his pickup with his dogs in the back. The leader of the pack was an old female named Maggie. As leader, it was her job to keep the others together and following the scent of the animal they were supposed to track. That night my uncle set them on the trail of a raccoon and off they went, baying and barking excitedly with old Maggie in the lead.

"We built a fire and sat under the stars listening to the dogs, as my uncle explained to me by the sound of their calls, what they were doing. Finally he said they had something treed. So we tramped through the woods until we found them. The dogs had split into two groups, each barking at the base of a different tree. My uncle looked at me and asked which of the trees I thought held the raccoon. In one of the groups I spotted old Maggie, barking furiously and jumping up at the trunk of the tree. Thinking she was the leader and the smartest, I said the raccoon had to be in her tree.

"My uncle laughed. He walked over to the other tree, shouldered his rifle and shot at something high up in the branches. A very angry, very ferocious raccoon fell to the ground, where he slashed and bit the dogs as they attacked him. It was a brutal, ugly sight that made me vow never again to go hunting.

"As the fight was concluding, old Maggie came trotting over to the melee, looking sheepishly at my uncle as she passed, pretending she had just made a mistake. But that wasn't it at all. Maggie was smart. She knew exactly what was going to happen when that wounded raccoon came crashing out of the tree, and she didn't want to get hurt. It was just too dangerous. She was 'barking up the wrong tree.'

"Let's set aside our aversion to this bloody business and see if, at least, there is something useful we can take away from it. I think there are two lessons to be learned. Lessons which, I think, apply to our case. First, it is very easy to draw the wrong conclusion from circumstantial evidence. The kind of mistake I made, thinking that if Maggie was there the raccoon must be in that tree. And second, that sometimes the truth is too dangerous or frightening to face, so some will choose to ignore it, just like Maggie did. It is just easier, less messy, to draw the wrong conclusion sometimes. I think that is exactly what happened here. The prosecution is barking up the wrong tree. Now, let me show you why.

"Our story starts when Crystal Robinson is charged with selling drugs. Along comes Officer Horgan. He is on loan to a Federal drug task force and arranges for her case to be dismissed. In exchange, she agrees to work for him as an informant. Not a bad job really, because in the Federal system informants get paid, quite handsomely. They get a share of the spoils. And Officer Horgan was the one who decided how much of the drug money recovered went to the informant. Some of the busts they made were quite big. A lot of cash was recovered. This should have resulted in a pretty good pay day for Crystal, except she told us she didn't get her money. Where that money ended up seems fairly obvious; it was sitting in Horgan's safe, the one she told us about. Horgan was just going to keep it."

"Objection," Jessup shouted. "There is no evidence of that."

"This is final argument, your Honor," Earl said. "The prosecution is asking the jury to draw inferences from the evidence. I'm entitled to do the same for the defense."

Jefferson looked down at his notes of the trial testimony, turning several pages of a yellow legal pad. Finally, he looked up. "Overruled," he said. Jessup plopped back into his seat and turned to Tanner with an exasperated look.

"When Crystal finds out Horgan is being transferred," Earl continued, "she realizes he won't need her anymore, not as an informant or as a girlfriend. So she goes to see her old friend Jake Snyder, thinking maybe he can help her. She tells him about Horgan and his scam to keep her money. That's where the story about the corrupt cop came from, the one Snyder would try to sell to Sergeant Brown. Crystal wanted that money in the safe and she wanted to get back at Horgan for walking away. Did she want him dead? I don't think so.

"Now, to understand what happened next, we need to understand Jake Snyder. Jake is a snitch. He is concerned about one thing and one thing only. Jake Snyder. So he goes to Sergeant Brown and tries to trade Crystal and Horgan for his freedom. But, no sale. Brown tells him he needs something bigger. Remember that. Something bigger. Snyder contacts Aradano, the bondsman, who visits him in jail. He tells Aradano he knows about this restaurant safe that has a lot of money. They work out a split. It's doubtful he even mentions Horgan. Now they need somebody who can get into the safe. Aradano calls out Mr. Seabrooke, a known safe-cracker. In exchange for Mr. Seabrooke doing a little job for him, Aradano posts Seabrooke's bail for free."

Jessup leaped to his feet. "Objection," he cried. "This is pure fantasy."

"Just state your objection, Mr. Jessup," the judge said. "I don't need a speech."

"No foundation. Arguing facts not in evidence," Jessup sputtered.

"It's a fair inference, your Honor, from the fact that Aradano posted bail for a complete stranger, without collateral or a premium, who just happened to be an expert locksmith," Earl said.

"Overruled," the judge said to Jessup. "You can reply in rebuttal."

"In the process of posting his bail, Aradano gets Mr. Seabrooke's contact information. Aradano returns to Snyder, who wants to know who Aradano has lined up for the job and how he can be contacted. Snyder probably tells him he wants the phone number so he can warn Seabrooke not to try and hold out on the take. Aradano reads him Seabrooke's phone number, the same way he read it on the witness stand. Incorrectly. Even Aradano can't read his own handwriting. The mistaken number he read off is the same number that ends up on that cellphone at the restaurant.

"To complete his plan, Snyder needed something more. That is why he befriended Emilio Chavez. Emilio has this friend, Deon Hawkins. You heard Detective Duncan tell you about Hawkins and his particular talents. Snyder and Hawkins meet in the jail visitor's room by switching seats when Hawkins visits Emilio and brings a visitor for Snyder. Snyder has a proposition for Hawkins. He wants him to kill a Los Angeles police officer. In exchange, Snyder will take on Emilio's case and Emilio walks free."

"Objection," Jessup shouted. "Judge, this isn't an argument, it's a fairy tale."

"Mr. Jessup," Jefferson said. "I warned you. State the legal grounds for your objection."

"Assuming facts not in evidence."

"Overruled," Jefferson snapped.

"Killing a cop, even for a man like Hawkins, is asking a lot," Earl continued. "It's way too risky. Unless, of course, there is a way to make it look like someone else did it. And Snyder has that all figured out. This is where Mr. Seabrooke comes in. Not only can they use him to get the money, they can also pin the murder on him. It seemed so easy. Mr. Seabrooke would crack the safe and leave with their money. Later, Horgan would arrive. Then Hawkins would show up to take care of Horgan and plant a cellphone with a call on it to Seabrooke's house. They would get the phone number from Aradano, the bondsman; he just misread his own handwriting. The plan was to make it look like Horgan had surprised Seabrooke. They never counted on Seabrooke leaving one of his tools behind. That was a bonus for them.

"Now all they needed to do was lure Officer Horgan to that restaurant. That was Crystal's part. We don't know what reason Snyder gave her for the need to have Horgan there. Maybe he told her they would force him to open the safe, I don't know. Whatever it was, she fell for it. She called Horgan that night, just like she told us. But it wasn't about any argument. All she would have needed to do was threaten to expose him unless he met her at the restaurant and gave her the money. So he went there and left the door open for her. What he planned to do about Crystal and her threats when they met, we'll never know.

"After Hawkins committed his bloody deed, only one thing was left to do. The final piece in Snyder's plan, the reason Snyder orchestrated this crime, the reason Officer Horgan is dead. Remember what Snyder was told, what he needed to trade." Earl's gaze swept over each juror. "He needed *something bigger*. Something bigger than just snitching off a corrupt cop. Big enough to buy his way out of a life sentence. And what could be bigger than getting a confession that convicts a cop killer? That's why Snyder asked Sergeant Brown for access to a private outside phone line. Remember that Mr. Seabrooke wasn't scheduled to be in that lock-up in Torrance. Snyder was. Mr. Seabrooke was there because of some supposed clerical error. Is there any doubt who arranged that? Any doubt what Snyder could do with a few unmonitored phone calls?"

Jessup heaved an audible sigh and rolled his eyes at the jury. Tanner sat staring ahead, deep in thought. Sam was scribbling notes for Jessup to use in his rebuttal.

"Just being in the same room with Mr. Seabrooke was all he needed. Making up a confession was child's play to someone like Jake Snyder. He already knew about the planted cellphone and the phony call home and he could get any other details he needed from Hawkins through Emilio, or over that outside phone line. He got his something bigger, and now he'll get his payoff." Earl paused and searched the faces of the jurors. "You should remember old Maggie, my uncle's dog, and how we can be misled by certain facts. Remember how easy it is to draw the wrong conclusion. You don't want to make a mistake, not in this case. Not with a man's life at stake.

"But I promised you a second lesson from my dog story, the one where drawing certain conclusions may appear so frightening or dangerous that some people refuse to consider them. That some truths are so disturbing that people choose to ignore them. So what is this dangerous truth? It has to do with the strange marriage between jailhouse informants and prosecutors. True, it is a loveless marriage. Prosecutors don't much like snitches, and I'm sure they would prefer not to use them. But they have fallen into this symbiotic relationship in which they need each other. Snitches make things easy, they provide prosecutors with confessions and convictions. Prosecutors allow snitches to avoid paying for their crimes. Now, in many cases these jailhouse confessions are probably true. Snitches are very cunning and quite adept at manipulating people. So in those cases, justice is served. It just smells a little funny. In the cases where snitches just invent confessions, well, that's for the jury to sort out. Prosecutors have come to live with this arrangement as a necessary evil.

"So where is the terrible truth I mentioned? It's right here. It's this case. Not the fact that Snyder made up a confession, you can figure that one out. It's that he *engineered* a crime just so he could *create* a confession. Snyder had nothing against Horgan. They were complete strangers. The only reason he had Horgan murdered was so he would have something worth selling. That's what is so dangerous. If you were the police or the prosecution, would you want to face the possibility that you had created such a nightmare, a system that not only did not suppress crime, but actually created it? No wonder they're afraid of the truth, it's too dangerous. It's safer to bark up the wrong tree."

CHAPTER 29

Earl sat on a bench outside the courtroom, leaning forward, elbows on knees, staring down at the marble floor. It had been four days since the trial had concluded. Since then, the jurors had been deliberating, closeted each day in the jury room. Just before noon on each of those days, Earl had stationed himself in the hallway, so the jurors would see him when they passed by on their way to lunch. A vigil he kept to remind them of his personal commitment. Today, as always, they walked by without making eye contact. Earl told himself not to worry, some juries were like that. But it was hard not to worry.

When the elevator doors closed behind the jurors, he removed a file from his briefcase marked "Penalty." It was thin. He needed to be ready for the next phase, just in case. If Seabrooke was convicted, the jury would be asked to make the grim choice of putting him to death or sentencing him to life in prison without the possibility of parole. It was difficult for Earl to concentrate. Without a verdict, his mind would not accept that the trial was over.

The hallway was empty. Then the elevator doors opened and he heard footsteps on the marble floor. He glanced up. Sam was walking toward him, her face showing the strain of waiting for a verdict. She sat down beside Earl without speaking. They sat in silence, both leaning back against the wall, staring ahead.

"I hate this waiting," she said at last.

"It's always the worst," he replied.

"You gave a good argument," she said.

"We'll see."

"You got one person thinking, anyway."

Earl turned to look at her. "Who's that?"

"Tanner, of all people."

"You're kidding? I knew he was a smart guy."

She gave him a skeptical glance. "That's sort of why I'm here. I've got an offer."

"I gather Jessup couldn't stomach talking to me."

"This comes from the top. Plead to a first degree murder and life without parole and we'll drop the death penalty."

"I'll convey the offer to my client, but the answer is no."

"I told them you would say that. So here's our bottom line. A straight first degree murder with parole."

"That's a generous offer on a cop killing, but we both know he'll never be paroled. Sam, I wasn't just playacting in there. I don't think this guy is good for it."

"I know," she said. "I also told them you'd say that." She sighed and stood up. "Maybe you'll get lucky." She turned and walked off down the hall.

In the lockup, Seabrooke confirmed what Earl already knew; he not interested in spending the rest of his life in a cage. Three hours later Earl received a call in the lawyers lounge. "Mr. Earl, this is the clerk in Department 102. The jury has a verdict." He limped for the elevator and pounded on the call button. He kept telling his brain to shut down, just move, don't think. Everything around him seemed out of focus, as if he couldn't see clearly. In the courtroom, he went into the lock-up to tell Seabrooke, then back out to sit at the counsel table. Suddenly he was exhausted, totally drained. The wait for everyone to assemble seemed endless. First they waited on Jessup to gather his entourage, then for the press to get there. The whole time he felt like there was an anvil sitting on his chest. He resented that he and Seabrooke were forced to wait like this, it seemed callous and cruel. He couldn't even begin to imagine what Seabrooke was feeling.

At last, Judge Jefferson took the bench, and Seabrooke was brought out as the jury started to file in. Earl studied their faces for some indication of their decision. Nothing. It was as if they had all agreed to wear expressionless masks. How cold that seemed. He would have thought that at least one would have had the decency to give him some kind of sign.

"Madam Foreperson," Jefferson said. "Have you reached a verdict?"

A heavyset woman stood up. It was juror Number 3, the one Earl had never been able to read. "We have, your Honor," she said, and handed the verdict to the bailiff. Jefferson studied it and passed it to the clerk to read.

"In the case of the People of the State of California versus Sydney Seabrooke, we the jury find him guilty of Count One, burglary." The clerk turned to the jurors. "Is this your verdict? So say you one, so say you all?"

"Yes," they answered in unison.

"And have you reached a verdict on Count Two, the murder charge?" Jefferson asked.

"No, your Honor. We are deadlocked."

"Without telling me whether it is for innocence or guilt, how does the count stand?"

"Eight to four."

"And do you think further deliberation might produce a verdict?"

The forewoman looked at her fellow jurors, most of whom slowly shook their heads. "I really don't think so. We're all pretty well dug in by now."

"All right, I will declare a mistrial on Count Two."

Jefferson went on to thank the jurors for their service, but Earl was numb, he couldn't listen. A mistrial meant the DA could try Seabrooke again. But that was for another day. Right now the realization was sinking in. He had done it. He had saved an innocent man. He reached out and put an arm around Seabrooke's shoulders. Seabrooke was trembling. Tears were running down his cheeks.

Earl pulled his car into the parking space behind his office. It had been two weeks since the jury deadlocked on Seabrooke. He had immersed himself in the trial, just as he did each time he faced a jury. All his thoughts, all his efforts, had been concentrated into a single-minded focus on winning the case. Everything else, including his other clients, had to take a back seat. To have allowed himself to be diverted by investing energy in anything besides this trial would have felt like cheating – as if he were robbing Seabrooke of his full effort. When he took a case, he took on a responsibility not just to the client, but to himself. In the end he had to be able to say to himself that he had given his all.

When he resurfaced after the verdict, his mind shifted to a more basic problem. Survival. Hawkins was still out there. Even though the trial was over, their scheme had been exposed, so the danger was not past. Hawkins might feel he owed Earl something. And it would not be hearty congratulations. Earl did not want to spend his days looking over his shoulder. He had to figure something out. A little self-help might be in order.

Back at the office, things had piled up. Martha had patiently waited during the trial, but no longer. Demands were made to restore order. So he set off to reassure clients by promising them the same focused attention when their turn came, placating judges by telling them he would get to his cases on their calendars, holding off prosecutors anxious to close cases. But the whole time his mind was elsewhere. What did Cavalli intend to do about Seabrooke? A deal? A retrial? What?

Today, when he walked inside the office, Martha met him with a silent stare, her lips clamped tight in concern. She extended her arm holding a phone message. Bob Bishop, Head of Trials, wanted to see him. It could mean only one thing. They wanted to talk. Let the bargaining begin.

Bob Bishop's office was as unassuming as its occupant. No framed commendations on the walls, no honorary Sheriff's badges perched on the desk, no photographs with smiling police chiefs. Just a bookcase stuffed with law books and a county issue desk piled with files and correspondence.

After shaking hands, Bishop dropped back into his chair. Earl liked Bishop, even respected him. Bishop had spent his career as a trial lawyer and a good one at that. He had a reputation as a hard-nosed prosecutor, but one who could step back and evaluate a case. He knew the pluses and minuses that calculated the odds on a case in front of a jury. Most importantly, he was someone whose word could be trusted.

"So where's Jessup?" Earl asked as he sat down across the desk.

Bishop gave him a bemused smile. "He won't be joining us."

"You're kidding? You bounced him?"

Bishop scrunched up his face in disapproval of Earl's characterization. "Let's say we thought a single prosecutor would give the case more focus."

"So who comes out of the bullpen?"

Bishop paused, holding Earl's attention. "Nobody," he said.

Earl raised his eyebrows in mock surprise. "So you're giving Sam a shot. Not a bad move."

Bishop nodded his acknowledgement.

"There's only one problem," Earl said. "The next time around, even Sam's not going to be able to change things."

"Really?" said Bishop. "That's not exactly the way I see it."

Earl leaned back in his chair and nodded for him to proceed.

"You tried a good case," Bishop said. "I'll give you that. You made something out of nothing. But now we know where you're going. There are no more surprises. It's not going to be like last time."

"That may be true," Earl said. "But that's not going to do you much good. Knowing Jessup, he put on everything you had the first time.

He never had a witness he didn't want to put on. And if you had anything new, you would have led off with that today." Earl paused for Bishop to deny it. "I thought so. So you're stuck with those witnesses and what might charitably be called their testimony." Earl paused again, but Bishop was silent.

"Of course," Earl continued. "Your wits could do me a favor and try to change their stories. But we know how that would go. Or, I suppose you could decide not to call them. But then I would just call them and it would look like you were trying to hide something. So, the way I see it, you try it again and we end up in the same place. A hung jury."

"That's possible," Bishop said. "But you're making a pretty heavy bet. You lose and it's the death penalty, you know that. No jury gives a cop killer life."

It was Earl's turn to sit in silence.

"Besides," Bishop continued, "one thing has changed. The jury tagged your man for the burglary. So right out of the gate we can put him at the scene of the killing. That's a bit of a problem for you. First impressions count. You know that."

Earl nodded, his face expressionless. Negotiating with a DA always felt to him like playing poker against someone who didn't have any of his own money in the game, while you just tossed in the deed to your house.

"I'll tell you what," Bishop said. "Let's split the difference. Plead him to a second degree homicide, fifteen to life. No death penalty, no life without parole."

Earl slowly shook his head. "I can't, Bob. I just can't." He paused. "Look, Cavalli has some skin in this game, too. If this thing hangs again, I wouldn't be surprised if Jefferson pulled the plug and dismissed it. That won't play so well in the papers." Bishop tilted his head in agreement. "Let me suggest another way that might get us both off the hook. What if you made Seabrooke your witness?"

"I'm listening," Bishop said, as if he knew this was where they were headed all along.

"Let's suppose Seabrooke was willing to testify that Aradano, the bondsman, approached him about a job. In exchange for cracking a safe at that exact restaurant, on that exact day and at that exact time, Aradano would post his bail and give him a cut.

"Go on," Bishop said.

"You take that to Aradano. There is no way he sits tight and rides a murder beef. He'll give you Snyder as the setup man. And Crystal, I'm sure, feels she was used to get Horgan there and never knew what was planned. She'll get on board. You jam Snyder with all that and he'll roll. He's a snitch, that's what they do. He'll offer up the only thing he has to trade, the shooter."

Bishop swiveled in his chair, pressed his fingertips together and stared off in thought.

"Seabrooke," Earl continued, "goes to prison on the burglary, which is exactly what he's guilty of, and you convict the real cop killer."

After a moment, Bishop grimaced and turned back to Earl. "The trouble is, that still leaves us short. It would probably work, but only until we get to Hawkins." Bishop paused to see if Earl was with him. "You're right about the others," he explained. "They would tip over on each other like a line of dominoes. Including Snyder. But that's where it ends. You say he'll give us Hawkins. But, so what? It's Snyder's word against Hawkins's. There's no corroboration. You think anybody is going to believe Snyder after his last performance?" Bishop's voice slipped into a "hillbilly" twang. "Last time I done tolt ya' that Seabrooke did it. That was a lie. But now I'm tellin' ya' the God's awful truth. Hawkins did it." He gave Earl a skeptical look.

Earl knew that Bishop was right. "All right. That's a problem. But listen, Bob. Snyder was the one who killed Horgan, just as surely as if he pulled the trigger. Whoever he used was just a tool in his hands. He's the real killer."

"You tell that to Detective Tanner. Right after your final argument, he was up in my office foaming at the mouth about Hawkins. This may come as a surprise to you, but when it comes to someone killing one of their own, cops sort of take it personally. Letting Hawkins walk will be a tough sell."

"Bob, this is the best you're gonna get. The cops may not like it, but they'll know you're right."

They sat in silence as Bishop continued to think. After a minute, he looked back at Earl. "Your man willing to do a queen for a day?" Earl recognized the prosecutor's term for an interview in which a defendant gives a preview of his potential testimony.

"You tell me you're serious about wanting to make a deal, and I mean you, Bob, personally. And that you've got the go-ahead to make it happen. Then he'll make a statement and answer all your questions."

Bishop swiveled his chair again and stared at the wall.

"All the usual conditions," Earl added. "You won't use his statement in your case if this goes sideways for some reason."

Bishop nodded slowly, continuing to stare off in thought. Finally, he turned back around. "All right. I'll need a couple days to clear this."

Earl tried to remain calm and not to appear unduly relieved. But it was hard. It felt like he was taking in a gulp of fresh air after being under water too long. They shook hands. Bishop stared into his eyes. Bishop's lips parted in a slight smile. He understood.

The street lamps cast a watery light on the quiet South Central street. The pre-war clapboard houses were set back from the sidewalk. All the windows had burglar bars and the front yards were fenced and gated. No one was out sitting on the stoops.

The dirt-coated Buick, with its crumpled fenders, had been parked on the street for some time. Cigarette smoke drifted from an open window. Deon Hawkins sat slouched behind the driver's wheel, dark eyes focused on a duplex down the block. Tattered shades were pulled in the darkened windows. The porch light was out. The uncut grass in the front yard was dotted with uncollected shopper saver newspapers. It looked as it always did, except something didn't feel right. He couldn't say exactly what it was, but he could sense it, like a scent on the wind. There was danger here.

Finally, Hawkins tossed his cigarette out the window and opened the driver's door. On the cool night air, a Mexican Ranchera ballad called faintly from someone's radio. He walked cautiously across the street and put a key in the front door. Slowly pushing open the door, he stared into the darkness, hesitating to step inside. He reached a hand around the door frame and fumbled for the light switch. Light filled the room, revealing a shabby couch, a carpet with a faded pattern and Detective Tanner tipped back in a plain wooden chair. A newspaper was folded across his lap.

"I was wondering when you would decide to come in."

Hawkins' body tensed, poised to run or fight. His eyes darted about the room.

"Now, don't go and do something foolish," Tanner said. "Stick around. Don't you want to know what happened to your little friend?"

"What the fuck you doing in my house?" Hawkins looked about. "Emilio," he called.

A muffled sound came from the next room. "Sorry he can't answer, he's sorta tied up right now," Tanner said with a grin.

Hawkins fixed Tanner with a hard stare as he slowly slid a hand behind his back.

"I wouldn't do that, Deon," Tanner said. He lifted the newspaper to reveal a revolver cradled in his hand.

Hawkins withdrew his hand. "You going on a vacation?" Tanner asked and nodded toward a suitcase in the corner.

Hawkins ignored him and looked over his shoulder. "I don't see no backup out there, little man. You plannin' to take me in by yourself?"

A mirthless smile spread across Tanner's face. "You don't' get it, do you, asshole? I don't plan to take you in at all."

Hawkins gave him a wary look.

"You see, it'll go down like this. I came here to ask about a few things that came up in Seabrooke's trial and I found you about to put it in the wind. It seems you were jumpy about something and tried to pull a gun on me." Detective Tanner shrugged his shoulders. "So what was I supposed to do? "

"What you gonna do about Emilio? Where's he fit in this little stitch-up of yours?"

"Oh, don't worry about your pal. I don't give a shit about him? As far as him talking, who's gonna believe him? The DA? I don't think so. But the people on the street will know, won't they Deon? They'll get message loud and clear. Nobody kills a cop and gets away with it."

The sound of the gunshots punctuated the night's quiet. A dog barked, then the street returned to silence. No lights went on, no doors were opened. In this neighborhood, the sound of gunshots was as common as a car alarm and just as consistently ignored. Being too curious was a recognized health hazard.

Earl parked his car, lifted his briefcase out of the trunk and trudged toward the office. He felt restless, unsettled. He had plenty to do on his other cases, but none of it grabbed his interest. It had been a week since he had read about the Hawkins shooting. The papers had identified him as "a person of interest" in the Horgan homicide. At first, Earl had been worried the DA would back out of the Seabrooke deal. Cavalli needed a show trial to reaffirm his fearless prosecutor credentials. No shooter, no star, no show. But Earl need not have worried. Cavalli just shifted his sights and put Snyder in the cross hairs. The prosecution still needed Seabrooke to start the dominoes falling.

Earl stepped inside the office. Martha was at her desk and fixed him with a mischievous grin. She was dangling a phone message between her finger and thumb like a matador's cape. "And who do you think just called and asked for an appointment?"

Earl pretended to think. "Thomas Glass. He's being charged with murdering the truth."

Martha smiled. "Detective Tanner. It seems the Justice Department has launched an investigation into the Hawkins shooting. The FBI wants to talk with him. He wants to retain you. We had a nice chat. He seems like a very nice young man."

"Does the fact that he's a police officer have anything to do with him being the first client you ever liked?"

"Just call him and see if you can help. Maybe it will get you out of that feckless mood you're in."

"Feckless is it? Was that in today's crossword?"

Martha shooed him into his office and turned back to her keyboard.

Earl dumped his briefcase on the carpet and dropped into his chair. Martha was right. Tanner's call did pique his interest, but it didn't surprise him. Cops were funny that way. Beat them in a case and they felt you had inflicted a mortal wound on justice. At the same time, you earned their respect. And when a cop got in trouble, principles got set aside. They might consider you on a moral plane with your clients, but when the bell rang, they wanted you in their corner.

Tannner's call, however, was not the first thing he needed to respond to. Something had been pulling at him, and he suddenly decided what to do about it. He dialed the phone.

"Sam, its Bobby Earl."

"So you're finally calling to apologize."

"You'll have to get at the end of a long line for that. But I don't exactly remember that particular transgression."

"Why, robbing me of my big case, of course. Now that Snyder's the target, I can't prosecute. I dealt with him one-on-one when he was on our team, so no telling what he's going to say about that."

"You're right. Sorry about that. But maybe I can make up for it."

"You're going to commit a big crime I can try."

"Not quite. I described your dog Beauty to my dog, the elegant Mr. Henceforth, and he seemed eager to meet her. He was taking his afternoon nap when we spoke and he opened one eye. That passes for wild enthusiasm on his part. So I'm proposing they have a playdate."

"Well, it would have to be chaperoned. Miss Beauty is a proper lady, after all."

"I understand. But at the same time, she might not be able to keep her paws off Henceforth once he swings his jowls for her, so I'll have to be there too. And I usually travel with a bottle of wine."

"That's good, because chaperoning is thirsty work." She paused. "It's about time, Bobby Earl. About time."

ACKNOWLEDGMENTS

The journey that culminates in writing a novel is never traveled alone, but there are some people, in particular, to whom I would like to express my gratitude.

Steve Greenleaf, the accomplished author of thirteen novels, was the first to apply a critical eye to the manuscript. His kind words of encouragement gave me the confidence to continue onward.

Tom Eidson, who was never too busy with his own successful writing career, to pause and lend a sympathetic ear and offer a savvy suggestion.

Steven Drachman of Chickadee Prince Books generously invested his time and energy in improving the book. His commitment to independent publishing provides a valuable forum for new voices.

And to all the criminal defense lawyers from whom I learned my craft, but more importantly, taught me the essential role the defense must embrace and fiercely champion if our justice system is to thrive and the rule of law is to flourish.

But most of all, I am grateful to my wife Susan, whose unflagging encouragement buoyed my spirits through the rough patches. Her tireless reading and re-reading of every passage, with her keen intelligence and thoughtful insight helped shape the tone and character of the book. We took every step of the journey together, as we have with all things.

Ed Rucker
September 2016

CPSIA information can be obtained
at www.ICGtesting.com
Printed in the USA
BVOW11s0718240417
482063BV00017B/434/P